Also by Bella Mason

Awakened by the Wild Billionaire

This is **Jane Holland**'s debut book
for Mills & Boon Modern.

We hope that you enjoy it!

Discover more at millsandboon.co.uk.

THEIR DIAMOND RING RUSE

BELLA MASON

HER CONVENIENT VOW TO THE BILLIONAIRE

JANE HOLLAND

MILLS & BOON

First published in Great Britain 2023
by Mills & Boon, an imprint of HarperCollins*Publishers* Ltd,
1 London Bridge Street, London, SE1 9GF

www.harpercollins.co.uk

HarperCollins*Publishers*, Macken House, 39/40 Mayor Street Upper, Dublin 1, D01 C9W8, Ireland

Their Diamond Ring Ruse © 2023 Bella Mason

Her Convenient Vow to the Billionaire © 2023 Jane Holland

ISBN: 978-0-263-30691-0

08/23

THEIR
DIAMOND RING
RUSE

BELLA MASON

MILLS & BOON

For the crazy redhead in my life.

Lindsay, this one's for you. You know why.

CHAPTER ONE

THIS ROOM HAD not changed in twenty years. From the books to the trinkets to the globe bar standing in the corner, everything was exactly as it had always been. And it made her feel like running.

Lily Barnes-Shah stood across the room from her brother, Devan. They'd used to love this room. Her father's office. Even though they'd never been allowed to play in here, somehow they always had. The dark wood furniture, massive carved desk and heavy drapes had provided endless hiding places for their epic hide and seek games. Her father would eventually find them and usher them out with a stern warning and a barely hidden smile.

Now it felt like a creepy monument.

And remembering that smile that had made her love her strict father so much brought mostly anger. As did her brother. Once her best friend, now she barely recognised the calculating man he'd become.

Her father Samar—Sam, as he'd been known—had passed away from a sudden heart attack a mere two months ago. Just weeks from his sixty-sixth birthday. Everything had changed for Lily that day. Her desperation had grown steadily since, and the one person she'd thought she could trust to help her was proving how little he cared.

It was a deep cut to her already aching heart.

Shah International had been passed down from their grandfather to their father, and now to Devan. And since he had joined their father in business she and Devan had grown steadily apart. All he focussed on was his work at the family company that dealt with everything from import and export and distribution to a series of chain store brands. Her father had got what he'd always wanted—his heir following in his footsteps—and she lost her best friend. Her brother.

'Dad planned all this years ago. You were fine with it then, so why is it a problem now?' Devan asked from behind the desk.

The drapes behind him were opened wide but the doors to the terrace were shut, and the hedge beyond was so tall that she couldn't see the blue San Francisco sky. God, he looked so much like their father. It took everything in her not to look away. They had the same golden-brown skin, dark brown eyes, thick black hair. He was the patriarch of the family now. His word was law.

'I was never fine with it, but what could I do? I was nineteen and studying abroad. I obeyed Dad, but still I begged, for five years!'

Lily had always wanted to please their father—had done everything she could to make him proud. He'd been a traditional man, and had expected obedience, but this arrangement was beyond what she could endure.

'I've been thinking about it a lot lately. The fact that Dad promised me he would find a way out. Well, Dad is dead now, Dev, so it's up to you. Only you can put a stop to this.'

That conversation with her father had been on repeat in her head. Yes, he was the one who had put her in this position, but he had given her hope that he would try to free her of the arrangement after he had seen how controlling Lincoln was. He'd promised her he would find a different way, and he'd never gone back on his promises.

Well, not unless a heart attack that no one had seen coming made him.

'Your engagement...'

Her temper flared. How could Devan try to dress up this madness as an *'engagement'*. She hadn't been asked. Hadn't said yes. This was being forced upon her. She wanted him to call it what it was. After all, she was the one being treated like a commodity.

'Arranged marriage,' she said through clenched teeth.

'Your engagement protects us both.'

It grated on her nerves that Devan, who knew her better than anyone, could ignore the way she felt. That he could see how angry she was and not care. It hurt. How had they gone from friends to this?

'It protects an investment. I thought my brother would want to protect *me*,' Lily said softly, the words slipping out before she had the chance to stop them.

She had hoped so hard that Devan might want to help her. But she could see now that the boy who had doted on her was gone.

'Lily, I am. This is what's best for us. Yes, Shah International is doing well, and is ours, but Arum Corp... Dad only owned thirty percent of that, and Arthur owned fifty—which was fine when Arthur was alive, and still fine when he died and Lincoln took over...'

'But not now that Dad's gone?'

Arthur Harrison had been her father's best friend. Both had come from old money. They had socialised in the same circles, gone to the same schools, and studied at the same Ivy League universities. They'd been more like brothers than friends and had remained so over many years. So when Arthur had approached Sam with the idea that they go into business together, it had been a no brainer.

They had started with a single bakery—a test to see how

well they could work together—but they had grown it into a supermarket, then a chain, and following that the company had moved into goods production.

Sam had agreed to a lesser share in the company for a few reasons, but primarily because going into business with friends was something he'd usually advised against, and a smaller shareholding would lessen his risk. It had been Arthur's first enterprise started from scratch, and there had been no telling how well it would do or if it would succeed at all.

To preserve their friendship, they had agreed to make a buy-back of shares possible if the partnership didn't work out. And, in a plan to protect the business they were starting, once they'd attracted other shareholders they'd agreed to a clause that said any shareholder could be voted off the board and their shares bought back should he in any way bring the business into disrepute.

So thirty percent had suited Sam at the beginning. After all, his main priority had always been Shah International... until Arum grew into the giant it had become.

Lily had loved Arthur. Just like her father, he'd been a shrewd businessman. Formidable in the boardroom, but loving when it came to his family. Which was why his son Lincoln had been such a surprise.

'Lincoln is the majority shareholder, Lil,' said Devan. 'We need you to marry him as planned and keep him happy. Keep him on good terms with us. He isn't his father. If I start buying back shares, it's going to sour the relationship. And you know he will find some way to implement that clause even if he has to fabricate a reason. We can't give him a chance to own eighty percent. What will happen to Arum then?'

'I don't want to marry him, Dev. I never did.' Lily felt nauseous. Beyond desperate now.

'I'm sorry, Lily. More than anyone, you and I know what Linc is like.'

How could they not? The three of them had grown up around each other. Devan had always been the responsible one. The leader of their group. When she was young, Lily had assumed it was simply because he was the eldest, and had thought it completely unfair. *She'd* wanted to be the leader, and thankfully Devan had always indulged her. She'd been a ball of energy. Making friends with everyone they'd met, always up for a game, but Lincoln... He had always been cold. Calculating. Spoilt and entitled. And it had only grown worse as they grew older.

When Sam and Arthur had joked about Lily and Lincoln getting married she had seen the look in his eyes. She knew the match wouldn't be because he wanted her—it would be because by tying himself to Lily, he would have complete control when the business fell to him and Devan. She would become a pawn he could use to control her brother.

After Arthur had died, Sam had approached Lincoln to talk seriously about the possibility of a marriage. Because as much as he'd known Lincoln would benefit, her father had also known Lily and Devan would too. Devan had already shown a strategic mind, and Sam knew that with Lily binding the families together he would be able to leverage things to his benefit. Lincoln would be less likely to attempt to push out a member of his family.

Lily remembered well the day her father had told her of the marriage he wanted to arrange. The shudder that had run through her body. In that moment she had known how awful life with Lincoln would be.

'Yeah, foolish me for thinking you would want to spare your sister that,' she said now.

Unable to look at her brother any longer, she turned towards a shelf packed with books. Foolish was exactly what she felt, and she couldn't bear the thought of Devan seeing the hurt that would be written on her face.

Devan's voice softened. 'I don't want to force this on you, but it is what it is.'

She refused to look at him, and there was steel in her tone when she replied. 'So that's it? The company is more important than me?'

'Lily…' It was a reprimand.

Screw this.

Enough of trying to be polite. Trying to ask for help. She didn't need it. She had made something of herself without Devan—she didn't need him now.

'Don't *Lily* me, Dev. That's exactly how it is. You say Shah International is doing well? You and I both know that's an understatement. That company makes this family more money than it knows what to do with. So what if Lincoln tries to push you out of Arum? You'd barely feel the pinch. But all you all want is *more*, and you don't care that *I* am the one who will have to pay the price.'

'You don't know what you're talking about,' her brother said quietly. 'You have never wanted anything to do with the company.'

That was true. She had no interest in working in a glass tower every day. The corporate life had never appealed to her. Which was fine, because all that expectation had fallen on Devan, who had welcomed it.

Instead, her father had indulged her in her dream. He had paid for her to attend pastry school in France, and she had managed to earn a business degree while doing so. She had used both to start her patisserie on Fisherman's Wharf and now, at only twenty-four, she was running one of the most popular eateries in San Francisco.

That didn't mean she knew nothing of the family company.

She huffed a laugh. 'What happened to us, Dev? The old you would never have said that, because it isn't true, but this new version of you…this one looking down his nose at me…? I don't know him, and I don't care for him.'

Lily stalked towards the desk, where he was still seated.

'You're right, I didn't want to work in the company. And looking at what you've become, why would I? But I still know what it's worth. You need to see that you're so hung up on that thirty percent of Arum that you won't even consider the wealth you already have with Shah, even if it costs you your blood.'

'So if you don't get your way you're threatening to cut all ties with me? Throw me to the wolves?' he asked.

Lily took a deep breath. Just the thought of letting go of her brother cracked her soul. The fact that their relationship had become so contentious was a constant ache in her gut. All they had was each other. After their father's funeral, their mother had announced that she couldn't live in the big house in Presidio Heights with all the memories it contained. But she couldn't let it go either. So she'd decided to travel. The last Lily had heard from Victoria Barnes-Shah, she'd been somewhere in Italy.

That was another conversation Lily wanted to forget. She had confided in her mother about not wanting to marry Lincoln, but Victoria had urged her to do so regardless—because, as she had put it, *'Your father loved you so much, and he only wanted the best for his children. You should obey his wishes.'*

Maybe that had come from a place of grief, but all it had done was make Lily feel more alone.

And that had left her and Devan in this giant house with all the silence between them.

'I wish you could see how unfair it is even to ask me that.' She stared unflinchingly at him. 'I'd never intentionally hurt you, but if you won't help me I'll find a way to fix things on my own.'

His expression became concerned. 'Don't do anything rash, please.'

She refused to respond to that. She would do whatever she needed to. All she wanted was a chance to live her life freely. Marry someone she chose—if she chose to marry at all.

'And don't forget we have that networking event tonight,' Devan reminded her.

'You have got to be joking!' Lily snapped. 'After everything I've said?'

Devan heaved a sigh. 'Look, if you don't want to go with Lincoln, you don't have to. Just attend with me.'

Lily studied her brother, unsure if she could trust his invitation—and wasn't that just a kick in the teeth? But it occurred to her that it could be an olive branch, so she would take it.

'Fine.'

But that didn't mean she wasn't going to work on a way out from this very moment…

CHAPTER TWO

SEATED BESIDE HER BROTHER, Lily toyed with her diamond bracelet as she looked out through the window of the limousine. She hadn't said a word to Devan after their chat earlier, and the atmosphere between them was still tense.

They drove in utter silence through the tree-lined streets until the Bay came into view in utter silence save for the soft crooning Devan preferred lilting through the speakers. She had nothing more to say to her brother, but if she was being honest she was grateful that he hadn't forced her to attend this event with Lincoln.

'Can you pretend that you don't hate me when we walk in there?' Devan asked.

Lily glanced at him. His face was drawn into a frown. 'I don't hate you, Dev. I hate what everyone is making me do,' she said softly, and then turned back to stare out of the window.

Tonight was important, she knew. It was the first big business event since their father had died and Devan had taken over his role. She wanted to offer her support.

'You look nice, by the way,' he said after a brief pause.

Lily looked down at the pale yellow fabric of her long, flowing designer dress, at her wrists cuffed in sparkling diamonds.

The event was being held at The Royal, a boutique hotel on The Presidio. Lily had always loved the place. It was beautiful in the day, but even more breathtaking at night, when the bridge was lit up. It was a small venue, close to the homes of those families with the most money.

As much as this was to be a business networking event, it was very clear who it was for. The tight-knit old money community that had begun this event many, many years ago. In fact, Lily knew only a few new people had ever made it in, and that was because their bank balances made them hard to ignore.

The limousine stopped under a portico. Instantly a young man in an impeccable uniform opened Lily's door and helped her step out.

As soon as they entered the large function room, lit by bright crystal lamps, Lily spotted the view of the Golden Gate Bridge, lit up and glowing against the inky sky, the Bay a glittering dark blue void beneath.

She felt Devan's hand between her shoulders, ushering her forward, and snapped her attention to all the formally dressed people in the room, dripping with wealth. Some held champagne or rich amber-coloured drinks in their hands. Others were gesturing animatedly with large smiles on their faces. The faint strains of classical music could be heard, though it was almost drowned out by the constant hum of voices.

Everywhere she looked there were groups of people, and in between, barely noticed, were black waistcoated waiters, circulating with trays of edible pieces of artistry.

She saw Devan scan the faces in the crowd before gesturing to her that they should head in one particular direction. Her stomach sank. She had hoped she would be able to spend the evening with her brother, despite their disagreement. Now she saw the impossibility of that. Felt hope die within her, only to be replaced by a burning anger she would have to cover up with a winning smile.

She turned to look at Devan and saw a flash of uncertainty in his eyes that quickly changed to a look of utter determination as he led her towards Lincoln Harrison. The bitter taste of betrayal coated her tongue. If it hadn't been clear to her this afternoon, it certainly was now: Devan was not going to help her.

Lily stared ahead of her at Lincoln, who had a look of sheer possessiveness in his eyes. He watched her as if she was a trinket that belonged to him, and in that moment that was how she felt. This was a business transaction and she was the commodity. It hurt.

She shook off her brother's touch. 'Hello, Lincoln.'

His blue eyes twinkled as he leaned in to kiss her, but she turned her face at the last moment, forcing his lips to press against her cheek. His blond hair brushed against her skin as he pulled away, his lips set in a grim line.

'Lily.' Lincoln slipped an arm around her waist, pulling her to his side.

His touch might as well have been a padlock and chain. That was how trapped she felt. She glared at her brother, but turned away. She couldn't look at either of them.

Her stomach roiled at the weight of Lincoln's hand on her hip. Not a sign of affection but a shackle. She couldn't breathe. Needed to get out of this place. Out of her life. Lincoln wanted them to wed in a year. How could she do that? How could she succumb to a life like that?

She couldn't. Would never survive it. Never survive being with this man who had asked her father if he *really* wanted to risk Devan's place at Arum when they had spoken once about calling off the arrangement. When Sam had tried to explain that Lily's goals no longer suited being married to him.

Bile rose in her throat when she thought of what freeing herself might mean for Devan. And she might displease her mother by going against her father's wishes, even though before he'd died he had promised to find a solution for her. But still she was stuck here.

Lily took a deep breath, trying to centre herself. To halt her panic and desperation to run. She needed to think, but when she opened her eyes a figure captured her attention. A man in a dark suit with red hair and no hint of a smile on his face.

He wasn't the tallest man in the room. Nor was he the largest or the brawniest. But he had a presence that shouted louder than any voice. It made him stand taller than anyone else. He had a predatory air that sucked all the attention away from everyone and everything else, focussing it all on him.

He was feral and beautiful, caged in a designer suit. But it didn't make him look trapped. No. It was the glossy coat of a jungle cat as it stalked its prey.

As if he felt her gaze on him he turned his eyes on her. While she couldn't tell the colour of them from where she stood, she felt a shiver pass through her, and even the constricting band of Lincoln's arm fell away.

Julian Ford stood at the bar, glass in hand. Raising the club soda and lime to his lips, he took a sip, rolling it around his tongue, relishing the tart bite. He hated these events, preferring to be at home or in his office, working. Growing his company or creating blueprints for new technology.

That wasn't an option tonight.

The exclusivity of this network was legendary. The only thing that had garnered him an invitation—and a reluctant one at that, he assumed—was his bank balance. No one would ignore a billionaire for too long. Especially one like him.

He hated having to make small talk with a bunch of rich snobs, but even he knew the importance of this kind of networking.

He glanced around the room once again, paying close attention to all the heads of industry he wished to win over. Mentally he sorted through the list of people who it would be most profitable for him to work with. To him, winning people over didn't mean playing nice and kissing ass. No. To Julian, winning meant making a success of the company he'd worked his hands to the bone to build. Winning meant showing people just what they would lose from *not* signing with him and how much they would gain from an association.

His attendance here was only the first step. What he needed was an in for the Zenith dinner in a few weeks' time. If this event was exclusive, it was nothing on the Zenith network. Much to his irritation, he had never yet received an invitation, and even his being here tonight didn't mean that was likely to change.

He took another sip of his drink, sliding his free hand into his pocket, and turned to face the older gentleman beside him, nursing a glass of Scotch as he ran his fingers through his salt-and-pepper hair.

'This turnout could work in your favour,' said Henry Cross, the man Julian owed so much to. He was his mentor. The one person in the world he trusted.

'I'm not interested in the numbers,' Julian replied.

'Of course not. I taught you better than that.' The old man smiled.

Julian had seen that smile so many times over the years, yet still he couldn't return it. Thankfully Henry never expected him to, which made being around him so much easier.

Julian had graduated from school early, which had meant he was far younger than anyone else at college. Far younger and far, far smarter. Henry had recognised the genius in a very poor, very serious, driven young man, and had taken him under his wing.

Now Julian owned IRES, a leader in renewable energy technology. His own invention—created while still a teenager— had made him a millionaire, and following that a billionaire, but the success of IRES had mostly come from overseas markets. He was still struggling to gain a foothold in the States.

It was hard to convince companies in the US to work with

him when even those in San Francisco—the city in which he'd placed his headquarters—stubbornly refused to work with him. But his overseas success wasn't enough. Julian needed to replicate that success on home soil.

His drive to turn nothing into the behemoth IRES now was had taken intelligence and an understanding of where exactly to focus his efforts. So, no, he would not be looking to get in bed with anyone in this room who had money—which was everyone—but the select few who would have the greatest impact.

After all, a predator didn't hunt an entire herd blindly…it selected its prey and went after it.

'You did,' he said now. 'The problem is I couldn't care less about the people who *want* to talk to me,' Julian added, looking around the room.

'That group will be hard to break into,' Henry agreed, glancing over his shoulder to the man Julian was looking at.

'Lincoln Harrison won't give me the time of day. He won't even take a call from IRES,' he said through clenched teeth.

'I heard a rumour that he's looking to invest in green energy for Arum…' Henry leaned against the bar.

'He is. But I'm betting he's hoping one of his associates with the correct pedigree will magically provide the solution he's looking for.'

This was the issue Julian kept crashing into. It didn't matter to people like Lincoln Harrison who could provide the best solution—what mattered was who from his approved list of old money sycophants could provide the best solution. Because in his world being born on the wrong side of the tracks was a blemish that couldn't be tolerated.

Just then a woman entered the function room. Skin golden-brown. Glossy black hair pinned up, exposing an elegant neck. Lithe and graceful, in a pale yellow dress that made him feel kissed by the sun. Such a change to the monochrome monotony in this room.

It was Lily Barnes-Shah.

And Julian couldn't look away as she and her brother Devan approached none other than Lincoln Harrison himself.

He watched with interest as she evaded his kiss, then stiffened at his touch.

Interesting.

With great effort Julian turned his attention back to Henry. It was hard to do, because everything in him wanted to keep looking at her.

'Why does he want to go green now? PR?' asked Henry.

'No...' Julian forced himself to pay attention to the conversation. 'And it's not out of moral responsibility either. He's found out how much money he would make in the long run, so he's prepared for the capital outlay now.'

'Well, as long as his money is good...'

Julian's gaze had started wandering back to Lily, but now it snapped back to his mentor. That wasn't all there was to it, but Julian didn't control his clients' motives, and as long as his own goals were being met he would have to be satisfised with that.

'That won't matter if I can't even get an in with Arum.'

'You know what the issue is, don't you?' said Henry.

Of course Julian knew, and he could do nothing about it.

'You're new money and your reputation. These people think you're too ruthless.'

His so-called ruthlessness followed him around constantly. For the most part Julian revelled in it, but occasionally it was a hindrance. He just always looked for the most efficient solution. Efficiency didn't leave time to care about feelings. Efficiency meant taking over companies, trimming away the fat, stripping it to its bare bones and then making it perform at its best.

Julian made things work. It was business. There should be no room for feelings. It wasn't logical. As for the other issue… There wasn't much he could do about that save marrying into that old money world. But marriage was not an option. *Ever.* Not with his past. His company and his money were good, and that would have to do.

'You need to show them a different side to you, Julian. Something they can relate to,' Henry continued.

'I'm not softening my edge just so that a bunch of elitist pricks can feel good about themselves. I'm the best at what I do. My work should stand alone.' Julian didn't raise his voice. He never let himself show anger. He could control himself. Had to.

'It should, but you'll catch a lot more flies with honey than with vinegar. Remember that. We'll talk more later—there's someone I need to see.'

Feeling someone's gaze boring into him, Julian looked over to see Lily Barnes-Shah staring right at him. He couldn't look away. Even from where he stood he could see there was something about the look in her eyes. Something like anger. She looked away first, but that was a feeling he knew all too well.

It was an interesting thing, watching a person make a decision of some gravity. Watching the emotions play out on their face. First uncertainty, followed by a ripple of fear, and then, as their will solidified, and they became certain of their choice, their features would set. Sometimes with determination, other times with confidence, at times even with aloofness.

Watching Lily closely from his place at the bar, Julian saw her push her shoulders back and lift her chin, as if she'd suddenly remembered she was San Franciscan royalty. With no small amount of curiosity he saw her pull away from Lincoln, whose questioning gaze had turned hard.

Julian realised his glass was midway to his lips, as if he'd forgotten what he was doing. He drained the rest of his drink, not tasting any of it, and watched Lily walk away from the two men. He had seen Lincoln's look before. Seen what it could do. It was a symptom of a much bigger disease. A subtle tell that wrote an entire book for Julian about what kind of man Lincoln Harrison was.

He knew he needed more information on what was happening, so he looked to her brother Devan, whose jaw was set. A look of frustration on his face.

Very interesting.

But the two men didn't hold his attention for long. Not when *she* was walking towards him. Not when this beautiful woman, who moved with effortless grace, and who had eclipsed every other being in this room, had her eyes fixed on *him*. It shifted something in his chest. Made every cell in his body come alive. Her presence called to him, and his body was responding without thought.

Julian rested against the bar just as she reached him, leaning his arms on the gold marble. 'I've never seen anyone look more like a lamb to the slaughter,' he said.

A flash of surprise was quickly covered by a polite smile. 'You must not attend enough of these things, then.'

Her voice was lower than he'd expected and he immediately craved hearing it again.

'Julian Ford.' He extended his hand.

She laughed—a delicate, musical sound that crept under his skin—and all he could do was stare.

'I know who you are,' she said, her eyes twinkling. 'And I'm—'

'Lily Barnes-Shah,' Julian responded, looking down at her diamond-shaped face.

The rich warm tones of her skin glowed in the bright light. Her espresso-coloured eyes were bottomless depths...black mirrors that sparkled. They were coloured with a hint of sadness her smile couldn't cover, and there was no discernible point where her irises ended and her pupils began.

Heaven help him if they weren't the most beautiful eyes he'd ever seen.

Lily took his hand in a surprisingly firm grip. A spark unlike anything he had felt before flared at the touch, and a jolt of pure want went right through him. He looked into her eyes and saw surprise and heat there. Julian could only assume it reflected his own.

What the hell was happening to him? No one ever affected him like this, and he was never deprived of female company. He could have anyone he wanted, when he wanted—although admittedly that had occurred with less and less frequency since those interactions had grown tiresome.

He wasn't expecting and wasn't prepared for Lily to jump-start his need with nothing more than her presence and a handshake.

And he wasn't the only one affected.

He had heard her gasp. Could see the flush now creeping up her skin.

Gently, she pulled her hand away—delicate and small in his—and as if someone had flipped a switch the people around them seemed to move once again. The hum of voices filled the air. His lungs began working once more, but the atmosphere remained charged. He half expected to see the crackle of electricity zapping between them.

Lily cleared her throat, turning towards the bartender, a pulse fluttering at her neck.

'A Cabernet, please,' she said.

Julian tipped his empty glass, indicating that he wanted a refill, then leaned on his elbow and crossed one foot over the other as he turned towards Lily.

'I wouldn't have expected you to know me,' she said.

'Should I be insulted? You don't know me, and yet you're already making assumptions.'

She let out a soft chuckle. 'I suppose you're right.'

Their drinks were placed on the bar and he watched her lift the red wine to her full lips, his cruel imagination making him think of all the things he'd like to do to those lips.

Get it together! he chastised himself.

'Shall I just assume you know everyone in this room?' she challenged with a cocked brow.

'Yes,' he answered simply.

'I suppose I should expect nothing less from the wunderkind of the Bay Area.'

She took another sip. It was driving him crazy.

Julian's genius had been extensively covered by the media. When you were an industry-leading innovator, with a rags-to-riches story, you were newsworthy material. He had learned to live with it, but hated the idea that one day someone was going to share the entire story of his childhood. The idea made him burn.

'Not just the Bay Area,' he said.

'Wow, you certainly don't have any issues with confidence.'

The teasing smile on her face made him eager for the next one that would appear.

'I see no point in denying the truth. What use do I have for false humility?'

'Is everything black and white with you?'

'I have room for a few shades of grey.'

'But not a rainbow?'

'Definitely not. I'm in technology. I like the simplicity of binary.'

'Maybe there's fun to be had in the complex?' Lily challenged.

Julian took a single step towards her, making her crane her neck to look up at him.

'I agree,' he said, in a darkly sensual voice. 'In taking it apart and reducing it to its simplest parts…understanding what makes it tick.'

Lily shivered under his gaze. She had never been with a man before, but for some reason she was certain Julian would be able to take her apart—which was a wildly inappropriate thought to have about someone she had just met. She had to regain her balance. Take this exchange into safer waters and away from what was pulsing between them.

'From what I hear, taking things apart is what you do best.'

'Then your sources must not hear everything.'

He took a lazy sip of his drink and Lily watched the bob of his Adam's apple as he swallowed.

God, she just could not tear her eyes away from his. There was no word for the colour of them. Hovering somewhere between green and blue, they reminded her of the most untameable seas. Fierce. Beautiful. Just like the rest of him.

A tiny gold hoop earring twinkled prettily in the helix of his left ear—so out of place with everything else about him. The impeccable suit, the perfect posture, the utter seriousness… It hinted at something hidden. Something she wanted to learn. And it screamed danger. Told her that he wasn't from her world.

She was drawn to him. If she closed her eyes she could still feel the current skittering across her body. The flare of her pulse. Reactions she hadn't ever felt before. Even though they were just bantering, she couldn't control her body's awareness of him. She felt the gruff rumble of his voice when he spoke like a tremor in her world. Lily wanted nothing more than to be around this man all night…

'Are you saying you don't?'

She picked up her wine glass for fear that if her hands were free she might do something terribly reckless. Like touch him again.

'Oh, I do. I will take apart anything that isn't working.'

'Brute.'

Lily thought she almost saw him smile then. Something flashed in his eyes before disappearing entirely.

'Sometimes you need to be.'

He looked away, for a moment, as if deciding whether or not he wanted to say more. Lily held her breath, hoping he would.

'If you had a tree you knew could produce the best fruit but was incapable of it right now, you would tend it. Cut away the rot. Find the source of the problem and eliminate it. Maybe you would have to trim it so far back that it would take a whole seasons for it to recover but once it did, you would have your perfect tree. What use is a business that is bound to fail?' he asked. 'How does that make money? Everyone it supports is in danger of losing their livelihood. It might not be pretty, but sacrifices have to be made—and if that makes me a brute, I'll happily wear the title.'

'Hmm, you care...' She smiled in playful accusation.

'Most would say I'm incapable of it.'

Lily saw the hint of hidden depths in those hard eyes. 'I get the feeling most people don't really know you at all,' she said.

He cocked a perfectly shaped brow. 'That's a bold assumption to make about someone you don't know.'

She jutted out her chin. 'Am I wrong?'

'Not at all,' he conceded.

'You know, you're surprisingly honest...' And after dealing with the machinations of Devan and Lincoln, she found it refreshing.

'Again, should I be insulted?'

'Definitely not. In any case, I don't think I *could* insult you.'

'And why is that?'

'Because to feel insulted you would have to care about what people think, and something tells me you don't.'

'How very astute.'

Having that confirmed shifted something in her. It told her she could trust this man—because if he didn't care what people thought, there was no reason for him to be dishonest or deceptive.

Julian was enjoying himself with Lily. Her quick, teasing wit and her readiness to go toe to toe with him was a massive turn-on and he was struggling to ignore the attraction.

'Still, everyone is talking about Helios,' Lily said, taking a sip of her wine while keeping her eyes on him.

Julian's last acquisition had been a PR nightmare. The company had had potential, but everything had been wrong with it. He'd had to clean house from bottom to top, and felt no remorse after taking it apart.

'I'm sure they are.'

He glanced over her shoulder to grant himself a small reprieve from her presence, noting that Lincoln had joined another group, but was staring at Lily with anger clear in his eyes.

'Your boyfriend seems to be rather put out that you're talking to me.'

'He's *not* my boyfriend.'

Her tone had a note of finality to it, but there was something else in it that rankled.

'That's a juvenile term anyway.'

The switch from playful to this combination of anger and frustration was jarring. 'I apologise,' he said. 'I assumed you were together.'

'You and everyone else.'

There was a hopelessness to her tone when mere moments before it had been bright and full of life. Something was going on here.

An instinct he'd thought long buried rose to the surface. 'Pick up your drink and follow me.'

She had no reason to do so, having only just met him, but he knew she would. So, without checking to see if she had in fact followed him out, he made his way to the balcony that offered unobstructed views of the spectacular bridge.

He was relieved to find her joining him at the railing. Having Lily out here might get him the answers he wanted, as well as some ammunition. Whatever situation she was in, Julian sensed she hated it, but knew she wouldn't easily reveal what that was. She had no reason to. He had to offer her something to gain her trust enough that she would tell him…

Lily had expected Julian to question her on what he'd witnessed in the ballroom, except he didn't.

'I was once in a situation where everyone thought my life was as good as it got, given where I lived.'

Julian looked out towards the water as he spoke. His tone careful.

'But it wasn't?' she asked.

'Far from it.'

'What did you do?'

Lily wondered if by sheer chance she had found someone who could understand what she was going through. What she needed.

'Everything I could to get myself out.' Julian turned to look at her then. There was something tumultuous in his eyes. 'To live on my terms. To have freedom and peace.'

Lily wanted that too. Desperately.

She didn't know what Julian had seen in her face when he had asked her to step outside with him, but she hadn't expected him to offer this bit of strength to her. A little piece of him, she realised. A kindness…a small offer of himself from a man who gave nothing away.

It made her feel reckless, and before she could stop herself—before she could consider that she had only known him for a few minutes—Lily found herself revealing her situation to this man who made her feel so inexplicably comfortable.

'My father promised me to Lincoln. I'm supposed to marry him. It's what my brother wants,' she said.

Understanding lit his features. 'You're a bargaining chip.'

'Pretty much,' she replied, suddenly realising how impulsive she was being. Wondering if she'd made a mistake telling him.

'And what do *you* want?'

No one had asked her that before. Not one person cared enough but here stood Julian asking how she felt. A lump rose in her throat and she had difficulty talking around it.

'I want the chance to live my life. Whether I end up marrying someone or remaining single for the rest of my life, I want it to be *my* choice. Everyone should get that. Why should I be deprived?'

His unflinching gaze held hers, sending goosebumps up and down her arms.

'You shouldn't.'

He looked away. Immediately she missed the way his eyes felt on her.

Shifting the focus away from herself, Lily asked, 'What do you want from this night?'

She watched him glance though the glass doors at a group of men talking animatedly. A group that included her brother and Lincoln.

'The one thing I can't have.'

She heard the note of frustration in his voice and understood. She knew exactly how reluctant this community was to let in new money. It was elitist and judgemental.

'I'm afraid they're going to take a lot of persuading.'

'Tell me something I don't know. You should probably go back inside,' Julian said.

'I probably should. They're going to wonder what we've been talking about.'

'Tell Harrison I'm looking to buy a cake,' Julian said, amusement twinkling in his eyes, even though he still did not smile.

Lily choked out a laugh around her wine.

'We'll speak again, sunshine,' he said.

'Julian!' she called, before she disappeared through the doors. 'Your secret is safe with me.'

'Likewise,' he replied.

CHAPTER THREE

WITH A THUNDEROUS RUMBLE, Julian brought his car to a stop in front of a large concrete building with industrial French doors in Fisherman's Wharf. The streets were busy. And there was a cacophony of sounds in the air as he stepped out of his car.

This was not a part of San Francisco he often visited. He had no reason to. He'd moved to this city because it had been the best place to start IRES. The only support he'd had as a young man had been Henry, so the fact that he resided here was a bonus.

Still, he could appreciate the place Lily had chosen for her store.

Lily...

She had been on his mind from the moment he'd set eyes on her. Of course she had been—she was beautiful. However, it was when he'd heard Devan Shah wanted to hand her over to Lincoln Harrison that the cogs of his mind had begun working. It was obvious how entwined those families were, and he knew they could unlock his success in San Francisco and, following that, in the wider US.

Experiencing that intense chemistry with Lily had him forming a plan. One that would greatly benefit him and, if he played it right, save Lily too. He would use her to get closer to Devan. Work on him to secure his support for the deal at Arum and then, once that was in hand, gain the vote of the rest of the board. It was risky, though, as it would spark the ire of Lincoln—the majority shareholder.

There were a few things Julian considered would work in his favour: firstly, Lincoln rarely went against any decision that Devan and the board backed, and secondly, he was more than willing to secure some insurance against Lincoln as a contingency plan. Julian suspected he knew the kind of man he was, so there would be plenty of dirt to find if he looked in the right places. And thirdly, once Julian had insinuated himself into their clique Lincoln would have no choice but to consider IRES. It would look suspicious if he discounted Julian without reason. Especially if he used Lily to garner an invitation into Zenith…

There was also the possibility that with Devan lobbying for Arum to go with IRES none of his back-up plans would be needed.

The first step was to get Lily to agree. Which was why he was outside her shop now.

Pressing the fob in his hand, he locked his black, futuristic sports car, buttoned his grey suit jacket and walked towards glass doors with a quaint sign above it that read *Crème*.

Even for this city full of food, the place was busy.

He opened the door and slipped in quietly. His first thought was how inadequate the word 'bakery' was. Lily's café-patisserie was a kaleidoscope of pastries in every colour fathomable. Every seat was taken, and queues formed at every cake display.

A ribbon of pride wound around his heart. Perhaps it had something to do with how happy she looked here, compared to the sadness he'd seen behind her façade when they had first met. There was something special about her that went further than her brightness and obvious intelligence. Although he didn't quite understand why he felt so strongly, given he had only met her the night before.

An apron with curly writing on it covered her front. Her glossy ebony hair was pulled back into a ponytail that Julian wanted to wrap around his fist. He wondered if she would gasp when he tugged on it. What the skin on her neck would taste like…

He shook away the thoughts. Or tried to. He had been failing at that since last night. He couldn't get her off his mind. From her smile and her eyes to everything she had said, Lily had imprinted herself on his memory.

His urge to pull her into his arms and kiss her wasn't the reason he'd come, but he did like getting a chance to watch her. She handed a box to a customer with a broad smile and greeted the next person. Every face brightened when she spoke.

He couldn't relate.

Being who he was, Julian brought out fear, frowns and clenched jaws. The best he would get were fake smiles.

But Lily wasn't like him. She wasn't made of darkness.

Julian decided to be patient. What he wanted to discuss would need her undivided attention. So he waited and watched.

Lily felt a prickling of awareness. A feeling she hadn't ever experienced until the night before. *He* couldn't be here, though. Why would he be? He knew how little power she had over her family and with the Harrisons. She wouldn't be in the predicament she found herself in otherwise.

Surely she was imagining things.

But one quick glance to the corner of the store told her she wasn't. Julian was in her patisserie, looking sinful and dangerous, with his hands in his pockets and no hint of a smile on his face.

She wondered what it would take to get one out of him. How handsome that would make him. Why didn't he smile? He was certainly capable of humour. She had found that out last night.

When Devan and Lincoln had interrogated her, Lily had

actually told them that Julian wanted a cake. She'd had to hide the laugh that had threatened to erupt when their faces had reflected confusion and then suspicion.

She had managed to keep it in until she shut the door of her bedroom later, when breathless laughter had escaped her. Lying in bed, she had found thoughts of Julian spinning wildly. Without even touching her he'd made her *feel*.

When he had stepped into her space it had been as if he had tugged her head back and made her look at him. It had made her achy and flushed. And when he'd walked away after calling her 'sunshine' she'd wanted to beg him to say it again, but she hadn't.

She'd played the sound of his voice over and over in her head until she'd fallen asleep…

She handed a box of pastries over the counter and told one of her assistants that she would be right back.

'Julian,' she said when she reached him. 'This is a surprise.'

'Do you have a moment? We need to talk.'

His eyes were burning into her the same way they had done the night before, making it hard for her to concentrate. The sunlight coming through the glass illuminated half his fair-skinned face while striking the other half in shadow. Her mouth went dry looking at him.

She wanted to touch him. Find out how hard his body was. Run her fingers through the short, soft red hair that was cut so perfectly that even though she expected it to curl over his collar, it never did.

'Um…give me a moment. It's a bit crazy in here. I need to deal with a few more customers then we can talk.'

He gave her a single nod. No words. Just one efficient movement.

She rushed back behind the counter and apologised to her customers before helping them as quickly as possible. In a matter of minutes the queue had cleared, leaving her free to deal with Julian.

'Let's go to my office,' she said.

Her stomach did a little somersault at the thought of being alone with him.

She led him through the passage at the back of the bakery, past the busy kitchen to a closed door at the end. She held it open for Julian, shutting it once he was through and inviting him to take a seat in front of her messy desk. Her computer sat idle to one side. A cork board on the wall was pinned with a slew of slips and papers and different types of ribbon.

To an outsider, it probably looked like chaos. To Lily, it was perfectly ordered.

She took the seat beside his, angling herself towards him. 'What did you want to talk to me about?'

'I need you to listen to me with an open mind. What I'm about to say could benefit us both.'

She was intrigued. But also, given the current state of her life, a little apprehensive. 'I'll try my best.'

'That's all I ask.'

She watched him study her, making her feel even more antsy.

'I have a proposition for you. A mutually beneficial one.'

'Oh...?' She frowned.

His eyes flicked to her forehead before landing on her eyes once again. Lily suspected nothing slipped by his notice.

'I can get rid of your Lincoln Harrison problem. In return, you can help me get close to your brother, and thereby gain access to a group of people that holds a lot of money and influence in this city.'

'What? How?'

Her heart began beating wildly. She was willing to listen to anything that would free her of Lincoln.

'All we have to do is pretend to be engaged.'

That drew her up short.

Lily was certain her heart had now ceased beating. There was certainly no air in her lungs. So she had no idea how she managed to say, 'Engaged...' It somehow managed to sound like a question, a statement and a panicked breath all in one.

'I realise this might seem a bit extreme, but you agreed to try to keep an open mind,' Julian said.

How the hell could he speak so calmly?

She swallowed hard. 'I did.'

'Clearly you are aware of my reputation...' He paused, continuing only once she'd nodded. 'Having you as my fiancée will soften my image. In addition, it will make people more amenable to me joining their circle. Zenith. In terms of your situation, being engaged will make it a lot harder for Lincoln to marry you. You could have your freedom. After an appropriate amount of time we will call the engagement off, by which point you should be out of your brother's house and free to seek any path you wish. I'll make sure you're free. You have my word.'

'Julian...' Lily said on a breath.

She didn't know what to say. How could she trust that Julian would let her go afterwards? She couldn't trust her own family to look out for her. Though she was willing to extend a small amount of trust towards Julian when she told him of the arranged marriage.

'I'll put out the word that we've been seeing each other secretly,' he went on. 'But with your father's sudden passing we realised it was time our relationship was out in the open.'

'I don't know what to say.' She pushed off the chair, pacing to the cork board and back, seeing nothing of her office. 'People already think I'm with Lincoln—or entangled with him in some way. This would be scandalous. And what about the fact that people are genuinely afraid of you?'

'*You* don't ever have to be. I need you to know that. I'll take care of you, Lily. I'm promising you your freedom and I *never* go back on my word.'

She didn't know... This seemed dangerous. Changing an arranged marriage for a fake engagement. Also, Lincoln was vindictive. He wouldn't take kindly to Julian stealing her away.

'The idea is insanity,' she said softly.

Glancing back at Julian, she suddenly felt she could trust that he would protect her. He would be able to handle Lincoln. She was fairly sure of that. This was just such an extreme solution.

She turned around again, closing her eyes. Then she felt his presence at her back. A feeling she wanted to sigh into and a current that made her alert of every little thing around her. The weight of his hands on her shoulders turning her around. The touch searing her right to her depths. There was a flare in his eyes too. The colour darkening, his grip tightening just as her core did. Her breath becoming rapid and shallow. Her body moving closer to his without her realising it....

'You need to get away from him. I can help you.'

Julian's voice had grown hoarse. His head dipped infinitesimally towards her.

'Why do you want to?' she asked.

'Because I've seen the way he looks at you. I've seen it before, and I know that you know what I'm talking about. Is that the life you want for yourself?'

She was right. He *did* notice more than anyone else ever had. She wasn't sure if Devan hadn't seen it, or if he just didn't care enough to protect her from it, but that look on Lincoln's face gave her a horrible feeling about the future.

'I need to get away from him. I just want to live my life... but I'm scared to get stuck in another trap.'

'I know you have no reason to trust me yet, but give me a chance to show you that you can. This will work for both of us. We have the chemistry to make it believable. I know you feel it.'

Lily did. Her body pulsed with the need to close the tiny gap between them. To run her lips up the strong column of his throat.

'We'll need terms before I consider this any further,' she said, forcing herself to think beyond the lust. 'A definite end point.'

'Agreed. Here's what I propose...'

Julian removed his hands and she wished he hadn't.

Sitting down once more, he gestured for her to do the same, then continued. 'Arum is looking to switch to green energy. I want that deal. A deal with them will open a lot of doors that have been closed to me in San Francisco and the country at large. Once I have it we'll no longer have to see each other, but you'll keep wearing your ring for a while longer. After an appropriate amount of time, you can take it off and move on with your life. You never have to see me again if you don't want to.'

'Ring...?'

'Of course. We'll be engaged.' His lips twitched, as if a smile had fought to be freed but lost the battle. 'We will go on three dates. I will propose to you on the first one. After the third, you will move in with me.'

'Move in? I don't even know where you live!'

Lily panicked. How could she live in the same house as him, as attracted to him as she was, while knowing their every interaction would be fake?

'I live in Sea Cliff. Now you know,' he deadpanned. 'My fiancée can't be living at home with her brother when she should be planning a wedding with me.'

'Valid point...' Lily choked.

'Once this is over you can live anywhere you wish. I will assist you if you require it.'

She had already been looking at apartments, but had held

off on making a decision. She didn't really want to leave Devan alone in that big house when it had been intended to be a home for their family as it grew. Except she also didn't want to stay in a place that reminded her of how badly her family had let her down.

'Lincoln might come after me after we break up.'

'I know men like him, Lily. All we need is time and plenty of public appearances to sell the idea that we're madly in love. Harrison won't want it to seem like he's waited for you. He wouldn't give anyone that kind of power over himself, would he?'

Lily didn't have to think about it. 'No, he wouldn't.'

'I guarantee, before we call it off Lincoln will have someone else on his arm.'

'He would want to seem like he's winning. Probably make some big public announcement,' Lily said, following Julian's thought.

'Precisely. The expectation would shift. When were you meant to have married?'

'Next year.'

'If you agree to this, that will never happen. What do you say?'

This whole idea was madness. Her heart raced just from thinking about it. She would be lying to her brother. Her mother.

But doing so might grant her a life that was all her own. That was what Julian was offering, and all he wanted was a fair shot at a deal that was unfairly being denied to him.

And Julian himself was an attractive part of the package. A fun, thrilling part. Of course this was all fake, but the idea of being around him and getting to know him better—this man who made her feel things she never had—was extremely appealing. Even now, when he was doing nothing more than looking at her, he turned everything inside her molten.

Maybe he could show her the passion she had been denied, even if it was temporary. And maybe…just maybe… she could finally have someone in her corner. Someone she could be honest with and confide in. Heaven knew how much she missed that.

It was hard to trust that everything would work out as he planned, though. It was hard to trust, period. Yet he had resources—power. He could more than adequately take on Lincoln if it came to that. Though she hoped it wouldn't.

If Julian could free her, the least she could do was help him. He was right. This was a mutually beneficial plan, and she could count more pros than cons to this arrangement.

This was insane.

A rash decision.

Don't do anything rash, please. Devan had asked.

Too damn bad!

This was a way out and she would seize it with both hands.

'Let's do it,' she said, surprised by the steadiness of her voice.

A small smirk curved one corner of his mouth and she lost the ability to speak as his face was transformed into something roguish.

'I'll pick you up tomorrow evening. Seven. Wear something you'd like to get photographed in.'

He winked and leaned down to place a quick kiss on her cheek. Sensation exploded throughout her body, but before she could turn her head, maybe kiss him back, Julian had already pulled away, his eyes smouldering.

She saw his jaw flex and then he was striding out of her office…leaving her a nervous, excited, heaving, trembling mess.

CHAPTER FOUR

A DRESS THAT she would like to get photographed in.

Ordinarily an easy decision to make. Not tonight. Lily stood in her large walk-in closet, riffling through rails of beautiful dresses bought off catwalks around the world. None of them seemed right.

There was a lot of pressure on this date and this night. It felt monumental. The first step in taking her life back. Getting out of this pit of desperation and frustration. What dress, if any, would be appropriate?

A part of her that she didn't want to pay attention to wondered if Julian would approve of what she wore. It shouldn't matter. What they had was fake. But when she thought of that kiss in her office, as innocent a touch as it had been, she couldn't deny that she was attracted to him.

For a hairsbreadth of a moment, when she turned her head, she wanted to be kissed by him. Wanted that light brush on her lips.

Lily couldn't remember a time when she wanted that so badly.

It made sense. Julian was, objectively, gorgeous. She couldn't be the only one to respond to him that way. Yet she hadn't felt so strongly towards anyone else in the past.

Caught in her thoughts, she slipped a dress on.

This is the one, she thought.

The dress she would wear when she announced her relationship with Julian to the world. And her brother.

A flicker of guilt burned in her sternum. She was exposing him, giving Julian access to him, letting him use her to win over Devan and thereby work his way into that elite circle of businessmen.

A voice at the back of mind told her this wasn't what good sisters did.

But what about good brothers?

Did they dangle their sisters in front of predators? No. And so she was left with no choice.

She zipped up the blush-pink dress. Its pleated skirt sat prettily around her knees and the sleeves covered her arms to just below her elbow, warm enough to stave off the mild autumn chill. Lily smoothed her hands over the crystal beaded bands around her waist and admired how the metallic silver threads woven into the fabric caught the light.

It was perfect.

She buckled a pair of strappy, red-soled stiletto sandals on her feet, checked her make-up in the mirror and went downstairs to wait for Julian.

'Are you going out?' Devan asked, the moment she reached the main floor.

'Yes.'

'With whom?'

'I don't see how that's any of your business, Dev.'

Lily walked away but he followed.

'I know it isn't with your friends.'

Lily wanted to laugh. Of course it wasn't. She was twenty-four, but instead of having nights out with people she liked, she avoided them. She couldn't tell them about her arranged marriage. Gossip like that would spread like wildfire. And constantly turning down invitations had seen them drying up altogether. So no, she would not be seeing her friends.

'If you know it's not with them then you already have a good idea of what I'm going to say.'

'Lily...'

Another reprimand. She was growing tired of them.

Heaving a sigh, she spun to look at her brother. 'I'm going on a date, Dev.'

Worry clouded Devan's eyes and then they quickly flashed with anger. 'Is this why you suddenly want out so badly? So you can date someone?'

'I want out because I want my life back. I'm dating someone because I want to.'

'Dating?'

Panic and disbelief warred in his tone. Lily couldn't bring herself to care.

Whatever else Dev was about to say was cut off by the sound of a growling engine. Lily hadn't expected the flare of anticipation in the pit of her stomach that it brought, but there was no denying that she couldn't wait to see Julian.

Julian drove through the tree-lined streets of Presidio Heights. The houses were old and beautiful. The blue and gold sunset sky reflected on their walls and windows. The money that flowed through these streets was clear.

This was where he should have bought a home if he'd been strategic. It would have placed him in the ideal location to move among the people with whom he was now trying to conduct business. The thought of being here, however, sent an involuntary shudder through him.

His home was the one decision he'd made with his heart, and the freedom he felt every moment he spent in it was worth any trouble now.

After the childhood he had had, being so monstrously trapped in that dark house, now being able to sleep while looking up at the night sky was something he absolutely would never give up.

He let his mind drift to Lily and how trapped she was. Even if she hadn't agreed to this ruse he would have found a way to free her, but she didn't need to know that. No one did. He would teach her how to live for herself, and maybe when she made her own home she would find it to be her sanctuary too.

He turned into the drive of an Edwardian-style mansion and killed the engine of his McLaren Artura. This agreement with Lily was necessary for both of them, and he had zero intention of letting any emotion into the arrangement. Especially after he'd kissed her cheek and burning hot arousal had coursed through him. He had wanted to seize her lips and push her against that ridiculously large cork board. Wanted her to push back against him.

This level of attraction was unexpected, and he had to treat it carefully. He couldn't lose control. There was too much on the line.

He had two goals: help Lily and get the Arum deal. That was what he must focus on.

Getting out of the car, he buttoned his black suit jacket and walked up to the front door, which swung open before he could push the bell. Every thought in his head vanished. There was Lily, with a nervous smile, looking far more beautiful than he could have imagined. The urge to kiss her kicked him so hard he wasn't sure how he didn't choke out a sound.

'Julian!' she greeted him, far too brightly. 'Come in. I just need to fetch my purse.'

He crossed the threshold, losing the battle with himself and leaning down, brushing his lips lightly against her cheek.

'Deep breath,' he whispered in her ear. He heard her exhale, felt pleased that she'd listened. 'Good. Now put your hand in mine.'

His fingers locked around hers as she threaded them together. It was the most peculiar feeling. His heart both sped up and fell at ease all at once.

He closed the door and noticed a suspicious Devan off to one side.

'*This* is who you're dating?'

Irritation burst through Julian. He didn't let it show as he approached. Standing a few inches taller than Devan, he looked down at him and extended his hand. 'Julian Ford.'

'I know who you are.'

'Good, then introductions aren't necessary,' Julian said, keeping his face neutral.

Devan turned his furious gaze on Lily and Julian pulled her closer to him.

'Do you think this is a game, Lily?' Devan asked.

'I assure you it's not,' Julian responded.

'I don't know what you think you're playing at, Ford.'

'I'm not playing at anything, Devan. All I'm doing is taking my beautiful woman out to dinner,' Julian said evenly.

'*Your* woman? Since when? Last night?' Devan scoffed.

'For months. We kept it quiet because your father assured Lily he would find an agreeable solution to her situation, but since he passed her requests for help have fallen on deaf ears, and things have become somewhat uncertain. That's why I wanted us to stop the secrecy.'

'Is this true, Lily?'

Julian turned to look at her, but she was already staring at him. Paralysing him with those eyes.

'Yes.' She smiled.

'Where did you meet?'

'At the patisserie,' Julian answered without missing a beat, making Lily smile broadly.

'The bakery?'

Julian turned his attention back to Devan. 'I don't think calling it a bakery does it justice, and before you ask, the building next door belongs to a client.' That much was true.

Julian pressed a kiss to the top of Lily's head and it made her shiver. Something inside him rejoiced at her reaction.

'Why don't you get your purse, Sunshine? We're going to be late.'

She nodded and walked away, directing an uncertain gaze at him as she stepped through the doorway.

'I don't know what game you're playing with my sister, Ford, but I won't tolerate it,' Devan seethed.

'I've already said that I'm not playing games. I don't intend to wait in the shadows while the woman I love is handed over to another man. Lily deserves better than to be treated like that and you know it. Despite what you may think of me, I have no issue with you, Shah, and all I'm here to do is take her to dinner. But just so you know... After tonight, I'm not hiding our relationship. I thought you would appreciate the forewarning.'

Drawing up beside him, Lily announced that she was ready.

'Let's go.' Julian took her hand, leading her out through the front door. He opened the door of his car for her, then rounded the vehicle and slid into his seat.

'A gentleman,' she said with a teasing smile.

The expression on his face was wolfish. One that didn't reach his eyes which were still cold. Predatory. 'Well, I am a man...but I'm certainly not gentle.'

If the words hadn't set her pulse fluttering, the wink surely did it. Lily couldn't help staring at him as they drove off. He looked so at ease. So capable. His white shirt was open at the neck, exposing just a hint of the smooth skin at the base of his throat. Now that she thought about it, every time she had seen him, or a picture of him, he had always been in an impeccably tailored suit. Clean-shaven. Nothing out of place. Not even a strand of hair.

That level of discipline and control was nearly unfathomable. Julian seemed beyond human. It had to be taxing...

Only one thing betrayed that cool, calm exterior—the twinkling earring was the first thing she noticed when she opened the door. It was so at odds with everything else about him and she wondered why—if he'd set his sights on getting into Zenith—he wouldn't just remove it.

'I'm surprised by your choice of car,' she said, breaking the silence.

He frowned. The first real expression she had seen him show.

'Why?'

There was genuine confusion in his tone.

'Given that you're all about renewable energy, I thought you'd be busy trying to save the world.' She grinned.

He let out a rush of air and she wondered if that was almost laughter.

'I'm not the hero of this story, Lily. You'd do well to remember that.' His light eyes flicked to hers, then back to the road. 'And it's a hybrid.'

She let out a peal of laughter that had his lips twitching.

'Thank you for what you did back there,' she said. 'I'm sure Devan is angry, but you were so convincing.'

'I lied to him. I told him I didn't have an issue with him,' he confessed.

'And you do?' Lily wasn't really surprised. After all, her brother was part of the group that had made growth in San Francisco difficult for IRES. 'I guess I can understand that. I am aware of the privilege of my birth. If it wasn't for my surname I wouldn't even be in this group, despite my success. So I want you to know I do get it.'

'That's good to know, but not what I meant. I have an issue with the fact that your brother isn't protecting you from Harrison. I was serious when I said you need to find your own place.'

'I do.' Lily fell silent, staring out of the window. 'Thank you for helping me, even though I'm basically a stranger to you.'

'You're not a stranger. We've been dating for months.'

Lily laughed. There it was again. That hidden humour. It felt so good to be pulled away from her wallowing. She had always possessed the ability to see the positives in any situation—the quintessential eternal optimist—but lately it had become harder to be that person. Especially when she was constantly trying to hide the hurt her family had caused.

'There's something we haven't discussed.' He was all business again. 'As of tonight, we'll be engaged. There will be an expectation for displays of affection.'

'I've thought about that too,' Lily replied. 'It would be weird if we never touched. Give us away... Would you like to set some ground rules?'

'I would.' His eyes softened, as if he was pleased. 'I will only ever touch you if and when you are comfortable with it, and I will only go as far as you want me to.'

'What happens if we need to kiss?'

Julian briefly glanced at her. 'Would you be comfortable with that?'

Lily thought back to his lips on her cheek in her office and how much she'd wanted to meet them with hers.

'Yes, I would.'

She didn't add the *with you* that was on the tip of her tongue. She had never been kissed properly before, never wanted it, so this desire was a little alien, slightly worrying and incredibly thrilling.

'What about you? Is there anything I shouldn't do?' Her cheeks heated. She couldn't believe she was having this conversation with him.

His lips quirked up slightly at one corner. 'No, I'll be fine.'

Of course he would. Unlike her, he wasn't inexperienced. Could he tell that she was?

'Okay, good... Yes. We will hold hands and touch and occasionally kiss. For people to see. Perfect.'

She could tell he was trying not to laugh.

'What?'

'It's going to be fine, Lily.'

She hoped so.

They drove the rest of the way in comfortable silence. Getting engaged publicly was a bold move, and she knew she should be feeling more apprehensive about it, but she wasn't. All she felt was this constant current between her and Julian.

The car came to a stop outside a brick building in the city. One of the many warehouses that had been converted into modern masterpieces. Julian pressed a warm hand between her shoulder blades, guiding her inside. She had to fight the tremor his touch unleashed.

'I can't believe you got a table here,' Lily said as they stepped through the glass doors.

'There's nothing I can't do.'

'Don't look now, but I think your humility is showing,' she teased.

The corner of his eyes crinkled, but still he didn't smile.

The waiting list for this Michelin star restaurant was months long, so she couldn't really blame him for being cocky. And, as amazing as the food was, it was also a place to be seen. No doubt there would already be pictures of the two of them entering together. And the fact that Lily could feel the heat from Julian's body as they moved told her exactly what those pictures would look like.

'Mr Ford,' a hostess in black greeted him. 'Your table is right this way.'

A small gasp left her when Julian took her hand in his, and a pleasurable tingle travelled all the way up her arm. She plastered a smile in place and walked alongside him as they were led up a flight of floating stairs and past a sea of tables. There wasn't an empty seat on either floor, and she could feel the burn of all the eyes on them.

'Your table,' the hostess announced, standing next to a table for two out on the small balcony.

They would be in perfect view of everyone inside, yet their conversation would remain private.

Julian pulled out a chair and kissed her cheek once she was settled, then rounded the table to his own seat. His eyes were intense.

There was a small soft smile on the hostess's face as she handed them their menus, then left.

The pull he had on her was so strong Lily had to repeat *fake engagement* in her mind until she could smile and speak without her words sounding like a plea for him to kiss her.

She picked up her menu for a distraction, but the words made very little sense. Thankfully Julian didn't force her to make conversation. At least not yet. But when his leg brushed against hers under the table her body stiffened. Finally, a waiter appeared and she heard Julian order, saying words she was grateful for because they would take her mind off all the ways her body was reacting.

'I'll have the poached lobster and a club soda with lime.'

'The same for me, please,' she said.

Julian could have ordered cardboard and she would have said that she'd have the same. She forced her scattered thoughts into some semblance of order, because if she was going to spend any amount of time with this man she couldn't let their chemistry derail her.

'Can I ask you a question?' she said.

'Of course.'

'Do you not drink alcohol?'

'No.'

'At all?'

She was curious now. She remembered the globe bar in her father's office. The brandy he and Arthur Harrison would sip during their long discussions. The golden liquid flowing whenever they entertained. It had almost seemed like a bonding ritual. If Julian didn't join in with that, he was setting himself apart from these people in yet another way.

'At all.'

'Why?'

She saw his jaw flex, a flash of anger in his eyes, but when he spoke his voice was even and smooth, as always.

'I grew up with an alcoholic. I've seen what alcohol does. There's no room for that in my life, and while you are with me you will remember that.'

That hard tone only made her want to know more. What had happened to him?

'I will. I promise. Can I ask who it was?'

'My stepfather.'

It seemed that was all he was going say so she didn't pry. 'I'm sorry you had to deal with that.'

She grew quiet, trying to put a picture of Julian together, but he was a highly complex puzzle and she only had a few pieces so far.

'Just ask me what's on your mind.' He smirked. 'I can see those cogs turning.'

She let out an embarrassed chuckle at having been caught, but she wasn't going to squander the chance to collect more information.

'Okay… You seem to have come up with this idea rather quickly, and I'm just wondering how you were able to. I mean, being my fiancé makes it impossible for you to have a partner.'

'That's easy. I don't have one.'

'How is that possible?' she blurted.

Julian leaned forward, elbows folded on the table. 'I'm glad you think I'm so desirable.'

'I just meant—'

'The answer is simple, Lily. I don't do relationships.'

That seemed ridiculous. The man was smart, sexy, and so far seemed like a good enough person.

'Why?'

'Why do you want to know?' He smirked again, but this time there was no humour in his expression. 'Think you'll be the one to fix me? I'm a grown man. I don't need to offer reasons for my behaviour.'

He was right. He was free to do what he wanted. It just seemed wrong.

'You don't. And I don't think that. One, I may not know you very well, but I don't think there's anything to fix. Two, I'm trying to get to know you since we will be engaged. And three, I'm very aware of what this is, Julian, but we don't have to be strictly business partners—we can also be friends.'

'I don't have those either,' he stated simply.

Didn't that sound lonely?

'Okay, so what do you do for fun?'

'I work. I tinker.'

Lily thought about Crème and all the time she spent there. All the late nights perfecting recipes alone. She loved that time, so she really couldn't say much to him because hadn't she become the same way?

'Ah, yes, the genius.' She grinned. 'It's funny, you don't *look* like a genius.'

Why was she trying to provoke this obviously tightly wound man?

'Why? Because you buy the media's narrow-minded depiction of what intelligence looks like?'

'Of course not!'

Yet that was exactly what she was thinking—purely because the idea of Julian as a shy, socially awkward person was highly entertaining.

His eyes twinkled in that way they did whenever they flashed the smile the rest of his face wouldn't allow. 'It's both good to know and a little concerning that you're such a bad liar.'

'That's a compliment, Julian. No one should be good at lying. Are *you*?'

'You have no idea…'

But she did. She'd heard him telling her brother he loved her. It was the first time a man had ever said he loved her, and it was a lie. A necessary one, but it left an awful taste in her mouth. And that was her problem, not his.

She pushed on with her questions, only pausing when their food was served before asking, 'How old are you?'

'I thought you'd heard all about me?' He cocked a brow and it was maddening.

'I don't keep a dossier on you.' She rolled her eyes.

He gave a chuckle! Finally! It seemed to surprise them both. 'Thirty.'

As their dinner progressed, Lily found she was able to interpret Julian's subtle tells. When he was amused, when he didn't want to answer a question, when something deeper stirred in him but he wouldn't let it see the light. And, as much as she hadn't expected it, she found she was truly enjoying herself. Talking to Julian was easy, and he made her feel lighter, unburdened in a way that she hadn't experienced in a long time. He drew laughter from her easily. Made her smile.

She watched him move their two glasses aside and reach over to take her hand in his.

'Are you ready for this?' he asked.

'Yes.' She was calmer than when he had collected her, comfortable now that she had got to know him just a little bit.

Her life waited on the other side of this decision and she was ready to live it.

He kept his eyes on hers, stroking his thumb back and forth across her knuckles, spreading a white-hot heat that pooled in her core. She watched him slip a hand into his coat pocket and withdraw a black velvet box that he placed between them, pulling his hand away from hers to open the lid with a click.

And even though Lily knew this wasn't real, and she knew Julian didn't love her, she couldn't breathe. Couldn't reach into the box and pluck that amazing ring out. And it was amazing. Timeless. Something she would have chosen for herself. A large princess cut diamond in a platinum band set with a series of pavé diamonds.

'Lily, marry me.'

It wasn't a question…wasn't a request. It was a statement convincing her that she could place her trust in him. Telling her that they were in this madness together.

'Yes,' she choked, surprising herself at how easily the word fell out.

She'd worried that it would be hard to say yes when the time came, but it wasn't. For whatever reason, her *'yes'* felt right.

Julian pinched the ring out of the box and slid it onto her finger then brushed his lips across her knuckles. The world disappeared.

'I'm going to kiss you now,' he said softly, his eyes on hers, and when she nodded with a whispered 'Okay', he pulled her to her feet and stepped up to her until their bodies were almost touching. Until she had to crane her neck to look up at him. At the hunger in his eyes.

Lily had always avoided kissing Lincoln, and had thought she must be wired differently because she hated the idea of it. It was why she had turned away so his lips never met hers. Why she'd felt less than nothing.

But now…

Now her heart raced and her body pulsed. Now she could hear nothing but thunder in her ears. Now all she could do was drown in those darkened eyes, crave the heat of his body.

Julian grasped her chin between his thumb and forefinger, controlling her with ease as his lips lowered to hers. Brushing softly, gently. Once…twice. And then his tongue followed, tasting her.

She mewled, felt her legs growing weak, but a strong arm wrapped around her waist, fusing her to his hard body, and she gasped, allowing him to slide his tongue into her mouth, coaxing hers to dance with him.

And it did. Nervously at first, but then Julian growled deeply at the back of his throat, and it was the single most erotic sound she had ever heard. It made her confidence swell. Allowed her to take his bottom lip between hers, to press her hands against the hard muscle of his stomach, push them up until they landed on his chest, his white shirt bunched in her fingers.

And still he kissed her. Dominated her mouth. His lips slid with urgency now. They were lost. Lost to this stormy tempest of a kiss that kept sucking them into its depths only to crash into each other again and again.

His taste and his smell, like rich leather and spice and a hint of coffee, submerged her. She thought she could kiss him for ever. But the sound of clapping broke the spell and Julian wrenched away from her lips, his chest rising and falling as if he had run miles. His eyes were dark.

Lily hadn't known what to expect in kissing Julian, but she couldn't have imagined it would be like this. Kissing him had been life-altering. And she wanted to do it again.

CHAPTER FIVE

JULIAN'S JAW WAS clenched so hard his teeth were in jeopardy of shattering. He held the steering wheel in a death grip. There was no air in the car. Only a tension so thick it was almost physically suffocating.

Lily wasn't looking at him. Her eyes were set firmly on the road ahead. Dainty hands neatly clasped in her lap. Still. So very still.

Despite this, every minute shift in her body set off a gong in his head. Julian half expected to see something physical, tethering them together. But there was just the invisible magnetism between them that had ratcheted up to alarming levels. He had never been so aware of a woman's body before.

It was all the fault of that kiss.

They'd had chemistry before, and now that they'd lifted the lid on it, it was like opening Pandora's box. Unleashing a power between them that they hadn't seen coming. One that had led to this tension...all the easy conversation from before obliterated.

Julian wanted to call out to Lily. Make sure she was okay. That would have been the right thing to do. But he couldn't. It would mean unclenching his jaw, and that pain gave him back his control and the ability to think straight, which was exactly what he needed now. He had to master himself, because if he didn't his mind immediately went back to the kiss.

He'd had to kiss her. People had needed to see. That was the whole reason he had chosen that restaurant in the first place. No doubt pictures of his proposal would already be flying around San Francisco at speeds that would seem incomprehensible.

So he'd slipped the ring on her finger and then had to kiss her—because what man would not do so after getting his *yes*? He'd been prepared for that. He'd thought it would be a simple kiss. But, Christ, he'd been wrong!

The moment their lips had touched something in him had bowed to Lily. As if he had been searching for an answer his whole life and here she was, giving it to him. He hadn't been ready for the surge of arousal, for her less than confident response.

Julian had kissed many women in his life, so the inexperience of her touch had been immediately noticeable to him, telling him he had to be gentle. But he hadn't wanted to be, and when she'd found the confidence to kiss him back he *really* had not wanted to be gentle. He'd wanted to swipe the table clear and pin her down on it, kissing her until her lips were bruised from the force of his want. And even though he'd had to hold back, he'd still drowned in her.

He could still feel the sweet touch of her hands on his chest. His eyes flicked down to his shirt. Deep creases wrinkled the fabric where her hands had fisted it. She'd wanted more of him and he had wanted to give it to her. If that clapping hadn't returned his senses to him Julian shuddered to think where they might have ended up.

Lily could make him lose control. Therefore Lily was a danger to him. To his goals. He had remained focussed on IRES for years. It was the only good thing in his life. He needed to make sure his company thrived, because the success of his company was what made him worth something. More than that, the greater the success of IRES, the further away from the poverty of his childhood he moved. But, despite all that, he still wanted to kiss her again.

It was not acceptable.

He had worked too damn hard to get where he was just to lose sight of what mattered because of some attraction. He hadn't walked out of his stepfather's house, never to return, only to fall down now, before he could have everything he wanted.

He had been through too much, sacrificed too much, to let his wayward libido screw everything up. Emotions…raging attraction—they all clouded the mind. After all his mother had been through Julian didn't want that. He needed Lily and she needed him for a purpose. If they blurred the lines it would help neither of them.

He couldn't let a kiss like that happen again. For both their sakes.

Now, his biggest concern was to get her comfortable with him again—because if she stayed this tense around him no one was going to believe they were engaged. Devan was suspicious enough already, and he needed the man to see how happy Lily was with him. It would get him on Julian's side for the Arum deal, and soon enough Julian would leverage this 'relationship' to secure other contracts.

All of it would start with Lily relaxing. The problem was it wasn't in Julian's nature to apologise—and he didn't want to apologise for that kiss.

'Lily…'

Her body stiffened, but slowly she turned towards him, her gaze averted. 'You don't have to say anything.'

He had only seen her confidence. The insecurity written in her posture now didn't sit right with him.

'I'm sorry,' she said.

Julian was taken aback. What on earth did she have to be sorry for?

'For what?'

'The kiss.'

Julian swung the steering wheel, pulling over under a large tree. He turned in his seat, studying her intently. 'What are you talking about?'

'I—I got carried away, and then I saw the look on your face...'

'Lily, look at me.' When she didn't, he held her chin and forced her to. 'You have *nothing* to apologise for. We're consenting adults, we kissed, and it was good. Clearly there is something here—and if there was anything written on my face it was frustration that I wanted you like that in public.'

She tried to look away, but he wouldn't let her.

'Would it help you to know that I want to kiss you again right now? Except that isn't what this is...so I won't.'

Julian could see doubt in her eyes as to whether she should believe his words.

'No one is going to believe you're happily engaged to me if you're this tense,' he told her. 'Is that what you want?'

'No,' she responded softly.

'You need to be as comfortable with me as you were before.' He had enjoyed that. Not something he wanted to dwell on right now. 'Give me your hand.'

'What?' She frowned.

'Give me your hand,' he repeated.

He waited patiently for her to place her hand in his. Once she did, he held the back of it and placed it on his chest, guiding her hand up and along his shoulder, under his jacket, ignoring the way it seared through him. He took her touch up to the side of his neck, watching the way her breathing had become even and the tension in her body had given way to fascination.

'I am just a man...' He let go of her hand, felt her skim it over his cheek, slightly rough from the day's growth. 'You're wearing my ring. You can touch me without apology, Lily.'

Because he liked it. He liked it so much he wanted her to keep touching him.

'All we have to do is just keep in mind what we're doing here. What we're both trying to achieve.'

Lily nodded, pulling her hand away.

Julian walked Lily to the front door with his hand pressed to her back. Devan's car was in the driveway, and he wondered if her brother would be watching to find some tell that this was all a ruse. He wanted to tell Lily to touch him, but he didn't need to. As if she could read his mind, she wrapped her arms around his neck, hugging him fiercely.

His own arms automatically came around her in response. He was learning how she felt against him. How small her waist was…how easily he engulfed her.

'Remember we're engaged now. If you need anyone, you call me first,' he instructed her.

Then, because the temptation was too great, he kissed her cheek. And when she let go of him he placed another on her lips.

'Goodnight, Julian.' She smiled broadly, then stepped into the house.

He climbed back into his car, ignoring all the things Lily made him feel. It was obviously a side effect of the near celibate life he had been living lately. It was catching up with him now. That was the only explanation.

He refused to dwell on how beautiful Lily had looked on that balcony. How her smile had made him feel, And as he approached his home he put all thought of her aside. Stepping into the modern house set into the cliff, with all its windows offering him unmatched views of the bay, Julian felt the familiar sense of peace that came from being here…alone.

He placed his phone down on the entrance table, and saw a message from Henry flash on the screen.

What are you doing? Lily Shah?!

Julian called his mentor.

'Are you out of your mind?' came Henry's voice, which was coloured with concern. 'The Shahs and the Harrisons are so intertwined everyone knows she's meant to end up with Lincoln.'

'Does everyone know or just expect it?' Julian asked. 'Because what I know is that *I'm* the one in a relationship with her and it's me that she's engaged to.'

Julian walked onto the terrace, felt the chill night breeze ruffling his hair.

'Is Lincoln Harrison really someone you want to anger? Christ, Julian, you want the Arum deal. How is pissing him off going to help?'

Julian thought back to the way Lily had tensed when Lincoln had touched her. How he'd looked at her... He felt his stomach roil as buried memories surfaced to torment him, as if living through it hadn't been enough. The familiar burn of rage rolled through him.

'Don't worry, Henry, I know what I'm doing.'

'Do you? Why now?'

'Yes, I do. And it's because her father's dead. I'm just letting the world know she's taken. That she has been for a while. Why do you think this has been such a secret? I know what the expectations were.'

'That still leaves Harrison. He's the one who could veto IRES getting the energy deal, even if you have Shah on your side.'

'I'm aware of that.'

Julian was also aware of the fact that Lincoln did not often go against a decision when he would be the only opposing vote, and if his plan to get Devan and the board on his side worked, then Lincoln wouldn't risk the scrutiny of his society peers.

'So what is this? Have you found someone you could love more than your company?'

Henry's question was ridiculous. Love would never be a consideration. Everything Julian was doing was for IRES. But that didn't mean it had to benefit only him.

From the moment he'd seen Lily he had felt a protective instinct unearth itself. He had failed his mother, but he was powerful now, and this time would be different.

'They're completely different. In any case it doesn't matter, because this whole damn city will know she's with me.'

'I hope you know what you're doing.'

Henry hung up, leaving Julian to stare at the phone in his hands. From the moment he'd stepped into Crème Lily had been under his protection. That was no lie. He wouldn't leave her to deal with people like Lincoln Harrison. The man had him thinking of his stepfather, in a crumpled heap on the floor, with Julian standing above him feeling pure satisfaction.

Which was exactly why he couldn't allow himself to get emotionally invested. It wasn't part of the deal, and at the end of the day the only thing he needed to keep sight of was where he was going to take IRES once these people accepted him.

CHAPTER SIX

LILY SAT IN her office, attempting to work. Her door was shut and she had asked not to be bothered while she dealt with everything that required her attention. Except only one thing had it...and it sparkled on her finger.

She couldn't stop thinking about their date. Sure, it hadn't been real, but she had genuinely enjoyed Julian's company.

She toyed with the ring. When he had said she would be wearing one she'd never imagined it would be something quite so beautiful. Something that suited her so perfectly. Of course Julian couldn't have known that.

Julian...

When she closed her eyes she could still feel his lips on hers. That kiss had made her forget where she was, who she was. Just thinking about it had her breath coming in pants. Just as his had done.

She'd been so convinced she had ruined everything by getting carried away. They'd just needed people to see them being affectionate. Acting. That was what he'd been doing. But no one could be that good an actor, could they?

No, the kiss had been real. He'd said he wanted to kiss her again, and she should be grateful that they had such intense chemistry. It would work in their favour. Even Devan had bought the act.

He had been waiting for her arrival home, and all he had said was, 'So it's real?'

When she had nodded, he'd left her standing in the hall. That was the last time she had seen him, but she hoped that his reaction was a sign their plan was already working.

Her mind was firmly focussed on a man who held the weight of the world in his sea-coloured eyes. She sensed that there was so much more to him that he was likely hiding behind thick, high walls. But why? He seemed so hard, but never cold. So controlled, never smiling, and yet his eyes often lit up with humour.

And in the car he had been kind. Reassured her. Made her comfortable. Yet he'd also warned her that he wasn't a hero. Something told her he really did believe that. In fact, there had been several warnings and they all said the same thing: *Don't get attached.*

There was no risk of that. Lily wouldn't let herself forget what was at stake. Her freedom. Her happiness.

That was a feeling she hadn't had much of recently. She was still mourning her father, but instead of getting a chance to work through it, she was having to deal with the anger she harboured at him not fulfilling his promise. The abandonment she was trying to convince herself didn't exist after her mother had left her to deal with her own grief and decided not to be around to help her children. The frustration of only having her brother to turn to now, when he didn't care.

That was why this plan with Julian had to work.

She would be getting just as much out of this as he would. Maybe she wasn't after a deal worth millions, but some things were worth more than money. If only her family would realise that.

It was at that moment that her phone rang. Lily snatched it off her desk, sneaking a quick glance at the name on the screen before answering.

'Hi, Mom.'

Lily's heart raced in her chest. She knew her mother would

most likely be disappointed in her, but she reminded herself that her family had broken her trust, so she had nothing to apologise for.

'Lily, is it true? You're engaged?'

It was the first conversation they had had in weeks, and the first words her mother said weren't full of concern for her daughter who had recently lost her father but rather about her engagement. It broke Lily's heart, but she refused to let the hurt show.

'It's true,' Lily said, injecting as much excitement as she could into her voice.

'To Julian Ford? I didn't even know you knew him! What about Lincoln? You're meant to marry *him*.'

Lily could almost see the frown on her mother's face.

'Yes, to Julian. I was never going to marry Lincoln, Mom. Julian and I have been together for a while.'

'So why haven't I heard about this? Or met him?'

'Because we had to keep it a secret while the Lincoln situation was supposed to be dealt with, but I couldn't wait any longer. I want Julian. I'm his.'

'Lily…' her mother said sternly.

It wasn't a tone she'd heard from her very often. Not when she and her mother had been close. But all that was lost now.

'Your father went to a great deal of trouble to secure your marriage to Lincoln. He knew what was best and now that he's gone—' her mother's voice broke on the word '—you should honour his wishes.'

'No,' Lily replied.

'Lincoln can secure your future, and your brother's future. What can Julian Ford offer you? Think of your family.'

'Lincoln means nothing to my future. This is about Arum. Julian can give me everything I want.'

That was true. He was helping her take her life back. Putting her in control of her destiny.

'Why can't you be happy for me?' Lily finished softly.

'You have never mentioned this man before. The Harrisons are like family...'

Lily wanted to point out that she could never have spoken to her mother about Julian when all she'd wanted was blind obedience to her father. She bit back the words only because she knew her mother was blinded by grief and wanted them all to hold on to every part of Sam Shah.

'You don't know Lincoln like I do,' Lily said evenly.

'I can't support this engagement, Lily. You belong with Lincoln. Honour your father.'

What about me? she almost asked.

'Then don't support it. None of you care about me anyway. Julian makes me happy and I'm going to be with him.'

Lily hung up on her mother. It took every bit of strength in her to do so.

She stared at the phone, willing herself not to cry. She couldn't trust her family to be on her side. To protect her or support her.

It didn't matter. She and Julian had a plan.

Lily took another look at her ring. 'I'm engaged,' she whispered to herself. 'What would a newly engaged woman do?'

The answer, she realised, was celebrate. She would show off her ring to her friends and family. Tell the world how happy she was. Well, she had no friends to speak of now, her family weren't happy, and posting all over social media would be unfitting for someone of her station. Which was fine. Because there was really only one person she wanted to see. The one in all this with her.

Deciding it would look good for them both, Lily locked her office behind her and made her way to the front of the shop, where she put together a box of pastries. Leaving one of her assistants in charge, she climbed into her car and drove to the financial district.

Though she had never been there before, she knew exactly where the IRES building was located. A tall glass and steel structure, it was the closest of them all to the pier. As she drove around it to park in one of the guest bays Lily saw at the entrance a large wireframe sculpture of the earth surrounded by a solid green circle with two leaves on top.

She made her way to the reception desk and was shown up to the top floor without having to say who she was. Realising that Julian had obviously cleared her to enter the building made her smile. He'd thought of everything, which was reassuring.

An immaculately dressed brunette greeted her as soon as she got out of the lift.

'Good morning, Miss Shah. Please follow me.'

Lily wasn't sure what she'd expected the inside of Julian's building to look like but, examining the white walls and floors with light grey furnishings and pops of green throughout the space, she figured she should have expected something like this. The no-nonsense décor seemed on point for him, but there was still a welcoming quality to the space. And the most impressive thing was that it didn't interfere with the spectacular view outside.

'Mr Ford, your fiancée is here to see you,' the brunette announced, holding open the door to a massive corner office.

Julian flicked his gaze up from his laptop and Lily was lost in the force of it.

'Thank you,' he said to his assistant. 'Hold my calls.'

Lily didn't hear the door close. She was too focussed on Julian's body as he rose from the chair and stepped around a large, frosted glass desk. He was in a dark blue suit today. Butterflies took flight in her stomach. An overwhelming urge to touch him seized her.

'Hi...' she breathed, then cleared her throat and tried again. 'Hello, Julian.'

His eyes flashed as he stopped in front of her. His thumb pulled her bottom lip free from her teeth. 'Is everything okay?'

'Yes, I just thought it might be nice if I brought my fiancé something from the bakery.'

She held the box out to him, and he took it with the utmost care. He leaned down to kiss her on her cheek. Her skin burned.

'Thank you.'

Lily kept her eyes on him as he lifted the lid on the box, his eyes crinkling with amusement as he set it down on the table.

'I thought I'd bring something for your employees…you know, because their boss is such a brute.' She grinned.

His arms came around her waist and she watched, spellbound, as a broad, beaming smile broke through.

She'd thought Julian would be handsome with a smile on his face. That was like thinking Michelangelo's *David* was a nice sculpture. A criminal understatement.

He was devastating. Deep dimples popping. Perfect white teeth gleaming. His eyes shining so bright. His face was transformed. Resplendent. It was like the sun coming out on cloudy day.

His smile was breathtaking…why did he hide it away? What had happened to him?

Lily resolved right then to bring a smile to his face as often as she could.

But she was already attracted to him…if he smiled like this often she would be in serious trouble.

'Need sweetening, do I?'

She wrapped her arms around his neck, still thrown by her reaction to him. 'Maybe…'

'Cinnamon rolls aren't very French,' Julian teased.

His usually low, smooth voice was somehow richer with the smile colouring it. As if he was one step away from laughter.

'No, they're not,' she replied, thinking that no doubt people on the other side of his glass-walled office would be watching. 'But the exclusion of them from any bakery is sacrilegious.'

'That's a strong opinion to hold on a bun.'

'And the only acceptable one.'

Lily barely paid attention to her words because her entire body screamed at her to kiss him. That once wasn't enough. She knew she had to marshal some control over herself before they fell into another embrace like the night before—except it would be far less appropriate in his office.

'Have you seen the news?' he asked.

When Lily shook her head, he unhooked her arms from around his neck, giving her engagement ring a quick kiss that had her melting before handing his tablet to her.

'I've been at the bakery since four this morning,' she said. 'But my mother did call me about it.'

'How did that go?'

'Not great,' she admitted.

There were several tabs open on his tablet, all with news of their engagement. Some of the media sites ran with pictures that had obviously been taken by other patrons at the restaurant, while others simply had individual pictures of them side by side.

'I had my PR people issue a release last night. Now our story is the only one everyone knows.'

'Perfect. Thank you, Julian.' She locked the device and handed it back to him.

He placed it on the table and leaned against the edge. 'Did Devan say anything?' he asked.

Lily shook her head walking towards the floor-to-ceiling window. She could see so much from here. The Ferry Building sprawled below her feet. The Bay Bridge stretching out to the horizon. The water glittering as if diamonds floated on its surface.

Her heart beat a staccato pulse as Julian's heat eclipsed her back. She told him of her interaction with her brother and he agreed that it had been better than anticipated.

'I had another reason for coming here,' Lily said, turning to face him.

'What's that?'

'I would like to plan our second date.'

Julian was struggling to keep his hands to himself. From the moment Lily had walked in all he'd wanted to do was hold her again. Kiss her like he had done on that balcony. The kiss on her engagement ring had been a slip of control that frustrated him, but he'd be lying if he said it hadn't excited him at the same time.

She had her hair tied up and a cobalt top over jeans, and Julian thought he had never seen a more beautiful woman. He could no longer recall the face of anyone who might have come before, and he didn't understand what it was about her in particular that made his blood sing.

'You would, would you?' he asked.

'Yes, all you'd have to do is be at Crème tomorrow evening. Eight.'

'The point is for people to see us,' he replied, even though the idea of being alone with Lily was rather enticing. Especially since he hadn't got much sleep the night before, because every time he'd closed his eyes he could feel the pillowy softness of her lips, or her hands on his neck, or the way she'd looked when she'd opened the front door...

'They will. I'll be closing up at five. Everyone will be gone by six. And when your car is parked for hours in front of my *closed* store word will spread.'

'Fine, I'll be there.'

'Great. Well, I have work to get back to.'

'I'll walk you out.'

He took Lily's hand, letting his office door swing shut behind him. It was like trying to hold on to the lightning crackling between them. The air became so heavily charged he was certain everyone on the floor could feel it. Certainly the craned necks as they passed people indicated as much.

He took Lily to a secondary bank of elevators. They had a lot less traffic. He didn't quite comprehend why he did this. After all, people needed to see them together. And yet he wanted a moment with her that wasn't on show...

He pressed the button to go down and the doors slid open instantly. He let her enter first, then pressed the button for the ground floor. Smoothly the doors slid shut, and with every moment that passed Julian's willpower slipped just that little bit more, until her nearness and her scent and the current running between them made it snap altogether.

He punched the red button on the panel, bringing the elevator to a jerking halt, and crashed his lips down upon Lily's, slamming her back against the black mirrored wall. There wasn't even the tiniest hint of hesitation from her as she kissed him back, her hands coming up to cradle his face. Their lips slid together as his body pressed up against hers, and a tidal wave of arousal crashed through Julian, burning him up from the inside out.

His hands slid down her body and she whimpered, the sound slicing through him. He grasped her wrists, pinning them above her head in one of his large hands, with the other pulling her thigh up around his hips, letting his arousal grind against her. A moan fell from her mouth and he growled. Beastly. Hungry. He kissed a path to her jaw, down her neck. His tongue tasted the sweetness of her skin. The scent of her flowery perfume and vanilla was on every inch of her.

'Julian...' she breathed against his ear. 'We can't do this here.'

Here?

In a lift. In his office.

He let his forehead fall to the crook of her neck, taking a breath. He eased her leg down, but his breathing still hadn't returned to normal.

'It might be a bit inappropriate to make out with the boss at his office,' she said.

He appreciated her trying to get them back on solid ground, but he could see the glazed look in her eyes, just the same as his.

He pulled himself up to his full height and dropped a kiss on her forehead. 'There's nothing inappropriate about me kissing my fiancée.'

He pressed the button once more and the elevator continued its descent. He walked her to her car and watched her drive away, cursing the way she threatened his perfectly ordered world.

CHAPTER SEVEN

HEADS TURNED AS a loud roar echoed through the streets of Fisherman's Wharf. Julian brought the car to a stop outside Crème but didn't immediately get out. Instead, he stayed where he was and looked through the large windows at the dimly lit store. He was dreading this date.

He had been irritated with himself since the incident in the elevator. Lily was challenging his control, and that wasn't something he could tolerate—because who would he become without it?

Images of his stepfather flashed through his mind. The man's violence. His own. Julian couldn't let his control be challenged because he refused to turn into the kind of man that his mother had loved despite all he had done to her. Refused to be the kind of person to fall in love.

The leather on the steering wheel complained at his wringing grip.

He had to reinforce his walls because he knew Lily had the potential to pass through those barriers. He didn't invite love or affection into his life. They were temporary. Inevitably ripped away by circumstance or time, leaving you battered and broken. Julian couldn't afford that. He had to guard himself against her.

Their touches in the office had been for show, calculated for the most part, so kissing her fingers, wanting for his own moment with her in the elevator—all that had to stop.

Julian got out of the car, shut the door and walked into Crème. The lights were low. A candle burned on one table that was perfectly set with shiny cutlery and tall glasses.

The table, while not directly in front of the window, was within perfect view of the street. Perfect to sell the idea of an intimate dinner with a bit of privacy. No doubt there would be pictures taken through the window.

Julian felt Lily enter before he saw her. He had to stave off annoyance with himself as he turned around. She wore a flowing red dress that tied around her neck. Her hair was loose, falling in a straight, silky sheath down her back. Diamonds sparkled in her earlobes. The punch of her beauty knocked the air from his lungs.

'Hi, Julian.'

She smiled, kissing him lightly on the cheek. He thought the kiss was far too fleeting—which was ridiculous, given that he had decided to keep his walls up around her.

'Have a seat. I'll be right back.'

She was gone before he had a chance to respond.

He took his seat and waited for Lily to return. This space felt too intimate. He should have insisted on planning this date. Then they would be elsewhere. Somewhere more public.

Lily returned with two large white bowls. The aroma emanating from them was heavenly.

'Here you go,' she said brightly, setting one bowl in front of him before placing the other on the table and taking her seat.

'You made this?'

Of course she had. Julian had thoroughly researched her before he'd ever set foot in Crème.

'I did. I know boeuf bourguignon isn't the fanciest French dish I could have prepared, but it's just so good.'

She reached for a carafe filled with chilled iced tea, but he beat her to it, pouring the cold reddish gold drink into their glasses, then setting it aside.

He picked up his cutlery and hesitated. She'd cooked for him. It shouldn't mean anything. It didn't, he told himself. So what if the last time a woman had prepared him a meal he'd been fourteen and dressed in thrift store clothes? It wasn't a big deal.

But as he looked into his bowl his mind was taken to a small table under a fluorescent light, with a nervous, scared, happy woman who shared his eyes. The person he'd loved the most and hadn't been able to save.

'Is everything okay?' Lily asked from across the table, watching him carefully.

'Fine.' He took a sip of his drink, bringing life back to his parched mouth, and then set about eating this meal that was definitely not making him feel anything. 'This is good. You're very skilled.'

'Was there ever any doubt? Did you not have one of my cinnamon rolls?'

He could see that she fully expected him to say no, but what fun would that be? She had him off balance tonight. It was time he returned the favour.

'I did.'

'You did?'

'Yes. All of them.' He smirked.

'A-all of them? I didn't expect… I didn't think you had much of a sweet tooth.'

'I don't, but as my fiancée personally delivered them to me the least I could do was eat them.'

Lily laughed. Not politely, the way someone would expect of her, but a deep belly laugh. 'Just when I think I have you figured out…'

'You shouldn't think that. Ever.'

No one ever got close enough to him to do so, and no one ever would. He dictated who entered and left his life, and he was quite happy for the only person who stayed in it to be Henry. As attracted to Lily as he was, he couldn't allow her in.

'A man of mystery.' She tried to hide her smile by taking a bite of her food.

'Don't you think mystery is important?'

'No,' she answered honestly. 'It means keeping secrets, and secrets ruin everything. Having to keep the truth of my relationship with Lincoln a secret cost me my friends, and a great deal of my happiness. So, no, I don't care for mystery. Give me honesty, let me understand you, and I'll never betray your trust.'

Julian agreed with her. But the truth required more faith and trust in people than he was capable of giving. And he hadn't been happy for a long time. Most of his life. At the very best he had snapshots of it when he was younger. A taste of what he couldn't hold on to. Something to crave and miss and make him bitter.

'When did your father make this deal with Harrison?'

'When I was nineteen. I was in France when Arthur died, and when I came back for the funeral my father told me what he had done. Lincoln seemed thrilled with the idea. I pleaded with my father to undo it, but I didn't want to displease him. I never did. Anyway, I went back to France to complete my studies...'

'You escaped.'

'I did.' Lily nodded. 'I was really grateful for the time I had left on my course, and the apprenticeship after that. I loved France, and I think I appreciated it even more after going back.'

'Do you miss it?'

'So much. On cold days we would all find a warm bistro and complain about the chefs at the school.' She chuckled with a faraway look in her eye. 'When it was warmer, we would fill up a pavement café.'

Julian couldn't help feeling caught up in her memories.

The smile she wore now shone brighter than any other he'd seen her wear.

'Things felt simpler there,' she went on. 'I wasn't Lily Barnes-Shah. I didn't have to live up to anything or fulfil anyone's promise. I could just cook.' She looked up at Julian, her sadness evident now. 'I love being here. I wouldn't want to live anywhere else. Crème is my life. But I sometimes wish I could go back to Paris. Pretend I'm still in a time when my father was alive and not arranging a marriage I didn't want. When my mother was still willing to be there for me. When Devan and I were closer. It's ridiculous, isn't it?'

Julian pushed his empty bowl away, leaning forward on his folded elbows. 'It's not ridiculous to wish things were different. It just doesn't help you to deal with what's actually in front of you.'

'Have you ever wished that?'

It was such an innocent question, but to answer would force Julian to reveal more than he wanted to. And yet he wanted to tell her.

'My father wasn't a particularly wealthy man, but he was smart.'

He felt a burn scratch at the back of his throat, like it often had when he was younger. It had made him feel so weak that he had eventually stopped himself from thinking about Conrad Ford at all.

'He was a professor of robotics in LA.'

'What was he like?' Lily was leaning in, and without thinking he pulled her hand towards him, wrapping his strong fingers around hers.

'I don't know,' he answered. 'He died when I was two. I have no memory of him. He feels a bit like some mythological creature I can't be sure existed. Except—'

'Except of course he did, because you're here.'

Julian nodded. 'I was told that he was almost single-mindedly driven. But also a family man.'

'Brilliant and driven?' Lily summed up. 'Like father like son.'

'That's how it would seem.'

And Julian was certain that was precisely one of the reasons that his stepfather had hated him.

'Do you know what he looked like?' she asked.

He huffed a humourless laugh. 'You could be looking at him now.'

'Oh, Julian. I'm sorry.'

He batted away her apology, but he could see the sincerity on her face. There wasn't pity there—just a deep sadness on his behalf.

'You mentioned you had a stepfather, though...'

He tensed, but Lily's free hand coming up to draw lazy circles on top of his had the tension melting away.

'My mother remarried a few years later and we moved to Lupine Heights.'

Lily's brows rose. Clearly she had heard about the small town just outside LA and all the things he'd had to avoid growing up in that place. The crime, the drugs, the gangs...

'We lived there until she got cancer, and within a few months she was dead.'

'Oh, my God...'

He gave her a small smile. 'That's life. You can wish things to be different, but at the end of the day it doesn't matter because it's all temporary.'

Her face softened. 'Is that when you came up with your energy storage invention?'

Julian saw right through what she was attempting to do. But he was grateful for the change of topic because he didn't understand why he was talking to her about his past. All the things he kept hidden. The only person alive who knew about this was Henry, and that was because he had needed to know what he was taking on in a mentee.

'It is. I was fifteen at the time. I knew I could make money from selling it, but I didn't want to. It was mine, and I was going to make more money from keeping it and using it myself.'

'That's really impressive,' Lily said.

Her heart was breaking at all that he had revealed and everything he wasn't saying. But he was opening up to her just a little, so she would take what he offered.

'Why that invention?' she asked. 'Why renewable energy at all?'

'You mean besides it being good business? Because I've experienced enough of people trying to destroy the world without thought about who it affects. What will we have left if we keep taking without care?'

Lily could see him so clearly. This real version of him that he kept hidden beneath so many layers. He wore his ruthlessness like a badge of honour, but beneath that veil was a man who was trying to protect a world that she could tell had been cruel to him. She wouldn't say it out loud, though. Something told her he would deny it if she did.

This man had a beautiful heart. She had seen glimpses of it before. Now she was certain it was there. He just protected it with impenetrable armour.

And that was when she realised that she was in serious danger of falling for her fake fiancé.

Lily stared into those soulful, heartbroken eyes, not realising she been leaning closer and closer to him until a large hand wrapped around the side of her neck. His thumb stroked her cheek, making her rise with him as he stood, moving into her space beside the table. The hand on her neck skated along to grasp her chin, and his thumb caressed her lips before sinking to her mouth. She flicked her tongue against the pad, watching Julian's gaze become stormy. He pulled his thumb free, trailing it over her bottom lip. She closed her eyes. A shiver racked her body. Julian was so close his breath ghosted over her lips.

'I want to kiss you,' he whispered.

Say no.

'Please…' she breathed.

But he didn't. Not immediately at least. She stood there, head tilted up to his. His face so close. Tasting the air between them. The only contact: his fingers holding her chin. She felt possessed, but it didn't bother her. Oh no, she craved more. Then, as if he understood what she couldn't say, couldn't ask for, he touched his lips to hers, spreading a liquid warmth through her that pooled in her belly.

Softly, gently, his lips stroked hers. Caressed hers. Sending wave after wave of scalding pleasure over her. But she wanted more. Julian was making her wait. Taking his time. Giving her so much, but only releasing it as he wished to. Warm, wet bites had her moaning in desperation. Begging.

And then he gave her a little more. His free hand moved to her hip. Fingers dug into soft red fabric and flesh alike as he drew her flush against his body. His heat was engulfing her. She savoured the hardness of him. That coiled wildness held at bay by an iron will.

And then he slid his tongue into her mouth and she ignited. She wasn't aware of anything but Julian's mouth now. Couldn't control her body.

Smooth, silky strands flowed between her fingers and she realised she was tugging on his hair. A deep groan rumbled in his throat and his kisses grew harder, his tongue urgent. Demanding. The hands on her hip and chin disappeared and she was being lifted into the air, but she didn't open her eyes to see where they were going. She couldn't bear to. All she cared about was keeping her hands around his neck and their mouths fused together.

She heard a door close. The office door. They were in her office. Away from prying eyes. Completely alone. This wasn't part of the show. This was for them. She should stop it, but she couldn't. She couldn't think of anything except that she burned for Julian.

Solid earth materialised under her feet, but it didn't matter because Julian was kissing her even more furiously now. Like a starving man having been denied food all his life finally finding nourishment. Her heaving breaths were rapid, and yet still she had no air. Her body was trembling. And even though she matched the ferocity of Julian's kisses, it wasn't enough.

'Julian...'

Was his name a plea or a prayer? She didn't know—but he did. Her back met the wall. She felt his thigh between her legs, propping her up, his hands skating over her breasts, his thumbs teasing her nipples. Lily moaned loudly. Sensation arrowed through her. Making her hips grind against him. She had never done this with a man before...

'Good girl,' he growled into her ear, before his teeth grazed the lobe.

His crazed, open-mouthed kisses covered her neck, her shoulder, and never once did his hands leave her breast. Hoarse moans and mewls flowed from her. And then without warning his hands dropped to her thighs and suddenly hoisted her up. She gasped as her sex pressed against the force of his hardness. It was the first time she had ever felt such a thing.

Her virginity was not something she held on to as some sort of treasure, rather that Lily hadn't wanted the intimacy when she was younger and definitely didn't want it with Lincoln, but now she found herself wishing Julian would take it.

She looked down at him through her lashes just as he was looking up at her through his.

Caught.

They were caught in a trap of their own making. The beast in him seemed barely tethered as he ground his hips against her, making her pulse race. Climbing to a height but she wasn't afraid of the fall. She craved it.

'Give it to me, Lily.'

His voice was low. Gravelly. Strangled. Raw.

And then she shattered. Plummeting through pleasure the like of which she had never known before. And Julian was kissing her again, until suddenly she found herself on his lap in a chair with no idea of how she'd got there.

He held her until her senses returned, and with it her voice of reason.

What had she done?

She had lost control so spectacularly. Lily couldn't think of a thing to say.

He dropped a kiss on her head and she had to hold in a sigh. This felt so good. Why shouldn't she indulge in whatever this was? She hadn't ever experienced attraction like this.

'I made dessert...' she said, and half laughed.

'I think that was it.' He kissed her neck. 'It's late.'

Lily nodded. They both needed a bit of space after what had happened. She got off his lap and saw his jaw tick as she left her office. She didn't know what he was thinking. Didn't know if he already regretted what had happened.

She cleared the table before he could emerge from the office, and once he did she locked up and allowed him to walk her to her car. When he kissed her cheek she hated it that she didn't know if it was part of their ruse or something more. The lines were blurred now.

She drove away thinking that even if this was a mistake, she couldn't bring herself to regret it.

CHAPTER EIGHT

THE LAST CUSTOMER had left Crème, and even though it was still bright outside Lily was happy to close up for the day. She had already sent everyone else home and the place was spotless—though one table in particular kept calling her attention. All day it had distracted her with flashes of the night before. Snippets of conversation playing over in her mind.

The world thought it knew about Julian, but hearing him speak of his mother and father had been something she wasn't prepared for. The matter-of-fact way he'd discussed them might have fooled most people, but not her. She was beginning to understand him, and she recognised that using his detached tone was the only way he could work around his sorrow.

She tried to imagine his loneliness. Tried to picture what it would have been like if her father had died when she was young, if she had lost her mother... But she couldn't because back then she'd still have had Devan.

She was starting to understand, though. Her mother's phone call was a wound that still throbbed, and yet she still had Julian—regardless of what they might be to each other.

It was surprising how much he cared. Which was made even more clear by the reasons he'd got into his business.

Lily walked into her office to switch off her laptop. She glanced at the wall, feeling her cheeks heat immediately. She really needed to guard her heart with Julian. It was becoming far too easy to forget her reasons for doing this.

With her laptop bag slung over her shoulder, she locked up the office before returning to the front of the store.

'Lily.'

She jumped, dropping her bag. Her heart nearly beat out of her chest.

'Lincoln, you gave me a fright,' she said, trying to get her pulse under control. 'What are you doing here?'

It was a fair question. He hadn't ever visited her store, always claiming he was too busy, which had pleased Lily as Crème was the place she was happiest. Where she didn't have to be reminded of promises made and broken. There was no reason he would come here at all.

'I didn't mean to scare you,' he said, taking a step towards her. 'I just came here to talk.'

'Okay...' Lily said uncertainly.

'You know what this is about.'

He fished his phone out of his pocket and handed it to her. On the screen was a picture from the night before, of her and Julian having dinner, and another of their kiss. It felt wrong to have that embrace splashed about. Especially after all they had shared.

Lily handed the phone back, her engagement ring twinkling in the light, and Lincoln snatched her wrist to get a better look at it.

'What are you doing, Lily?'

She could hear how angry he was.

'I'm doing exactly what I want to. Marrying Julian. I love him, Linc.' She pulled her hand away from his and took a step back.

His blue eyes grew frigid. 'You love him?' he sneered. 'You can't be that naïve. He's using you to get to me—and, in case you've forgotten, you will be marrying me.'

Lily tried to remain calm. She wasn't afraid of Lincoln and she wasn't going to give him the satisfaction of getting angry. 'I won't be. I have chosen the man I want.'

'We had an agreement,' he spat.

'No, we didn't. *You* had an agreement with my father, but he's dead now and your arrangement should be too. I'm not anyone's property.'

In a flash, Lincoln's hand was wrapped around her arm, his grip nearly bruising. 'You're mine! Do you understand?'

'You're hurting me.'

'You're going to take off his ring. People expect us to be together. I won't have you embarrassing me.'

His teeth were clenched. There was a wild look in his eyes.

'People expect us to be together because you let them think that. You didn't have to agree to this madness.'

And for that Lily would never forgive him. She wasn't a trinket to be given or owned. She was a successful business-woman with a first-rate education.

'Stop. Being. Stubborn,' said Lincoln. 'You're leaving with me.'

'I suggest you take your hands off her right now.'

Lily nearly sagged with relief at hearing that low, smooth voice dripping with fury. Rage had turned Julian's eyes more vividly green than she had ever seen them. She didn't know why he was here, she was just happy that he was.

Julian looked at the hand around Lily's arm, and then at the man holding her in place. A blistering rage overcame him. He wanted to rip into Lincoln. Tear him away from Lily. Only violence would satisfy his fury.

'Ford.' Lincoln curled his lip. 'This doesn't concern you.'

His muscles coiled beneath his expensive suit, Julian prowled towards them. 'You're touching what's mine. It very much concerns me.'

He stepped between Lily and Lincoln, prising his hand off her using a deathly grip that had Lincoln blanching.

'Leave. While you still can,' he growled.

Because if he didn't Julian was certain that Lincoln would only be leaving in the back of an ambulance. The image of another bloodied and broken man on a stretcher came to his mind, but this time Julian wouldn't feel a shred of guilt for putting him there.

At university it had taken him one moment to lose control—one snap of his temper to get his fists flying. He had been so far gone in his anger that he didn't remember a great deal of what had occurred. What he did remember was the satisfying connection of his fist, over and over again, with the guy's face and body. Pummelling him. Seeing the blood coating his own knuckles and shirt.

It had taken Henry's intervention to smooth things over. Julian had got lucky. But his mentor had made sure he had another outlet for his rage after that, and Julian had recognised the violence he was capable of.

Now, both men stared each other down, but with Julian shielding Lily, he would not be the one to cave. He hadn't meant to call her his, but now that the words had left his lips he liked the way it had sounded. Lily *was* his.

In those extra minutes he'd needed after she'd left the office last night, he'd realised how consumed he was with her. Which was dangerous to his goals. To his need for control. That was why he'd come here now. To make sure she understood that nothing further could come from what they had shared. That he had Arum and Zenith to consider. Neither of them was looking for more. That wasn't part of their agreement. He'd wanted to have that conversation in person. Now he was thankful for deciding to do that.

Lincoln spun on his heel and left.

Only once the door had slowly swung closed did Julian turn

around. He took Lily's face in his hands, lowering himself to look into her eyes. 'Are you hurt?'

'No. No, I'm fine,' she reassured him.

'Let me see.'

He pushed her sleeve up to see light red bands on her tanned skin. His breathing grew ragged.

'Julian, I'm fine,' she said, touching his cheek. 'Look, they're already fading.'

'Don't worry, baby, I'm fine.'

He flinched at the memory. He wasn't going to let that happen again. Not to Lily. He would protect her from everyone.

'I'm moving up our timetable. You're moving in with me now.'

'Julian…'

'You're not safe alone, Lily.'

His voice had still not returned to its normal register.

'I'm not afraid of Lincoln. I refuse to be. I've known him my whole life. I think we should stick to the plan.'

Julian stood to his full height, settled on his decision. 'If you don't move in with me tonight, I will just have to take you everywhere you need to go personally, and I will be hiring a security team that will shadow your every move. Up to you, sunshine.'

He knew she would never go for that. He was forcing her to pick the only acceptable option. Even though he would have to figure out how he would keep her at arm's length when she was under his roof.

'This is a gross overreaction,' she told him. 'You do realise that, right?'

Defiance burned in those obsidian eyes.

'One way or another, I will keep you safe. Now, you can come with me, or I can rearrange my entire life for as long as we are together.'

'You're impossible! Fine. I'll move in with you.'

'Tonight, Sunshine.'

'You really are one to close every loophole, aren't you? Yes, tonight. Now. Let's go.'

Julian sat behind the steering wheel of Lily's car while she furiously texted her brother. After having his own car sent home, he'd insisted on going with her to fetch her possessions—which surprisingly hadn't taken long. Devan hadn't been home, and when Lily had tried to call she'd reached his PA.

Julian had helped her load her bags into her car and she'd handed over the keys, saying she had to let her brother know what was happening.

'He's not happy,' Lily said, staring down at her phone.

Of course he wouldn't be.

He would have likely already heard about Lincoln's visit.

'He thinks I'm making a mistake.'

'He'll come around, Lily.'

Julian couldn't explain his need to constantly reassure her. Make her happy. He needed to get a hold of himself—especially if they were to live together.

'And even if he doesn't, at least you will be able to live on your terms. You don't need his permission or his blessing.'

'No, I don't,' she agreed.

But he heard the note of sadness in her tone and hated it. He had grown to care for her beaming smiles, even though he knew they covered up a world of hurt. And the fact that he craved them told him that he was growing far too attached.

He lived alone for a reason.

He rounded a corner onto a road lined with lush green from its grassy, well-manicured pavements to the hedges and tall trees. The houses here were large and stood close together. Except his. It was the only property with land to spare on either side. The trees almost completely blocked the house from sight.

'I didn't expect this much privacy here,' Lily said as the

gate swung wide and he drove down a short driveway to an underground garage, where he parked her car next to his and killed the engine.

Thinking it was the perfect opportunity to show Lily who he was, and stop her from getting closer, Julian turned to face her. 'I bought the houses next to mine and razed them.'

He saw shock, maybe a little horror on her face, and climbed out of the car just before she did. She did not wait for him to open her door, which annoyed him. He got her bags and Lily followed close behind, as if she was trying to process what he'd said.

'Just to have the land?' she finally asked, sounding scandalised.

'To be alone,' Julian responded simply.

To have peace.

'Why not just buy elsewhere?'

Julian placed her bags on the floor and walked out onto a terrace that overlooked the cliff face and the water below. He could feel Lily behind him.

'Because this is what I wanted, and I make damned sure I get what I want.'

'Why?'

She wasn't asking why he went after he wanted—he was certain she already understood that from their conversations. No, this question begged to know why *here*. It revealed only her curiosity, but an answer from him would reveal so much more.

Julian looked at her but said nothing as he picked up her bags and walked away, leaving her outside. He climbed the glass staircase. There was so much glass in his home. The Bay was visible from virtually every spot in the house. Julian loved being alone here, where he could breathe.

Lily fell into step beside him, not saying a word. He pushed open a door and gestured for her to enter first. Apart from his room, this was the room he loved most.

There was a wash basin and large tub in the corner beside a low wall that offered both privacy and a breathtaking view through the massive window that angled into the room turning the ceiling into a wide rectangular strip. The king-sized bed sat on a plush carpet, the headboard against a wood-panelled wall. The view of the sky uninterrupted from the bed. An ever-changing work of art.

'Closet is through those doors,' he said, setting her bags on the bed.

'Thank you, Julian. It's beautiful.'

He watched her walk to the window, looking out with a small smile on her face.

'Would you like me to send for the rest of your things?'

'That's not necessary.' She spun around and stepped around him to place a miniature Eiffel Tower on the bedside table. 'I have everything I need.'

Was he expected to believe that this woman who had grown up with such excess was going to live out of two suitcases?

She must have seen the scepticism on his face because she said, 'I have Crème, and I'm on the verge of getting my freedom. I don't need anything else.'

The words resonated too deeply with him. Because wasn't that his life too? What this place was meant to represent? IRES and freedom.

IRES had given him wealth and power, and that had given him freedom. Freedom to leave his past behind…freedom to create this sanctuary…freedom to live his life any way he damn well pleased.

'Join me downstairs when you're ready.'

He turned on his heel, leaving the room before he did something foolish. Because all he could think of was how much he would rather have her sleeping in *his* bed. Something he'd never wanted before.

Julian felt conflicted over having her in his home. He was maddeningly attracted to her, but having another person in his space had him ill at ease. And yet he still wanted to spend every moment with her, protect her... Which had him gritting his teeth.

He couldn't want that. He never wanted that kind of chaos in his life. He found peace in his home and Lily affected that far too much. He needed to take back control. Not let his affection for her grow. Because he had seen what loving someone, letting them in, could do to a person. Had seen his mother suffer day after day.

Needing a moment to clear his head, Julian stepped out on the terrace, taking a deep breath and focussing on his plan instead. Having royally angered Lincoln, Julian knew he had to find the insurance he needed to trump Lincoln's vote—but now he didn't just want to do it for his plan. Seeing the man's hand on Lily had Julian craving retribution, but he knew now he'd have to work harder on Devan.

He pulled out his phone and made the call.

'Shah,' he greeted him.

'What are you doing?' Devan demanded, not bothering to conceal his anger.

'I'm sure I don't know what you're talking about,' Julian said smoothly.

'Making Lily move in with you. You're using her.'

'I think you're projecting.'

'What?'

The word was a low threat that did nothing to move Julian.

'This arranged marriage to keep the power at Arum between you and Harrison. Here's the thing... When I walk in to find Lincoln Harrison manhandling my fiancée, I tend to become somewhat unreasonable.'

'Lincoln hurt Lily?'

Just like that the man's anger disappeared, to be replaced by a concern that made Julian want to laugh. How concerned could her brother truly be if Lily was having to move into *his* home?

'I could show you the marks if you'd like,' he said. But provoking Devan further wouldn't help, so he softened his tone. 'Lily is safe with me, Devan. I can protect her. Always will.'

That wasn't a lie. Even after all this was over and they were nothing to each other he would still protect her.

'I just thought you should know.'

There was a pause on the line before Devan responded. 'Thank you for telling me.' It seemed like he wanted to say more, but instead he said, 'I'll be keeping an eye.'

'I'd wonder what kind of brother you were if you didn't.'

Julian ended the call and slid the phone into his pocket. Devan should have seen the marks on Lily. He knew it wasn't serious but it did nothing to quell his rage.

Being around Lily made memories surface that he worked every single day to forget. But he would never forget.

Blood and bruises. Who could forget that?

Julian wanted to protect Lily. Except he knew his feelings didn't stop at protection. He could barely exercise restraint around her. The night before had proved that much.

There was only one thing he could really do. Pretend to be her doting fiancé in public but keep his distance at home.

The first thing that had struck Lily about Julian's home was how tranquil it was. It was so silent that she could barely hear the sounds of waves lapping on the shore. She could see why he would have wanted this place, but it had taken her more than a moment to get over the shock of him ruthlessly tearing down houses to get it.

And he was ruthless.

To buy a home, with all its memories, and then raze it…
She couldn't imagine it. It seemed callous. And that was a
part of Julian. Yet it seemed at odds with the person she was
discovering him to be.

It was something she should try to remember.

He kept his eyes fixed on his goal and she would have to
as well.

She made her way downstairs and found Julian standing out
on the terrace, hands in his pockets, face turned up to a sky not
quite dark enough to see any stars. He was so utterly, heart-
breakingly beautiful. She could see in the set of his shoulders
and in the expression on his face that for once his guard was
down, and it allowed her to glimpse the sadness within him.

There was more to his story. She wasn't naïve enough to
think he had confided in her about his whole life, but what he
had said was already more than any child should bear. Maybe
that was exactly what had sowed the seed of callousness in
him. She couldn't imagine what else he had been through.
What had scarred his soul.

Yet, even so, his determination was clear in every part of
him. Those suits and his perfect appearance did nothing to
hide that barely leashed power, and she wondered what would
set it free.

She stepped out to join him, felt goosebumps rising in the
chill breeze coming off the Bay. Julian shrugged off his jacket
and draped it around her shoulders. His warmth was already
so familiar.

'Settled?' he asked.

'As well as can be expected.' She walked up to the railing,
seeing the startlingly blue infinity pool below her and the
beach far below that. 'You have a beautiful home. So light.
Airy…'

'I sense a question there.'

'I just didn't expect it.' She hadn't seen drapes or blinds on any of the windows. 'I guess I'm wondering why. You are so private and this is so very open.'

'Because when you've spent your whole life in the dark, Lily, all you do is crave light. How's your arm?'

'My arm? Oh, fine.' She had almost forgotten about Lincoln altogether, even though he was the reason she was here.

'He won't get away with it.' Julian joined her, resting his elbows on the railing as he gazed over the water. 'I'll make sure he pays for hurting you. I made you a promise.'

Lily was struck that he should want to protect her so ferociously from the one person who held what he really wanted. It made her feel she was a priority. Not something she was used to.

'No,' she said, and he turned to look at her. 'Don't do anything that could hurt you later—and I'm not just talking about the Arum deal.' A boldness gripped her, and she placed her hand over his heart. 'Some things are more important.'

His eyes shifted into softness, which then morphed into something scorching, before all emotion was cleared away and he pulled away from her, stalking inside, leaving her feeling unbalanced.

She was growing to care deeply for Julian. Especially after what had happened on their date at Crème. But maybe she was reading the situation all wrong. After all, he was far more experienced than her. Maybe for him it was nothing more than a physical reaction and she was overstepping.

Why was it so much harder for her to remember the fake part of their relationship?

Lily lay in bed, staring at the sky as it was transformed from a black void to a blue and gold painting of sunrise. She threw off the covers and changed into her work clothes, despite it being so early, because she couldn't remain in this room any longer.

She took a look around the house, noticing the absence of

anything sentimental. There were no knick-knacks nor any in-dication of childhood memories, no pictures on the walls save for artistic photographs clearly purchased at a gallery. It was all so careful not to hint at the past. As if all that mattered to Julian was right now.

She went down to the kitchen, wondering if he would soon join her, but she found a note on the countertop saying he had an early meeting and wouldn't be back until later.

The note didn't sit well with her. Surely he would have mentioned the meeting the night before or knocked on her door earlier.

There was a nagging voice in the back of her mind telling her that he was avoiding her.

He didn't have any reason to, did he?

She got her answer later, after she'd arrived back at his home, having heard nothing from him all day. It was just a simple text saying he was tied up at the office and wouldn't be back before dinner.

He was definitely avoiding her.

He couldn't have gone from wanting to rearrange his entire life to being so busy he barely had time for meals that weren't at his office. Something was going on, and she was determined to find out what it was.

She waited up, finally hearing him enter late into the night.

'Welcome home,' Lily said, stepping into the light of his open-plan kitchen.

'Lily. What are you doing up?' He gave her the barest of glances before placing a cup down on the counter.

'Waiting for you.' She saw his eyes close momentarily, a tick in his jaw. 'We need to talk.'

'Whatever it is, I'm sure it can wait.'

'No, it can't. I want to know what I've done to make you avoid me.'

Her voice was strong. Whatever his answer was, she was

resolved not to be hurt by it. There was a problem and they needed to fix it.

'I'm not avoiding you,' he said impatiently, placing his hands on the counter on either side of his cup.

'That's the first lie you've told that I genuinely don't believe.'

'I don't know what you want me to tell you.'

'The truth. Why are you avoiding me?' She stood beside him now, not giving him the chance to evade her.

'Lily…' he growled.

'We're doing this thing that requires us to be honest with each other, Julian. I'm not backing down until you tell me what's going on.' When he did nothing but heave a frustrated sigh, Lily pushed. 'Is it because I'm here? Do you regret it?'

'*Yes*, damn it!'

Lily recoiled as though she had been slapped.

Julian pushed away from the counter, running his fingers through his thick red hair as he stepped away from her before whipping around, fire in his eyes.

'Do you know what you do to me?' he almost yelled. 'You make me want to lose control!'

Lily was stunned. The words sent sparks through her body. She'd thought she had done something wrong. Something to push him away. But she was wrong. He also felt whatever was building between them, and it wasn't just attraction.

'Then do it,' she said evenly, standing her ground.

Julian stared at her, a scorching look in his eyes. 'You don't know what you're saying,' he said slowly.

Lily lifted her chin. Every bit the confident Shah she'd been raised to be. 'Maybe I do.'

Julian stalked towards her, barely restrained, grabbing her arms in a vice-like grip. 'You have no idea.'

Lily thought of everything she knew about him. How much

he wouldn't let out. Maybe he needed to. Maybe she could be the one he let go with.

She raised herself up on her toes and kissed him softly. An innocent touch before lightly licking his lip. 'Show me.'

'Lily…' he groaned.

She could feel the tension in his muscles.

'Julian…' she whispered, and he seized her mouth.

Lifting her onto the counter, he stepped between her legs and she wrapped them around him. He held her face as his teeth tugged at her lip, making her gasp. Lily had thought their other kisses had set her aflame, but they were nothing on this. His control was in tatters. His need was speaking to hers, turning into an all-consuming storm with both of them in the centre of it.

There was nothing gentle about this kiss. Nothing gentle about the grip he had on her or her fingers pressing into his back under his jacket. There was no masking the sounds of want he made, in conversation with her own moans. But just as quickly as his lips were on her, he was yanking himself away, his chest rapidly rising and falling.

'Not like this,' he said. He moved back, pressing his forehead against hers. 'Not like this.'

'Julian, I want—'

'Tomorrow I'm taking you on a date.'

Her heart fell. 'Our third date…'

CHAPTER NINE

THAT EVENING LILY made sure she was home early. Having no idea where Julian was taking her, she paced back and forth in the walk-in closet. To be honest, she was rather unsettled by this date. After Julian's admission, and that kiss that had felt so real, she'd thought they were making progress to something more. Something she'd realised in that moment she desperately wanted.

She had made the first move. Had felt liberated enough to decide for herself that she wanted Julian. Then he'd said he would be taking her on a date, and it had felt as if the rug had been pulled from under her.

Always their arrangement.

That was his shield, wasn't it? Whenever he was pushed into real feelings, Julian put those walls back up. And while Lily had no illusions of what this was meant to be, no one could have predicted their intense chemistry.

Maybe she just had to be patient.

She pulled her satin robe tighter, taking another look through the racks.

'Lily?' Julian's voice came through the door.

She pulled it open, revealing him in a black suit, his hair just slightly damp. The scent of leather and spice wove around her. She gestured him to enter the room, which was generously sized, but with him in it suddenly felt very confined. Especially with his eyes trailing over her robe and then moving back up to her face. The unmistakable flare of want was there.

'Can you tell me where we're going?' she asked.

He cleared his throat. 'That's why I'm here.' He reached into his jacket pocket, revealing two tickets that he handed to her. Her eyes widened when she read them.

'How…?' she breathed. 'It's been sold out for months.'

His fingers grazed over her cheek. 'When are you going to learn? There's nothing I can't do.'

A smile stretched across her face. He was taking her to a French play that she had wanted to see so badly, but the tickets had been snapped up before she'd even had a chance to buy one. Lily had consoled herself by saying it was for the best, because she would have had to attend alone.

'Happy?' he asked tenderly.

'Yes! So happy!' She hugged him tightly, trying to convey how much this meant to her. 'Thank you, Julian.'

'You don't have to thank me, Sunshine.'

'I guess I should get ready.'

She pulled away and Julian caught her around her nape pressing a quick kiss to her lips. 'You can keep those.'

He left the room, leaving Lily holding the tickets and trying to keep tears at bay. He had understood how much she had loved her time in France. Understood what this would mean to her. This might be a fake relationship, but no one had ever treated Lily like this. As if what she said and loved mattered in a massive way.

Julian waited at the foot of stairs, his nose buried in an email that he was replying to without paying much attention. He really had wanted to keep his distance from Lily, but when she'd pushed, leaving his precious control in pieces, he'd realised he couldn't stay away. He didn't want to.

He wanted her. He wanted her more than he wanted any-

thing else. And while he didn't deserve her, he could enjoy what they had while it lasted. Why shouldn't he? Everything came to an end. Everything was taken away at some point. So until then he would soak up all he could from her and then, when it was done, he would tuck those memories away with all the others he tried never to think about.

That was why he'd had to stop that kiss. Lily deserved more than a frantic, lust-filled ravishing on a kitchen countertop. She deserved to be taken care of, to be worshipped—which was why he'd bought those tickets to the play. It had stung when she'd assumed it was another date for their arrangement, but it was good because she wouldn't allow herself to get too close to him.

The click of a heel was the first thing he heard. Slipping his phone into his pocket, he looked up. His breath caught. How was it possible that this woman wanted him? She was perfect.

Thin purple straps sat on tanned shoulders. The neckline of her dress dipped into a V in the valley of her breasts. The skirt was gathered at her tiny waist before falling to the floor in layers of rich purple chiffon. There was a long slit up her left leg, and he could see flashes as she stepped onto the stair below. Her hair was pulled up, and he could almost taste the skin at her neck.

'Exquisite.' He held out a hand to help her down, revelling in her glorious smile.

'You don't look too bad yourself, Ford.'

He flashed a smile at her—something he found himself doing more frequently these days—and led her to the car, sneaking glances at her all the way on their drive to the theatre.

When they finally took their seats in gold and red opulence, Julian lifted their threaded fingers to his lips. It wasn't enough.

'So, are you going to require a translator?' Lily teased.

He chuckled. 'I'll manage.'

'Good, because I can't promise that I would remember.'

Julian knew he would try his best to remember this moment. Her unguarded happiness. He heard the play start, caught glimpses of it, but all that really held his attention was the woman beside him. Every emotion was displayed on her face, and yet, throughout, that smile never wavered.

His thumb stroked across her knuckles and he leaned over to kiss her hair. And then, almost without realising it, he was on his feet, clapping with everyone else as the cast took a bow and the curtain fell.

A tear fell from her eye, kissing her cheek before falling. He brushed it away with the back of his finger, proud that he could have brought her to something that had moved her so deeply.

'Did you enjoy that?' he asked.

Lily nodded enthusiastically. 'So much. You don't know what this means to me.'

'Come on.'

He led her out of the theatre, avoiding anyone who might want to speak to them, ignoring the unmistakeable flashes of a camera, and helped her into his waiting car.

Tipping the valet, he slid into the driver's seat and turned to Lily. Not quite ready to put an end to the night when she looked so happy, Julian asked, 'Would you like to take a drive with me?'

'I'd love that.'

They drove along the darkened streets in comfortable silence. Words were unneeded for whatever was passing between them...building between them.

It wasn't long before they were meandering through the winding roads of Golden Gate Park. Vibrant green foliage illuminated by his headlights flashed by, and soon he parked at the side of the road, climbed out, and rounded the front of the car to assist Lily, before taking her hand and walking over the bridge.

The bright full moon was their only source of light, casting a silvery glow on everything it touched. It was enough to see where they were going, but Julian still scooped Lily up in his arms as if she weighed nothing and set off on the path.

'What are you doing?' She laughed.

'Saving you a twisted ankle.'

It was an excuse, and they both knew it, but she let it drop.

Julian had, of course, been to Strawberry Hill before. He had seen couples and families walking the paths or sailing in the paddle boats and he'd never understood. Not until now. When he had someone special to appreciate this place with.

A pagoda with bright red pillars and a jade roof appeared at the water's edge and Julian set Lily on her feet once he'd climbed the stairs and stood at the stone banister.

'It's so beautiful out here…and quiet,' Lily said, leaning into his warmth.

Julian wrapped an arm around her shoulders, pulling her against his side, tipping her head up to kiss her just once.

'Cold?'

She shook her head and gazed out at Stow Lake, but his gaze was firmly on her. As it had been all night.

'I know I've already said it, but thank you for tonight.'

She looked up at him and he was lost in those bottomless eyes that seemed as if they could hold an entire universe.

'My family used to go to the theatre together when I was younger,' she said.

He could tell it was a happy memory. It was clear from the longing in her voice. 'You miss it,' he stated.

'I do. I used to be so close to my father… I thought he was perfect in every way. I think we were just a very close family—especially Devan and I—but this arranged marriage with Lincoln changed all that. My relationship with my father wasn't ever the same. It became…'

'Strained?' Julian offered.

'Yes. And it was like that until he died. I wish we could have fixed things. It's the one regret I have. But I'm also so angry with him. Angry that he promised me to Lincoln. Angry that he died before he could fulfil his promise to me to undo it. Angry because I feel like he didn't do all that he could, and now I have all this anger towards Devan and my mother.'

'It's okay to feel that way, Lily. The people who should have protected you didn't. You have every right to be angry.' Julian shook his head, thinking of how everyone responded to her. All those bright smiles in her store. 'You have no reason to treat everyone as kindly as you do. This world has failed you.'

'No, it hasn't. *You* haven't.' She smiled at him. 'I know I have the right to feel betrayed and angry, but I don't want to live my life under a dark cloud. I refuse to. There are good people in this world too, so I choose to see the best where I can.'

Like she did with him. But would she still think so when she knew of the darkness in his heart? Why he didn't let himself love?

He found himself talking before he'd consciously thought about the words. Words he hadn't uttered in years. Maybe ever.

'The man my mother married was an alcoholic. I don't remember much of our lives in LA after my father died, but I do remember the day we moved to Lupine Heights. I was six at the time, and from the moment we stepped into that small dark house I knew I didn't want to be there.'

Julian felt Lily's arms wrap around him, but he couldn't see her. All he could see was the stream of memories.

'From that first day I hated the way he looked at her, but I didn't understand it then. After their wedding his drinking got worse. It stopped being something that happened at night and became a constant. He was volatile at the best of times, but when he drank he was completely out of control. My mother tried to please him. Keep him happy. Hoping that if she made things easier for him he'd have no reason to turn that volatility on us.'

He looked at Lily then. Hoping she would understand what he was saying. Why he wanted to help her so much. Protect her from Lincoln like he never could his mother.

'It was a ridiculous hope. The first time he hit her she made me hide in the closet, but I could hear, and when I couldn't take it any more I burst out and ran to her. She was cowering on the kitchen floor, and that was the first time I felt rage.'

He shook his head, trying to clear away the fear, the anger.

'I leapt at him, but I was just a kid and he easily slapped me aside. So I kneeled beside her...'

'Don't worry, baby, I'm fine.' He could still hear his mother's voice in his head. See her weak, tear-stained smile.

'It became a constant thing after that. And I tried to protect her, but I was weak. Eventually he had enough of me interfering and turned his violence on me.'

Julian still remembered the bruises. The pain of his broken arm.

'You weren't weak. You were young. Didn't anyone help you? Report him?'

Julian smiled serenely down at Lily, brushing her tears away and kissing her forehead.

'Who would?'

He was certain that the abuse had been suspected at his school, but no one had helped him, choosing instead to believe whatever lies his stepfather had told.

'He would just explain everything away. I begged my mother to leave, but she never did.'

Again, he hadn't been chosen.

'She tried to defend me, but that only put her in harm's way. There was no winning. And then, just before I turned fifteen, she died. It was his fault. He drank away every penny we had. There was nothing left for her treatment.'

And he had done nothing. It had just been him and his

mother against the world and he had done nothing. How had his genius helped him then?

Guilt and shame ravaged him.

'When did it stop?' Lily asked, her voice hoarse and scratchy.

'For her? When she got sick. For me? After she died. He didn't realise how much bigger than him I'd had grown. I hadn't either, until one day he came at me, and I swung for him, and the next thing I knew he was across the room in a heap.'

He felt a phantom pain spread across his knuckles. Felt a savage satisfaction settling in his belly as if the wound was still fresh. He had enjoyed it then. Had got high on the power of beating his stepfather. It had been the first real slice of elation he had felt in years. That explosion of violence had made him happy, and he had known what he was because of it.

'What happened to him?'

He could see she was hoping for some retribution. He had wanted that too.

'Nothing. I graduated from high school early, studied on a full ride and never went back. I haven't seen·him in over a decade. This is why I need control. Why I don't have relationships or friends. I can't risk turning into him. I can't risk falling in love.'

'Julian,' she cried. 'Vincent is not your father. You are not him.'

'I don't remember my father, Lily. It doesn't matter what blood I have in me when that was the man who raised me. I'm vengeful because of him. I'm ruthless because of him. I watched my mother die because of him. All of that is in me. You say you want to see the good in people? Some of us don't have any good left.'

'That's not true.' Her hand caressed his cheek and he wiped away the tears that wouldn't stop. 'You're a good man, Julian. If you weren't, you wouldn't be helping me. Wouldn't have protected me from Lincoln. Wouldn't own the company you do. You're *good*.'

Julian took her face in his hands, lowering his lips to hers slowly. His eyes were on hers, and just as their lips touched her wet lashes fluttered closed, but his didn't. He couldn't bear not to look at her.

'Lily…' he whispered.

He wanted to devour her but he took his time savouring her, kissing her sweetly under the stars. Not a soul in sight. Just him and her and the give of her soft lips, salty with tears shed for him. A crack formed in his chest at that alone.

She grabbed the lapels of his jacket, pulling herself up, trying to be closer to him, so he lifted her, holding her tightly, letting her kiss him deeply, a little clumsily. Her inexperience endearing. And then he was pushing her back against a pillar, his tongue demanding. Wanting Lily to give him more. For her to seek out her most hidden desires and present it to him.

Furious.

That was what this kiss had become.

Mouths moving together.

Biting. Licking. Sucking.

Pleading.

And then Lily was whispering in his ear. 'Take me home, Julian.'

CHAPTER TEN

THEY BURST THROUGH the door of Julian's house. Lips frantic. Hands in hair, on chests, under shirts. No time to speak. No time to breathe.

His body was coiled, begging him to take her where they stood, but he wouldn't heed that call. There was only one place he wanted her.

He slid his hands under her thighs, through the slit in her dress, picking her up and walking up the stairs to his bedroom. Lily wouldn't let him stop kissing her, making his blood pound. He couldn't remember a time when a woman had driven him this crazy.

Julian took her into his bedroom, releasing a string of profanities as he let her slide down his body, bringing her to stand in front of him. He was painfully hard.

Holding Lily's heavy gaze, Julian trailed his fingers up the back of her neck to the elegant silver clip holding her hair up. As gently as he could, he pulled the long, shiny stick away from the barrette, dropping both pieces to the floor with a clatter. Her hair fell in a waterfall of luscious black. An oil spill over his light hands.

Doing the one thing he had wanted to since stepping into Crème, Julian wrapped the length of her hair around his hand, tugging her head back in a fist to expose her throat. He groaned, tasting the skin there.

Sweet. She was so damn sweet.

That flowery scent, with a hint of vanilla intoxicated him—it was almost as if the bakery had permanently etched itself into her skin.

He kissed her again. Slowly this time. Reverently.

'Julian…' she moaned. 'Stop teasing me.'

But he wasn't. He was driving himself mad. Wanting to take his time. To taste and kiss every inch of her. Discover her every secret. Find out if she would beg or plead or pray…

'Sunshine…' his voice was gruff '…tell me you want this.'

He needed to hear her say the words because he had never wanted something so badly in his life.

'I want this…' she breathed. 'Julian?'

'Hmm?' He was kissing the spot below her ear that had her melting in his arms.

'I have to tell you something first.'

He pulled away to look at her. At the serious look on her face. So uncertain…

He tugged on her chin. 'You can tell me anything.'

'I'm…' Her face turned crimson. 'I've never done this.'

He frowned, before understanding took hold. 'You're a virgin?'

She nodded, trying to look anywhere but at him. He'd known she was inexperienced. Could tell from her kisses. But he'd never once suspected she would be a virgin. Not especially with her being promised away. Christ, she never had a single moment to enjoy her life.

'Are you mad?' she asked.

He couldn't help but laugh. 'No, Sunshine. I'm not mad. I am very, *very* not mad.'

He smiled. A primitive part of him rejoiced.

Lily was his. His and his alone.

He was overcome with relief that he hadn't lost control the night before, and determined to make this night unforgettable for her.

* * *

Lily's face was on fire. Embarrassment was curling through her after having to admit her inexperience, but at the same time her heart was racing. Full to the point of bursting. Because she wanted this so badly and she wanted it with Julian.

His warm hand caressed her cheek and she leaned into the touch.

'Look at me,' he said.

She obeyed without thought.

'I'm glad you told me.'

His lips on her forehead sent a shiver down her body.

'And I'll offer you a first too.'

Lily looked at him, confused.

'I have never brought a woman here.'

'To your bedroom?'

'My home. Just you, Sunshine.'

Lily was so happy that she had waited. So happy that her first time could be with Julian. She realised how deeply she trusted him. And he trusted her too. If he didn't, he would never have told her everything he had tonight.

'Take me, Julian.'

She was jittery with anticipation. Excited and just a little scared of the unknown. He had already shown her pleasure once, and they had both been fully clothed. How would tonight change her?

He sucked her lip between his, sending tingles throughout her body, making her open to him, begging for him to deepen the kiss. But he didn't. She watched him step away and kick off his shoes and socks before standing before her.

'Undress me.'

The whispered command had her gasping. Excited to touch all the hardness that she had felt under his shirt. Every bit of him was accessible to her now. It was exhilarating.

She swallowed thickly, her gaze meeting his heated stare.

A gentle smile of encouragement on his face. God! Those dimples were going to be the end of her.

Slipping her hand under his jacket, she saw Julian's eyes close, and he let out a slow exhale. She pushed his jacket off his shoulders, letting it fall, then trailed her fingers over the buttons of his perfect white shirt. Then a sudden impatience seized her and she couldn't wait. Grabbing the placket in her delicate fists, she looked at him, gave him a wicked smirk that he returned, and ripped it open, sending buttons popping and scattering all over his hardwood floor.

His eyes darkened even further. Lily hadn't known she could feel this wild...this uninhibited. This demanding of what she wanted. She tugged down his pants and his underwear with them. There was no waiting now. And when he kicked them aside she got to see him. *Really* see him.

Nothing could have prepared her for the wave of arousal she felt at the sight of his body. Lean. Muscular. Every muscle was carved into him as if he was made of marble. Power kept at bay by the silken veil that was his skin. Every inch honed perfection. And then there was the tattoos that had been hidden by his suits.

Bold and black and so striking against his fair skin, it wasn't a pretty piece, but she could tell it wasn't meant to be. It was a massive dying tree, with a knotted, twisted trunk and gnarled roots inked over his ribs and ending at his hip. Bare branches curled towards his nipple.

Lily traced the pattern with her fingers. Followed the branches as they curled and grew around his side towards his shoulder blade. The dead, barren branches slowly grew. Burls giving way to tiny leaves that became lush and full. From death to life. And on his left pec was a series of roman numerals separated with two little dots.

She noticed his breathing had become ragged. His lips were

pressed together, studying her. She didn't want to think about what the tattoo meant. He had given her enough this night.

'Kiss me,' she ordered.

One arm wrapped around her waist and the other held the back of her head as he fused their mouths together, gliding his tongue over hers. Each swipe speared to her sex, making her gasp loudly. Then she felt his hands on the back of her dress, tugging the zip down until the fabric parted. She shivered when his fingers trailed lightly over her bare spine.

A groan coming from deep in his throat.

'So soft…' he said against her lips, peeling the dress away.

Her stomach fluttered as he scooped her up without warning and placed her in the centre of his massive bed, crawling over her exactly like the jungle cat she'd thought him to be the first time she saw him.

His lips trailed over her jaw, down her neck, over her chest…kissing, tasting, biting in a lightning trail that had her breathing hard. Lily hadn't ever felt anything like this. As if she was floating and drowning all at once. And then his mouth closed over her nipple and she arched off the bed but then Julian was running a hand down her side soothing and igniting at once. An earnest supplication of pleasure so intense it had to be sinful.

His lips returned to hers as his fingers trailed up the inside of her thigh, but he didn't stop there, easing her lace panties aside and stroking her sex. She knew how wet he would find her.

Lily had always assumed being this intimate with someone would be difficult, maybe even mortifying the first few times, but it wasn't. A voice at the back of her mind told her that Julian made the difference. She believed that she was safe with him. That he would take her pleasure and treasure it.

'I'm going to go slow…' He kissed her sweetly. 'You can stop at any point, Lily. Do you understand?'

She nodded.

'I need to hear you say the words, Sunshine.'

'I understand.'

'Good.'

He reached into a drawer in the nightstand and pulled out a foil square. He reared back and she watched him roll latex on his daunting length. She was suddenly nervous. Excited, but tense. Falling into her head were questions and possibilities, and it was Julian's teeth biting her lip that had her coming back to him.

'I'll take care of you, Lily.'

She watched him move to the foot of the bed, pulling off her underwear. She stopped breathing entirely when his mouth lowered to her sex. His tongue had her awash in sensation, her hips bucking to meet his mouth and a large arm curled around her, his hand pinning her to the bed, and he licked and sucked and soon had her drowning in a river of pleasure.

The bedding fisted in her palms, she uttered a melody of whimpering cries she had no capacity to understand as they filled the room.

Further and further away she was swept in this torrent. Her toes curled. Her body was his to control. She was relaxed, and yet strung impossibly taut, and as she begged him...*begged* for release...just before she could be taken over the edge she was in Julian's arms, foreheads connected, his hardness at her entrance for one eternal moment before he thrust into her and held her tightly.

A cry fell from her mouth and he kissed it away. Keeping still, he held her close until she could adjust to his large intrusion.

'You're okay, Sunshine. Take as long as you need.'

His voice didn't sound like his at all. It was strangled. Tense.

The burn faded quickly and she tried moving her hips, shocked at just how good it felt. So Julian began to move.

Slowly at first. And then he bent her leg, which she wrapped around his hip, and she couldn't think. Couldn't breathe.

How could anything feel this good? It was killing her in the best possible way.

'Breathe, Lily,' he whispered in her ear, which only sent her soaring that much higher. 'You're incredible.'

She wanted to respond. Wanted to say something—anything. But there were no words in the world. There never would be. All that existed was Julian and how he made her feel.

She opened her eyes—that she had no idea when she had closed at all—to see their bodies joined, moving rhythmically together. Julian's body chorded, betraying the strength that lay in those muscles that treated her so gently. His light eyes—so dark—heated but there was something more than heat in them and her body pulled tight, caught in a raging torrent. Her pleasure crested until she crashed around him, shouting out his name as he grunted his own release.

Panting was the only sound in the silence.

She felt Julian's head in the crook of her neck, tried to stroke his hair but she was boneless.

Lily wasn't sure what she'd expected, but it certainly hadn't been this. Pleasure so intense that a tear fell from her eye, cutting a wet path down to her temple.

She felt Julian's lips there. Kissing away the tear before the next one fell. His tongue was tracing up its path. Licking away the overwhelming emotion. A gentle kiss was placed on her closed eye. Then the other. He kissed her cheeks and her nose and her forehead, and lastly her lips. Lingering there. The taste of salt on his tongue.

Then he pulled away from her, disposing of the condom before collecting her in his arms and covering their bodies in a thick duvet.

As she lay in his embrace, sated and happy, Lily wondered

if she did herself a disservice by waiting so long. Could she have had this before?

'No,' she heard Julian say. 'I know what you're thinking, and it wouldn't be like this with anyone else. This is us.'

Her eyes began to droop as Julian stroked his fingers through her hair, and it wasn't long at all before Lily was sound asleep. Her last thought was that this date wasn't just for their plan. This was more. This was so much more...

The first thing Lily noticed when she woke up was the empty bed. She had woken briefly earlier, to the warmth of Julian's naked body pressing against her, his arms wrapped tightly around her. Deep steady breaths had told her he was fast asleep but now the sheets were cold where had lain.

She emerged from under the covers that were so carefully tucked around her, brushing her hair away from her face. Rubbing the sleep from her eyes, she finally looked around the room she had slept in.

The ceiling and two walls were made entirely out of panels of glass. Above her the sky was still a deep blue, slowly turning lighter. The panoramic view allowed her to see the golden rays as the sun slowly began to rise. The wall behind the headboard and the one on one side of the room were the only solid ones. There wasn't much in this room. A massive bed, two lights fixed above the nightstand, and in the corner where the three glass walls met, sat a solitary chair with a lamp arching over it.

So much space to hold so little, but it didn't need more. Didn't need art or ostentatious furniture when all she could imagine doing was sitting in bed and watching the Bay. The unmistakable bridge was silhouetted against the morning sun, slowly showing hints of that bright orange colour.

Julian had created this for himself. A little piece of heaven that he didn't invite anyone into. And she couldn't blame him.

Not after what he'd said. This was obviously his refuge, and he had invited her into it.

Her heart thumping at the knowledge, Lily tried to keep her head. Moving in with him was a necessary part of their ruse. They had chemistry—that had been evident from the start— and maybe he was coming to trust her, but if last night had been such a mammoth step in whatever their relationship was, wouldn't Julian still be here this morning?

She thought back to how he had avoided her before. Was he doing the same now? Trying to push her away because he regretted saying too much? Being with her? After all it had been her first time. She had nothing to compare it to. What if it hadn't been as good for him? Not nearly as life-altering?

That was entirely possible. She was inexperienced. He might have just been leaning into their attraction. Maybe in being with her he was trying to indulge so it wouldn't be as potent any more. Would make their interactions more bearable for their plan.

The problem was that for her the lines were becoming blurred. This relationship wasn't real, but everything she had felt the night before had been. Julian had confided in her and she had given him her virginity. Those things weren't fake. So where did they go from here? Because she still wanted her freedom and Julian definitely wanted that energy deal.

Lily had to get out of this room.

But she was naked.

She stomped over to his closet, sliding the door open and stepping into a space that lit up when she walked in. Rows of suits and shirts sat neatly, evenly spaced on the rails. Ties, watches, shoes—everything perfectly displayed. Perfectly ordered.

'This is why I need control, Lily.'

This was beyond control. This was keeping himself on an impossibly tight leash.

'You make me want to lose control!'

She was chaos to him…and order and chaos were mutually exclusive. They could never have anything beyond this fake engagement.

Breathing suddenly became difficult, especially when she felt as if her heart was being split in two. She wanted more with him, but now she was faced with the evidence that it wasn't possible, and it hurt so much more than she could have imagined.

She found a neatly folded white T-shirt and slipped it over her head. It was far too long on her, but that suited her just fine.

Fully intending to go to her room, dress as quickly as possible and leave, Lily stepped into the hallway and heard a metallic clang followed by a series of other strange noises. Following them, she came to the open door of a gym, and just as she reached it Julian walked through. Shirtless and sweaty.

Her mouth dried as she looked at him. Sweatpants sitting low on his hips. Buds in his ears. His hair damp and sticking to his forehead.

Lily reached to pluck one of the buds out of his ear and placed it in her own. She wrinkled her nose at the screamed-out lyrics, the aggressive thumping beat, and placed it back into his ear. She saw his lips twitch in amusement.

She'd just about turned to go back the way she'd come when he caught her wrist and pulled her back. The ear buds were in his hand now, which he was sliding into his pocket.

'I was hoping you would sleep in,' he said.

'I'm late. I should be at Crème already.'

Why was this so awkward?

'I'm certain you don't have to be the one to open up every day. So why don't you tell me why you're really up so early?'

'You weren't in bed. I just thought… It really doesn't matter. I should get dressed.'

'You just thought…?'

She could see he wouldn't let it go, and knew he'd probably be able to see straight through any lie. 'I know last night was different for each of us,' she said. 'It probably wasn't that enjoyable for you. But for me…'

Heat burned her face. She could only imagine how red it would be. And now, to her absolute mortification, he was trying not to smile.

'That's what you're worried about?'

He tugged her into the gym, sitting her down at the end of a padded bench and kneeling in front of her, his hands on the tops of her thighs. Lily tugged the hem of her borrowed T-shirt further down.

'Sunshine, last night was beyond words. I could have you every day in every way and it still wouldn't be enough. I'm greedy for you. And leaving you asleep in that bed this morning, not waking you with my tongue and my fingers, took more strength than I knew I possessed.'

Lily opened her mouth but no words came out. Not when his words had her growing moist.

'My leaving that bed had nothing to do with how much last night meant, or how much I want you, and everything to do with who I am.'

'What do you mean?' Lily asked softly.

'I'm awake before sunrise every day so I can do this.' He gestured around the gym. 'So that I can be at my best for every moment of my day. For IRES.'

'You work every day?' But Lily already knew the answer to that, even without his solemn nod. 'Julian, that isn't sustainable.'

'It is for me. It's what I do. No matter where I am.'

'Why do you work so hard?'

'IRES is all I have. For what was sacrificed…' Julian shook his head '…it has to mean something. I need IRES to be a success. It makes me worth something.'

'You already are.' She cupped his cheek. 'You can't just work. You need to relax too. Do something you enjoy.'

'I do.'

Lily didn't believe him, but she asked anyway. 'What's that?'

'Krav Maga.'

'Krav...? Julian, that doesn't count!'

She realised how lucky Lincoln had been to leave Crème unscathed.

'Would it make you happy if did something different?' he asked, and there was a spark of mischief in his eyes.

'Maybe...'

He gave her a wicked grin and pushed her down onto the bench, bunching the T-shirt shirt at her waist and lowering his mouth to her sex.

Before all thought could be pushed out of her head she held on to the new goal she had. To help Julian really live his life.

They were well and truly late now, but Julian didn't care. Not when his lips were sliding against Lily's as steaming water rained down on them in his cavernous shower. Holding her back to his chest, he slid his fingers in and out of her, heard her moans echoing off the tiles until she loudly came apart for him.

Then he lathered and soaped her, bringing her to the edge and leaving her there.

'A promise for later,' he whispered in her ear.

Seeing her in his T-shirt had punched such a wave of possessiveness through him he'd very nearly told her that was all she must wear in his home. But somehow he had managed not to act like a neanderthal when she'd sought reassurance.

Julian couldn't believe Lily had thought he hadn't enjoyed himself. He was certain sex would never be the same for him again. It certainly wouldn't be after she'd left his life—and she did have to leave. He still couldn't give himself over to love, or whatever this was.

Stepping out of the shower, he wrapped a towel around his waist before picking up his razor in the routine he had performed every morning since leaving his stepfather's house. Work out, shower, shave, work hard for as long as it took to achieve his day's goal—and repeat it all the next day. It had served him well. But now he wanted more than that.

His gaze flicked to Lily in the mirror. He wasn't worthy of her. He would lose her. It was inevitable. Everyone left. By choice or not—it was immaterial. His father had died before he'd had a chance to know him, his mother had lived a tortured life before she died, and Lily would leave because all she was looking for was her freedom.

So he was faced with his own choice: he could push her away or he could enjoy this while it lasted.

So, no choice at all then. Because he craved her like air.

'Arum is hosting the Zenith dinner the day after tomorrow,' Lily said while drying her hair.

Zenith was the exclusive network started by the old money families of San Francisco. Julian still hadn't received his invitation, and this would be the first test to see if he was making any impression with this plan that they had embarked on.

'I know,' he replied.

'You know you're my plus one, right? Even if you don't get an invitation, you'll still attend.'

'I know that, but getting one will make convincing those people to work with me much simpler.'

'You still have time,' Lily offered.

He did, but it wasn't all that much. The longer it took for him to be accepted into the ranks of this group, the further away the Arum deal would get.

CHAPTER ELEVEN

THE INVITATION LANDED on Julian's desk that very same afternoon.

Step one was complete.

Now he would have to gauge how his relationship with Lily affected Zenith's perception of him.

But for the first time since coming up with this plan, Julian was unhappy. Something between him and Lily had shifted. He no longer wanted to flaunt their relationship in the faces of those who wouldn't accept him without her. He wanted to protect what they had behind very thick walls. Except it wasn't just up to him. Lily would benefit too, and any change in the plan would affect her life. She had given him no indication that her wishes had changed and he couldn't expect them to— especially when all he could commit to was something temporary. His goals hadn't changed either.

So he would continue with his end of the bargain and when Arum signed it would all be worth it.

He hoped.

Julian up picked the invitation card, eyeing the Zenith logo. These people advertised their power and wealth unapologetically. It was ridiculous to him that he could create an international powerhouse and still have to cater to their whims to get a real foothold in his own city. But he had to. Because not achieving this goal meant failure, and he couldn't withstand that.

While it irritated him, it wouldn't have bothered him as much before. Now it felt like the price was growing. And that price was his relationship with Lily. Yet everything rested on this event. His future and the future of IRES.

What he needed was time with Lily away from all this. Time that was just theirs.

Julian had Lily pressed against his side in the back of the car. He noticed her fingers tracing along the stones of the elaborate yellow diamond choker he had given her before they'd left the house.

They were both clad in black, as per the invitation, but for some reason he'd hated the idea of Lily in something so lifeless, so he'd presented her with a gift. A little bit of the colour that he had grown so accustomed to seeing her in.

She was staring out of the window, but he knew she was looking at nothing in particular.

Raising the partition between them and his driver, Julian pressed a kiss to her temple. 'Don't be nervous. I'm not letting you out of my sight.'

She leaned into him with a sigh, but said nothing, and Julian suddenly wished they were anywhere but here.

But he couldn't take his eyes off the goal.

For either of them.

They approached a magnificent high-end hotel, recognisable immediately by its carved façade and towering stone pillars and a landmark in San Francisco. It was fitting that the dinner should be held here, where business had been conducted by the wealthy and influential for over a hundred years.

Julian himself had used their boardroom facilities to secure several deals. It seemed like a sign.

The car pulled up to the entrance and once the door was opened for him Julian stepped out and offered his hand to Lily.

Every head looked their way when they entered the room. Everyone saw her hold on to Julian's hand. Watched as she stepped even closer to his side.

He leaned down to whisper in her ear. 'Are you ready for this?'

'Funny, I was just about to ask you the same thing.'

Lily smiled. She could have fooled anyone else here, he thought, but not him. He could see she was nervous about being here. Facing the repercussions of their actions. But he also knew she would do anything to have her life back, and with or without him she would handle these people with grace.

'Here comes our first test,' Julian said, watching Devan approach with an impassive look on his face. 'Shah.' He held out his hand.

'Ford,' Devan greeted him, taking it.

Julian's eyes never once left his and he noticed a shift there. Instead of outright animosity there was just caution. He looked at his sister and kissed her cheek.

'How are you, Lily?'

'Happy.'

She beamed, and Devan clearly believed it, because his shoulders sagged. With relief or resignation Julian didn't know, but it was a start.

'Good. That's good,' Devan said quietly.

There was a hint of sadness in his tone that irked Julian.

'The house isn't quite the same without you,' he went on.

'You're going to have to get used to that, Dev,' she told him.

Lily smiled up at Julian and he felt a fist clench around his heart. He kissed her temple without thinking. A small smile broke through his features without his permission.

Devan noticed. Everyone did.

'Would you like a drink?' Julian asked her, offering Lily a moment alone with her brother.

'Yes, please.'

Except she didn't let go of him. Chose to remain by his side instead of her brother's. He wasn't prepared for how that felt...

'Ford, wait,' Devan said as the two of them turned away. 'I want to talk to you.'

'About...?'

'The energy deal.'

Julian tensed. Then he pivoted to face Devan.

'You want in, and I'm prepared to help you. Under one condition.'

'What's that?'

'You make Lily happy. I know you can keep her safe, and I thank you for doing so, but if I find out that you've used her, not only will you not get the deal, I'll see to it no one in San Francisco works with you again.'

'Dev!' Lily reprimanded.

'Easily done.'

Julian extended his hand and Devan shook it firmly.

They stepped towards the bar, but didn't make it very far before they were swallowed up by a group of people. Julian already knew every single one of them, but still he stood there through the introductions, shaking hands and paying compliments.

These were the people he needed on his side. The shareholders of Arum.

'Congratulations on your engagement!' gushed an older woman covered in glittering diamonds. 'Can I see the ring?'

Julian wrapped an arm around Lily's waist, fusing her to his side as she held out her left hand.

'Oh, that's beautiful!'

'Julian chose it.'

Lily was the very definition of a charming fiancée. He re-

membered what a terrible liar she was, so seeing her so effortlessly playing the part should be worrying him. Except he
realised that when it came to Lily his walls had come crashing down, and he wanted every bit of affection she had it in
her to give.

'He has great taste.'

'Clearly.'

Julian looked down at her with softness in his heart.

'I have to say, Ford, I was rather surprised to hear about
your engagement. I think we all were,' said a greying man in
a sharp suit.

'Some things aren't for the world to see,' Julian replied
easily.

Whatever this was budding between them, it was theirs
alone.

'I couldn't agree more,' the man said with a twinkling smile.
'I saw you having a chat with Devan?'

'He is Lily's brother.'

Julian would give nothing away. He wanted to know where
they stood before he said anything.

'Yes, but you must know how the shareholding in Arum
is. If you can convince Devan to vote in your favour, we may
be inclined to do the same.' The man handed Julian a business card. 'Give me a call. I expect to see a lot more of you at
these events, Ford.'

It was music to his ears.

When they finally made it to the bar Julian placed their order
then pulled Lily aside. He had been so attentive all evening,
she thought. He could clearly see that she was apprehensive
about seeing Lincoln again. Not that she anticipated him making a scene—he never would—but he had been so angry the
last time she'd seen him.

She felt warm fingers brush against her cheek, followed

by soft lips on hers. Julian's tongue caressed hers sweetly, his kiss obliterating the worry from her mind.

'We should be mingling,' Lily said softly.

Julian's breath kissed her ear, sending tingles right through her.

'I don't really care about that. I just want to take you back home, lay you out and feast on you until you're breathless and panting my name.'

It took every ounce of self-control she had not to moan right there. The self-satisfied smirk on his face told her he knew exactly what he was doing. She would have dragged him away herself if she hadn't understood how important this night was.

'Well, you're just going to have to wait.'

'Am I?'

Julian pulled her body flush against his. Powerful thighs pressed against hers. His manhood and his muscular torso.

'Yes.'

He was making it very hard for her to think clearly. Especially because he was allowing her to see his playful side. This man who didn't smile or laugh did so freely around her, and he was doing so now, in the presence of others. And they noticed.

How could they not when his hands had been all over her all night? Every touch sending shockwaves to her core.

'Lily… Ford.'

The chilly voice made the smile drop off her face. She felt Julian put his arm around her shoulders as they both turned to face Lincoln.

'Hi, Linc,' she greeted him.

He said nothing. Blue eyes boring into hers.

'Harrison.' She heard Julian say.

'I suppose congratulations are in order,' he said stiffly.

'Thank you.'

He was only doing this to keep up appearances, because a

Harrison very clearly giving a Shah the cold shoulder would set tongues wagging. And they couldn't have that.

'The board can't stop talking about you two. Seems like you're a changed man, Ford.'

'I'm the same man. Lily just brings out a different side of me.'

Flashes of that night in the pagoda came to her mind. Of being in his bed for the first time. Of him giving her the necklace she wore. All the hidden pieces of himself he'd shown her. They were always there. No one else cared to see it, and Lily couldn't think of a greater travesty, but it made what they had all the more special.

Lincoln was looking at her again. Something wavered in his gaze. The look of someone having lost a prize. She hated it.

Julian must have noticed the change in her, because he excused them, leading the way to the tables that were now filling up before dinner was presented.

And that was when she met Henry Cross.

Of course she knew of him, and had wondered what he would be like since the first time Julian had mentioned him, but she hadn't expected to meet him here.

'I'm glad you made it, Julian,' Henry said. 'And you must be Lily. Pleasure to finally meet you.'

'And you.'

Lily smiled politely. The tables were filling quickly, and she noted that everyone around them was from Arum. Her brother was seated opposite her, looking uncomfortable next to Lincoln, but Julian wouldn't let her focus on that.

Throughout their meal, and through all the chatter, she relished the touch of his thumb on the back of her neck. The whispers and the kisses. All of it distracting her from the fact she was sharing a table with the people she was hoping to get away from. The very people Julian was trying to win over.

The feeling she'd had when she'd walked into his closet

swarmed over her. She wanted him so much, but this could never last. Not when they had such opposing goals.

When the meal was done and most of the seats vacated, Henry asked Lily to stay.

'You can go, Julian. You have work to do.'

Lily watched with shock as Julian rolled his eyes and then obeyed and stood. He kissed her cheek and turned to his mentor.

'Don't steal my date,' Julian warned, before walking away.

Lily wanted to burst out laughing. She hadn't thought there was a soul on earth that Julian would listen to. But maybe it was more that Henry understood what Julian needed, and in turn Julian had shown her how much he trusted Henry.

'I have not seen him this happy in my life. You've done this, Lily,' said Henry, as he watched Julian walk away.

'Thank you.'

Lily's heart squeezed at the tenderness in his kind brown eyes. 'You care for Julian a lot.'

'I don't know if he's told you how we met?'

'Not much.'

Lily was on tenterhooks. Eager to collect every little piece of Julian she could.

'I went to give a talk at his college. I could tell there was something special about him, and when we spoke I saw a young man with a massive intellect in worn-down thrift store clothes. I knew then I couldn't let him languish, just because he didn't have the privilege of his fellows. So I took him under my wing. He was so serious. Never smiled. Not even on the day of his graduation.'

'You were there?' Lily was so glad that Julian had found someone to care for him.

'I was. I taught him everything I knew about business, but it became clear very quickly that he saw things differently, and soon the young upstart was giving me advice.' Henry laughed with clear affection. 'But I didn't want him working for me.'

'You didn't?' Lily asked, confused. Henry seemed to love Julian so much, and it seemed rather strange that he hadn't wanted to give him a place in his company.

'No. No doubt he would have made me a great deal of money, but with everything that young man had been through he needed someone to support his dreams.'

'How did you do that?' she asked.

'He gave me the capital to start IRES.'

Lily started at Julian's voice.

He sat elegantly in the chair beside hers.

Henry chuckled. 'He's like a son to me.'

'You're growing sentimental, old man.'

He seemed unbothered by Henry revealing so much of his past.

'Maybe I am.'

Lily loved the fact that she was being allowed to witness the special relationship they had with each other. Loved it that Henry had never been put off by Julian's coldness. He just accepted him.

'When I found out about this engagement I will admit I was concerned, but you've done well, Julian.'

'I have.' Julian's fingers curled around hers. 'We should go…'

All three rose from their chairs and Henry leaned in close to Lily. 'I'll be grateful to you for ever. If you ever need anything at all, you need only ask.'

He gave her a peck on the cheek and placed his card in her hand, then he shook Julian's and left.

CHAPTER TWELVE

'THAT WENT WELL,' Lily said, once they were settled in the back seat of the car.

It had gone far better than either of them had anticipated. All Julian had to do now was solidify the relationship with Devan and the shareholders were his. Yet that was far from the reason tonight had been so momentous.

Henry had told Lily things that Julian often wished his mentor would forget, but he wasn't upset. He wanted her to know him. On some level he understood that even when she eventually walked away, a little piece of him would be tucked away with her and it would be safe.

He pulled her across his lap, kissing her neck, holding her as she melted against him, wanting so desperately to make her happy.

'I have a surprise for you,' she said breathlessly.

'For me?'

'Yes, but before I can tell you what it is, I need to know if you trust me.'

'Of course I do.' Trust wasn't something Julian often did, but he trusted Lily. Trusted her with his past, his plans…

'I want to take you away,' she said.

'Where to?' he said against her neck, trailing his fingers slowly up her leg.

'Paris. I've made arrangements for Crème. All you have to do is say the word.'

'Paris?' He stopped his hand on the inside of her thigh, felt her tremble.

She touched his forehead to his. 'Come to France with me.'

'Of course I will.'

Hadn't he been wishing for time alone with her? She was giving him exactly what he wanted.

'We can take my jet.'

He saw relief flood through her and trailed his hand further. The damp fabric between her thighs kissed his fingers and he groaned, eyes burning into hers.

'You've kissed me and touched me and teased me. And I've been aching for you all night,' she told him.

Julian's lips swooped down on hers in a fiery kiss that had him growing hard in an instant, cursing the fact that they were in this car that would be arriving at his home within minutes.

They broke apart and without a moment's pause he had his phone to his ear, issuing quick commands.

'We're going to have to wait, Sunshine. Give me an hour and I'll make it up to you.'

As promised, in an hour they were buckled into plush cream seats on Julian's jet and taxiing down the runway. Julian sat opposite her, with a table between them, making no move to touch her. Though his face remained neutral, there was a glint in his eye, and Lily knew then that he wasn't breaking his promise...he was just making her want him even more without laying a finger on her.

Finally he grinned, covering it up with a large hand as he looked out of the window.

San Francisco was a web of golden light as they lifted into the sky. No sign of the steep roads and iconic houses. Up here she could find no reason to be anxious, no anger towards her family. Those were all problems left on the ground.

Lily hadn't felt this serene in all the years since she had returned from France. But now it was as if a heavy cloak had been cast off and she was free. She wanted to help Julian live, and Paris did just that for her. This way she could take him away from everything that weighed on his shoulders, from that maddening discipline, and help him relax.

In the back of the car she had seen the understanding in his face when she'd invited him on this trip. He appreciated how much it would mean to her, and she wanted to share this part of herself with this man who was not going to be around for much longer, if tonight was anything to go by. Because once Devan and the board voted to sign with IRES, Lincoln would too. He wouldn't vote against his partner.

The smart thing to do would be to distance herself from Julian. She was already too close. She wanted him so badly. But he had never once said that he was considering any kind of future with her.

Even after he'd told her about his stepfather, he'd said he couldn't let anyone in. But maybe it was time for him to let go of the fear of what he might turn into. Maybe she could show him who he really was.

Would he let her?

The plane levelled off and drinks were served. A short glass of something red, diffused slowly into clear liquid. The glass, frosted with condensation, sat on a coaster and she reached to stir it with the black straw before taking a sip. She didn't bother asking what it was. It refreshed her and that was all that mattered.

'Tired?' Julian asked.

'I'm fine,' she said. But when she leaned her head back she could feel the tendrils of sleep creeping over her.

She felt him undoing her seat belt and carrying her to the back of the plane. She should have protested, but it was comfortable in his arms, warm and safe, so Lily let him carry her to the bed and drape the sheets over her. But she wouldn't let him leave.

'Stay.'

She held her breath while he watched her. For a second? A minute? A pause in time. Then he took off his shoes and jacket and slid between the sheets, pulling her to him. She went willingly into his arms.

'You should sleep. I'll be right here when you wake.'

'Kiss me, please.'

He didn't hesitate. Not for a moment.

This kiss was soft, gentle. Sweet beyond imagining. It didn't ignite her, like his lips usually did. No... It melted her. Stirred her slowly. His fingers combing through her hair had her sighing into his mouth. But before she was ready to stop his lips were gone, pressing a kiss to her forehead.

His fingertips stroked lazily back and forth on her scalp, lulling Lily to sleep. She thought she heard him speak, but she was too far under a thick cloud of sleep to parse his words.

Only once they had begun their descent did Julian rouse Lily. After landing there was a blur of activity, and soon the two of them were in an electric sports car that Julian drove through the streets with such ease Lily wondered just how familiar he already was with Paris.

That question was soon answered when they reached a beautiful old building in the Seventh Arrondissement. They went up to the very top floor and she watched Julian pull out a key to unlock a door, which he held open for her.

'Welcome home.' He smiled.

'Home? You own this place?' she asked, stepping into a light foyer with wooden herringbone floors and large windows.

'Yes. I have properties all over the world.'

Of course he did. She should have considered it before. But

when they'd been in his house she hadn't been able to picture him anywhere else.

He slipped his hands into his pockets. 'Why don't you take a look out of the window?'

Lily gasped. She felt as if she could touch the Eiffel Tower if she stuck her hand out far enough. Just a handful of trees separated them from the breathtaking landmark.

'You have a beautiful home.'

It really was. A beautiful blend of modern and classical French design.

She felt his arms wrap around her. 'Come on, we've still got plenty of light left in the day. We're going out.'

His bedroom was just as exquisite as the rest of the apartment. After a quick shower Lily dressed in a flowing skirt and light jacket. She was just draping her bag across her body when Julian stepped out of his walk-in closet.

She was at a loss for words.

This was what he looked like when he relaxed.

There was just a hint of stubble on his face, long, powerful legs were sheathed in light denim, and a white T-shirt stretched across his chest. The gold ring that pierced his ear was twinkling, as if it held the secret of Julian's transformation.

It took nothing away from him. This Julian still had that air of danger his suits advertised so flawlessly, except now he looked more human somehow. Not the man who had to shave every say, who had to only wear those suits and workout at precisely the same time each morning because he had to be—had to be—so perfectly disciplined for every moment of his life.

'Ready to go?'

No, she wasn't. She didn't want to leave this apartment at all now. Didn't want to waste a single moment of this Julian when she knew he would disappear the moment they went back to San Francisco.

'Where are we going?' Lily asked.

Maybe she could convince him to make it a short outing…

'Where do you want to go?'

Her very first thought was the pavement café that held so many great memories. And so that was where they went.

Sitting outside at a wrought-iron table, they were nothing more than a couple having coffee. The Arum deal, Lincoln and Devan all seemed like faraway concerns that couldn't touch them here.

'Sunshine,' Julian said as she reached the end of telling him the story of something that had happened at the café. 'It's okay to come back here because it brings you happiness, but you can't use it to escape to the past. Look forward. You need to create new memories.'

He was right—she did. And she would. With him. Those were the only new memories she really wanted, but she was too afraid to say that. Afraid to break the spell. Because he still hadn't said that they were done with faking. That this was real. She wanted to believe that it was. It *felt* real.

'The future seems a little uncertain right now,' she admitted.

'It always will—but you make a plan and you stick to it and all the pieces will fall into place.'

Would one of those pieces be him?

In those days spent in Paris, creating new memories was exactly what they did. Lily took Julian to all the places she wanted to share with only him, and he did the same for her. They'd be driving for hours, only to realise that they would rather be holed up in his apartment.

On their second day she learned that his French was perfectly fluent and cringed at the thought of her teasing when he'd taken her to that play.

Every single day was perfect. There wasn't a camera to be found, and that allowed them to carve out precious moments for themselves.

One moment was made all the more special as Lily stood alone in the Hall of Mirrors at the Palace of Versailles. Bright sunlight poured in through the large windows, reflecting off every sparkling surface. The golden statues were nearly glowing. Above were chandeliers so breathtakingly intricate she couldn't stop looking at them. And the ceiling… It was beauty beyond words.

Julian had managed to arrange a private tour, just for them. Another memory made with him for her to pocket away.

She glanced sidelong at him as he studied a statue of a golden woman bearing a crystal lamp. This man had brought her here, showed him a piece of himself and made her happy. Simply looking at him made her heart race.

'What's on your mind?' he asked, turning to her.

'Nothing,' she lied. When he cocked his eyebrow, she chuckled. 'It's just unfair how you affect me.'

'You think it's not the same for me?'

Julian was incredulous. How could she not see what she did to him?

'Come with me.'

He was going to set the record straight. He was in France with her because she had asked him to come, but still she thought he wasn't completely under her spell.

It was ridiculous.

He took her hand and led her through the palace and the magnificent gardens to the hotel in the palace grounds. They entered a grand apartment with its gilded walls decorated similarly to the palace that could be viewed from the window.

Julian had booked it for complete privacy but he did not stop until they were in the largest suite allowing her to walk a few steps away from him. She pivoted on the spot, watching him. He knew she would be reading clear want on his face. This was how he would show her exactly what she made him feel.

'Take off your clothes and get on the bed.'

Lily cocked a brow at his command, but he knew she would obey. It was written in the way her eyes grew heavy, in the breaths that seemed to come a little more raggedly, and the blush creeping up her neck. Julian watched, cataloguing every minute detail, every change in her body.

She drew her shirt over her head, letting it slip through the tips of her fingers to the floor.

Julian stood still. Trying with all his might to control the want ravaging him. Trying not to cross the distance between them and take her in his arms. He couldn't do that. He had to show her what he couldn't say. What he might never be able to say. Even though the words had been dancing around his mind constantly.

'I love you.'

They had been the last words he had said to his mother at her bedside. The last time he had said them at all. There was no way he would ever be able to say them again.

Julian pulled his own shirt over his head and threw it to one side. Lily paused her movement, her gaze raking over his body, and he could have sworn he felt it like a touch. Drawing the corner of her lip between her teeth, she removed the rest of her clothing, with Julian just a step behind.

Then she climbed into the centre of the large, four-poster canopied bed and leaned back against the pillows.

'Touch yourself,' he said, hoarse.

Her skin flamed, and he could see her swallow hard, but despite her shyness Lily raised a hand and trailed it down her stomach. Teasing.

As hard as he was, he knew it wasn't just arousal that coursed through him, but pride. He was so proud of this woman who didn't back down from any challenge. She just reached within herself and pulled from her limitless reserves of strength.

So he would make her invincible. No one was ever going to try to control her again. She wouldn't be shy about her pleasure, wouldn't worry about her freedom, nor care if anyone was there to support her. Because he would make sure she knew she needed no one. The world should be bowing to her, begging to be allowed into her universe.

And even though he couldn't say the words playing in his mind, Julian knew that he loved her. It was an absolute, immutable truth. Even though he'd tried to fight it. Even though he knew what love could do to a person. Even though he knew this couldn't be for ever. Julian had fallen in love with her.

He watched her fingers slide lazily over her sex, heard a gasp escaping her at her own touch, and with eyes locked on hers he grasped his hardness, matching her slow, languid pace.

The muscles in his abdomen tensed, pleading with him to go faster, but he wouldn't. He leaned against the wall behind him. The cool surface was welcome against his heated skin. Lily was flushed, her breathing growing more uneven the longer she watched him. And as her fingers moved faster, so did his hand. A moan came from both of them, the two sounds intertwining in the quiet room.

'Lily…' he rasped. An invocation.

Through the haze, he could see understanding light her eyes. She slowed her hand right down and so did he. His obedience to her order was unwavering, making him groan…a rough, strangled sound.

A feline smirk curved her lips. She controlled him. Controlled his very pleasure. Her eyes sparkled with an excitement that made his pulse hammer even harder. She pushed up on her elbows, a look of challenge in her eyes, and it was the sexiest thing he had ever witnessed to see Lily come into her power.

She'd taken a wrecking ball to his high walls, exposing him. All of him. Raw and unguarded. She saw his smiles and laughter. His ability to joke and be playful. Not because he'd let her, but because there was no other way he could exist around her.

Lily had become his safe space. And, to his immense surprise, he didn't hate it. There was a settling in him almost like peace, knowing she saw him. Maybe not the brutal truth of him—not yet—but he would hide nothing from her now.

Nothing except those three words he would never utter.

Julian's muscles tensed and bunched. His shoulders chorded as she toyed with that control. Her breasts were heaving just as much as he struggled for his next breath. But he would say nothing. He would revel in all that she did to him.

He could tell the game was becoming too much for her, that she was on the verge of losing control, and she closed her eyes, throwing her head back on the soft down pillow.

'No, keep your eyes open,' Julian instructed in a low, tight voice. 'See what you do to me.'

And she did. That obsidian gaze never wavered as her fingers slipped between her folds, faster and faster. Julian could feel the coiling beginning at the base of his spine. And then Lily was calling out his name as she shattered on the bed.

Her fingers stilled.

'Keep going. Don't stop.'

Despite her writhing and mewling she listened to him. He knew how sensitive she would be, but she listened because he had power over her too. Her fingers moved as quickly as his hand, and then he felt his entire body go taut as his release burst from him, clouding his vision and stealing his breath... his strength.

Julian dropped his head against the wall, needing a moment before he was able to prowl to the bed, climb over her. One hand held him up while the other slid over her smooth skin. Over her thighs and her ribs and her breast.

His fingers wrapped around her neck as he indulged them in a firm but gentle kiss. His lips blazed a trail to the base of her throat. Slowly, so slowly, kissing their way up her neck, his lips brushing her ear.

'Now do you see what you do to me?' he whispered. 'You hold me in the palm of your hand, Sunshine.'

'Julian…'

She breathed hard against his neck. A tremor went through him.

'You do that to me too.'

He scooped her against him, rolling onto his back and holding her tightly. She settled with her head on his chest. There was an end point looming, so Julian was determined to savour this with Lily while he could—because he was certain he would never experience it again.

Legs entwined with his, her arm draped over his rippling stomach, Lily trailed her fingers over the pattern of the tree inked into his side. She smiled as his skin pebbled from her light touch, but he made no move to stop her.

She drew over the black lines. 'Was it painful?'

'Yes.' His voice was soft.

'When did you get it done?'

Her voice was as soft as his as her finger followed the line of a dead branch reaching towards his nipple.

'While I was at college.'

After he'd left his stepfather's house.

'After I met Henry and he showed me what it meant to own a company. Understanding the dynamics was easy, and I let myself believe in a future where I had all the power.'

Despite his quiet, even voice, Lily could feel how his heart sped up. Hazarding a look at his face, she saw that he was looking out of the window. Who knew what he saw? But that sadness she often caught a glimpse of seemed to be leaking out of him now, and she had to turn away lest she dissolve into tears and this wasn't about her needing comfort.

'Before that I was still convinced I just had to survive. It was all I was used to...'

Lily had to shove aside the burning anger clawing at her throat. He shouldn't have had to be used to that. How was it fair that Julian had had to deal with the aftermath of abuse and his stepfather had paid no price?

'But once I saw what I could achieve I just looked forward.'

'And that's when you had this done?'

'Yes.'

She looked again at the knotted bark and gnarled roots. The stunning leaves were hidden from her right now, but she refused to move from her position. She could guess the meaning of the tattoo now. To grow from something dead, something just trying to remain anchored into something that flourished. That triumphed. He'd survived his abuse, but when she thought about how disciplined he was, how he never wanted to lose control, she knew he hadn't healed. He was still running from it. From that life.

'And this one?' she asked, running her fingers over the numbers on his chest to keep him talking.

He was silent for a moment. She looked up to see his eyes were closed.

'My mother's birthday.'

Her heart crumbled at the raw pain in his whispered words. The long string of roman numerals stood out boldly against his smooth, light skin. She pressed a kiss to it, then another. His fingers sank into her hair, their gentle touch only fuelling her anger further. Her devastation on his behalf.

It was a long while before she could trust herself to speak without her voice trembling. 'What was she like?'

Something told Lily that, while he carried a constant reminder of her, Julian didn't let himself think of his mother very often—and he needed to. She wanted to help him while he was being this open with her, because she had no idea when he would clam up. Which question would be one too many. When he would decide this was much too real for their arrangement and push her away.

The idea that he would was like a knife in her chest...

'Alice Sullivan was...'

Sullivan? Lily thought. Probably his stepfather's name.

'She was wonderful. When it was just us two, she was happy and bubbly. Everyone loved her. But the more conspicuous her bruises became, the less she would go out or interact with anyone. Slowly that light died...but she still loved him.'

Lily tightened her arms around him.

'Did you ever wish for things to be different? For your mother to have left?'

'Yes.' Julian answered. 'I quickly realised that while she loved me, she couldn't choose me. Nothing will change that.'

Lily's heart broke. Julian was still angry—she knew that much. He had accepted what had happened but he hadn't moved on. No matter what he said. Because if he had, he would have love and a family. Friends beyond Henry.

'She was as protective as she could be,' he said. 'But I don't think she was terribly brave.'

No, because 'brave' to a little boy would mean a mother who would have picked him up and left that house. She must have been broken too if she'd thought she couldn't leave. No one was at fault here except Julian's stepfather.

Lily could only imagine what that must have done to Julian. For him to know every day that his mother couldn't choose him. To know that he was too young or too weak to protect her, even though he'd tried.

He was quiet for a long time before he added, 'It was my fault.'

'What was?'

Her heart had almost stopped beating. Surely he couldn't think he was to blame for what they had been through.

'Her death. The abuse.'

'No,' Lily said firmly.

'I could have found the money for my mother's treatment... stood up to him sooner. I was capable. And I enjoyed putting him on his ass.' Julian smiled but it was more a baring of teeth. 'But I was filled with so much hate that I didn't realise I could do it until it was too late.'

'Julian...' Her voice was strangled.

'Was?' He laughed out the word. 'I still am full of hate.'

And Lily heard it then. Hate. Not just for his stepfather, but himself too.

'That's not true.'

'You think I didn't already have the idea for my invention when she got sick? I did nothing with it. I could have sold it and got us the hell out of there. But I did nothing. I held on to it until it could make me money and the cost, Lily, was my mother's life. That's why I need unparalleled success for IRES. I sacrificed my mother, and I need that loss to mean something.'

'You were just a child, Julian. You can't take that on yourself. You were surviving as best you could.' Silent tears trickled down Lily's cheeks. His voice was so lifeless. Hollow.

'That first time he beat her was after they got into an argument over me.'

Lily stopped breathing. She was certain he had never said those words to anyone before. Wondered how often he had dwelled on it. So much heartache. It wasn't fair for one person to carry this much.

She shifted on the bed, nuzzling his ear with her nose, and was rewarded with the smallest of smiles. 'It wasn't your fault—you hear me?' she said adamantly.

She would keep saying it until he believed it. Even when whatever they were to each other came to an end.

He didn't respond.

They were quiet for a long time. She would have thought

him asleep had it not been for his fingers, rubbing lazy circles on her skin.

'And this?' She touched the gold ring in his helix, hoping he would keep talking.

That got a bigger smile out of Julian. 'A little bit of rebellion,' he said.

'Oh?'

'I quickly learnt the best way to avoid my stepfather was not to be at home, so as soon as I had grown enough I got a job after school, working at a tattoo and piercing shop. I was underage, but I was tall and sufficiently well-built enough to pass for older, and they paid me in cash. I saved every penny for my escape. Whether it was going to be through college or another way, I was determined to get out.'

'But you held on until the scholarship came through?'

'I did. I knew it would be the most permanent way to leave, and besides, I was due to graduate early.'

'So when did you get the piercing?'

'Shortly after my mother died. I knew *he* would hate it. I wouldn't have dared before then...'

'In case he took it out on her.' Lily finished for him.

Julian nodded. 'I wanted him to dare him to do something about it, but by that point he could do nothing against me. The shop used to get some really rough types coming through, so they taught me how to fight enough to make anyone think twice about causing trouble. They didn't realise that they were helping me with my stepfather too.'

His jaw clenched and a look of utter desolation crossed his face. Whatever thought he'd just had, it was obviously agonising.

'I like it,' she said.

'You do, do you?'

'Yes, but I have been wondering...'

'Why don't I just take it out and fit in?'

There he went—reading her mind again. 'Yes.'

'I don't want to fit in, Lily. This little thing—' he flicked the earring '—is a constant reminder of where I came from.'

Lily understood then. The suits were his armour, but they covered up his reminders. The earring, though, was unmissable. Any time he caught his reflection he would be reminded of who and what he was. So would everyone who encountered him. He wasn't part of their world. He wasn't spoilt and entitled. He hadn't been raised with privilege. Julian had fought. He'd fought for everything he had. Earned it.

His reputation said 'ruthless', but his appearance told everyone of those Zenith businessmen that he was something different. Dangerous. Because he could surpass them even having come from nothing.

Lily kissed his jaw, and when he turned to look at her she kissed him with all the passion he brought out in her. Trying to be a balm for his soul. Wanted to tell him she accepted him. But she didn't know how he would react to that, so instead she kept kissing him. Gliding her tongue along his. Enjoying the sounds he made as he pressed their bodies together.

He needed to be broken out of his cage, and after all that he'd told her she was adamant that she would be the one to do it. Not because he needed fixing, but because he deserved to live a life free of the weight he carried.

And if anyone understood how much freedom meant, it was her.

CHAPTER THIRTEEN

BUCKLED AGAIN INTO the cream leather seat, Lily caught up on the news on Julian's tablet. After reading through article after article, she finally reached the society section.

A headline caught her attention and she froze.

Heart racing, she opened the article and began reading.

'What is it?' she heard Julian ask.

But she couldn't form a response. Not even when he came over to read over her shoulder.

On the screen, in a big close-up photo, was Lincoln with a tall blonde on his arm. Lily recognised her face. She was the daughter of one of her father's business associates, who obviously would have been one of Arthur's too.

There were several pictures, all taken on different days while Lily and Julian had been in France. The article stated that they were in a committed relationship. Lily didn't care if that was true or not, because now everyone would know that she and Lincoln were not in any way expected to be together and he had very clearly moved on.

'How does it feel to be a free woman?' asked Julian.

'I don't know…' She laughed nervously. Her family no longer controlled her destiny. It no longer mattered that she couldn't trust them, that they didn't protect her. 'I'm just hoping I'm not dreaming.'

'You're not, Sunshine.'

She was free. Really, truly free. She could live her life as she wanted to now. There was nothing holding her back. And it was all thanks to the man beside her. The one who had liberated her.

'Thank you, Julian. I'll never be able to say it enough.'

'You never have to at all.'

When she looked up at him she saw he had the strangest expression. Pleasant, but closed off. Was it because part of their agreement had come to an end? She was more than willing to help him still, and it wasn't just because that was the deal.

She wanted him to get the Arum contract because she knew that he was the best at what he did. That he cared. She wanted the old money businessmen to accept him because of who he was. To her, he was perfect. It didn't matter what he thought of this arrangement any more, because what they'd shared in France had been the most real thing she had ever experienced. It had for him too. If he needed time to see that she would give it to him, but she wasn't going to let him think that she was willing to leave.

Getting off her seat, she stood before him, curling her fingers in the lapels of his jacket. 'I am grateful, Julian, but Lincoln doesn't matter. None of them do.'

Not any more. Not when she felt so deeply for the man in front of her.

'What *does* matter?'

There was an apprehension in his eyes that he either couldn't mask or didn't bother to. Lily hoped it was the latter.

'This.'

She placed a soft kiss on his lips that had the strong bands of his arms wrapping around her. He took her with him as he sat down, on his lap, with her arms around his neck and their lips connected, and that was where she stayed for the rest of the flight.

* * *

The sun was only just going down when they returned home. And the fact that Lily now considered this house 'home' was testament to her growing feelings for Julian.

Not wanting to say goodbye to this time they had to themselves just yet, they spent most of the afternoon in bed, tangled in the soft sheets. But despite this she could see that whatever had been bothering Julian on the plane had not gone away.

She wanted to help him, but even though he had opened up to her, she didn't think he would tell her what was wrong now. She had been trying to process everything he'd told her in that bedroom. It crushed her that he blamed himself. That part of him hated himself.

He needed to come to terms with the abuse. See that none of it was his fault. Maybe then he could finally start healing. He deserved that. Deserved peace and love and acceptance.

And Lily wanted to be the one to give him those things.

Love…

She knew she was falling for him. Had known it for a while. But it had been on that plane, when she'd seen the picture of Lincoln and her first thought had been of Julian, that she'd known it was love. But he hadn't said he felt that way, so neither could she. The line between what was fake and what was real had never quite been cleared.

All she could do was trust her feelings.

She loved him. So she would help him.

'Julian…'

'Hmm?'

'I was thinking.'

'Should I be worried?' He smirked.

She rolled her eyes, and even though his were closed, an amused chuckle rolled through his chest.

She didn't know how he would react to her next words, and

he must have picked up on her apprehension because he said, 'Sunshine, you can tell me anything.'

'I didn't like something you said earlier.'

He opened his eyes to peer at her. 'What did I say?'

'That you blamed yourself.'

He took a deep breath but she pushed on.

'And I was thinking that you should visit your stepfather.'

His body went rigid. Any warmth lingering in his stare dissipated. 'No.'

'Julian—'

He flung the covers away and got off the bed, pulling on his underwear with jerky movements. 'I'm not seeing that man.'

'I think it could help you.'

She sat up, trying to reach for him, but he stepped out of her path. She tried not to let the hurt show on her face.

'That man hurt my mother, Lily.'

His voice was low now. Dangerous. He was buttoning his pants, snatching his crumpled shirt off the chair in the corner of the light-filled room.

She didn't like it that he was getting dressed. It seemed too much as if he was erecting a barrier between them.

She vaulted out of bed, stepping between him and the door. 'Just please listen.'

'I'm not seeing that man and that's final.'

He stepped around her and went through the door, leaving her alone in the room.

She dressed as quickly as she could, in another one of his T-shirts, and set out in search of him. She had to try to convince him. Help him have closure so he could move on with his life. A life that until now had centred only around IRES.

He wasn't anywhere in the house. It was only when she went down to the lower level that she spied him on the terrace. Sitting on the edge of a pool lounger. Sunset rays glinting off his red hair. Elbows braced on his knees.

'Julian…' she said softly, sitting on the lounger next to his. An arm's length away. 'I just want you to be happy.'

He said nothing. Simply stared at the cement floor as if it contained some answer he was searching for.

'And you're not,' she went on. 'I see you—all of you—and I hate that you've been blaming yourself for something you shouldn't.'

She looked over at him, still he said nothing.

'I think talking to him now could give you some closure. Allow you to move on with your life.'

Lily sighed, looking across the Bay towards the bridge.

'I want so much more for you, Julian. More than just IRES. You deserve life, and you have so much of that in you, but you've got it all shackled. I want you to see that you're not like him. That you don't have to keep running from your past. Because it's only going to hold you back from what you could have. What you might want to have. I'm not presumptuous enough to believe that's me, but there's a whole world out there for you.'

She looked at him then, to find he was staring at her. Still silent, but listening at least.

'Please just think about it.'

She moved to stand up, wanting to leave him in peace, but his voice stopped her.

'I vowed never to go back there.' He was looking at the floor again. 'I'll think about it.'

Julian looked at the small bungalow. The blue paint that haunted his dreams was peeling away. The yard was overgrown with weeds. The windows were nearly opaque with crusted dirt.

His hands tightened around the steering wheel of the rental car.

Lily placed her hand on his shoulder. He didn't have a smile to give her. He had nothing right now. His shoulders were tense beneath his black suit.

This place brought back nightmares. He could still see himself entering the house for the first time. Could see his mother take her last breath. Julian would never have come back here at all. He had left Lupine Heights and everything in it behind. Yet Lily had said she didn't believe she was what he wanted, he'd wanted to scream. She was *all* he wanted and didn't deserve. So, for her, he would try. Try to put this place and this man behind him. And maybe then, for as long as she would let him, they could be happy together. Until she had to walk away.

Julian wasn't foolish enough to think it wouldn't end, because of course it would. He hadn't changed and neither had she. The stakes were still the same.

He tried to push all that away as he climbed out of the car. All he needed was for his stepfather to accept accountability for what he'd done. Nothing more.

He walked around the car, but Lily had already climbed out, was holding her hand out to him. He took it, keeping her a little behind him as they set off up the broken concrete path.

Climbing the stairs to the front door, he felt his stomach turn with disgust at the sight of the empty beer bottles all around the porch. Anger was growing within him, burning a trail through his veins.

He took a breath. He didn't lose control these days and he wouldn't give his stepfather the satisfaction of doing it now.

Raising a fist to the door, Julian knocked three times, then waited, shielding Lily just a little bit more with his body. He had asked her to stay behind, even though he'd wanted her with him. The idea that she should be around this vile man had made his stomach churn. But she'd refused, saying she wanted to be there for him just as he was for her. As much as he appreciated it, everything in him was now screaming to protect her.

'Well, well, well… Look who it is,' said the man with the sneering face who came to the door.

He was a head shorter than Julian, with cruel blue eyes that held no beauty at all, and he was portly, with a yellowish tinge to his skin and the whites of his eyes.

'Vincent.'

Julian had avoided saying that name as much as he could throughout his life.

'What do you want, boy?'

He felt Lily tense and couldn't blame her. No one else would dare speak to him this way.

'To talk.'

Vincent stepped aside, allowing them to enter, and a horrible sense of déjà vu overcame Julian as he stepped over the threshold into the dark house. It reeked of alcohol, stale cigarettes, and whatever it was that was rotting in the kitchen.

'You better sit, then.'

'We'll stand,' Julian said, looking down at a small brown stain on the carpet.

He could almost see a small, pretty woman curled around that spot.

'Suit yourself.' Vincent dropped into a couch, taking a swig from a half-empty bottle of whisky, watching them. He looked at Lily. 'What are you doing with *him*, sweetheart?'

'Don't you dare talk to her,' Julian growled.

He was burning. Burning from the inside out. Every shout and echoing through time in his head.

'Then what do you want?'

'For you to listen.'

Lily squeezed his fingers—a tether so that his fury didn't sweep him away.

'I left this place intending never to see it again, but the idea of you living your life in peace after what you did to my mother is not acceptable.'

Vincent scoffed, but Julian ignored him.

'I want you to admit what you did. What you did to my mother. Not just the beatings, but drinking away any money for her cancer treatment, what you did to me...all of it. I want you to take responsibility and then tell me why.'

Vincent huffed a remorseless laugh.

There was true evil in this world, Julian thought, and he had been raised by it. He never should have brought Lily here. Bright, sunny Lily, in her violet dress, with her loving heart and empathetic soul. She should never have had to set foot in this hell.

She let go of his hand and pressed herself into his side. Her arm moved around his waist and his around her shoulders.

Vincent's eyes narrowed.

'You want me to admit to what *I* did? What was that? Teach a runt some manners? Encourage my wife to behave as she should?'

Julian's hands curled into fists.

'Easy...' Lily whispered beside him.

'Maybe I was tough on you both, but look at you now.'

'Tough? You call what you did being *tough*? You killed her. You know that, don't you?'

Julian's voice was low and menacing. Anyone else would be cowering.

'What help were you?' Vincent threw back. 'All that intelligence and still your mother died. What use were you?'

Julian had no defence. Those were questions he had asked himself time and time again. Selfishly, he'd wanted time away from this house. Away from the bickering and abuse. And instead of using that time as he knew he should have, he'd just looked for an escape. He was just as responsible.

'You think you're so much better than me, boy? You forget I raised you. We're the same. Don't think I didn't see the enjoyment on your face that day.'

The day he'd fought back. As surprised as he'd been, he had enjoyed it. For a moment he'd made Vincent hurt and he'd revelled in it. Played it back in his mind several times in the days and weeks that had followed. A savage smile curling his lips every time he thought of it.

'I'm nothing like you, old man. I'm not the one who beat a woman and a child. I made something of my life.'

Vincent took another swig of whisky and the motion had Julian wanting to grab the bottle and shatter it across the wall.

'Maybe you did, but you're still a monster—no matter how fancy your suits or how rich you are. Remember that.'

'You're wrong.'

'Lily, don't.'

He frowned when she ignored him.

'He isn't a monster. He has never been one. But I can see all the lies you tried to fill his head with for so many years. I'm glad we came here today, so he could see exactly what he left behind. Exactly what he *isn't*.'

Julian couldn't help himself. He dropped a kiss to the top of her head. Just when he thought he couldn't love her any more, she did something like this and took his breath away.

He looked at his stepfather, once more prepared for this to be his last goodbye. 'How much time do you have left?' he asked.

'What?'

'The skin…the eyes. Yet you're still drinking. How much time do you have left?' Julian asked again.

'Maybe six months,' Vincent replied. 'Less.'

'You don't deserve this but you're getting it anyway. I'll make sure you get treatment at the local hospital. I'm not getting you a carer to abuse. You dug this hole for yourself, and you can die alone.'

Julian led Lily out of the house, saying nothing until they were both in the car. Leaning his head back, he gave himself a moment—just one—before starting the car and easing it into the road, not bothering to look back at the house disappearing behind him.

Vincent wasn't wrong. He was a monster. He'd been raised by one, after all.

CHAPTER FOURTEEN

VINCENT'S WORDS WERE still spinning around Julian's mind when they walked into the house. Nothing he'd said had been a surprise. They were all words he had said to himself.

Julian shrugged off his jacket, depositing it on the couch on the way to the massive window. It was dark over the water. Lights reflecting off the black surface.

'Julian?'

He spun around at the sound of Lily's voice. She had been so quietly supportive...hadn't said anything on the drive home. No offerings of hollow words. Simply a presence beside him.

'You know none of what he said is true, right?' she said softly, padding over to him.

He put his hands on her hips as soon as she was close enough to touch.

'None of it—I mean it.'

He closed his eyes for moment, but before he could say anything he was met with a very firm, 'Julian...'

He couldn't help but smile at that. Lily could see right through him and he had done nothing to deserve her.

'I want you to listen to me very carefully,' she said. 'Just because that man raised you, it does not mean you will turn out like him. *You* are kind and protective, Julian. The only monster is Vincent.'

How could he tell her that wasn't true? What kind of son

didn't do everything in his power to help his mother? Looking back, he knew he'd had options to get them out. Or, when he'd become the main source of conflict, to remove himself from the equation. Maybe not at first, but afterwards he could have thought of something.

'Talk to me, please,' Lily begged, cupping his cheek.

'I know we're not the same, Sunshine. But that doesn't make me good,' he said softly.

He wasn't good. Not like her.

'Yes, you are. Please don't doubt that. I know today was hard…'

That was an understatement. To see his stepfather showing no remorse had infuriated Julian, and that tension still riddled his body, but he couldn't explode. He had no way to let it out.

'But you have to see how different you are. Will always be.'

'Lily, I'm nothing but darkness.'

'Julian, if it weren't for the darkness we'd never see the stars. Despite everything you've been through, your heart is pure. I feel safe with you, and I haven't felt that way in a long time.'

The words made a lump form in his throat, and all he could do was take her lips in his…swallow the gasp that made him burn for her. Sweetly, his lips roved over hers, sliding together and pulling apart. He felt her hand grip the shirt at his waist and he licked at the seam of her lips, which parted with a moan that had arousal arrowing through him.

He slid his hands down to her thighs, lifting her up, and then climbed the stairs to his bedroom, setting her back on her feet at the foot of his bed.

After everything that happened during the day, after Lily's words, Julian wanted only to ravish her. To mark her with his mouth. To have her scream his name, but he didn't deserve that. Neither did she. She should be worshipped.

Standing on the tips of her toes, Lily brought her lips up to his ears, sucking his earlobe into her mouth. He groaned.

THEIR DIAMOND RING RUSE

'You once told me you're not gentle. Show me how not gentle you can be,' she whispered. 'Let go, Julian. Break free with me.'

Her teeth grazed the shell of his ear while she ran her nails down the front of his shirt, then down, down, down over the bulge in his pants, and his leash snapped free. He crashed his lips down on hers on a rushed breath. A hard, bruising kiss full of desperation and fervour. Then his tongue was in her mouth, and the clipped, uncontrolled noises she made just drove him wilder.

Teeth were tugging on her lip that she bit down on so often. Julian wanted to lay her out every time she did so. And then he was cutting a blazing trail with his own lips and tongue along her jaw, kissing that sensitive spot beneath her ear and feeling her shudder like it was his own. He moved down her neck to the hollow at the base of her throat. Licking, tasting the sweet skin there, as she threw her head back, offering herself up to him.

Julian pulled away. 'Do you have any attachment to this dress?' he asked, voice low, breaths uneven.

'No…'

'Good.'

The sound of tearing fabric rent the air, and before it had properly fluttered to the floor her bra had joined it. Arching her back in his arms, Julian closed his mouth over her nipple, sucking hard, making her mewl. But he didn't stop. Not when he was so enjoying the litany of gibberish that fell from her mouth.

And then he dropped to his knees, peeling her panties away and closing his mouth over her sex. Groaning at the obvious evidence of her arousal. Her honey taste.

His tongue was relentless. Her nails scraped against his scalp, delicate fingers tugging his hair, and it had him pulling her harder against him. She was swaying as if her muscles

BELLA MASON

159

couldn't cope with the onslaught of pleasure, but he wanted more. Wanted to give more. So he hooked his arm tightly around her hips and slid a finger deep within her. The loud moan had satisfaction curling through him, pushing him to pleasure her until she exploded spectacularly.

Her body had gone limp. But he had her. Wouldn't let her fall.

He laid her on the bed, stomach down, and reached into his nightstand for a foil packet. Then he kissed her back, all the way up her spine. Brushing her hair aside, he kissed her nape. His hardness pressed against her entrance.

'Please, Julian...' Lily said breathily.

The words set his blood on fire.

He pushed into her, one arm moving under her to press her against his heat. His body curled protectively around hers as his hips set a merciless pace.

He cursed under his breath. 'Sunshine...' he moaned beside her ear.

God, he loved her! So much that he couldn't get close enough or have her fast enough. And then there was the way she said his name, over and over. Like a chant. Like a prayer. And it was all cracking him open. She was the only person he wanted to see him. To know him. All of him.

'I can't get enough of you, Sunshine...'

He threaded his fingers through hers, pressing her palms down onto the bed. The sheets pleated and curled in their joint fisted grip. This intensity of pleasure was a blow to his body and his mind with every thrust. But he needed to see her. To look into those obsidian eyes.

So he pulled away and turned her over...

Lily had wanted Julian to let go. She had seen from the moment they'd got in the car that he needed some sort of release.

A means to explode. Because he was feeling too much and locking it all away.

And now he was unleashed. With her.

Beads of sweat coated his body. Every muscle was pulled taut. A predatory gleam in his eyes, but there was something more in that darkened gaze. She couldn't decide if she loved it more that he had opened himself to her, or that he was making her see stars.

He pushed all the way into her, banding both his arms around her body. They were pressed together, his head in the crook of her neck, and he was kissing her, whispering to her of her perfection, as his substantial length slid in and out of her at a rapid rate.

Lily didn't know any more if she was moaning or if her ragged breathing had just turned this loud. In Julian's embrace, surrounded by his heat and his scent and his voice, all she knew was a burning pleasure that had her heart thundering and her toes curling.

She wished she had known that she could feel like this. Feel taken and loved, safe and yet still dangling over a precipice. To feel so connected to someone and still lust after them.

'Mine.'

It was a guttural declaration that made Lily shiver.

'Yours,' she managed on a broken breath, and his arms seemed to hold her even tighter.

He was coming apart now—just as she was—in a firestorm. She couldn't get enough breath. They were going to set this whole house aflame. And those flames grew. From the depths of her, through her blood and her body, until she couldn't hold it at bay any longer. And she erupted just as she heard Julian's shout, felt his body tensing with hers. Rolling. Swaying. Holding on until they were both ash.

Limp.

Spent.

Bit by bit his grip loosened, as if he was coming back into his body and the animal was being caged away. He lifted his head, but only to press his forehead to hers, and she looked into glazed blue-green eyes and saw love and no small amount of caution.

He had let go, but she was still here. This bed, this home, was where she would always want to be, and tears slipped from her eyes at the realisation. She tried to dash them away, but he gently brushed them off her cheeks first.

She didn't know why she was crying. She was happy. Happier than she ever remembered being. Despite the tears, she smiled. Broadly. Warmly. As if the sunshine was inside her.

Her face lit up like the sun, squeezing the breath from his lungs. Lily was so beautiful. So pure. Utterly perfect.

What are you doing, Julian? he asked himself.

And he knew then that he had to end this right now. It couldn't go on a moment longer. He couldn't be the one to extinguish that light from her eyes. Because he would. He knew it. He was dark, violent, filled with rage, and she would never deserve that.

She deserved a good man. As much as he hated the idea of her with anyone but him, it was the truth. He didn't deserve her. And if he truly loved her he would let her go, so she could find a happy, free life.

But because he was weak, like his stepfather had always said he was, he let her pull him in for another kiss.

One more night. He'd give himself that. One more night.

So he lost himself in her lips and her scent and her sweet satin skin one last time.

CHAPTER FIFTEEN

LILY WAS FAST ASLEEP, curled against Julian, when he woke. Her scent was all around him. Pulling him under. Drowning him in everything he felt for her. This was a once-in-a-lifetime love. He knew it as he knew his own name. He loved her so much he couldn't breathe.

He had barely slept. When he had, he'd dreamed of her, and when he'd lain awake he'd held her close, as if she would disappear at any moment.

Mine.

That was what he had said the night before. The word played in his mind but he hadn't intended to say it out loud. And she had said she was his. He wanted that desperately—but she couldn't be. Nothing had changed.

She turned towards him in her sleep and he pulled her against him, his fingers threading through her hair. Forehead pressed against hers. He loved her, and he knew she loved him too. It should have made him happy, but it was only breaking him apart.

Love wasn't enough. Not for him. It had done nothing to save the mother he'd loved, who had also loved his stepfather. The mother who had loved him so fiercely but who had never been able to choose him. It wasn't enough for her to leave Vincent. Not even after he had broken Julian's arm.

All that love but it didn't make him worthy. He hadn't been

worthy enough for her to save, and he wasn't worthy enough for Lily.

Vincent had called him many things over the years. To Julian, they were all true. He had been weak when he was younger. He wasn't good enough, and he was most certainly selfish. Why else would he have taken Lily's affection, knowing there could never be anything between them? And now she'd returned that affection, but he was going to cut her loose and fade into memory.

He had to.

She hadn't chosen this relationship. She'd been thrust into it. By him. By his idea that they could use each other. But he had just used her desperation. He was going to make millions from their arrangement, and all she'd get was the life she was owed.

Opportunistic—that was what he was.

He had pulled her into his darkness. And there was only darkness in him. His soul hadn't seen light. Not until she'd walked in at least. Julian couldn't do this to her. He needed to protect her light. Couldn't let her be tainted by him. He just had to look at all that he had done. In life, in business, Julian *was* ruthless. He'd earned that reputation. Revelled in it until it became a problem. Until it had hurt IRES.

Now he didn't care about his company as much as he did Lily. He didn't know when that had happened. He just knew that his mother was gone but Lily could still be protected— even from him. He would walk away and make her do so too. She would find happiness without him. His heart was in pieces now, but he would do this. For her. Anything for her.

Julian held her against his body tightly. Trying to imprint her into his soul. She would always be there. There would be no one else.

Kissing her head, he silently said his goodbye to her.

Scrunching up his eyes, clenching his jaw, Julian tossed aside the covers, careful not to wake her as he left the bed.

He watched her then. Hair fanning out over his pillow as she sought out his warmth in her slumber. Committing the way she looked to memory, Julian left the room.

He showered and changed into a dark suit in one of the guest rooms before going downstairs, where he would make the call he had hoped not to have to make. Since the Zenith dinner he had been called by several businessmen who had never shown any inclination to work with him before. As a result, several deals had been signed with IRES. But Julian knew the moment he broke up with Lily—the moment he broke her heart—the Arum deal would be lost. Devan's vote would be gone.

He didn't care. It would be a fitting punishment to lose it. Except his employees didn't deserve that. And, more importantly, Lily wouldn't be fooled into leaving.

Their agreement was that they would pretend until the deal was signed. Well, there was only one way he was getting that done now—and it wasn't through the support of the board.

He had his phone to his ear, waited three rings before it was answered by a hostile drawl.

'What do you want, Ford?'

'Harrison. I want the Arum energy deal and you're going to give it to me.'

Julian wished he didn't have to do this, but he did. He was already in bed with these people, and showing them just how ruthless he was would change nothing. All his contracts were iron clad, and once people worked with him they didn't look elsewhere.

'And why is that?' asked Lincoln.

'Two reasons,' he responded. 'One, you know how good I am. How good my technology is. You've already done the research and you know you would be a fool to discount IRES.'

He waited, but there was no denial.

'And two, I know you looked in to me the moment I spoke to Lily. I did the same the day you accosted her at Crème, and I am damn sure you don't want what I found out to become public knowledge.'

There was an amused huff on the line. 'Are you blackmailing me? You'll find nothing sticks to me, Ford.'

'I'm incentivising you to make the right choice, because you and I both know I can make your past misdeeds hurt. Do you really want to try me, Harrison?'

There was a long pause before Lincoln spoke again. 'You seem to think you're going to lose the other fifty percent of the vote. I wonder why that is.'

'Every good businessman has contingencies in place. I'll leave nothing to chance.'

'If you do lose the others' support, you realise my vote counts for exactly half.'

Of course Julian knew that. 'Yes, and I also know that you hold the tie breaker vote. So what will it be? Giving IRES the deal or facing your reckoning? I can count your crimes if you'd like. Let's see…there's bribery, assault of various degrees, that I'm sure you can thank your father for burying. Then there's—'

'Enough. Fine. You'll have your deal, Ford, but this won't be forgotten.'

'I'm sure it won't.'

Julian slipped the phone into his pocket and turned around to find Lily descending the staircase, freshly showered and ready to leave for work. Not just leaving for work, Julian reminded himself. This would be the last time he saw her, and he had to fight the crumbling inside him.

'That was the news we've been waiting for. The board has voted to go with IRES,' Julian said.

She walked over to him and kissed him lightly on his cheek.

It knocked the breath from him. He knew he would never have that touch again, but he had to stand firm and do at least one good thing in his life.

'That's wonderful news.' She smiled, but it faded quickly, to be replaced by a frown. 'Julian, what's wrong?'

'Nothing's wrong,' he said, taking a step back.

She tracked his movement.

'We've achieved what we set out to do,' he told her.

'I don't understand…'

'You've got what you wanted out of this arrangement and now I have, too.'

'Arrange…? Are you breaking up with me?'

He would hate himself for the rest of his life for the hurt he saw flash across her face. And it would only get worse.

'Breaking up would imply there was something real to begin with. It's time for you to leave.'

Julian's heart was tearing itself to shreds.

Don't leave. I need you.

But the thought would never be heard.

Her features had set in a determined look. The first time he'd seen it was when she'd walked over to him in a room full of people.

'A lamb to the slaughter,' he'd said that night.

'I know what you're doing,' she said. 'I won't leave you.'

'I want you to go.'

His ring was on her finger and yet he was pushing her away. This felt wrong. It was all wrong. But he had to do it. He would never make her happy—he wasn't capable of that. He'd let his mother die, failed her, but he could save Lily.

'Julian, don't do this. Please…'

Her eyes welled up, her voice breaking on that last word, but he wouldn't let himself comfort her. He would have to endure her hurt. Bear his punishment.

Julian shook his head and looked out through the window at the water stretching to the horizon.

'I'm a monster, Lily. Haven't you ever wondered why I never seem to have much competition? I put people out of business. You yourself brought up Helios. I do whatever I need to win.'

He turned back to her, removing any emotion from his voice. Making it as cold as he could manage. He was a good liar, after all.

'I've been doing that with you, too. So, please, just go.'

Her tears fell. 'You're not a monster…' She dashed the wetness away with the back of her hand. 'If this is about yesterday… You're not him. You're good and kind.'

'You've just seen what you want to, Lily.'

He couldn't call her 'Sunshine'. Not now. It would undo him.

'Vincent was right. I did enjoy beating the shit out of him. And he wasn't the only one. That's who I am. I told you at the start I'm not the hero of this story. And I'm telling you for the last time—leave. I don't want you.'

He saw her throat bob as she lifted her chin. She wouldn't beg, and he was so proud of her. She was strong. She would be fine. And since Lincoln had moved on, he was no longer a threat either.

'Fine.'

She prised the ring off her finger and he couldn't bear it.

'Take it back,' she said.

'No. Keep it.'

He wanted to say that it was part of their plan, but really it was just his selfish need to have her never forget him.

She curled her fingers around it, regarding him with those remarkable eyes. 'Thank you for what you've done for me, Julian. Good luck with IRES. I'll send for my things.'

Without so much as a goodbye, she turned around. And he watched the woman he loved walk out of his house.

The walls were closing in. His clothes felt too tight. Too constricting. He couldn't breathe. Something was trying to break free of him.

He watched the door. And he watched, and he watched— until he snapped, flipping the glass table over and sending it crashing to the floor, shattering in a snowfall of razor-sharp ice.

She was gone.

And he was alone in his house. Just as he had always preferred.

CHAPTER SIXTEEN

LILY COUNTED THE number of steps to the door, then to her car. She kept counting. Anything...*anything* to keep her from falling apart. To stop her from focussing on the man she was leaving behind. The man who didn't want her. Who had never said this was real.

Except she had felt it. She had felt his love with every touch the night before. But if he couldn't take that step towards her, she wouldn't force him. If he wanted to be left alone, then he would be.

It was that thought of never seeing him again that had the first tear falling.

Fracturing. Her heart, her soul...it was all fracturing. A fissure was opening up right through her, and into it fell all the memories they'd made. She couldn't think of any of them.

Starting up her car, Lily took a deep breath and drove away from the house. Not to Crème, but to her brother. Why? She had no idea. He hadn't been a supportive brother lately. But she had just lost her home—not the spectacular house perched on a cliff, but the man who lived in it—and maybe she craved something familiar. Something that might once have been comforting.

She drove along the street she had grown up on and turned into the drive of what was now her brother's home. She took a moment, trying to breathe around the suffocating knot in her chest, but every breath hurt. As if she was choking on it.

Still, she tried not to let the tears fall. Because if she started, she likely wouldn't stop.

Fishing the key she had not returned out of her bag, Lily reached for the lock—only to have the door swing open. And there, ready to start his day, stood Devan.

'Lily?' Surprise turned to concern, and then to anger.

'Dev...' she managed hoarsely, through the burning in her throat, and let out a muffled sob when he pulled her into a crushing hug.

'What happened?' he asked.

She swallowed, opening and closing her mouth several times, but no words came out. So much had happened. A lifetime fitted into such a short period. And all those memories she'd thought had fallen into that fissure now crashed upon her.

Devan led her to the kitchen, let her perch on one of the tall chairs around the large marble island where they used to spend their time. They hadn't shared the same space in an age.

She watched her brother shed his jacket and take the seat next to her.

She toyed with the ring on her finger. Big and beautiful and sparkling. She pulled it off, turning it around and around between her fingers.

'He called it off.'

She didn't look at her brother. Didn't want to see the smug satisfaction on his face. It had probably been a mistake, her coming here.

'He couldn't do it,' she said in a small voice.

He couldn't accept that he was good. Had pushed her away because of it.

'I knew he would hurt you,' Devan said lowly. 'He never deserved you. Don't worry, Lily, I can make him pay.'

'No!' she rushed out. He had been hurt enough. 'Don't ruin the deal for him, please.'

'How can you ask me that?'

'Because a lot has happened, Dev. Julian…' Something caved within her just at saying his name. 'He's a good man. He just has his own battles to fight.'

Still she didn't give up that ring. She was supposed to keep wearing it until the time was right to take it off. The time would never be right because all she wanted was to tie herself to him. She accepted him. All of him.

Over and over he'd said he was the villain, but he wasn't. No matter what he did, she loved every part of him. Yet she couldn't keep his ring on her finger because it hurt too much to see it there.

'You love him…' Devan said, sounding almost as if he still didn't truly believe it.

'I do.'

'I have to admit, Lil…part of me hoped that this was all some sort of elaborate game.'

Guilt slammed through her. Maybe that was how it had started, but she thought back to their first date and realised it hadn't ever been. Not really. She and Julian had been special from the start and now it was over. It was always meant to end, and she should have done a better job of barricading her heart.

'I don't want to talk about him.' She sniffed. She couldn't bear it. She missed him already—as if a piece of her soul had been ripped away.

'He was my home, Dev. No one cared for me like he did.'

Devan flinched, then shifted closer. 'I haven't been a very good brother to you, have I?'

'No, you haven't,' she said softly, and saw him wince.

'I hate seeing you hurt, Lily. And I'm sorry that I was also a cause of it.'

Lily said nothing, focussing instead on the way the sunlight danced on the diamond.

'I have no excuse,' he went on. 'I guess I wanted to do right by Dad. I had something to prove. But I should have been there for you. I should have helped you with Lincoln. That should never have been placed on your shoulders. I'm sorry I tried to force you.'

Lily finally looked at her brother, seeing genuine remorse on his face. 'What are you going to do about him?' she asked.

'Don't worry about it. I'll find a way.'

He snaked an arm around her and she rested her head on his shoulder.

'I've missed you, Dev.'

'I've missed you too, Lily.'

Julian sat behind his desk in his office, high above San Francisco, just as he had done for the last three weeks. The rest of the floor was dark. Everyone had left hours ago. Not one of them, not even his PA, had said goodbye. They had all been giving him a wider berth than usual.

The sky behind him was pitch-black. Twinkling lights spread out as far as the eye could see. He had no mind for it. No mind for the beauty. It didn't matter. All that mattered was his work.

In the weeks since Lily had left, Julian had focussed only on IRES and he had been productive. Of course he had, when he'd had to keep busy every waking hour. It was all he could do to stop himself thinking about Lily. To spend as little time as he could in that bed where they had come together every night. In his home that now felt too big. Too empty.

His life was empty without her, but he couldn't let himself dwell on the ache in his chest that hadn't let up since he'd made her leave. He had always known he would have to let her go, and still he'd let himself love her. Still, he'd carried that love in every breath.

His phone rang, pulling him out of the thoughts he had fallen into. Thoughts of Lily. Glancing at the screen, he let it go to voicemail. If it wasn't about work, he didn't need to hear it.

It didn't help that while people suspected they were no longer together, Lily hadn't said anything to anyone. So everyone asked how was she? Where was she? What was going on? And every time he barked that it was none of their business.

He scrubbed a hand down his face, barely able to keep his eyes open any longer. Grabbing his laptop, he left his office, went down to his car and drove home in silence, mentally planning out his next day.

IRES had been awarded the Arum deal. It was a massive undertaking, which thankfully kept him busy. And, as reluctant a partnership as it was, Lincoln was clearly impressed with what Julian had brought to the table.

But it felt like a hollow victory.

He had wanted to earn his way in. Show the elite just what his company could do and make them choose him. After all, if these contracts were handed out on merit, there would never be any doubt that IRES would be their first choice every time. Except they weren't. And Julian had had to resort to ruthless means once again. It had been the only way to ensure his goal and thereby set Lily free.

His home loomed dark and unwelcoming as he parked his car in the underground garage. He wondered, as he walked into the house and went straight to the fridge, what Lily would have said if she'd known what he'd done to get the contract.

'Don't do anything that could hurt you later.'

Her voice in his head made him flinch. He had already done that, even though it had been for the best. One day she would find someone who loved her—not as much as he did…no one could love her like him. Someone who would make her happy.

Julian slammed the door shut. His appetite had disappeared in an instant.

He dragged himself up the stairs, feeling more like a shadow than ever before, and let out a heavy breath before entering his room. He could have avoided it—just like he'd avoided going anywhere near Crème. He did have other rooms that would have suited him.

But he was stuck here. Wanting the memories of her and the freedom this room had been meant to grant him. But all it had become was a prison he'd sentenced himself to.

CHAPTER SEVENTEEN

A WEEK LATER, Julian was home before dark for the first time since Lily had left. He'd barely had a moment to place his belongings down when the doorbell chimed. He knew who it was before he opened the door, and when he did so his mentor's concerned expression greeted him.

'Henry.'

'It's been weeks, Julian.'

It had been. He'd sent Henry's calls to voicemail more often than not, and when he had spoken to him it had usually been to postpone whatever plans Henry had included him in.

After weeks of being cancelled on, it seemed he'd had enough.

Julian stood aside, holding the door open to allow Henry to enter. 'I've been busy.'

Henry didn't seem convinced.

Julian led him to the plush couches out on the pool terrace, where the two men sat opposite each other.

'You've been busy since you were a teenager, Julian. This is about Lily, isn't it?'

Julian looked away. Past the thick trees that offered him complete privacy and over the water.

'Tell me the truth this time,' Henry said, and there was a softness in his voice that made Julian grit his teeth.

Of course Henry had seen through the ruse, even though

he had never said anything. Likely he'd been waiting for Julian to sort out his own mess.

He swallowed, thinking of the night he'd first seen Lily, and then he said, 'It was just meant to be a convenient arrangement. A mutually beneficial one.'

'It was more than that,' Henry said, as if it was an undeniable truth.

'Yes.'

Julian ached. He missed Lily so much it was a physical pain. He walked to the edge of the pool, staring at nothing in particular, and slid his hands into his pockets. Lily was gone. It would make no difference if he told Henry about it now. So he did. Leaving his feelings well and truly out of it.

'Julian,' Henry said when he'd finished, but he refused to turn around. 'I know you love her. Look at what you did. You wanted into Zenith, wanted a deal with the man whose—for all intents and purposes—fiancée you took from right under his nose and threatened him, then blackmailed him. You made an enemy of the client you wanted to attract and I can tell part of you still wishes to destroy him. You took Lily from her home that she shared with her brother knowing what was at stake, telling yourself she'd help you get closer to Devan, accepted by him and his clique. It was never about any of that. Just admit that you wanted her from the moment you saw her. No matter what you've been over the years, son, you were always honest. So be honest now.'

Still Julian said nothing, because Henry was right.

'I knew she was special when I saw you two together,' said Henry. 'You realise that was the first time I ever saw you smile? I've known you all this time and finally I got to see you happy because of her. Look at you, Julian…you're a ghost of your former self.'

'I do love her,' Julian said finally, in a calm voice. 'That's why she had to go. I don't deserve her.'

'Julian…'

'Don't tell me it's not true. You're right. I'm not happy. But I couldn't take her happiness away for my own.'

'Did she tell you she was unhappy?' Henry challenged.

'She didn't need to. I had a reminder of who I really am, and I couldn't do that to her. I failed my mother, Henry. What if I do the same to her?'

The visit with Vincent was still fresh in his mind. Though he never intended to see the man again, his medical bills had been steadily flowing to him. They kept the wound open. Wouldn't let that last interaction fade into the background.

'What sort of reminder?'

'I saw Vincent.' Julian glanced over his shoulder to see the frown on Henry's face replaced by something fiercer. Anger.

'You know better than to listen to that…' Henry floundered, unable to find a word to adequately describe Julian's stepfather.

'He was right.' Julian looked away again. 'What use was this intellect when I didn't use it to help my mother? I could have. Instead of being selfish, and trying to find ways to stay away, *I* could have done something. But I didn't. I couldn't risk being that selfish again, Henry.'

'Julian…' Henry's tone was firm now. In a way it had never been with him before.

'He was right,' Julian repeated. 'Vincent did raise me. I'm every bit the monster he is. How could I not be? He is what I know. What if one day I lose control and turn into him? That's a possibility. We both know I have that violence in me.'

Julian's greatest fear. The possibility of becoming his stepfather scared him senseless. It was the reason he had to keep himself in check all the time. He had so much anger and resentment in him—where would a slip lead him? He'd still been a teenager when he'd put someone in hospital.

'You forget that I know you,' said Henry. 'You didn't leave it at that. What did you do?'

Julian dropped his head. 'Nothing. I did nothing.'

He had gone in wanting him to acknowledge what he had done to Julian and his mother, but he hadn't pushed for it.

'He's dying,' Julian said after a while. 'His liver is failing. I told him I'd pay his medical expenses and left.'

'Julian, sit,' Henry instructed.

He looked over his shoulder at his mentor with a cocked brow. Neither backed down until Julian let out a long breath and dropped into the couch opposite him.

Henry sat forward. His brown eyes were hard. It was a look Julian had seen him use in business.

'Now, you're going to listen to me. None of what Vincent accused you of is true. Yes, you may have been raised by him in part, but you were always your own person. You tried to protect your mother, but protection is an adult's job, and you were a child. I know you like to take responsibility, but you can't do that for everyone's actions. *You are not to blame.*'

Julian rubbed his eyes with his forefinger and thumb but didn't interrupt.

'You are a good man, Julian. Better than you realise. You helped that scum and left. Do you know what strength that takes? And what about Lily? You helped her because you wanted to. I'm willing to bet you would have even without the Arum deal hanging over you.'

He would have. Of that Julian had no doubt.

'You have accomplished so much, but until now, you have only been surviving. And you're barely doing that right now. You need to live, Julian. Let yourself be happy. Did you not let go just a little with Lily?'

'I did,' he admitted, thinking back to how she had unleashed him and hadn't turned away.

'Your happiness isn't a crime. It's okay to be ruthless in business—you need to be—but not in your life. Don't cut things out that bring you joy because of a fear you shouldn't have to bear.'

'I pushed her away, Henry. I doubt she would want to see me.'

He could still picture her hurt when he'd told her to leave. For that alone, he was the villain.

'You know Crème has the best *cannelé*?' Henry smiled.

'You saw her?' Julian breathed.

'I did. Don't worry. I said nothing to her. I went only to check in.'

'How is she?'

'Miserable. She misses you too.'

His heart fluttered back to life. She missed him. Despite what he had done. Could he allow himself to see her? See if she still loved him. But what then?

'You know, there aren't many regrets I have in life,' said Henry. 'Hardly any, in fact. However, I do regret never settling down. Starting a family. I wish that I had. I got lucky, though. I found a son on a campus.'

Julian smiled at that. It was small and quick, but it felt like waking up from a haze. Henry had been there for him from the moment they'd met. Taken him in. Taught him. And, Julian realised, protected him. Helped him succeed. He had done everything a father would have done for his son.

'Vincent is not your father,' Lily had said, and Julian had been so hung up on all the ways he might have been that he hadn't seen what was right in front of him. Vincent had never been his father. Never his role model. He fought everything the man was. But Henry...

In every way that mattered, Henry was his father. Julian listened to him, emulated him when he could, had moved to San Francisco to be closer to him. Why had it taken him so long to see it? He couldn't have loved the man more even if he was blood.

'Not many people get that lucky,' Henry went on. 'You might not because you have something special in front of you right now. Are you going to let the woman you love slip through your fingers?'

He didn't want to. No part of him wanted to say goodbye to Lily but it was so hard to think of himself as someone worthy of her. What if he hurt her? He couldn't survive that. What if one day he grew angry and lost his temper with her just like Vincent had done? That would be unforgivable. Except he really wasn't like Vincent, was he? His darkness grew out of hatred and pain, but he always tried to be better than his stepfather. Tried to be more like Henry. The man who was looking at him with love and pride. Even when he had made a mistake Henry never turned his back on him.

If a man like Henry was willing to believe in Julian, why wasn't he willing to believe in himself? With Lily, he was everything he'd ever wanted to be. She brought out the best in him and he loved her. So much that he was willing to let her go and find love with someone else. He'd suffer for it, but he'd be at peace knowing she was happy.

Except she wasn't, from what Henry had said, and if being together could make them both happy why should he keep punishing himself? Punishing them both?

Their love wouldn't be like his mother's. It wouldn't be a trap filled with torment. His and Lily's love was something bright and pure.

'No, I'm not.'

He looked at his watch. If he rushed, he could make it to Crème before Lily closed up.

'You can lock up on your way out.'

Henry sat back, his expression a mixture of smugness and pride.

Julian paused on his way inside the house and threw over his shoulder, 'I met my father that day too, Henry.'

* * *

Crème was still open when Julian came to a screaming stop in a parking bay close to the entrance. Relief, fear and excitement all coursed through him in equal measure. It had been weeks since he had last seen Lily, and as he got out of his car and quietly walked into the store a strange sense of peace overcame him. The feeling of coming back home after a long time away.

He watched her smiling at customers, but the moment they left that smile vanished. He had done that, and he would beg her forgiveness for it.

She didn't look up. Not once. Paying attention instead to the display she was refilling, her back turned to him. For a moment he was frozen. Stuck on everything he should say. On whether she would let him say the words. If she would let him hold her.

'How much are the cinnamon rolls?' he asked, in his low voice over her shoulder.

Lily whipped around. Surprise, happiness, anger, sadness— all passed over her face in quick succession. A rainbow of emotion that ended with nothing...just a blank look when she saw him standing before her in jeans and a sweater.

'Julian.' Her voice was careful. 'What are you doing here?'

His heart beat frantically. He wanted her back, but it had to be her choice. He would lay himself bare to her and then she could decide if he was worthy. Whatever her decision, he would accept it. But he had to try.

'I needed to see you. Talk to you.'

She shook her head. Swallowed once. Then twice. 'It's been weeks, Julian. I think the time to talk is gone.'

She pushed past him to the door, which she locked, flipping the sign to closed. She tried to walk past him again, but he grabbed her wrist, making her stop.

'Please listen to me and after that I'll go. Will you allow that?'

A light sweat broke out at the back of his neck.

'You didn't want me. You told me to leave,' she said, pulling out of his grasp.

He tried to hide his wince. It hurt that she'd moved away from him, but if he was honest he deserved it. 'I lied. I had to. I told you that you had no idea how good a liar I was.'

'Was?'

He nodded. 'I'm done with lying to myself...to you...to the world. I wanted you from the moment I laid eyes on you, Lily.'

She regarded him coolly. Carefully concealing her feelings from him. And now he understood how she'd felt when she had wanted him to let go. To give up his control and just feel. Because he wanted so badly for her to yell at him, or pound her fists on his chest. Anything but this stillness.

'Fine. Say what you came here to say and then you can leave.'

'Thank you.'

He wanted to reach for her, but didn't think she would appreciate that after the way he had behaved, so he took a deep breath instead.

'There was once a boy who knew only darkness and grief and pain. He was told he was brilliant, but all he felt was hopelessness. Each day was the same. Each day he had to fight that same darkness until he was consumed by it. He didn't know if he was still fighting it or if it was inside him any more, so he grew up trying his best. But with each passing day hate and pain were the only things that grew. Eventually whatever light was left in him was extinguished and that left only darkness. And so he believed that was what he was...that he didn't deserve the light.'

Lily was looking at him with a mix of concern and sympathy—and no small amount of anger. Not at him, though. He could tell. It was the same way she'd looked at him the night he'd told her about his past.

'I wanted to send you away because I had to save you from

my darkness,' he told her. 'Do you know why I call you Sun-shine?'

Lily shook her head.

'Because that's exactly what you are. What you've always been. My sunshine. You bring light to my very dark life, Lily. You make me see a path…a life that I couldn't see in that black void I lived in.'

'You're not filled with darkness, Julian,' she said brokenly.

He ran his thumb down her cheek, giving her a sad smile. 'Yes, I am. I've lost everything good in my life, so I was convinced that it was just a matter of time before I lost you too. The way I grew up…it was chaos. So I controlled everything. But you, Sunshine, bring order to my life—and yet at the same time the most beautiful chaos.'

Lily took a step towards him, closing the distance between them and he could have dropped to his knees.

'I just wanted to give you a chance to live a happy life on your terms,' he said. 'To save you from me. So that day, when I told you I would make sure Lincoln paid for hurting you, I started looking into him and I dug up a lot of dirt.'

Lily's eyes turned hard. But he was prepared for that.

'I told you not to do anything you'd regret,' she said.

'I know you did. So I sat on that information until the morning when I knew you had to go. I called Lincoln and told him I would use what I'd found if IRES didn't get the Arum deal.'

'You didn't need to do that,' she said in a hard tone.

'I didn't think I would have a chance with them after I sent you away. I didn't care about the deal anymore, but I knew you wouldn't leave me in the lurch. But we had an agreement, so the only way I could get you to leave was to get that contract. I did what I thought I had to.'

'Why didn't you just talk to me?' she asked.

'Because I wanted the best for you and I didn't think it was me.'

She scrunched her fingers in her ponytail and he watched her trying to sort through everything he'd told her.

'You shouldn't have done that,' she said.

'I know.'

'I wish you had talked to me about this, Julian. After we saw Vincent I blamed myself for pushing you too hard. But all I wanted was for you to get closure.'

'I needed that push, because you were right. But what he said was everything I had already said to myself. All the reasons I hated myself.'

'I wish you could see yourself clearly,' she said, her eyes welling up. 'I wish you could stop punishing yourself and live.'

'I want to—but I can't do this alone. Living instead of surviving. I thought I could, but I need you. You're my light when everything in me is just the darkest night. You give me hope that I can be a better man. Maybe even a good man. I love you, but I don't know how to do this.'

'You love me?'

Her tears finally fell free, cutting him to the quick. Julian took her face in his hands. He should have told her every moment of every day that he loved her.

'Yes! With everything I am. I want to protect you, and care for you, and take a ridiculous number of trips to France with you, and sit at that table—' he pointed to the spot where they had shared a meal on their second date '—eating dessert with you.'

'Julian…' Lily let out a sob. She loved him too. Had never stopped—not once in these long weeks.

'But I want…' Julian trailed off.

She had never seen him stumble or struggle for words, but she understood then. No one had chosen Julian. Not his mother, who tried to protect him but not leave for him, not his stepfather, who had so terribly hurt him, and definitely not all the business people who'd excluded him for no reason.

'You want me to choose you,' she said.

Julian didn't answer. She could see that he couldn't. Those blue-green eyes were flat. There was no mischief or humour or sadness. Just nothing reflected back at her. It broke her heart that he was too wary to ask for what he wanted but he never had. It was time he finally understood the depth of her feelings for him.

'Julian, I chose you from the start.' When he was still a beautiful stranger. She had left Lincoln's side and went to him that first night. His eyes twinkled at the memory. 'I'll always choose you. But I knew it was all just meant to be fake.'

That was the reason why she had never said she loved him.

'It was never fake for me,' he said earnestly. 'That first night, Lily, I saw you walk in with Devan and I felt kissed by the sun. I couldn't stop looking at you. Watching to see where you would go and what you would do. I thought I loved you when I kissed you in your office. Knew I loved you when I took you to bed, and again that next morning. I let myself believe it when we went to France, and I hoped...*hoped* you could see it in what you did to me.'

Lily's last defences against Julian crumbled. She wanted him to be hers for the rest of her life.

She threw her arms around his neck, hugging him fiercely, felt his arms tighten around her the instant she did. 'I love you.'

Julian's head tucked into her neck. When he spoke his voice was muffled against her skin.

'You're my sunrise. My first spring blossom. My hope and my happiness. You give my world colour and meaning. You're everything I don't deserve but desperately want. You make me believe—and I love you so damn much!'

Lily felt as if a fog had lifted. As if the sun had finally come out and warmed her soul. Maybe she was light but Julian wasn't darkness, he was the darkest night sky in a remote location. Maybe he was hard to reach, but once she did, his beauty was breathtaking.

'You're the best person I know, Julian, and I love you, too.'

He pulled away from her embrace, only to kiss her hungrily. Impatient and uncontrolled. Showing her just how naked he could be with her, how much he loved her, and she felt it. It was in the press of his lips and the touch of his tongue. In his hands fisted against her back and his tightly shut eyes.

She would stop the clocks so they could spend this moment tangled in each other for eternity, but he slowed the slide of his lips and broke the connection. He pressed his forehead against hers, his breath uneven.

'Do you still have my ring?' he asked hoarsely.

'I do. Do you want it back?'

'No. When you're ready to be my fiancée again—whether it's a day from now, or a week or a month or a year, I want you to leave it in the middle of our bed and I'll know you're ready. You'll have to say nothing else.'

He was giving her the choice. Letting her make the decision about her future. Their future. And she knew if there was ever a way for him to prove how much he loved her, respected her, it was this.

'What if I'm ready now?' Lily asked with a broad smile.

Julian chuckled, his breath brushing against her lips. 'Then we'll go home right now and you can show me that you want me.'

'Home? I've bought my own apartment, Julian.'

'*You're* my home, Sunshine. Whether it's my house—*our* house—or your new apartment, it's home.'

Those words made butterflies take flight in her stomach. Made her so happy she had to make sure she wasn't glowing.

Lily stood on tiptoe to whisper in Julian's ear. 'Race you there.'

EPILOGUE

One year later

THE SUN STREAMED into the pavilion at Strawberry Hill, cutting dark shapes into the floor. Stow Lake glittered beyond, but Lily could barely remember where she was. Nor could she pay attention to the small, intimate gathering of friends and family seated a few feet away from her.

She looked at her hands, held in Julian's grasp, trying not to let her vision blur with tears. Slowly, she raked her gaze up to meet his and, just like every time she did, her breath caught. In his tux, with his earring twinkling and the sun gilding him in golden light, he was magnificent. And he was hers. In every way. From this moment on.

Lily had thought she was happy before, but it was nothing compared to how she felt now.

The officiant said something she could not parse because she was still spellbound by Julian. And in a few minutes he would be her husband.

He had once told her he couldn't make her happy, but he'd been so wrong. Every day was happier than the last, and they were only just starting their fairy-tale.

It had only been a year, but so much had happened in that time. Lily had opened a dessert bar, to rave reviews, she and Devan had completely repaired their relationship, and her mother had moved back to San Francisco. Things weren't perfect there, but they were working on it. She'd even rekindled the friendships that she'd been certain she had lost. Her friends had welcomed her back with more than a few tears. And those same friends now sat amongst the small crowd sharing this day with them.

And Julian... He had worked every single day to show her how much he loved her. He had finally stopped blaming himself for his mother's death and accepted that he was nothing like his stepfather. While he was still supremely disciplined, he had started to relax. Let go a little. There was still a long way to go, but she planned to hold his hand throughout it all.

'Julian and Lily have prepared their own vows,' the officiant said now, and turned to Julian.

'Lily, I promise to always protect you. To support you in all that you do. To listen to you.'

He smiled broadly, dimples appearing in his cheeks, and her heart stuttered.

'To be your best friend and closest ally, just as you are mine, and I promise to give myself to you wholly in every way.'

He already had. Julian kept nothing from her. Let her see his bad days and nightmares and she loved him all the more for it. She thought back to the surprise that awaited him at the house. The pregnancy test she had taken the night before and couldn't wait to tell him about.

'Julian...' Her voice was thick with tears. 'I promise to always choose you. To support you in all that you do. To listen to you. To be your best friend and closest ally, just as you are mine, and I promise to give myself to you wholly in every way.'

Julian couldn't stop looking at Lily. At her curled hair with the pretty flowers braided through it, at the beaded, toga-like dress, white against her golden skin, with the sun shining through the long drapes of fabric. At her night-sky eyes, glistening with tears. She was a goddess and she was his. Though not his alone.

Julian knew about the pregnancy test, but he would wait for her to tell him the way she wanted to. They were going to have a baby which would be perfect in every way, because it would be a part of her. He couldn't wait for its arrival—which, judging by how flat Lily's stomach was, would be a long way away.

'I love you, Sunshine...always,' he said, sealing his promise by sliding on to her finger a diamond wedding band that perfectly matched the engagement ring that had started them on this journey.

'I love you, Julian...unconditionally and for ever.'

A tear slipped down her cheek and he brushed it away with his thumb. He would never tire of hearing those words. He offered her his hand, and she slipped a simple titanium band on his finger. The weight was satisfying. Calming. Like a piece of him clicking into place.

'Titanium,' she had said. 'Because it doesn't break easily. It's strong...just as you are.'

He'd had no words for her then, and he wondered if he would wake up every day just as pleasantly surprised that he got to spend his life with Lily—his wife.

He took her face in his hands as her fingers curled around the lapels of his jacket and he kissed her. Softly, sweetly, gently. With all the love he held in his heart.

For the rest of their days their life would be perfect, he knew. Because right now he vowed to make sure of it.

* * * * *

HER CONVENIENT VOW TO THE BILLIONAIRE

JANE HOLLAND

MILLS & BOON

In memory of my mother, Charlotte Lamb,
a much-beloved Mills & Boon author herself
and an amazing woman.
This one's for you, Mum!

CHAPTER ONE

'SABRINA,' BARKED THE voice on the other end of the phone, prompting an instinctive flush of guilt. 'What on earth are you doing back on Calista?'

It was the same question Sabrina had been secretly asking herself for the past twenty-four hours, couched now in her father's terse tones and delivered directly into her ear. Even though she had doubts about this return to the Greek island where she'd been born and raised, his peremptory demand prickled at her nerves. She wished he would trust her a little more, the way he trusted his other two children, Tom and Pippa. But they were his own flesh and blood, unlike her.

'Um…unfinished business.' Switching to speaker phone, she set her mobile on the stone step beside her. She needed to listen out for a vehicle approaching. 'It shouldn't take long, Dad, I promise.'

'What unfinished business? What are you talking about?'

Sabrina sat down in the shade of the old orphanage and began to smooth out the tangles in her wayward blonde hair. She'd forgotten how intense and unrelenting the heat could be on this tiny island. She'd hired a sports car on the mainland and brought it over on the ferry last night—the island was too small for a proper airfield—and driven here from her harbourside hotel this morning with the top down, wind in her hair. Now her ordinarily sleek hair more closely resembled a briar patch.

'Nothing important.' Stumbling over the little white lie, she winced. 'I'll tell you when I get home.'

'I'd rather you told me now...'

Her father's voice deepened, his sympathy triggering the anxious little girl still inside her.

'This is me, Sabrina. You don't have to pretend. I know you haven't been back to Calista since...' He stopped, abruptly changing tack. 'Look, just tell me what you're up to, darling. Let me be the judge of whether it's important or not.'

Sabrina rested her forehead on her hand, groaning inwardly. She loved him, this extraordinary billionaire who had rescued her from an ignominious existence, brought her into the heart of his family and allowed her to blossom into the high-flying executive she was today. She would always be grateful to him. But he couldn't keep interfering in her life. Even now she was heading towards her thirties, he still seemed to view her as a child.

'Sorry, Dad. You're... You're breaking up. Poor reception.' She rolled her eyes at this unlikely excuse, finishing apologetically, 'Call you back later, okay? Love you loads.'

Turning off her phone with a grimace, she stood up, brushing dust off the white silk dress she'd chosen for this difficult meeting.

Andrew Richard Templeton, OBE, would be angry at her for terminating his call. She admitted to some trepidation at that thought, for she hated disappointing him by not acting the obedient daughter. But right now she couldn't deal with his mother hen approach to parenting. Not today. His well-intentioned desire to shield her from life's knocks would only sap her confidence, and she needed all her strength and focus for the negotiations to come.

Assuming anyone turned up to negotiate, that was…

Against the rhythmic *chi-chi-chi* of cicadas in the heat, Sabrina gazed up at the orphanage, tilting her head to take it all in.

The cracked, whitewashed walls had been softened since her time by fragrant ropes of bright, flowering bougainvillea that were gradually taking over the place. The sloping roof where she and her friends had sometimes crept out to sunbathe was missing a few terracotta tiles. As she descended the steps into the deep hollow where the orphanage nestled, a lizard with jewelled eyes blinked at her, and then zigzagged up the sun-baked wall to disappear behind a clump of brilliant magenta flowers.

The front entrance, a flaking blue door that sagged in its frame, stood closed. There was an official-looking notice nailed to the door. She scanned the warning, written in Greek, that stated the building was due to be demolished.

Tears flooded Sabrina's eyes and she struggled against the urge to shout furious obscenities at the innocent air. Instead, she contented herself with a muffled sob. 'How dare he? I won't allow it.'

The painted sign above the door said, *Calista Orphanage.*

This was where they'd brought her as a terrified orphan, lost without her single parent mother, too scared to raise her head in case anyone saw her scar-ravaged face.

Yet, despite her fears, the orphanage had become her home, and since nobody had liked the look of her enough to adopt her until she was sixteen, this place had dug deep into her heart and refused to be dislodged.

Here, she'd run wild and free, lost herself in books and poetry, skinned her knees playing games of tag, and made the best friend in the whole world. As much as a girl could ever be friends with a tough young urchin with jet-black hair and fists permanently clenched for battle.

Trying the door, she found it unlocked. The orphanage stood several miles from the island's main port, deep in dusty, sun-drenched countryside. Nobody would come all the way out here to rob an empty building.

Sabrina wandered through familiar rooms long since emptied of their contents. Her high heels—unsuitable for the terrain, but providing much-needed extra inches for to-day's meeting—echoed on the worn stone flags. She paused in each doorway, hearing the ghosts of laughter and teen-age chatter in her head, and even peered up the stairs into the honey-coloured gloom, half expecting to see Yannis or Melantha standing there.

Clenching her jaw, she felt abruptly furious again. She couldn't allow this place to be knocked down. Whatever the cost, it must be renovated instead. But she could al-ready hear her father's calm, prosaic analysis. *A waste of money*, he would say, and he'd be right. But not everything was about the bottom line. Sometimes the heart needed to be reckoned with as well.

The choice was not hers to make, though. That was the difficulty.

Sabrina took a deep breath and let it out unsteadily. It was by the merest chance that she'd heard of the decision to demolish the former children's home. Nobody could have guessed, herself included, how vehemently she would react to the news.

Kind and generous though Andrew Templeton was, there had always been something missing from her relationship with her adoptive father. His fabulous wealth was no sub-stitute for the close bond she'd enjoyed with her mother here on Calista. Perhaps that was why she still felt such emotion for this ramshackle old building with its homely rooms and cosy corners. Losing it would be like losing her mother all over again.

Peering into the small hall where they'd used to gather for performances or indoor sports, Sabrina froze, her head raised to listen.

Only it wasn't a car engine she heard.

Her heart began to thud.

It was a helicopter. Which meant only one thing.

Sabrina hurried up the stairs for a better vantage point. From his PA's email, sent three days ago, she'd assumed he would be sending a lackey to this meeting—some representative who would listen politely and report back to him.

No lackey would arrive in a helicopter.

Upstairs, sunlight struck through the dusty first-floor windows with a fierce glow. As a child, she'd had to stretch on full tiptoe to peer out of this window. Now she stood in imposing stilettos with a platinum heel and stared across the orphanage grounds to where a helicopter was majestically descending. Its rotor blades winnowed the leafy trees and shrubs, dragging up dust in an ever-growing spiral. His company logo was on the side panel, but the glass was tinted, making it impossible to see who was inside. Then the helicopter touched down and, while the blades were still spinning, the door was thrown open and a man jumped to the ground.

Sabrina gasped, her heart in freefall.

Both hands wide against the window, fingertips white with pressure, she thrust her face against the dirty glass to stare down at him, still unable to believe he had chosen to come to the orphanage himself.

Hadn't he realised she would be at this meeting? Or perhaps he had imagined she would be accompanied by a personal assistant or two. But she'd deliberately left her entourage behind for this trip, guarding her past even from the people who worked for her. Besides, she'd preferred the idea of walking about the orphanage alone beforehand, revisiting the sweetly scented haunts of her childhood home without being observed.

Now he was here too. And alone, just like her.

It had been five years since their disastrous last meeting, at a charity ball in Paris—the first time they'd seen each other since their teenage years. Sabrina had greeted her best friend with shy excitement, giddy to see him again, her heart thumping. She'd watched his meteoric rise in a business career with interest over the years but never quite dared contact him, knowing how bitter he'd felt when she'd been adopted at sixteen and left him behind. He had never replied to her letters, she'd thought, so why would he welcome her with open arms?

But then he'd hugged her in greeting and she'd forgotten her fears in the joy of catching up. That night in Paris had seemed like an ideal opportunity to renew their friendship, to discover who they had both become since leaving the orphanage and growing up. So after the charity ball had ended she had gone with him for a leisurely late dinner, and then back to her hotel.

By the time she'd realised her mistake, and that he was longer the inexperienced boy she had known on Calista, it had been too late; the damage had been done.

He was leaner now than he'd been in Paris, dark hair slicked back, his black jeans casual yet perfectly tailored, his white shirt immaculate. He took four or five confident strides away from the helicopter and stopped there, just clear of the blades. As if sensing her gaze on his face, he raised his head, looking towards the orphanage as he began to unbutton his jacket.

'Rafael...' she whispered.

Through whirling dust their eyes met with a force that knocked the breath from her. In that instant she flashed back to a doctor in the hospital, telling her apologetically that her mother was dead and she was alone. The self-same dread crept through her now…the shiver of abandonment.

Momentarily dazzled, as though she'd looked too long at the sun, Sabrina staggered back a few steps, dazed and disorientated.

Then she turned and fled.

The helicopter had barely touched down before Rafael was out and striding towards the orphanage, unbuttoning his jacket against the familiar Calistan heat. Throwing one swift glance up at the building he had viewed as a prison during his childhood, he checked abruptly at the sight of a pale oval at an upper window.

Sabrina was already there. A ghost in the condemned building.

Of course it didn't have to be her at the window. But then she moved, and he knew her at once. The turn of that blonde head, the light, natural way she moved her hair, like a field of ripe corn dancing in sunlight, rustling and bending with the wind. Everything inside him clenched at the memory of that fair hair spread out on the pillow, her laughing eyes…

Damn it!

Gritting his teeth, Rafael slipped on a pair of reflective sunglasses and kept walking, his face carefully wiped of emotion. He sucked in a sharp breath that he couldn't seem to exhale, his lungs burning as he struggled against emotions he had long since refused to acknowledge. It was one thing to feel such weakness as a child, physically inadequate in the face of his father's cruelty. But he was a man now.

Why the hell had he made this crazy decision to travel halfway across the world to attend this meeting in person? His PA had been right, calling it dangerous and a colossal waste of his time.

'Let me staff it out for you, sir,' Linda had said crisply,

plucking Sabrina's letter away to study it for herself. 'Oh, yes, this has trouble written all over it. Andrew Templeton's daughter? Wasn't she the one at that charity ball in Paris?'

Spotting his frown, his PA had adroitly changed tack, snatching up the phone instead.

'Don't worry, I'll ask Christopoulos to deal with her. He's local to Calista and did a good job over the sale of the orphanage.'

None of his other staff would have dared handle him like that. But Linda was fifty-odd, acid-tongued and married with kids, one of them close to his own age. He was one of the youngest billionaire CEOs in New York City, so he valued her experience and even occasionally her maternal instincts.

'No, I'll speak to her myself.' Rafael had signed the paperwork on his desk, pushing his own internal voice of warning to the back of his mind. 'Get the jet fuelled and tell Johannes to file a flight plan to Athens. Have a company helicopter meet us there to fly me over to Calista.'

'Respectfully, sir—'

'The decision's made.' He'd played with his shirt cuffs, thinking hard. 'I'll need Villa Rosa opened up for me too.'

'You're planning a long stay, then?'

'Maybe.'

Rafael had barely known what he was planning at that stage. But he had known that this might be his only opportunity to meet Sabrina Templeton again face to face.

There was something he had to tell her—a deeply personal communication that could not be made by email or over the phone—and he had put it off long enough. He had no idea how Sabrina might react, and he owed it to his childhood friend to do it gently and in private.

Despite that, he agreed with Linda's astute analysis. Given his history with Sabrina, it was a scenario fraught with danger. Yet once the idea had taken root in his brain, growing with the wiry tenacity of a weed, he'd been unable to shake it loose.

'Sir, your schedule is pretty full-on this month.' Linda had flicked through his calendar app. 'I'm not sure it's practical.'

'Then clear my schedule,' he'd said curtly, dismissing her concerns. 'I'll need a car too. Sort it for me, would you? And call our stables there... Have them take a selection of my horses over to the villa.' Seeing her amazement, he'd given his PA a cool smile. 'Come on, you were only saying yesterday that I needed a break.'

'I meant a weekend in the Hamptons. Not an indefinite stay on a tiny Greek island. Besides, I've seen photos of that villa of yours, built into the cliff. Talk about remote...' Linda had rolled her eyes. 'Not terribly comfortable either, I should imagine, unless you're a Tibetan monk. Remind me, does it have hot and cold running water yet?'

Rafael had grinned appreciatively at his assistant's flippant zingers. 'Actually, it was a monastery back in the day, and I had the place renovated three years ago. Installed a pool and gym and extended the property. There's even plumbing in the kitchen now. No more jogging to the spring every morning for fresh water.'

He'd laughed at her theatrical shudder.

'Relax, would you? I'll fly out there, talk to...' He'd struggled to say her name without showing the turmoil inside. 'To Miss Templeton. And then fly back after a few weeks of sun, sea and snorkelling.'

It might take him that long to recover from facing Sabrina, he had thought grimly.

'What about the monthly board meeting?'

'I'm sure the board can manage without me for once.'

Rafael had shrugged, treading restlessly to the window

to stare out across Manhattan. It was a view he'd grown to love since making New York his home nearly ten years ago: sunlight glinting off skyscrapers, a forest of steel and tinted glass everywhere he looked. Although he got the occasional glimpse of the Hudson River when he was walking through the city. He liked seeing that bright flash; it reminded him that this was an island too, albeit very different from the one where he'd grown up.

'Look, why don't you sit in for me at any major meetings? You know where I stand on most things.'

Linda had looked pleased, but queried, 'And the new deal? You can't deny we've hit a roadblock, sir. We could really do with you at the negotiating table.'

Rafael had gritted his teeth at that reminder. They were in the middle of delicate negotiations with a US company founded by an ultra-conservative family. But recent talks had stalled after one of the major shareholders had complained of Rafael's multiple high-profile flings with beautiful women, calling these short-lived affairs 'decadent and outrageous'.

'Tell them I'm working on a solution.'

With that, he'd shrugged into his jacket and headed for the door, his mind already elsewhere—in the dusty sunlit land of his youth, where he and Sabrina had run wild together, two kids bound by the bonds of friendship.

Now here he was, his feet firmly planted on the dry soil of Calista, back at the orphanage where it had all begun for him... The sickening aftermath of his parents' brutal deaths and his long climb out of the depths of poverty.

Rafael eyed the orphanage with creeping abhorrence. He had hated this place for so long he'd demolished it a thousand times in his imagination, or let roses and briars grow up around it like an enchanted castle in a fairy tale.

Then fate had struck. The director of the orphanage had

contacted him out of the blue about some renovations, seeking a charitable donation. Rafael had jumped at the chance to buy the place outright and flatten it instead—to bulldozer its cruel walls into oblivion and give the kids there somewhere new to live. A fresh start for the orphans as well as himself.

Somehow Sabrina had got wind of his scheme and put in an objection. Far too late, of course. It was a done deal. The kids had already been moved and the demolition was scheduled for a few weeks' time.

He'd been intrigued by the half pleading, half threatening note of her letter. Her silence for the past five years had been eloquent: she had not forgiven him for Paris. Yet she felt strongly enough about the orphanage to break cover and contact him at last. It had seemed the ideal opportunity for him to do what he ought to have done years ago and come clean about what he knew.

Since Sabrina was based in London, and he was in New York, suggesting a meeting at the orphanage itself had struck him as a reasonable compromise. Neutral territory.

Now he was regretting that decision.

His visceral reaction just now, on glimpsing her face at the window, told him starkly that he wasn't over her. That he would never be over her. Not after their astonishing night together in Paris. But he could handle Sabrina Templeton, he told himself. He just needed to keep *business* at the forefront of his decision-making process. Not the tug of deep-down desire he still felt whenever he thought of her.

The front door was ajar. Rafael stalked into the familiar hallway, finding it empty. He stripped off his sunglasses, pushing them into his top pocket. Head up, chest out, every inch of him exuded a confidence it had taken him years to construct.

'Sabrina?' he called. 'I saw you at the window just now.

I know you're in here.' He paused, turning on his heel. 'Where are you hiding?'

Silence greeted him.

Possessed by a gnawing frustration, he took the stairs two at a time. He didn't like spending even a few minutes in this godforsaken building. The sooner it was knocked down the better. His heart was thumping, his palms damp. Memories dogged his footsteps every inch of the way. Older boys calling him names, throwing stones and punches… He had always fought back, despite being outnumbered.

There was no sign of her upstairs either. But he heard a distant clatter—like a broom falling. A grim smile touched his lips and he retraced his steps down the stairs.

There was an alcove under the back stairs where cleaning tools used to be stored. There was a low space beyond it, just big enough for a child to crawl into and hide. In their day a filthy curtain had covered it, but someone had replaced this with a low door which now stood closed.

Rafael hesitated, taking a deep breath. As a child, his father had often locked him in a dark cavity under the floor as a punishment. Now he disliked elevators and avoided tight spaces, despising his own weakness but aware that they made him slightly crazy.

Wrenching open the cupboard door, he bent and peered into darkness. The mops and buckets had gone, but there was a dusty broom leaning at an angle, as though hastily replaced. He could see the tips of two elegant shoes poking out of the shadows and heard a disconcerted gasp as her hiding place was violated.

'Sabrina.' He held out a hand to her, as if trying to coax a wounded animal out of hiding. 'Come out,' he said in Greek, instinctively using his native tongue now that he was back on the island where he'd been born. 'This is no place for you.'

Sabrina had often hidden here as a child, when the taunting had grown too much, pulling the curtain across and listening, knees tucked under her chin, while the staff hunted high and low for her. As her closest friend, Rafael had always known where she would be hiding, and had come along once the coast was clear to persuade her out again.

They'd been the two misfits of the orphanage. Sabrina with her scarred face and brooding silences. Rafael with his hot temper and criminal background.

When the other kids had picked on them, Rafael had always acted instinctively to divert attention from Sabrina, had been guilty of fights and breakages. 'Like father, like son,' some of the wardens had sneered at him. Rafael had ignored that lie; he was nothing like his mean, vicious father. But when one older boy had spoken disrespectfully of his mother, mocking him over how she'd died, he had lost control.

After that particular dust-up, the wardens had put him in solitary for a week.

Sabrina had come to visit him, sneaking extra food through the window.

They'd been inseparable as kids.

There had never been anything between them but friendship, of course.

Until that night in Paris…

'Go away, Rafe.'

Her voice was a mere thread of sound.

He repeated his request more firmly, adding, *'Parakalo…'* his voice cracking on that final word, *Please*.

'No,' she whispered.

Her rejection hurt, exactly as it had done the day she'd left him behind, smiling up at Andrew Templeton, her new father, as he steered her out of the orphanage and into the sunlight. Rafael had been happy for her all the same, knowing she was better off with a rich family, and had written her dozens of letters, hoping for news of her life in England.

No reply had ever come.

What a fool he'd made of himself over her. And for what? Sabrina had soon forgotten him, whisked away to a life of wealth and privilege.

'Don't be such a little coward,' he said roughly, pushing the hurt aside. 'You asked me to meet you and here I am.' He lurched forward and, despite his claustrophobia, stretched his whole arm into the space, his hand rigid and wide-fingered, hunting about for her. 'So you might as well stop hiding in the dark, obsessing over how hard your life has been. Because I can tell you now: mine has been harder.'

'Oh!'

There was outrage in that tiny explosion of sound, and then Sabrina came squeezing out of her hiding place on all fours, a flushed and indignant goddess with dishevelled blonde hair.

She clambered to her feet, knocking away his hand with violent disdain. They faced each other in the echoing hallway. Her breasts were heaving in a white dress that was wholly unsuitable for rustic Calista, its expensive clinging silk smudged with dust. Despite Paris, it was still a shock to see the cool oval of her face smooth and unmarked, no longer the scarred face he'd known and loved as a child. The plastic surgeons had done their work well.

'How dare you?' she ranted, standing almost eye to eye with him in stylish stilettos that emphasised her slender ankles and long legs.

Yes, Sabrina had grown up, all right.

'You of all people should know…'

Then her voice died away as their eyes met.

CHAPTER TWO

SHE HAD FORGOTTEN how his presence tugged at her. Though it was mostly a physical allure now they had grown up. God, yes, it *was* physical. That sharp tilt to his cheekbones, his broad chest and shoulders, the long, athletic legs and the arrogant way he held himself...

But the attraction she felt for him dug deeper than mere physical desire. Once it had been friendship—two lost children finding solace in each other's undemanding company. But in Paris their friendship had shifted abruptly to something more profound. The hurt in her had resurfaced and reached out to his own pain, hearing it answer her cry. And making love that night...

It had been a revelation. Like finding the lost half to a broken bowl and fitting the two pieces together so perfectly you knew it would hold milk again and never spill.

'Hello, Sabrina,' he was saying, still in the Greek island dialect they had both spoken as children. 'It's good to see you again.'

Then Rafael paused, long dark lashes sweeping down to hide the expression in his eyes.

'Know what, exactly?' he asked.

'I beg your pardon?' she said huskily, thrown off balance, trying not to let her hunger show in her face.

'You said, *"You of all people should know..."* but then you didn't finish.'

His dark eyes were deep, velvety wells of blackness that urged her to fall in and willingly drown herself.

'What is it I'm supposed to know? Or is this another of your elaborate guessing games?'

She caught a hint of bitterness on the end of that question and stiffened, instantly on her guard. In Paris, she had gone to bed with the Rafe she'd known and loved for years, ignoring the alarm bells that came with his pleasure-seeking reputation, and woken up with a stranger—a man who'd spoken to her in a voice full of light contempt and walked out of her life, leaving her hollowed out like a breakfast egg, all brittle shell and emptiness.

'I don't want to be reminded of the past, Sabrina,' he'd told her on the phone, heading to the airport for his flight back to New York. 'You were a part of the old Rafael, and all I want in my life is what still lies ahead. The future.'

Left alone, she'd flown back to the rainy streets of London in more agony than she could remember feeling since the accident that had claimed her mother's life. But she had emerged from that refining fire as a new Sabrina, colder and harder, the last vestiges of her innocence ripped away by one wild night of passion.

Rafael was waiting for an answer, his eyes locked on hers.

'That I'm not a coward,' she told him, switching abruptly to English and tilting up her chin when his lips compressed into a thin line. 'That's what you should know. Also, I wasn't obsessing over how hard my life has been. I got lucky here. I was rescued.'

'Unlike me?' he suggested, also in English, with the faint hint of an American accent behind his words.

Again their gazes clashed.

'No, you're a self-made man,' Sabrina admitted. 'And that's something to be proud of. You made it on your own and worked hard to be successful.'

'Damn right I did,' he said, almost between his teeth.

'I haven't had everything handed to me on a plate, if that's what you think. My father...' She hesitated, seeing an odd expression in his face and realising too late what she had said. 'My *adoptive* father,' she corrected herself carefully, 'made sure I wanted for nothing. But he didn't make it easy for me either. I've had to fight for what I wanted. Prove I'm worthy of—'

'His love?' he supplied when she paused.

'Of course not,' she snapped, instantly protective of the kindly, generous man who had adopted her. 'Not everything in this world has to be dog-eat-dog. Of course Andrew Templeton loves me—as I love him. We're father and daughter, even if that's a legal position, not one based on genetics. I was going to say worthy of his *support*.'

It was true that her adoptive father was capable of withholding love at times—usually when he disapproved of her choices—and even of stomping on her feelings if she dared exhibit any. But he meant it for the best.

'The world of business is tough,' her father often said, 'especially for women. You've got to be tough in return, Sabrina. Show no emotion...even when it's going badly.'

Andrew Templeton had given her money, opportunity, a roof over her head. But she'd still needed to work hard to earn his approval. Luckily, that had never been a problem for her. She enjoyed the challenge. Hard work kept her demons at bay.

'So he'll agree to bankroll your projects,' Rafael said flatly.

Sabrina gritted her teeth against a rising tide of fury. 'I

enjoy bringing new opportunities to Andrew's attention, yes. But they're all profit-makers. It's a quid pro quo.'

'Spare me,' Rafael said, and turned on his heel, stalking away.

'Hey, where are you going?' Impatient, she strode after him, elegant heels clicking loudly on the stone flags. 'I haven't finished.'

He didn't stop or look back, and Sabrina found her gaze drawn to his fast-moving body.

Stop ogling him, she told herself crossly.

But it was impossible when the black denim of his well-cut jeans hugged his taut behind and outlined his muscular thighs as he walked—a sight which soon had her thinking of one thing only… How his lean body had felt, sliding over hers that night in Paris, skin against skin, her desperate fingers pinioning his flesh against her.

'Why did you come here today, Rafe, if you're not even prepared to talk to me?' She threw the words at his back.

The question brought him to a halt at last. He turned, dark eyes glittering in the gloom.

They had reached the hallway. The front door stood open, heat and fragrance drifting in from the overgrown sunlit gardens outside. The sun was rising higher in the sky, and already she could feel sweat breaking out on her back, the white silk clinging stickily to her skin.

She ought not to have picked such a revealing dress today. But she'd wanted to make a bold statement at this meeting…just in case he turned up. She'd wanted Rafael to know she was his equal now—a hard-nosed CEO, too worldly-wise to roll over at his command.

Then she'd run and hidden like a scared child.

He must have read her mind, for his gaze narrowed before dropping over her bare shoulders in the strapless white dress and then, disconcertingly, moving even lower.

'Why did you hide from me under the stairs?' he tossed back at her in turn. 'Like a wild rabbit fleeing in terror for some hole in the ground.'

Angry colour bloomed in her cheeks. 'As you said, Rafael, it was a game. Hide-and-Seek, like in the old days.' Her smile was false but she thought he might buy it. 'I wanted to see if you remembered my favourite hiding place.'

'How could I forget?' he replied slowly, still looking her up and down.

There was a restless heat in his eyes that Sabrina recognised from last time. She turned away to avoid that devouring look, heading out instead into the hot, cicada-rich morning.

'It's so peaceful here,' she said hurriedly, to hide her discomfort. 'A beautiful building in picturesque surroundings. I can't believe anyone in their right mind would wish to knock it down. Not when you could so easily turn it into a hotel or a community centre. Maybe even a museum.'

She turned abruptly, startled to find that he'd followed her outside and was standing close, only inches away. But she refused to be intimidated.

His hands were thrust into his pockets, his eyebrows tugged together in a frown, and he was looking back at her stonily. Her heart sank at that closed demeanour. She had negotiated enough business deals to know the signs of someone determined not to budge.

She met the challenge of that obsidian gaze head-on, trying to break through his defences with a cry from the heart. And her heart *was* crying. Both at the demolition of the past and at what they'd become to each other. Once so intimate, now deadly enemies. And she had no idea how they'd got there.

'Why did you come here today?' she repeated. 'In person, I mean. It's a long flight from New York. Why not send a flunky?'

He did not answer at first, then he said slowly, 'I was curious to hear what you had to say, that's all.' His face was shuttered, harder to read than ever. 'So far, it's the same tired argument I've already heard.'

'Because I haven't given you my personal view,' she said earnestly, trying to appeal to the old Rafael—the one she hoped was still in there somewhere, if only she could reach him. 'I want to preserve this building because it represents love. Love and protection. Good people looking after children who have nobody else in the world.'

She saw the flicker of hostility in his eyes and took a deep breath.

'Okay, I can see I've touched a nerve. You didn't get an easy ride here. I remember the bullying you faced. But the wardens took you in and cared for you, didn't they?'

A low blow, perhaps, but she had to get through to him. He'd been a rebellious, wayward child, but with good reason. His father had been an Italian drug dealer who'd shot his Greek wife and then killed himself, all when Rafael was only ten years old. After that Rafael had claimed his life was cursed. But he must have broken the curse—else how could he have become such a successful and powerful man, outwardly a million miles from that troubled boy from a lawless family?

'I didn't come here to reminisce about the old days,' he said bluntly. 'The point is, this place is obsolete. Today's Calistan orphans want to live somewhere more modern.'

He paused, running a finger inside the collar of his white shirt, as though uncomfortable in the rapidly increasing heat of the day. They had both grown accustomed to the luxury of air-con, she thought wryly, feeling much the same discomfort herself and realising she had barely noticed this heat as a child.

'They want Wi-Fi and big bathrooms and a skate park,' he went on.

'So you say. I'd like to hear the kids themselves tell me that. And if it's true, why not rehouse the kids but leave this old place in peace?' she pushed on, sensing a shift in him. 'I know you struggled to get permission to knock the orphanage down. Why not sell it to me instead? Or consider alternatives to demolition? A sympathetic redevelopment, for instance?'

'Because I hate it,' he said hoarsely, shocking her. And then stopped, his jaw set hard. He looked away, his lashes once more hiding his expression.

Sabrina did not know what to say. He *hated* the orphanage?

'Forgive me,' he continued stiffly, after a moment's silence. His accent was harsh, and yet flowing at the same time, like water running over boulders in a mountain stream, his half-Greek, half-Italian heritage making itself known. 'I accept that you feel differently. But this place is mine now and it's my decision to make. The building has structural issues and it's coming down.'

'Structural issues that could be fixed with a little investment.'

When he didn't respond, Sabrina stared at him in despair, wishing she could break through that tough façade.

'I don't understand. Why do you hate this place so much? I always thought—'

He raised dark brows at her, his expression fierce. 'That I was *happy* here?'

The interruption was almost a slap. She took a few seconds to steady herself.

'That *we* were happy here,' she corrected him softly, her gaze searching his face. 'Rafe…'

He took a step closer at the sound of his name, his eyes locked with hers, and she instantly recoiled, unable to help herself. The thought of him touching her was too much to bear.

Rafael checked at her recoil, his mouth thinning into a smile so bleak it made her shiver.

'So that's why you ran to hide when you saw me arrive.' There was zero emotion in his tone. 'I repulse you. Yet you were so responsive that night in Paris…as though you'd never been touched before.'

He reached out, one fingertip brushing her cheek. She felt a rush of heat there and knew she was blushing.

'Ah…' He let out his breath in a long sigh. 'We were perfect for each other at sixteen,' he continued softly, 'long before we knew what to do with those feelings. Now we know, but it's too late.'

His gaze tangled with hers. She could smell honeysuckle on the warm air, drifting in from the gardens, its fragrance heavy and sweet, drugging her senses.

His dark eyes grew sensual under heavy lids, moving over her again. 'Or maybe not.'

Why had she ever thought his eyes were like black stone? They were dark, shifting pools, reflecting her startled expression.

She swallowed and took a shaky breath, struggling to break free of his spell. 'I don't know what you're talking about.'

'Liar,' he said, and gave a short laugh when she spun away.

'I want to save Calista Orphanage,' she said. 'Is that such a terrible thing? You may hate this place, but I love it with all my heart, and I still believe it's a beautiful place for children to grow up.' She looked back at him in hopeless yearning. 'Sell it to me, Rafe. I couldn't bear to see it torn down. It reminds me of happier days.'

He came close and she could smell his maleness now, in the alluring citrus scent of his aftershave, and she caught the faint shadow of stubble on his strong jaw.

'*"Happier days"?'* he echoed grimly. 'About that...' Rafael drew breath, as though to say something further and then stopped, his brows tugging together.

She waited, watching in puzzlement. What was on his mind?

'Let me get this straight. You love the orphanage *with all your heart*?' he quoted, his speculative gaze on her face. 'You'd do anything to get it?'

'Yes,' she agreed, aware of how weak that admission made her in his eyes.

But this was Rafael. Despite Paris, the past still bound them together. She could trust him.

'In other words, there's something you want here and only *I* can give it to you,' he mused, and now the glittering black stone was back in his eyes, blocking her every attempt to read his thoughts. 'Maybe we could trade.'

There—it was done.

The suggestion had been thrown out there so lightly, so carelessly, as though it weighed nothing. And yet the inherent danger had his whole body tingling with shock, his breath trapped in his throat.

His original intention had been to reveal what he knew about her past and then get back into the helicopter and fly across the island to his villa, for a few weeks of rest and relaxation by the pool. He certainly had no wish to waste any more time in this hateful place, mesmerised by mussed-up blonde hair as it trailed over the bare shoulder of this woman in a knock-out white dress held up by nothing more than the impressive anchor point of her breasts.

Yet, however hard his emotions snapped at him to complete this unpleasant task and get the hell out of there, his cold, logical business brain was busy formulating a more strategic plan.

'Excuse me?'

It seemed Sabrina hadn't got his barely veiled proposition. Or was pretending she hadn't understood.

'You want a stay of execution for the orphanage.' He smiled. 'And I'd like a chance to make up for what happened in Paris. I shouldn't have cut things short. I see that now. It's become…unfinished business.'

Her eyes flashed and she took a quick step backwards. No, she hadn't forgotten Paris either. He'd hurt her pride. No woman liked to be dumped. But he'd been in danger—serious, gut-wrenching danger—of losing his head over her. Something he'd sworn never to do with any woman. A terrifying thought had crossed his mind on waking up beside Sabrina, and he'd known he had to get out of there straight away.

Now, though, he could see a way to solve two problems with one solution.

An alarm bell was ringing insistently at the back of his head but he ignored it. Nobody was on fire. Not yet, at any rate.

His groin tightened at the thought.

'What do you say, Sabrina?' he asked huskily. 'How about a quid pro quo?'

He was deliberately echoing what she'd said earlier about her relationship with Templeton—the billionaire businessman with a finger in so many pies nobody knew exactly what his empire stood for, except that it was huge, a global web of companies with one man at the heart of it, constantly spinning straw into gold.

A quid pro quo. One thing in exchange for something else. Nobody being cheated…everybody winning.

'Let me get this straight.' The blue of her eyes had darkened. 'You want me to…?' She licked her lips as he took a step closer, and his gaze narrowed on the nervous movement. 'What? Spend the night with you again? Like we did in Paris?'

'Tempting,' he drawled, his heart beating erratically at the memory. 'That *was* quite a night.'

Part of him wanted to drag her into his arms and kiss her, see if lightning would strike twice. But once the stopper was drawn out of that particular genie's bottle he wasn't sure he'd be able to contain the explosion. No, it was better to keep his distance physically.

Besides, he still had something to tell her—the kind of bombshell you couldn't simply drop on a good friend and walk away. This way he could bide his time. Pick the moment carefully.

'But a one-night stand is always so unsatisfactory, don't you think?' he added, and saw her flinch.

She said nothing in response, her gaze dropping away. Rafael tried to read her expression and failed.

Into the burning silence, he said persuasively, 'Look, enough messing around. How about I put a serious deal on the table? Something that will meet your needs as well as my own?'

They were standing very close, almost touching. The fragrant heat off her body was driving his senses crazy… His pulse was racing, his mouth dry with longing.

'What kind of deal?' she asked suspiciously.

Did he dare make the offer he was so impulsively contemplating? It was off-the-chart outrageous. But hell, why not throw it out there and see what the reaction was? It would be the perfect solution to his current difficulties.

'Marry me.'

'What...? What did you say?'

She seemed stunned by his husky command—as well she might be. It was a fantastical proposal, of course it was. And yet he meant it.

Her lips parted, as though she was sensing the seriousness of his intent, and her eyes widened, a confused, storm-tossed blue. 'You must be mad.'

'You want the orphanage. I'll sell it to you in exchange for...' He drew an unsteady breath, not quite believing he was actually going to say it. 'My wedding ring on your finger.'

Her eyes widened even more and grew turbulent. 'Don't mock me, Rafe.'

'It's no joke.'

He needed to move this conversation to negotiation level, he realised, seeing her accusing expression, and he effortlessly shifted gear.

'I'm embroiled in a business deal with a deeply conservative US company,' he explained, his tone matter-of-fact, 'and they've made their objections to me plain. The playboy reputation...my refusal to settle down... Their doing business with me is making their stakeholders nervous.' He paused. 'My advisors tell me marriage would silence their concerns.'

There was a pulse jerking in her throat. 'So get married. Any woman would do. You don't need me.'

'On the contrary—you're the perfect choice. Intelligent, presentable, quick-thinking. A wife who understands the high-pressure world I live in.'

'Sounds like you ought to marry your secretary,' she snapped.

'My PA is already happily married.'

His gaze flickered over her, punctuated by another hot stab of desire that he ruthlessly suppressed. Once they were married he would get used to looking at her and that problem would go away on its own.

'Besides,' he added pointedly, 'I need a woman who can grace my arm on red carpet occasions, and while Linda is a wonderful wife and mother, she's not one for high heels and ballgowns. In fact, there's a public event coming up soon that would be perfect for us to attend together,' he mused. 'It would certainly get the paparazzi talking.'

'Stop it, Rafe. I'm not going to marry you and that's final.'

Swiftly, he foregrounded her needs. 'Look, do this and you can keep your precious orphanage.' He dangled that prize in front of her and saw how tempted she was. 'I'll gift you the deeds as soon as the ink's dry on the certificate. You can do whatever you want with the building. Move the kids back in or redevelop it for your own uses.' He waited, impatient now for her agreement. 'Well? Is it a yes or a no?'

'This isn't fair. You're…pushing me.' Chewing on her luscious lower lip, Sabrina ran a hand through her wayward blonde hair. 'Anyway, I don't understand… I thought you hated this place—that you were determined to demolish it.'

Rafael gritted his teeth, considering that. Yes, he would have rejoiced to see the orphanage torn down, brick by brick. Its existence reminded him of all those taunts about his weakness as a boy, his inability to look after his mother and stand up to his bullying father.

But he'd been through therapy to deal with those horrors—not entirely successfully—and he was also a businessman. He could see the worth in rejecting one vision for the sake of a better one.

He disliked being quizzed about his background when

the majority of his peers were the products of wealth and privilege—not like him, an orphan who'd dragged himself out of poverty through sheer hard work and determination. This marriage of business equals—to a Templeton, of all people—would seal his position in the global community and allow him to move forward with those deals that had been put out of his reach by more traditionally-minded shareholders.

Besides, the orphanage wasn't the only thing in his past that needed to be dismantled. His attraction to Sabrina was another dangerous hangover from that earlier phase of his life. However, familiarity bred contempt, as the saying went. Once Sabrina was his wife, constantly by his side, she would cease to hold the same allure for him, he was sure.

'I can be flexible where necessary, and I'm willing to revise my decision on this.' He raised his brows. 'How about you?'

She looked away without saying a word.

Rafael pressed on, confident in his ability to persuade her. Now that he had voiced his impromptu plan, he could see it was the perfect fix for their problems.

'We'll spend our honeymoon here on Calista. I have a villa on the island—only a few minutes away by helicopter. Villa Rosa. It's quiet, very beautiful, very remote…' He saw her unfocused blue gaze lift to his face and added roughly, before she could protest, 'There's only a few days' wait for a wedding licence on Calista. We can be married as soon as the paperwork's gone through.'

'You're forgetting something,' she said defiantly.

'What's that?'

'I haven't said yes.'

He curbed his frustration, seeking instead to address her concerns. 'What more do you need? My reassurance that this is strictly a business arrangement? That I only need you to attend a few public events as my wife…enough to convince the doubters?'

They were standing so close her sweet, female fragrance tugged at his senses, tangling itself around his heartstrings and jerking hard, making his breath suddenly constricted.

'I can do that,' he said, more slowly. 'In fact, let's make this a paper marriage. I'll have a contract drawn up and we'll both sign.'

'Paper marriage? What does that mean?'

'No sex,' he said briefly, and saw shock in her widening eyes. That had been too blunt for her tastes. 'All you need do is accept my terms,' he added, deflecting her moment of uncertainty, 'and the orphanage is yours, Sabrina.'

His hands had clenched into fists while they were talking. Aware of that tell-tale sign, Rafael consciously relaxed his shoulders, forced his too-tight muscles to loosen, and allowed his facial expression to shift into polite neutrality. Any obvious nerves on his part would only give her the upper hand in this discussion.

Sabrina drew a ragged breath. 'I can't,' she said huskily, and turned away.

Something akin to desperation flashed through him. He had come here to perform a grim task, then managed to talk himself out of it and offer her marriage instead, and now she was refusing him.

'In that case,' he ground out, his jaw clenched against a need so laser-hot it was burning away at his soul: the compulsion to conclude whatever this was between them and move on as fast as possible, 'you leave me no choice.'

The words were out before he could take them back.

She spun, staring at him, something in his tone clearly alerting her to the seriousness of this moment. 'What—? What do you mean?'

'I have something to tell you. Something…hard.'

Her chin rose. 'So tell me.'

Rafael knew that stubborn look. His heart went out to her, for he also knew how this information would crush her. But what choice did he have? This secret couldn't be concealed for ever. They had been soulmates once. Better him tell her than a stranger.

'Templeton is your father,' he burst out.

Her smile was crooked. 'Of course he is. He legally adopted me. You were there the day he collected me from the orphanage. So what?'

'No, you don't get it.' His voice dropped, became husky with emotion. 'He really is your father, Sabrina. Your *biological* father.'

CHAPTER THREE

SABRINA'S INSIDES CHURNED with anxiety as she studied his lean, dark face. Rafael seemed serious, and yet... How could he be?

'What on earth are you talking about?' she demanded.

'Wait here a minute, would you?'

He strode off towards the helicopter, leaving her stunned and uncertain on the orphanage steps.

'I'm sick of these games—' she began angrily.

But he called over his shoulder. 'Sabrina, trust me. I'll be right back.'

Irritated, she considered stalking to her car and simply leaving. But something about his ridiculous assertion nagged at her subconscious, and she made the decision to wait, even though she was sure that he was just messing with her head again.

There was a stone bench in the shade of the orphanage walls. She sat there, gazing up at the intense blue sky she remembered from her youth, trying to collect her shattered nerves. Andrew Templeton her biological father? It was simply impossible. Rafael couldn't be serious. Could he?

Two minutes later he was back, his jacket gone, top button loosened, and a fawn-coloured dossier in his hands.

'Here,' Rafael said, handing her the dossier, 'this is for you.' He ran a restless hand through his short dark hair.

'There's no easy way to say this, but... Templeton has been lying to you. And this is the proof.'

'Lying to me about what?'

He nodded to the dossier in her hand. 'Everything's in there.'

Sabrina stared up at him, fury and disbelief tugging her brows together. 'Rafael, if this is your way of discrediting the man who's been responsible for shaping my life since—'

'Read the dossier,' he insisted, cutting her off. 'Look at the printouts. The emails and letters he exchanged with the orphanage director. I found them here after I acquired the building. I've collected newspaper cuttings too—plus the results of a private investigation I ordered once I'd realised what I was looking at. It's all there. Witness statements, flight records, charitable donations...' His voice deepened. 'Details of Templeton's visits to Calista before you were even born,' he added grimly, 'and again in the years prior to your adoption.'

She still didn't believe a word of it. But she was curious to see what evidence he could possibly have gathered to prove this ludicrous assertion.

Reluctantly, she began to flick through the dossier. Her body stiffened and she turned back a few sheets, rereading the documents more carefully.

'Oh, my God...' she whispered. Her eyes flew to his face, horrified, and then she returned to the dossier. 'This can't be true.'

'I wanted to tell you earlier,' he said huskily. 'But I knew it had to be done discreetly, in person, and away from your father. Templeton would have stopped me speaking to you if he'd got wind of my discovery. And I meant that offer of marriage, by the way. If you'd said yes, I would have picked my moment to tell you about your father. As it is... I'm sorry.'

Rolling up his sleeves, he left her to read the dossier in peace, seating himself a short distance away on the orphanage steps.

'Let me know when you're done.'

Sabrina's hands shook as she read, her hope that it might be a lie soon fading. The billionaire who had rescued her from poverty and transported her so miraculously to a life of luxury beyond her wildest imaginings was not the hero she had always thought him to be. In fact, he was a liar and a cheat—and her biological father.

It was a simple tale.

Andrew Templeton had come to Calista as a wealthy man on a business tour of the Greek islands. Hiring a private villa, he'd entertained his business associates with wild parties that had turned into full-blown orgies, according to the investigator's report. A year later he'd returned to the island and spent time with an Englishwoman, Cherie, an ex-pat who'd lived on the island and had recently given birth to a daughter. Soon afterwards she'd been seen driving a new car and wearing expensive clothes, even though she was out of work.

A decade later, following the terrible car crash that had killed Cherie and left her daughter scarred for life, the girl had been taken in by the orphanage on Calista. A large anonymous donation had been made to the orphanage at around the same time—a donation repeated annually for as long as the girl remained there. This money trail led back to Templeton's first company, AT Holdings.

Emails exchanged between the orphanage and an unnamed executive at AT Holdings revealed the secret instruction that the girl was to be kept at the orphanage and never adopted, with any prospective parents warned off, while further substantial payments to the director and some of the wardens had been made privately, no doubt to ensure their silence and co-operation.

In the same year that his wife Barbara had died of cancer Templeton had returned to Calista, visiting the orphanage in person. Declaring himself enchanted by the sixteen-year-old Sabrina, he had whisked her back to England to become his 'adopted' daughter in the eyes of the world.

With a crash, the heavy dossier fell from Sabrina's hands, papers scattering about her feet. She sat with her head bowed, a curtain of golden hair hiding her face.

A pair of shining black shoes appeared in her line of vision. Then Rafael was kneeling beside her, his hand on hers.

'You okay?' he whispered.

'Of course I'm not. Andrew Templeton is my real father.' Her voice faltered as she said those words out loud for the first time and felt their cruel sting. 'But why lie about it? Why the elaborate pretence? The whole adoption charade? Why didn't he just tell the truth?'

'Templeton was already married when he met your mother,' Rafael pointed out. 'Your brother Tom would have been five at the time, your sister Pippa only two. From my investigations, it seems to have been a whirlwind affair with your mother. But although he supported her financially after your birth, there was never any suggestion that he would acknowledge you publicly as his daughter, despite his insisting on a paternity test… Which proved, of course, that he was your father.'

He paused, and she flung back her curtain of hair, staring into his face at last.

'Even after his wife died and Templeton came to find you, he must have decided to keep your true identity secret to avoid a scandal,' he added. 'And to spare his other children pain and embarrassment.'

'And what about *my* pain? *My* embarrassment?' Sabrina

dragged her hand away from his. 'I was the one left to rot in an orphanage for years while my billionaire father ignored my existence.'

'I know.'

Horrible realisations were rushing through her mind one after the other, and she gasped. 'Everyone thought he was so kind…adopting an ugly little orphan girl that nobody else wanted, fixing my scars, helping me into the business world. Instead, he was just *gaslighting* me.' Her hands clenched into fists. 'He did it all out of guilt.'

'I expect Templeton thought you'd hate him if you ever found out the truth.'

She jumped to her feet, unable to sit still a moment longer, treading carelessly through the scattered papers. How could Andrew Templeton have done this to her? To his own daughter…his flesh and blood. Every bit as much his child as Tom or Pippa.

Fury flooded her. 'What I can't forgive is how he instructed the orphanage director to put off any prospective parents and lie to me about it. To say nobody wanted to adopt me because…because of my…scars.'

A scalding tear rolled down one cheek. Gulping back a sob, she bent to pick up one of the sheets, holding it out to him.

'Did you read this?'

'I've read the whole dossier…cover to cover.'

'A local doctor suggested cosmetic surgery after a check-up on my facial scarring. And Templeton said no. He said it was b-b-better to leave me as I was…so nobody would look twice at me.'

She was sobbing now.

'Come here.'

Rafael took her in his arms and she did not resist, comforted by the reassuring embrace of an old friend. The boy he'd used to be was showing at last through the ruthless mask of the billionaire.

'I'm sorry,' he said softly, close to her ear.

'For what?'

'For causing you such pain.'

'No, I… I'm glad you told me.'

Sabrina swallowed what felt like a throatful of broken glass and took a deliberate step back. Without a word, he released her. Wiping her damp face with the back of her hand, she turned away and sucked in several deep breaths, struggling to get herself back under control.

'What I don't understand is why you didn't take this dossier to Templeton. He would have paid you a fortune to suppress it.' She glanced round at him. 'Maybe even smoothed your way with those narrow-minded conservatives of yours.'

His mouth compressed into a thin line. 'You seriously think I'd have used your pain to blackmail my way into the big boys' club?'

She shook her head. 'No, of course not. I'm sorry. That was unfair of me.' She ran a hand through her hair, turning away. 'But things are starting to make sense at last. The way the wardens treated me so kindly. Why the director always favoured me above the other kids.' Her voice wobbled. 'Because my father was paying them a fortune to keep me prisoner here.'

'Say the word. I'll hunt Templeton down and punish him for this.'

She stopped pacing and turned to look at him wonderingly. 'You'd really do that for me? Go to my father and—?'

'Make him suffer?' Rafael finished for her in a low voice, his gaze on her face. 'You know I would. We're still friends, aren't we? What hurts you, hurts me.'

'Yes… That civilised air doesn't go much deeper than your designer wardrobe, does it?'

As a kid, whenever she'd been bullied, he would chase after her tormenters and then spend hours in solitary for fighting them. All on her account.

'Scratch the expensive surface and it's the old Rafe under there.'

He said nothing, but his face darkened and he thrust both fists into the pockets of his black jeans, straining the material.

'But no,' she continued slowly, 'I can think of a better way to make my father suffer.'

He waited, brows raised.

'Let's do it,' Sabrina said daringly, not quite able to believe the way her thoughts were going.

She took a few steps towards him, swaying on her high heels, her hands twisting together.

'Let's get married. If there's one thing Andrew Templeton can't stand, it's another man taking away his possessions.' She swallowed. 'And I'm one of his possessions, aren't I?'

She met his startled gaze, hoping he hadn't changed his mind after her stark refusal earlier. Rafael might have behaved like a prize bastard in Paris. And he only wanted a wife so he could clean up his image for business purposes—not because he intended to stop playing the field. But she knew this man inside-out, faults and all, and he had brought her this information rather than use it as leverage against Templeton, which would have been more to his advantage.

Right now, she needed someone in her life she could completely trust.

Better the devil you know. Wasn't that the saying?

'If your marriage deal is still on the table, that is?' she added.

* * *

The helicopter rose slowly above the orphanage, rotor blades whirring, and soon they were leaving the old familiar buildings behind, along with her hire car.

Sabrina gripped the seat as they climbed into the sky, her stomach lurching. She often flew in helicopters now, but was never truly comfortable in them. In the window glass she caught her own scar-free reflection and was momentarily shocked, sucking in a startled breath.

Coming back to the orphanage and seeing Rafael again had messed with her head. For a second she'd half expected to see the old Sabrina looking back at her, her face scarred and, to her mind, unsightly. The terrified child who had crawled out of the raging inferno of her mother's wrecked car after it had plunged off the cliff road.

'Freak!' the kids at the orphanage had used to shout, seeing her burns, and it had taken all her persuasion to prevent Rafael from punching them for it.

He had seemed surprised just now, when she'd changed her mind and agreed to his absurd marriage proposal.

'Just to be clear…you're agreeing to be my wife?' he'd asked, eyes narrowed.

'If that's what it takes to get the orphanage.' She had hesitated. 'But only if we can include a time limit clause.'

He had stared at her. 'Meaning?'

'I'll marry you for one year. Then I want a no-contest divorce.' She had glared when he'd begun to protest. 'I'm not chaining myself to you for ever, Rafe. One year will be perfectly sufficient to get under my father's skin and sort out your issues with those conservative businessmen.'

She had stuck out her hand.

'Deal?'

It had not been an easy offer to make. Her heart had been

hammering violently and she'd found it hard to breathe. Accepting his proposal was insanely dangerous, both for her heart and her psyche. But she wanted that damn orphanage, and if marrying Rafael would also drive her duplicitous father crazy it made the deal suddenly more attractive.

Besides, it was only for one year.

It went against the grain to make a marriage commitment with a divorce date already lined up. She had always intended to marry for love, positive that she would know and recognise that 'for ever' feeling when she found it. Yet nobody in her life had even come close to the overwhelming, sheet-clawing passion she'd felt with Rafael in Paris.

Except his desire had been for the new and improved Sabrina, the one with perfect skin, not the person she still was deep inside… Which made it all wrong—an off note in a beautiful song, jarring her psyche whenever she thought of it.

Rafael had hesitated a fraction of a second before shaking her hand with a crisply delivered, 'Very well. One year and then we'll divorce. Now, let's get out of this place. It's going to be a busy few days.'

Rafael had gone off with his mobile to hustle through the paperwork and organise the return of her hire car, while she'd called the hotel to settle her bill and arrange the collection of her belongings. She was too accustomed to her father's own high-handed behaviour to question the lightning speed with which this marriage plan was being executed.

But as he'd escorted her to where the helicopter waited in the hot sun his hand had brushed her back and she'd stiffened, turning to face him, sharp as a rattlesnake.

'I've agreed to be your wife,' she'd reminded him coldly, 'not your lover. A paper marriage, you said. No hands, Rafe. Or the deal's off.'

A line of dark red along his bronzed cheeks, Rafael had grimaced. 'Forgive me. It won't happen again.' He'd opened the helicopter door for her. 'You have my word.'

Her response had been partly electric shock—a shiver up the spine that had set her nerve-ends tingling—and partly a test to see how serious he was about this marriage being strictly platonic.

Now, she felt doubly reassured that Rafael could be trusted to keep his side of the bargain. But it was still puzzling. Seated beside him in the helicopter, Sabrina risked a sideways glance at his profile and wondered again at his motives.

Since making his first million in shipping, Rafael Romano had grown into a notorious playboy, his name linked with a series of beautiful models, actresses, even elite sportswomen.

Most recently, he'd been seen out with a professional snowboarder, and Sabrina had winced, scrolling through a few jokey memes about the couple on social media. She'd switched off her phone after reading about their affair and lain down with a headache, wishing she didn't care so much and that he meant nothing to her.

She, on the other hand, had made the decision after Paris not to bother with men again. It simply wasn't worth the anguish when things went sour. Not that she'd had much experience of men before that night with Rafael. Her father had taken pains to shield her from the world after she'd left the orphanage, even hiring a bodyguard to follow her everywhere as a college student. And he'd never allowed her to write to her old friends back on Calista.

'You need to think of your future,' Andrew Templeton had told her early on, after settling her in his luxurious English mansion. Expressionless, he had read and then torn up the letter she'd written to Rafael. 'Those orphan kids are

in your past. Besides, they won't want to know you now.
Unless they want money out of you.'

'That's not true,' she'd insisted, horrified by such cyni-
cism.

Yet when she'd finally managed to post a few letters secretly to Rafael, care of the orphanage, he had never written back. After several years of silence she had given up
and tried to put him out of her mind.

Once she'd left business school, her father had put any
prospective boyfriends through such a rigorous grilling that
none had ever asked her out on a second date. Even now,
whenever she started seeing anyone, Andrew Templeton
would find an excuse to interfere.

'It's for your own good, darling,' he would say.

It was true that he had managed to steer her away from
fortune-hunters and undercover journalists. Yet his attitude
towards her dating anyone had always been conservative
and patriarchal in the extreme, and it was only now, knowing what she did about her true parentage, that she saw
through his veneer of 'caring' to the coercive, controlling
behaviour that lay beneath.

Meeting Rafael again in Paris had been a watershed moment for her. Far from her father's oppressive influence,
she'd been bowled over by Rafael's charm and good looks,
and sweetly nostalgic for the lost days of her childhood in
Calista. She'd tumbled eagerly into bed with him—only to
wither and die inside when he'd walked out of her life the
next morning without a backward look.

Her faithful companion in dark times as a girl had rejected her after one night together. It had been hard to recover from that blow.

Thanks to her father's over-protectiveness and her own
shy hesitancy she had been a virgin with Rafael. It had
been the most magical moment, giving herself to him and

discovering a hitherto unsuspected world of pleasure in his arms. She had woken the next day shy and smiling, sure they would spend the rest of their lives together...

'What are you thinking?' Rafael asked now, raising his voice over the roar of the rotor blades, his dark gaze on her face. 'Last-minute regrets?'

Sabrina shook her head. 'Not if this marriage teaches my father a lesson. He can't control me any more, and it's about time I made that clear.'

His jaw tightened but he turned his head, looking away across the beautiful green-gold landscape of Calista. She wondered what was going on inside that heavily defended mind of his. Apart from the emotion-free *kiss, conquer, move on* attitude she'd read about rather too often in the gossip columns.

At least that wild night in Paris had not resulted in a pregnancy. Her periods had always been erratic, and her doctor had suggested taking the pill to regulate them. So when they'd made love that night she'd known herself to be safe. Rafael had not held back after she'd admitted that she was on the pill, perhaps assuming she must have been with other men before him. He had certainly given no sign that he'd known she was a virgin.

They were flying along the barely inhabited western coastline of the island, passing sun-bleached rocks washed by the blue sparkle of the Aegean, only a few isolated dwellings to be seen.

There was a large, whitewashed villa in the distance, built in a quasi-Eastern style, with elaborate archways and a section of domed roof, perched on a crag high above the sea. On the sea-facing side a pool had been built into the cliffs, its blue oblong dazzling against a white surround, a few loungers set around it at intervals under striped um-

brellas. The whole place looked beautiful and luxurious…
and eerily remote.

'Villa Rosa?' she asked, pointing.

Rafael nodded, following her gaze. 'I phoned ahead and
asked the housekeeper to prepare a guest room for you. Your
bags should arrive later this afternoon, so you can change
into something more comfortable.'

After a quick glance at her revealing white dress—a look
that made her shiver—he settled a pair of reflective sunglasses over his eyes, blocking his expression.

'I'm told the official paperwork should be processed
within a few days,' he said. 'Then we can marry. Thankfully, the rules are more relaxed here than on the mainland.'

Only a few days.

Her breath hitched but she said nothing.

'It's important to make a splash with the wedding,' he
continued, 'but without risking your father trying to put a
stop to it.'

She knew this was no idle concern. If her father got wind
of their impending nuptials he would certainly find some
way to interfere—legal or not—or at least to postpone the
ceremony while he raked up dirt on her proposed bride-
groom. She knew Andrew Templeton would not be above
using Rafael's unfortunate family history to destroy him
in the eyes of the business community if he could possibly manage it.

Part of her longed to confront her father over the way he'd
treated both her and her mother. But she knew she would
only lose her temper. The emotions churning inside her
were still too raw. She was determined to keep her dignity
and speak to him calmly, as an adult and an equal, not as
the badly hurt child she was inside. But preparing for such
a difficult conversation would take some time.

Besides, until the deeds to the orphanage were safely in

her hands she dared not risk her father derailing their arrangement with some unexpected manoeuvre.

'What do you suggest?'

'We should marry somewhere even he would find it difficult to access,' Rafael mused. 'I have a large yacht moored at Piraeus that we could use for the ceremony. We'll invite a few trusted members of the media, but only if they agree to keep news of our wedding a secret until we're safely on our honeymoon.'

'And we'll spend the honeymoon on Calista?'

'At Villa Rosa, yes,' he agreed, gazing ahead at the property. 'It's secluded and under twenty-four-hour guard. But we'll tell the paparazzi we're going somewhere else, to throw your father off the scent. The Caribbean, perhaps. I have a small island there that I use occasionally. While everyone's looking in the wrong direction we can relax here without any fear of your father hunting us down.'

Soon they were circling the tiled roofs, and the pilot was instructed by Rafael to make for an area of pasture a safe distance from the house. As they flew over the villa the shadow of the helicopter fell across an inner courtyard with a fountain at its core and a peaceful colonnade, its walkway shaded by leafy green vines.

After landing it was only a short walk through an avenue of dark cypresses to the villa, but Sabrina was fiercely aware of Rafael's presence beside her the whole time. Looking ahead, she focused on the villa instead, admiring its sunny terracotta roof…the whitewashed walls draped in swathes of reddish pink bougainvillea. The path to the front door was lined with pots of tumbling scarlet and yellow flowers, and the air was rich with a sweet, heady fragrance.

As they approached the front entrance the door opened and a stout, smiling woman in a grey and white uniform stepped out to welcome them.

'My housekeeper, Kyria Diakou.'

Politely, Rafael introduced her to Sabrina in Greek, and then listened as the woman, whose first name was Thea, explained the arrangements she had made for their stay and asked if she could bring them anything to eat or drink.

'I propose a light lunch of salad with feta and a bottle of retsina,' he instructed the housekeeper, ushering Sabrina inside a cool hallway with marble floor tiles, its plain white walls decorated with several large, classical style statues and framed gold icons, the saints depicted as bronze-faced and long-lashed as Rafael himself. 'We'll eat outside on the veranda, thank you.'

When Kyria Diakou had hurried away, he led Sabrina into a sitting room dominated by a vast window that over-looked the azure gleam of the Aegean, its blue dotted with speedboats and the white sails of yachts.

'Villa Rosa was a shell when I first bought it,' he told her, walking to the window. 'It's taken years of renovation, and I'm still working on plans for a tennis court. But the privacy and the views…'

'It's beautiful,' she agreed softly.

'I'm glad you like it.' Turning, Rafael came towards her, a slight smile in his eyes, hands outstretched. 'I want you to be happy here.'

As he reached for her Sabrina could not help her instinc-tive recoil, doing exactly as she'd done before boarding the helicopter. Her heart began to thud wildly.

He stopped and his hands fell back to his sides. 'I wasn't going to try anything,' he told her grimly. 'I gave you my word.'

'I know. I just…'

It was remembered pain that did it, she realised. The an-guish he'd caused her in Paris might be buried deep, but it was still there in her heart.

'Sabrina?' He was still waiting for an explanation, his dark brows tugged together.

'I'm sorry,' she whispered.

Rafael nodded, seeming to consider her apology, then said lightly, 'Forgive me. I've just remembered something urgent I need to do. You'd better eat lunch without me. Just ask Kyria Diakou when she returns,' he added, 'and she'll show you to your room. I'll see you at dinner.'

With that, he strode away.

CHAPTER FOUR

IN TRUTH, HE had nothing urgent to do except brood on the insanity of his impulsive decision to offer her *marriage*, of all things.

In his vast sea-facing bedroom, Rafael found the pristine white covers turned down on his bed and the luggage he'd sent ahead already unpacked, everything hanging ready for him or folded neatly in his walk-in closet. He turned to study the familiar view from his window, his mind still reeling from the enormity of what he'd just done.

Asking her to marry him, out of the blue, and then hitting her with the truth of her parentage when she turned him down.

Small wonder she'd looked so shaken.

Yet she'd said yes.

Before recoiling from him in fear.

Her reaction had hurt. But no doubt he deserved it. Had the way he'd behaved in Paris destroyed the trust between them for ever? Or had he disappointed her in bed that night, so that every time he so much as reached out a hand to her now she would automatically shrink away?

Abruptly, Rafael recalled the violence of his response that night in Paris—his unexpected tears, his head thrown back in agonised pleasure as he climaxed. The emotion had left him floored at the time, unable to comprehend what was happening. Even now he felt strangled, his lungs burning for air, and fought to regain his balance.

Why the hell had he proposed like that?

He had meant simply to tell Sabrina the truth about her father and then walk away from her for ever. Instead, they were going to be married.

He'd always had an issue with impulse control, even after leaving the troubled days of his youth behind. It was something he'd tried to address in therapy over the years. It could be helpful in business, that urge to take crazy risks others might walk away from, but when it came to relationships it was far more damaging. He now had ample proof of that.

Hands in his pockets, he stood at the window for a long while, staring out at the Aegean. It was a view that had always afforded him peace in his high-pressure, trouble-strewn life. He focused on the blue-white haze of the horizon and sought to clear his mind, drawing deep breaths into his lungs and expelling them slowly to a count of ten as he battled to regain some semblance of calm.

But his gaze refused to stay focused on the horizon, dropping instead to the sparkling blue pool set about with sun loungers. He hoped Sabrina would approve of Villa Rosa, though it hardly mattered if she didn't.

Checking his fitness watch, he noted that the calming view was doing nothing for his pulse rate today.

Changing tactics, Rafael stripped off his travel-creased clothes and dragged on fresh black shorts and a T-shirt. Since a meditative state of Zen was apparently impossible to reach with Sabrina under his roof, he would blow off steam in a tough physical workout instead.

Heading down to his newly installed state-of-the-art gym, he was pleased to find everything had been laid out to his exact specifications—a carbon copy of the personal gym in his Manhattan penthouse suite. He set the treadmill timer and pounded away for thirty minutes, as though running from the devil, dripping with sweat and breathing heavily by the end.

He wiped himself down with a plain white towel before hitting the free weights area. Trying to block out the image of Sabrina shrinking from him, fear in her eyes, he hefted barbells to the point of exhaustion and worked out on the floormat with a medicine ball—crucial for maintaining his core strength. Another half-hour later he strode to the shower and doused himself in painfully icy needles of water, grimacing and wishing he could cleanse his mind as easily as his body.

After his workout, he relaxed on his balcony with a stack of magazines on elite cars and motor racing, two of his favourite interests. Yet even they failed to distract him from the throbbing awareness that Sabrina would soon be his wife.

He flicked through the magazines with rigid intent, studying glossy photographs of racing cars without really seeing them.

It was to be a paper marriage. No sexual contact. Remembering Paris, he reminded himself it would be safer that way. And he could handle it—no problem. He'd never encountered a challenge he couldn't conquer.

Besides, this villa was a former monastery. The perfect environment for embracing his celibate side.

Something about Sabrina triggered his deepest complexes, that was all. Perhaps they'd been so close as kids he still associated her with the early bond he'd felt for his mother. The mother he'd lost so traumatically…

He buzzed down to the staff quarters and asked Nikos Diakou to come up. He was his housekeeper's husband, who oversaw security at the villa, and also worked as chauffeur and gardener. Villa Rosa had an extensive array of cameras and multiple perimeter alarms which Nikos monitored for him. There were also guards discreetly patrolling the exterior of the property while he was in residence.

'I want double the usual number of guards on this visit,' he told Nikos, a smiling, bearded man in early middle age. 'I can't risk any security issues. Not with Miss Templeton here. She is a very special guest.' He hesitated. 'In fact, we're engaged to be married.'

'Congratulations, sir,' Nikos told him, his eyes twinkling, before slipping away to make the arrangements.

When Rafael finally ventured downstairs it was past the dinner hour and Sabrina was waiting for him on the veranda.

Her luggage must have arrived, for she was clad now in a saffron-yellow wraparound skirt with matching midriff top. There were jewelled sandals on her feet and a silver anklet dangling above one foot, delicate and eye-catching. Leaning on the stone surround that divided the veranda from the pool below, she stood with her face turned towards the sea, her burnished golden hair descending in waves down her back.

The dining table, set under a rustic roof, had been laid for two, silver cutlery glinting, red and white roses artfully arranged in a central display. Champagne was on ice, a thick white napkin wrapped about the bottle.

He stopped in the sliding doorway to admire her rear view. The wraparound skirt fitted snugly, outlining the curves of her tempting behind, while the anklet made him wish to stroke a hand up and down her shapely calf and ankle. A flare of lust lit him from within, but he forced the heat away, aware that she had sensed his presence and was already glancing round to see who was there.

'Oh.' Her hand clutched nervously at the stone balustrade as she met his gaze. 'I didn't hear you open the door.'

'I apologise if I startled you.'

Thee mou! He sounded so formal. Like a stuffed shirt. But her sensual appearance had knocked him off balance again.

She was lightly made-up and looked eminently kissable, especially when her eyes widened, taking in his outfit. He had chosen dark green linen trousers and a pale silk shirt for this evening, worn open-necked. He had decided against sandals, going barefoot instead. The glide of her gaze over his body was like a physical touch, and his arousal stirred again, hard to restrain.

'Wow, that's a very different look for you,' she said. Her cheeks were slightly flushed as she turned fully, her gaze taking in his bare feet. 'I feel distinctly overdressed.'

'In New York I spend my life in suits and tuxedos. I prefer to dress more casually at Villa Rosa. Feel the ground under my feet. I hope you don't mind the informality.'

'No, I'm the same. It will be good to lounge about in flip-flops for a while.'

'I'm sorry to have left you alone all afternoon.' He poured out the champagne and handed her one brimming glass, clicking his own against it in a salute. 'To a restful few days. *Yiamas!*'

'*Yiamas…*' she muttered, and downed the entire glass in one long, thirsty swallow. Then she bit her lip, staring at him over the champagne flute.

He raised his brows but dutifully refilled her glass and replaced the champagne bottle in the ice bucket.

'Is something wrong?' he asked. The possibility had him frowning. 'Not a problem with your room, I trust?'

'Oh, no, the room is lovely—thank you.' She took only a sip of her champagne this time, her expression suddenly wary. 'It's just… I tried to call my office but there's no mobile signal.'

Rafael couldn't help smiling at her naivety. 'Have you

forgotten what life is like on Calista?' He indicated the deep blue Aegean. 'This is one of the least populated of the Greek islands. And Villa Rosa is my refuge from the outside world. No internet, no mobiles, no television or streaming. The housekeeper keeps a satellite phone for her own needs, and so that I can alert her to my visits. But I prefer a clean break. A complete digital detox, I believe it's called.'

Sabrina's eyes hardened, her chin jutting dangerously. 'So, just to be clear, I'm stranded in the middle of nowhere, with no way to call my assistant and let her know where I am or tell her that I'm about to marry a man she's barely even heard me mention.'

'Barely?' he echoed softly.

Not responding to that provocation, she glanced over the balustrade instead, taking in the sheer drop to the sea below. 'I thought by marrying you I'd be escaping my father's obsessive control. But maybe I've jumped out of the frying pan into the fire.' Turning to him, she flicked back her blonde tresses, her look defiant. 'Have I?'

Their eyes met, and something crackled in the air between them—a sudden flash of electricity. He put down his champagne and stalked towards her, torn between anger at her suspicion and humour at this wildly off the mark appraisal.

'You fear I want to control you too?' he demanded.

Sabrina had backed away, coming up against the stone balustrade, her eyes wide, breasts heaving in the tight, shiny yellow top. Heat flared deep inside him and he shifted uncomfortably.

'I didn't say that.'

But her face told him a different story.

'You implied that I'm a tyrant, keeping you shut off from the outside world, when you yourself agreed only a few hours ago to come here of your own accord. Nobody forced you into that helicopter, Sabrina.'

The blue of her eyes matched the restless swell of the Aegean, with darker flecks of defiance and determination within their patina of vulnerability. His gaze dipped to her mouth, a rich bow of shimmering pink, and he struggled against the dangerous impulse to kiss her…to taste that delicious, willing mouth he still remembered.

'But perhaps you need to believe that so you can set me up as the villain of your little fairy tale.'

Sabrina did not move away, staring up at him, wide-eyed.

'Maybe you *want* to be stranded here alone with me,' he continued huskily. 'With nothing to do but relax, swim, sunbathe…and reminisce about the old days.'

His voice, deep and husky, sent shockwaves through her nervous system and made her blood pump faster. Avoiding the complication of any relationship since her last painful encounter with him, Sabrina had begun to consider herself invulnerable to men. Now she realised what a fool she had been. Trying to handle a man like Rafael was like juggling dynamite.

She was fighting for breath, trembling and unsteady before the raw power of his physical attraction. It took all her strength not to turn and flee back to the sanctuary of her bedroom. Since leaving the orphanage, though, Sabrina had learnt not to hide away any more, so she raised her chin and planted her feet instead.

She glared at him. 'Reminisce? I would have thought nostalgic tales about our years at the orphanage were the last thing you wanted to hear.' His eyes narrowed, and she added more coolly, 'But we definitely need to put our heads together and come up with a story to keep my father from suspecting anything. If I don't contact him soon he'll mobilise Interpol to find me. He's very protective, and he likes to know where I am all the time.'

Their eyes clashed, his face was hauntingly close, and for a moment she was struggling to breathe, her voice dying away...

To her relief, though, he turned away and stared out to sea instead, his broad shoulders tense. 'You ride, don't you?' he asked, tangentially.

She blinked, thrown. 'I... Yes, of course.'

'I own a riding stable a few miles from here. A selection of horses is always brought over to the villa for use during my stay. Shall we take a ride out tomorrow morning before it gets too hot?' Rafael swung back to look at her, his gaze once more enigmatic. 'There's a mobile signal further up the coastal road. You could take your phone and contact your father once we're in range, reassure him that you're safe and well. That should keep him off our backs for long enough to put our plan into action.'

Before she could reply, she heard the quiet footsteps of the housekeeper behind her.

'Should I serve dinner now, sir?' the woman asked Rafael in Greek.

He nodded, and she disappeared again.

'It's a good idea to ride out and call my father,' Sabrina agreed.

She was relieved, although her heart was still racing from that unexpected confrontation. It seemed the dangerous moment had passed. For now. Besides, she loved riding and would take great pleasure in exploring the surrounding Calistan countryside on horseback.

'I've brought jeans and boots in my luggage,' she told him. 'But I'll need a riding helmet.'

'I'm sure that can be arranged.' Politely, Rafael pulled

out the chair at the end of the veranda table and gestured her to sit down. 'Shall we?'

Sabrina wasn't terribly hungry, but sat anyway. Eating dinner was something to do that wouldn't involve staring at his lithe body until her hands began to shake. Assuming she could even focus on her food with him sitting at the other end of the table, his gaze steady on her face...

'Talking of reminiscences,' Rafael murmured, the ghost of a smile on his lips, 'do you remember those appalling meals at the orphanage? I still have nightmares about that spinach mush they seemed to serve at every other meal.'

'Ah, but we had a different cook at the weekends,' she reminded him. 'I think her name was Iris?' When he nodded, she added, 'Her cooking was at least recognisable as food. It was only weekdays when we got the green slop.'

He laughed. '*Green slop*. Yes, I'd forgotten we called it that.'

The housekeeper reappeared, bearing a tray of silver-lidded dishes, her face impassive as she served the food, poured more champagne into their glasses, and silently withdrew.

'Thankfully, my diet has improved since then,' he drawled, studying the silver dishes with a sardonic look before raising his glass in a toast. 'To success.'

'To success,' she echoed, sipping her drink with a guarded smile.

Rafael began to eat at once, intent on his meal. Sabrina took a few more nervous gulps of champagne before following suit, her appetite soon revived by freshly shelled crevette prawns served in a fan over a bed of rocket and baby lettuce leaves, a trail of spicy cream dressing adding a piquant note to the dish.

She glanced at him secretively as they ate, finding it hard to connect the powerful, elegant billionaire opposite with the dishevelled tearaway who'd befriended her at the orphanage. Rafael had been a troubled youth, always suggesting some crazy escapade or other. He'd certainly smoothed off his rough edges since then. But she had so many unanswered questions…

By the time she'd finished her spicy prawns and Kyria Diakou had borne the plates away, replacing them with roast lamb served on a bed of fragrant rice, with bread soaked in rosemary oil, the question uppermost in her mind had come back to destroy her appetite.

Why on earth had he demanded she marry him in return for selling her the orphanage?

He'd claimed his having a wife would remedy his playboy reputation with some conservative US company he hoped to do business with. But any presentable woman would have suited his purpose just as well.

'That look on your face… What are you thinking about?' he asked.

She choked on a mouthful of fragrant lamb, glancing up to meet the pair of level near-black eyes staring straight at her, and swallowed carefully. 'Me? Nothing.'

'Hmm…' was his dry rejoinder.

Rafael rose and came loping barefoot towards her, his eyes intent on her face. Sabrina held her breath, watching him. What was he planning? Her gaze was drawn irresistibly to his hard body. The ripple of his pale silk shirt was doing little to conceal the taut six-pack and broad, muscular chest she remembered.

The man was a walking blood pressure spike.

But he merely seized the champagne bottle from the ice bucket and poured more wine expertly into her fluted glass. 'You were running dry.'

'Hardly,' she muttered.

'Sorry?'

'I said, thank you.'

His eyes narrowed on her face, but he refreshed his own glass without comment before returning to his seat.

She gulped down more 'champers', as her father called it, and stared out across the wide blue sea. The rugged cliffs and smooth villa walls glowed with soft golden light as the sun set in the west. The rhythmic click of cicadas in the dry cliffside brush tugged at her—a familiar sound from her childhood. Being back on Calista was like stepping back in time…back into her own troubled past.

Her body was hot and feverish—and not merely because of the heat. She found herself wondering which of the rooms above was his, and whether his bed was as vast and seductively luxurious as her own…

She felt her cheeks heat slowly, much to her embarrassment. Never mind what Rafael was doing… What was *she* doing?

'I hope the guest suite is to your satisfaction.'

His deep voice broke in across her thoughts again.

'It was short notice, but I asked the housekeeper to do her best.'

He hesitated, perhaps taking her silence as a sign that something was wrong.

'Is there anything else you need?'

Her gaze met his with a jolt. She thought of a wave crashing against the dark wall of a harbour and leaping high, its white foam fizzing like the bubbly in her glass.

'No.' She took another sip, felt the heady wine tingling on her tongue. 'The villa is beautiful. And my bedroom is very…well-equipped.'

He raised his eyebrows at her choice of words.

This time she gulped at her wine and choked, unnerved by that intense, unwavering scrutiny.

In fact, she'd been deeply impressed by the guest quarters.

His taste was indisputable. The immaculate white walls and huge bed with its ornate dark wood frame and scrolled ends were both opulent and classically simple. Beyond the near-transparent floor-length curtains she'd found a sliding door with discreetly darkened glass that led onto a long stone balcony overlooking the Aegean, its stark lines softened by lush colourful plants spilling at intervals from terracotta urns.

She had stood on that balcony for a long while, staring down into the sparkling turquoise depths, trying to work out why she had agreed to marry him.

It seemed crazy, and not quite real—like something out of a dream.

She had done it primarily to spite her father. To show Andrew Templeton that he might have deceived her and manipulated her for years, but she was no longer his idiot plaything.

But that was not the only reason.

In this moment of supreme turmoil, when all her easy certainties in life had been torn down to reveal the lie that lay behind them, she needed Rafael's constancy.

He was her one still point in a shifting world.

Was it any surprise she had grabbed hold of him to steady herself?

Besides, every time she made the decision to fly back to London and confront her father, she abruptly recalled that Rafael still held the orphanage, and that this marriage was her only way of ensuring it would be saved from demolition.

More than ever she needed to preserve her beloved orphanage. What else did she have in her life that was *real*?

After her bags had been delivered from the mainland that afternoon Sabrina had taken a cooling shower while Thea Diakou had insisted on unpacking her luggage. The marble ensuite bathroom held every possible perfumed shampoo, bath salts, and soap she could possibly want, along with a stack of soft gold-coloured towels.

Cool and clean, she had wandered through the suite afterwards, in the white silk robe discovered on the back of the bathroom door, and found a private sitting room through another door, as expensively furnished as the bedroom, with a deep white leather sofa, a gold ceiling fan quietly whirring overhead, and a display case filled with the most exquisite carved crystal.

Villa Rosa was a far cry from Rafael's dark and twisted roots in the back streets of Calista's main port. Its sumptuous luxury felt decadent, especially compared to their simple lives at the orphanage. And yet this was Rafael's retreat, his place of 'digital detox'. True enough, she had seen no televisions, telephones or computers. And her own electronic devices had failed to find any wireless network.

He was still watching her, and she raised her chin.

'Though I'm going to miss being able to check my emails,' she added, aware of heat in her cheeks. 'Being cut off from the internet and all.'

With a slight smile on his lips, Rafael said, 'It may feel old-fashioned to you, but a more simple way of life suits Villa Rosa. This was a monastery once, you see. The house on the edge of the world, the monks called it.'

'How ironic,' she said without thinking, reaching for her glass again. Goodness, she had nearly polished off the lot. Shrugging, she knocked back the last drop. 'Given you're about as far from a monk as it's possible to get.'

There was silence from the other end of the table.

Oops, she thought, with a barely suppressed hiccup, and put down her glass. *That's torn it.*

Rafael had not expected his childhood soulmate to turn the tables on him so swiftly. He had asked about her room with secret eagerness, hoping she was pleased with what he'd achieved here. It was one of the showpieces of his growing empire, the large and beautiful Villa Rosa, built on the rugged crags above the Aegean. Yet instead of being impressed by his wealth and status she was openly mocking him.

'Given you're about as far from a monk as it's possible to get.'

That was the old Sabrina, laughing as she sharpened her teenage claws on his vulnerable boy's ego. A throwaway jibe, perhaps. All the same, his breath grew shallow as he pondered her words for hidden meaning. She knew of his playboy reputation, of course. But was it possible she was jealous of his past girlfriends?

Once dessert had been offered and declined, Kyria Diakou lit four candles that flickered in milky white containers on the table and began to clear the table. He caught the housekeeper's eye as she removed his plate and she withdrew discreetly, leaving them alone together.

Sabrina was looking out to sea, her chin resting on her hand, her profile even lovelier by candlelight. With all his instincts driving him towards seduction, Rafael felt the distinct press of desire and shifted uncomfortably in his seat, his gaze drawn to the answering flame in Sabrina's eyes.

He had agreed not to touch her. To do so would risk destroying the fledgling trust between them, not to mention endangering his own equilibrium.

Frustration gnawed at him like a physical pain, and he stood abruptly. 'Let's walk down to the sea before bedtime.'

At her look of surprise, he pointed out the low gate at the far end of the veranda.

'The monks carved steps into the cliff, leading down to a diving platform. They're steep, but lit by solar-powered lamps these days. It's perfectly safe.' Seeing her hesitation, he could not resist taunting her. 'Come on, you and I have scaled cliffs together before. Even in the dark.'

'I remember.' There was a glow in her uplifted face.

'Very well, then.' He held out a hand. 'Unless you're afraid?'

Sabrina stood, scraping back her chair. Her eyes flashed blue as summer lightning. 'Show me these steps. I'll go first, if you like.'

One after the other they descended the steps cut deep into the cliff wall. Below them the constant whisper of the Aegean sounded in the dark, its water lapping against rock as it had done for millennia, a warm violet swell in the dusk. The occasional seabird wheeled past their heads. A gentle breeze lifted Sabrina's hair and ruffled the thin fabric of her skirt.

The lower steps were not as deep-set or as well-preserved as the upper ones, and on a narrower part of the descent Sabrina stumbled and lost her footing.

Rafael, whose hand had never been far from her elbow, righted her at once. 'Careful...'

'Thank you,' she muttered, not pulling away from his touch as she had done before.

When they reached the diving platform he pointed out the small alcove in the cliff behind them, which had once housed a religious icon, and the Greek words carved into the smooth stone flags at their feet, left there by the monks.

She studied these with interest, her fair hair shining in the darkness, loose gold strands tumbling across her forehead, hiding her face.

Watching her, he felt his breathing quicken. He longed to brush back her hair, to tilt her face up towards him and set his lips against hers.

Sabrina turned to face him, her blue eyes almost as dark

as the Aegean, and put out her hands as though to ward him off. Had she sensed what he was feeling?

Hunger growled inside him. Yes, he'd offered the restriction of a marriage on paper only. And he knew the potential danger she represented to his peace of mind. But the core of his body was molten with desire. Somehow he must turn it back to stone in order to honour their bargain.

It was asking the impossible. Heat gripped him as their eyes met and he began to burn.

'Rafael, no,' she whispered, shaking her head. 'Let's not make a mistake.'

Their eyes clashed, but her lips parted as though in invitation and he felt the warmth of her breath on his skin. Electricity shot through him and he dragged in the warm night air instead, struggling to maintain control.

The temptation to move closer was strong...so strong. To place his mouth on hers and plumb those sweet, hot depths until she moaned in his arms.

'Let's not make a mistake.'

She wasn't immune to their chemistry either. Her whole body told him that without a single word being exchanged. Her wide gaze was fixed on his face, there was a flush in her cheeks, and her chest was heaving as though she were drowning. He almost wanted to laugh, recognising the same symptoms in himself, but there was no amusement left inside him.

They were being whirled away on a dark current, lost to all reason. Had he miscalculated so badly, thinking he could handle her proximity, that a marriage between them was simply a matter of logic trumping desire? Because they had been together only half a day and already his self-control seemed to be deserting him.

Thee mou, he thought hotly. *I have to break this spell.*

Another few seconds and he would be kissing her...

CHAPTER FIVE

BALANCED ON A narrow ledge in the darkness, above the dusky waters of the Aegean, one palm spread wide against the cliff at her back, Sabrina hardly dared breathe. She stared into his eyes and it felt as though time were standing still, locking them both into this endless moment.

The sun had long since dipped below the horizon, yet the island rock behind her was baking to the touch. Its rough, earthy heat reminded her of Rafael. Fierce, fertile, unyielding.

A vision flashed through her head: the two of them in bed together, her thighs locked about his bull-like strength, her softness melting into his volcanic embers.

Champagne was singing in her veins, stripping away her inhibitions. Her cheeks flared with colour as they stared at each other, bodies almost touching, the tension between them sky-high. Frustration gnawed at her as she fought the urge to drag him close by those short, silky strands of hair and press her lips against his.

But even as she weakened and reached for him Rafael straightened, turning his gaze up towards the villa and swearing under his breath in Greek.

Confused, she didn't understand at first what had angered him.

Then she heard it.

Somewhere in the gloom above them a telephone was ringing.

'What the hell?' Sabrina exclaimed. Her own eyes widening in shock, she studied the upturned oval of his face, lit by the solar-powered lamps near the steps. 'I thought you said there was no telephone at the villa?'

Fury flashed through her as she realised he had deliberately prevented her from making contact with the outside world.

'"Digital detox",' she scoffed. '"*A more simple way of life.*" What else have you lied about?'

'I wasn't lying,' he growled, but he was grimacing as he stepped back. 'That's Kyria Diakou's satellite phone. It must be important. Incoming calls are strictly for emergencies only. I'd better go and see who it is.' He held out a hand to help her up the steps. 'You first.'

'I can manage, thanks.'

Stiff with outrage, Sabrina marched to the steps and began climbing. She didn't bother arguing with him. But she was fuming. Always these lies... First her father, now the man she was supposedly about to marry. Was she a liar-magnet?

Her first impulse was to seek out the housekeeper and her satellite phone, call her assistant Shelley and organise a helicopter of her own to whisk her back to England. But by the time she reached the villa, breathing fast, her flush of champagne courage had begun to wear off and she was able to consider the matter more soberly.

He *had* told her about the emergency phone, she recalled. And if she abandoned their arrangement now Rafael would be furious, and might even be inclined towards an act of revenge. She couldn't risk losing her precious orphanage to a bulldozer.

One year.

She just needed to control her impulsive side a little longer—until the novelty of spending time with Rafael had worn off. And that included the almost irresistible urge to tumble into bed with him again.

Having followed Sabrina back to the villa, Rafael waited until she had stamped upstairs to the guest quarters before heading in search of the housekeeper.

'What else have you lied about?'

Frustration churned inside him. Damn that satellite phone. Now Sabrina was angry—and he couldn't blame her.

But part of him was glad she hadn't remembered about Kyria Diakou's phone, nor asked to use it. The fewer people who knew about their arrangement the better.

Sabrina was a high-powered executive, which meant if she was anything like him she must be itching to call her PA and check on the status of her latest deals and companies…perhaps also explain what she was doing on Calista. He didn't doubt her PA's loyalty, but there were ways for calls to be monitored and for information to be leaked out to the highest bidder.

As soon as Templeton heard about their proposed wedding he would doubtless swoop in and try his level best to persuade Sabrina against it. And even though Rafael was determined he would not succeed, she would still be forced into a painful confrontation with her father that she was not ready for. Not so soon after discovering the truth of her parentage.

He could not allow that. She had suffered enough at the hands of that man.

Kyria Diakou was apologetic. 'I'm sorry, sir. I left the phone in the kitchen and the window was open. The call was from your assistant, Linda. She asks you to call her back as soon as possible.'

'Thank you.'

Rafael waited until she had gone before returning Linda's call. It would be late afternoon in New York, he realised, glancing at his watch.

'This had better be good,' he ground out when his PA answered. 'You know how I feel about being disturbed at Villa Rosa.'

'It couldn't be helped,' Linda said hurriedly. She sounded flustered, which was unlike her. 'I thought you should know... Andrew Templeton has been calling your private line all morning. He seems to think you've abducted his daughter.'

'That was quick,' he muttered.

'Sir?'

He heard the shock in her voice and moved quickly to dispel it. 'Miss Templeton is my guest at Villa Rosa and is here of her own accord. That's all you need say if anyone asks.'

He left orders that she was to contact Templeton and let him know Sabrina was safe and would speak to him in the morning, then he rang off.

Furious at Templeton's interference, he stalked out onto the veranda where they'd eaten dinner. The dining table had been stripped of its pristine white cloth and only two flickering candles were still lit, almost burnt down to nothing in their translucent containers. The air was warm, cicadas chirruping fiercely in the darkness.

Rafael stood looking out to sea, even though the dark swell of the Aegean was masked by night. Templeton's accusation was a problem, but not one he hadn't anticipated. The important thing was to keep the billionaire from coming out here to see his daughter in person. Templeton was a clever and cunning manipulator, and Rafael was determined to keep him away from Sabrina for as long as possible. He had no interest in behaving like her protector, but he'd known her long enough to recognise how vulnerable she was feeling right now.

Rafael bent his head and went through the series of breathing exercises taught to him by his therapist years ago, seeking refuge in a state of inner calm.

But inner calm proved elusive. His mind jangled with hot, erotic memories he couldn't shake loose. Her soft lips parting as she stared up at him. The drift of her perfume in the evening air. The rise and fall of her breasts in the figure-hugging midriff top, her flat abdomen just visible below. That tantalising slit in her wraparound skirt, from where a smooth golden-brown thigh had teased him again and again as she'd climbed the steps above him.

His chest expanded and his hands clenched into fists. It was the absolute opposite of calm.

He had nearly lost control tonight and ruined everything with a kiss. Because one kiss would be all it took to crack the foundations of this marriage deal.

The friendship between him and Sabrina ran as deep as the roots of an ancient tree. Everything at the top of the tree was twisted and gnarled with disillusionment, yet below the soil those thick roots still lay tangled together, and they grew limb against limb, merging as one in the trunk. And this shared history was needlessly complicating what ought to be a simple business transaction.

Rafael lifted his head to the fragrant Calistan night and took a deep breath, scenting the air as though preparing himself for battle.

In the past, he'd struggled to feel more than sexual desire for any of the women he'd dated. Several had even accused him of being emotionally cold. But none of them had been friends with him beforehand. Now he needed to channel that bachelor energy into his relationship with Sabrina and stay focused on keeping things professional.

Which was ironic, given they were about to marry...

Sabrina had seen a few wild ponies on Calista as a child, but never ridden one. She had learnt to ride much later, at the exclusive boarding school she'd attended after her adoption had gone through. To sit astride the broad back of a horse, reins in her hands, and control such a vast beast with the mere touch of a heel or the turn of a wrist had been a revelation. Riding had become one of her favourite pastimes and one at which she'd excelled, both to her own delight and that of her father, who had encouraged her to compete in gymkhanas and other riding events, where she had even lifted the occasional trophy.

The only disappointment had been how rarely her father had come to watch her compete, after telling her, 'Money doesn't earn itself.' As a child, she'd contented herself with the hope that one day he would be proud of her business know-how instead. Now she knew better, the realisation stung.

Nothing would ever be good enough for that man. Deep down, Andrew Templeton didn't care about her. She was an inconvenience, that was all. The child he had never intended to have but had grudgingly felt he ought to provide for—especially once his wife had gone and he'd been able to do so without awkward explanations.

And to think the man had been her hero once. Her *hero*!

Tears pricked at her eyes.

Rafael had told her at breakfast about her father's ludicrous accusation that she was being held here against her will. They'd both agreed she should call him, but be careful what she said. Yet how on earth could she talk to him on the phone and not reveal that she knew he was her biological father?

She was bursting to vent her bitter hurt and grievance upon the man who had soured the sweetness of her past with lies. But she knew how to keep a poker face during negotiations in the boardroom, never letting the opposition know what she was thinking. Andrew Templeton himself had taught her that. Now he was about to have those same skills turned on him.

It was a secret pleasure to find that Rafael also knew how to ride. Not merely that, but he seemed born to the saddle, his command of the majestic black beast beneath him stemming from gentle hands and a low, persuasive voice.

Her own horse was also magnificent—a black gelding with a white diamond on his bony forehead and a tendency to shy at gates or unexpected obstacles.

Thankfully, the track they followed was marked as private, and they passed no vehicles to startle either of the horses. Soon leaving Villa Rosa behind, they rode at a brisk trot for about a mile, eventually turning onto a hot, dusty trail with tiered vineyards rising on one side and the sea on the other.

Catching her look, Rafael smiled, throwing her a quizzical glance. 'What have I done to amuse you now?'

'I never figured you for a horseman,' she admitted.

'Doesn't quite fit the profile? Is that it?' His smile hardened into a sneer. 'Low-life street kid…more likely to be seen stealing a horse than riding one.'

There was a distinct snap to his voice.

Her hands tightened on the reins and she drank in a gulp of air, filling her lungs to slow down her automatic urge to counter-accuse.

'I'd forgotten how touchy you are about your background,' she muttered. 'That wasn't what I meant, and you know it.'

'Do I?'

His dark gaze raked her as she sat upright, the reins gathered in her hands at exactly the correct angle, just as she had been taught.

'My apologies, princess. I don't have the benefit of your expensive education. Everything I know I had to teach myself—here at the library on Calista, and later in Athens. Sometimes I get things wrong.'

Goaded by the sharp note in his voice, Sabrina pressed her heels gently to the horse's flanks and the animal leaped forward in quick response. The easy trot became a canter, and she left Rafael behind in a cloud of dust.

She leant forward over the horse's neck, her fingers twined instinctively in its thick black mane. The wind was in her face and it felt as though she were flying, escaping from the tangle of desire that clouded and confused her mind whenever she and Rafael were together.

But the sweet respite did not last long. Soon she heard a thunder of hooves on the dusty trail at her back, and then he was alongside her, one strong hand grabbing for the bridle.

'Are you mad? Or are you trying to get yourself killed?' he barked as the two horses slowed to a sweating trot and then a sedate walk.

'Oh, stop overreacting. I was never in any danger.' She knocked his hand away from the bridle and eased the horse to a stop herself. 'I'd better phone my father now.'

His dark eyes snapped at her. 'Very well. You'll be careful, though? Because he's a smart man. He'll be listening for signs that you're not telling the truth.'

'I know how to deal with my own father, thanks. Is there a mobile signal here or do we need to keep riding?'

He levelled a glare at her that spoke of his frustration,

but gave a terse shrug. 'We've gone far enough now. You should be able to make the call.'

He hesitated, leaning forward to pat his horse's shiny neck as the animal snorted and breathed heavily beneath him.

'Look, I'm sorry about what I said back there. You didn't choose someone so privileged to be your father.' Narrow-eyed, he studied her flushed face. 'Before you make this call, I hope you haven't changed your mind about our deal. The paperwork's all in motion—there's no turning back.'

'I haven't changed my mind,' she snapped, still annoyed by how he'd wrongly assumed her horse had run away with her.

In some ways Rafael reminded her of her father, who had insisted she should operate independently of his wealth and influence, yet would still sweep in at the first sign of trouble to 'rescue' her.

Gathering the reins, Sabrina dismounted and looped them over a nearby fence pole. Then she fished her mobile from her pocket, walked a few paces out of earshot and turned it on, keeping her back to Rafael.

The screen displayed several signal bars and a dozen anxious messages popped up from her father, all chiming at once. She skim-read the texts before calling him back, hands trembling as she primed herself for a difficult conversation.

Her father answered almost immediately. 'Sabrina, thank God. Where on earth are you?'

Without waiting to hear a reply, Andrew Templeton pressed on, an explosive mix of fear and fury ticking behind every word.

'I received the most insolent message last night from that thug Rafael Romano. Are you okay? Has he hurt you?' He snatched a breath before exclaiming, 'I swear, if he's touched so much as a hair on your head I'll kill him with my bare hands!'

Every fibre of her being wanted to scream defiance at him, yet somehow Sabrina heard herself say coolly, 'Calm down, Dad. I'm fine.'

'Are you?' Templeton sounded frustrated, and more than a little suspicious. 'When we spoke yesterday you said you were on Calista and your mobile was playing up. I couldn't get hold of you again. So I notified the local police that you were missing.'

'You did *what*?'

'What else did you expect? If you've been trying to give me a heart attack, I congratulate you on nearly achieving it.'

That had to be his usual dramatic hyperbole. But she felt a flutter of anxiety. However badly he had behaved towards her, he was still her father.

'Dad, please tell me you're joking.'

'Not entirely. I've been out of my mind with worry. Your hire car was returned by an unknown third party. The hotel where you'd been staying claimed you'd checked out by phone and asked for your luggage to be collected—also by some unknown person. Then I learnt you've been travelling solo instead of with your team. All major red flags.' He was breathing heavily. 'Do you have *any* idea how much you're worth, sweetheart? You're a kidnapper's dream.'

'Yes, but I still can't believe you called the police without even waiting twenty-four hours.'

Sabrina took a few deep breaths, reminding herself to keep a tight lid on her emotions. Besides, it wouldn't do any good to yell at him. The man was as stubborn as an ox.

'I'm not an idiot. I didn't want anyone to know I was on Calista. The publicity might have derailed the deal I was trying to broker. That's why I was travelling unaccompanied.'

'It only takes one person to kidnap you, Sabrina,' her father pointed out. 'I did some digging to find out what exactly you were doing there. I even spoke to that ditzy assistant of yours—'

'You spoke to Shelley?' Her voice was a squeak of dismay. Her assistant was terrified of Andrew Templeton and would never have been able to withstand one of his trademark interrogations.

'Yes, and she eventually admitted you'd arranged a meeting with Rafael Romano, of all people.' He expelled a noisy breath, his voice grating with disapproval. 'You can imagine my reaction. I got on the phone to his people at once, but nobody seemed to know where he was. Finally, I got a call in the early hours, letting me know you were safe and spending a few days with Romano on Calista.'

She closed her eyes at the suddenly dangerous note in his voice.

'Darling, you need to come home straight away. I haven't forgotten the state you were in after Paris.'

She counted to five before replying, suppressing the words in her head. Words of anger and disillusion that would expose what she knew about him.

'Dad, please…'

It still irked her that, unbeknownst to her, Andrew Templeton had been secretly monitoring her movements during the Paris trip. On her return home to England, the humiliation of her father's lecture on one-night stands had been one of the most cringe-worthy experiences of her life. She had thought it embarrassing, but also rather endearing that he cared enough to keep an eye on her like that. Now it merely underlined how possessive and controlling he was over everyone in his life, and her fury grew.

She turned, shooting a wary glance over her shoulder, to

see that Rafael had also dismounted and was close by, his gaze intent on her face. Could he hear what was being said?

'Look,' she muttered grittily into the phone, 'I can't talk right now. There's something I need to think about, so I'm going off-grid for a few days. I'll call you after the weekend.'

'Is Romano there with you now? Is he the reason you're going "off-grid"—whatever the hell *that's* supposed to mean.'

She swallowed, hot-cheeked. 'He's an old friend and he's been supporting me through some issues, that's all.'

'Romano was more than a friend once, though, wasn't he? I haven't forgotten.'

'I have to ring off now.'

'Sabrina, wait—' he began, but she interrupted him.

'This is my business, Dad, not yours. Please don't ring Shelley and frighten her again. I can't afford to lose her—she's an excellent assistant.'

'Fine, but at least let me help.'

Her father seemed to be almost pleading with her. That shocked her… It was so out of character. But it also made her suspicious.

'Whatever you're facing, tell me what these "issues" are and I'll sort them out for you.'

He was shifting tactics, trying to probe her for weak spots.

'I'm sorry, Daddy,' she insisted. 'Not this time. This is something I have to do on my own. I'll be in touch as soon as possible, I promise.'

She ended the call while he was still protesting, and hurriedly turned off the phone before he could ring her back. Then she looked up to find Rafael still watching her, his hands in his pockets, his face expressionless. But she sensed what he was feeling, all the same. Satisfaction that his plan was still working—that she hadn't betrayed him and they would soon be man and wife. But also irritation.

Fury whipped through her—a fury she had wanted to direct towards her father but hadn't been able to. 'Well? Spit it out. Whatever you're thinking.'

'Going "off-grid" to think about something?' he said, his brows raised. 'As cover stories go, that's a bit weak. Anyone would think you wanted *Daddy* to come and find you.'

'Don't use that word,' she snapped.

'You did.'

'Only because I didn't want him to think anything was wrong.'

'I'm not sure you did a great job. But let's hope I'm mistaken.'

Unlooping its reins from the post, Rafael brought the black gelding towards her, his gaze lifted to the deep blue skies above.

'The sun's getting high. We should probably think about turning back.'

She mounted the horse with easy skill, ignoring his proffered hand. 'I thought there was *"no turning back"*?' she pointed out, quoting what he'd said earlier.

He said nothing to this jibe, merely mounting his own horse. Soon they were both thundering back along the track to Villa Rosa, side by side in the dusty sunshine.

The day felt curiously the same. Light glittered on the blue Aegean exactly as it had done before. Calista looked as wild and beautiful as ever. Yet something had shifted between them during that brief phone call to her father. She'd pushed past her inner misgivings to accept their marriage as a done deal, and seen triumph flare in Rafael's eyes as he'd noted and understood that change.

Let him gloat, she thought, her mouth compressing as she brooded over that call to her father. This would still be a marriage on her own terms, not Rafael's. She'd made that clear from the start. His ring on her finger, the orphanage deeds in her possession, her father's control left behind. No more, no less.

So what was this fluttering dread in the pit of her stomach? Why did she feel as though she'd broken free from one over-protective male only to weld herself to another?

CHAPTER SIX

THE COMPLEX MULTI-PAGE contract Rafael had instructed to be drawn up for their one-year marriage was brought over by his local lawyer, Christopoulos, along with a date and time for their wedding. Among its many clauses was a stipulation that Sabrina must attend a minimum of three high-profile social events as his wife over the course of the year, with the first coming up soon, its details highlighted so she could make a note in her diary.

He saw her eyes widen as she read through the document. The named event was the annual charity ball in Paris where they had met five years ago.

'Everything all right?' he asked, his jaw clenched, wondering if she was about to renege on their agreement.

But Sabrina replied, 'Perfectly,' with total composure as she accepted a pen from Christopoulos.

She signed her name at the bottom of the last page with no change of expression, but Rafael felt his own heart jerk as he took the pen from her. Still, he signed his name with a flourish before handing the contract back to Christopoulos, convincing himself that he was doing the right thing.

This bloodless union might frustrate him, but it should cure him of his obsession with Sabrina. After that, he could finally begin to live his life…

'Congratulations,' the lawyer told them, shaking hands with them. 'You may rely on my discretion, Mr Romano.'

* * *

On the morning of their wedding they took a speedboat out from the jetty below the villa, accompanied by Kyria and Kyrios Diakou, who had enthusiastically agreed to be their witnesses. It seemed his housekeeper and her husband believed this to be a love match, for they kept smiling at him and Sabrina with undisguised approval.

Sabrina herself had taken his breath away on emerging from her room that morning. She was wearing an off-the-peg wedding dress bought in Athens on a quick helicopter trip yesterday. An up-and-coming Greek designer had created a gown which would have been dismissed by most of the glamorous, high-maintenance women he'd dated in recent years, their tastes being more exorbitantly expensive. On Sabrina, though, it looked a million dollars. Its ruched bodice cupped her breasts with delicate ivory silk; spaghetti shoulder straps exposed sun-kissed skin. The frou-frou skirts of layered tulle ended just above the knee, displaying an expanse of thigh as he helped her into the speedboat.

Arousal taunted him, and his heart beat a little faster as he imagined what delightful silky scraps of lingerie she might be wearing underneath... Seconds later he was slapping himself down for even allowing his thoughts to wander in such a dangerous direction. This would be no ordinary marriage and he needed it to remain platonic.

'Get a grip...' he muttered.

'Sorry?' Sabrina looked round at him with wide blue eyes.

'I said, you might want to hold on to something.' He planted himself in front of the speedboat wheel, running through the engine checks. As his bride found a seat and gripped the side rail he glanced at Thea and Nikos. 'Ready?'

Kyria Diakou smiled up at him, her arms bristling with fragrant floral arrangements, all white roses and spreading greenery. Her husband was beside her, distinctly uncomfortable in formal wear. 'Ready, sir.'

The speedboat trip did not take long. His luxury super-yacht had been sailed from Piraeus and was now anchored out in the deeper waters between islands, swaying slightly in the sea breeze. The hull gleamed white in the sunlight, chrome rails glinting, and the whole crew was assembled on deck and standing to attention as they boarded the vessel.

'Welcome aboard, Mr Romano,' the captain said, saluting him before bowing slightly to Sabrina. 'Miss Templeton. Congratulations.'

'Thank you,' Sabrina said, smiling warmly.

Rafael caught her eye, a smile tugging at his own lips. He was remembering a time when the two of them had watched a Calistan wedding party assemble for photographs with the picturesque harbour as a backdrop. A couple of urchins themselves, they had mocked the bride in her finery and the groom in his stiff, formal clothes, never guessing they might one day be marrying each other.

Even now he couldn't quite believe it.

Him and Sabrina…

No, it couldn't be. She had always been too good for him. Her warmth and generosity, the sparkling beauty in her eyes… How could a boy from the backstreets reach for such a star? It would burn his fingers to the bone.

And yet here they were.

'This way, if you please.'

The captain led them to a beautifully constructed wedding area on the open deck, laid out with deep red carpets, white floral arrangements in high urns, and chairs for the crew, witnesses and select members of the world's press, who were already gathered, watching in excitement for their first glimpse of the happy couple.

'Miss Templeton, over here!' one of the photographers shouted.

Sabrina turned that way, an apprehensive look on her face, as the woman climbed on a chair to take a shot of the two of them together, standing arm in arm, with the smooth Aegean a blue haze behind them.

He could see why the few press they'd invited were lapping this up. Sabrina's blonde hair had been dressed with flowers, and long burnished gold strands trailed delightfully over her shoulders and down her back. She looked more like a wood nymph, one of the dryads of Ancient Greece, than the hard-headed businesswoman he knew her to be. The perfect image for some glossy socialite gossip piece or wedding column.

Rafael smiled down at her while more pre-wedding photographs were taken. 'You look radiant,' he murmured, and brushed her cheek with one knuckle. 'Smile more. Your father will be studying these pictures with a magnifying glass, remember?'

'You don't need to tell me that,' she responded, but turned a smiling face towards his. 'You look…um…very handsome in that tux.'

His brows flicked up. 'What? This old thing?'

Sabrina gurgled with genuine laughter, and on impulse he snaked an arm about her waist, drawing her towards him as though for a kiss. The photographers went crazy, snapping candid shots and shouting out impertinent instructions as he stared down into the turbulent blue depths of Sabrina's eyes, their mouths bare inches apart.

Her laughter died away, and her lips parted as if in shock. She whispered, 'Erm…does this need to be quite so realistic?'

Her gaze locked with his, her tulle skirt rustling against him, and everything about her felt maddeningly feminine.

'It's important to put on a show,' he reminded her, his voice unsteady, but he released her, turning to the waiting minister. 'Shall we do this?'

The ceremony seemed to fly by. The sun beat down on them, and those watching murmured a sigh of appreciation when the minister asked for any objections to be aired and none were. The deck rocked gently beneath them as they exchanged vows in soft voices that nonetheless seemed to carry across the water, for even passengers on passing vessels applauded and called out congratulations.

Rafael kept smiling throughout, keeping up the charade for the paparazzi, but he wasn't as calm and controlled as he'd expected to be today. Quite the opposite, in fact. His chest felt tight and his heart was thumping so loudly he was sure everyone on deck could hear it.

Meanwhile Sabrina never lost her poise, repeating the minister's words on cue, no hint of uncertainty in her voice. Rafael had to admire her single-minded focus—especially given how much she valued her independence. Sabrina punched through the day, her eyes on the prize, and did not even flinch when he pushed a heavy gold band onto her finger—the wedding ring that had arrived only that morning, express couriered from Cartier in Paris.

Finally, it was done, and they were man and wife.

'You may kiss the bride, if you wish,' the minister said, beaming at them.

The photographers shifted, hurriedly leaving their seats and scrambling for a better view of the married couple. Rafael felt the irritation of their presence, but accepted the necessity of having at least a few of the world's media here.

It was no good their marrying in secret, after all. He had to signal to the world that he was now a respectable married man. And she wanted her father to know about it too.

As Sabrina lifted her face towards him, dutifully playing the role of newly wedded bride, Rafael looked down at her with a sudden stab of trepidation. This would be their first kiss since Paris, and already his nerves were flaring up, memory kicking him back to the morning after...

'Rafael...?' she murmured, faint surprise in her face.

Frustrated by his own weakness, he bent his head and kissed his bride.

Thee mou!

At the touch of his lips to hers his heart rate rocketed, his body instantly aroused, blood pumping to every extremity. His senses spun and drowned him. He was overwhelmed by her warmth, her curves, the light fragrance of the flowers in her hair. It was all he could do not to drag her against him like a sex-starved caveman and slot his mouth firmly against hers, plundering her sweetness until she could no longer stand...

But they were in public. In full view of the yacht's crew—not to mention those members of the press, whose laughter and amused whistles brought him back to his senses.

Stunned, he straightened slowly, his hands releasing her, and saw the same shock in her dazed blue eyes.

It felt surreal to be married to his childhood friend, he thought, forcing a smile back to his lips. Like waking from the strangest dream to find it reality...

Back at Villa Rosa, he gave the Diakous the evening off, insisting he would himself serve the cold supper which his housekeeper had already prepared and left in the fridge on his command. The couple only lived a short distance away, in the villa grounds, in a self-contained annex. But he wished to guarantee that he and Sabrina would be alone together that evening, even if their marriage was destined not to be consummated.

'We're leaving now for our honeymoon on Paradiso, my

island in the Caribbean,' he had blithely lied to the carefully selected group of reporters after the ceremony. 'We're delighted and honoured that you could share our special day with us,' he had said, linking hands with Sabrina. 'Aren't we, Sabbie?'

When she'd nodded, he had kissed her hand and turned back to them with a pleading smile.

'All we ask is a little privacy for the next few weeks while we settle into married life together. Thank you.' He had led his new wife back towards the waiting speedboat. 'Feel free to enjoy the champagne and canapés for as long as you like before leaving. My on-board chef is *excellent*.'

The paps had shouted questions after them, Sabrina in particular, but she had already said she would not speak to the press, only pose for photographs.

'I'm not shy,' she'd explained to him beforehand, 'I'm just not terribly good at dodging questions.'

'That's because you're an honest soul,' he'd told her, and meant it.

Now they were safely back at their real honeymoon destination he took a moment in the gatehouse, to check the camera array and the perimeter alarms that kept them safe from intruders. He needed to be sure none of the paparazzi had found a way to follow them after they'd left the yacht, perhaps stealthily by drone.

But everything was quiet and still outside, only the cicadas chirping in the sunny warmth of the early evening.

Satisfied that the villa was secure, he followed Sabrina into the cool, air-conditioned interior and stood watching as she removed the headdress of flowers the hairdresser had arranged for her earlier that morning.

'Shall I pour us a drink?' he asked, thrown off balance by how silent the house was without his housekeeper. His nerves felt raw and unsteady.

'Yes, why not?' she said, her voice unnaturally high, and then kicked off her shoes before running upstairs. 'I... I'm going to change.'

Rafael hesitated, and then followed more slowly, heading for the sanctuary of his own suite. There, he changed out of his formal dark suit and tie into shorts and a crisp white T-shirt. Barbed thoughts and volatile emotions kept intruding into the orderly calm of his bedroom and he pushed them away, even stepping out on the balcony at one stage to meditate on the sea and breathe deep, struggling to regain control.

He wanted tonight to be special, but not as it would be for most married couples. More an outward symbol of how their marriage would work—calmly, and with the gentle affection of old friends who were gaining mutual satisfaction from an arrangement that would further their plans and ambitions.

Back in the bedroom, he fetched the deeds to the orphanage and a small, brightly wrapped gift from his bedside cabinet. The gift he turned over in his hand, unsure what to do with it, before slipping it into his pocket. He would see how the evening went.

Barefoot, he was about to head downstairs again when he heard a tiny, breathless noise from Sabrina's bedroom suite.

He stopped on the top stair, breathing harshly through gritted teeth, one hand gripping the banister until his knuckles showed white. He had heard that noise often enough as a child not to recognise it now...

It was the sound of a woman struggling not to cry.

Not since waking up in hospital the day after the car crash that had killed her mother had Sabrina been so unhappy.

Then, it had been the horrific discovery that her beloved mum was dead, and she would never hug her or speak to her again, while she herself had been left orphaned and disfigured, with no idea who her father was nor if she had any living relatives at all.

Now, uppermost in her head was the fear that she had made a terrible mistake, and one from which she might never recover. In punishing her father for his perfidy, had she merely punished herself?

She had told herself that securing the orphanage was all that mattered. Now Rafael's ring was on her finger and she was no longer Miss Templeton but Mrs Romano, with all that implied. Too late, the magnitude of what she'd done struck her.

While she might only have one year in which to endure this loveless marriage, she could not walk away without the deeds to the orphanage. But they had been married several hours and he had not mentioned their bargain yet.

What if he *never* handed her the deeds?

What if she had missed a legal hitch in the contract, for instance? Some carefully worded clause in the small print that would prevent her from ever owning the orphanage?

She had seen that tactic in business deals too often not to know how long a legal wrangle over the wording of a contract might drag on. Not simply months, but years... Long past the stated period of their marriage, in other words.

Sabrina stared at herself in the full-length mirror. The unhappiest bride in the world looked back at her, a perfect snapshot in ivory silk, but with both hands clasped to her cheeks, tears spilling from red-rimmed eyes. Still, she gritted her teeth and held back her sobs, too proud to let him hear her misery.

A creak as the door opened brought her around, rigid with embarrassment. Wiping her face with her hands, she glared at her new husband, framed in the doorway.

Rafael had changed into casual clothes, and was no longer

the austere stranger who had stood by her side throughout their perfunctory wedding service. Yet he was also unrecognisable as the rebellious, weed-tall youth she had grown up with. That boy would have understood her pain and rushed to comfort her—not looked back at her so blankly.

She could barely recall speaking her vows today. Yet she must have done so, for here they were—married. The heavy gold band on her finger proved it.

What she did remember was his kiss.

It had been Paris all over again. Pure molten electricity, flashing from her lips to her core in three seconds flat. How did he *do* that? Her shoulders had been warm and tingly from his touch long after he'd released her, and there had been a memory in her head, spinning round and round like a glitterball, of her and Rafe in bed together, making love. As her eyes had opened they'd met those dark depths and she'd known she was tempted to repeat the same mistake...

'I didn't hear you knock,' she snapped, thrusting her hand with its incriminating glitter of gold behind her back.

Rafael's gaze narrowed on her face. 'You've been crying. Why?'

'Brides always cry on their wedding day—didn't you know that?' She had been trying for matter-of-fact but it came out flippant. The shake in her voice didn't help. 'It's tradition.'

He came further into the room, searching her face. He was barefoot again, and in shorts, his legs lean and muscular, with a dusting of dark hair.

'I told you. I need my privacy—' she began fiercely, but then she saw he held out a large envelope.

'Here,' he said, his gaze unreadable. 'The deeds to the orphanage, made out in your name. Now you're free to do whatever you want with the place.' He took a step back as she took the envelope. 'A deal's a deal.'

'Oh.'

She had misjudged him.

'Thank you,' she whispered, and opened the envelope, peeking inside to see a wodge of legal documents and associated papers. Her heart flipped as she realised what this meant. The orphanage would no longer be demolished. 'That's... That's wonderful.'

Sadly, her memories of the place were tainted now, by what she'd learned about her father. But at least Rafael had kept his word.

Hesitantly, he drew a small gift-wrapped object from his pocket and held that out to her too. 'A wedding gift.'

Stunned into silence, Sabrina stared at his expressionless face, and then at the gift resting on his open palm. 'For...? For me?'

Inhaling sharply, she dropped the envelope on the bed, scrubbed at her damp cheeks again, and took a few tentative steps towards him.

'I didn't get you anything, I'm sorry.'

He said nothing, merely waited.

Scooping the gift from his palm, she tore off the tasteful gift wrap and found a tiny blue-white crystal dolphin inside the package, its smooth body arched in flight. Gasping in delight, Sabrina ran a fingertip appreciatively over its cool, delicate shape. The detail was exquisite, right down to its intelligent, gleaming eyes.

'Oh, Rafe, how lovely!' She closed her hand over the glass dolphin, warmth rushing to her heart. 'Thank you.'

He had been holding himself tense, but seemed to relax at this, his lips curving in a rare smile. 'I thought you'd like it. You always loved dolphins as a girl. You remember how we used to lie on the cliffs and watch them leaping in the bay?'

She nodded.

'I found that one on a market stall at the port. It's not worth much, but—'

'It's perfect.'

Rafael inclined his head, and she sensed pleasure in the brief gesture. 'Now, why were you crying? And don't try to deflect the question this time.' His jaw tensed. 'I thought you were happy to marry me. Have you changed your mind?'

Carefully, she turned to place the crystal dolphin on her dressing table, next to her make-up case and bottles of perfume. 'Of course I'm happy.'

'You don't look it.' His voice vibrated with tangled emotions.

She lifted her gaze to his face, trying to guess what he was thinking, but it was impossible. She hated that. Rafael was a closed door to her now, when once they had been able to read each other's thoughts freely. The loss of that intimacy pierced her heart, like steel thrust deep into her chest. Where had their friendship gone?

Another hot tear crept over the brim of one eyelid and rolled down her cheek. She turned her head and rubbed it away with her fist, hoping he hadn't noticed.

'Sabrina...' His voice was husky.

'I'm fine,' she insisted, and flashed him a bright, false smile. 'It's been a long day, that's all. And I was worried my father might suddenly turn up and—'

'You don't need to fear him ever again,' he interrupted her. 'You're my wife now. He can't touch you.'

She lowered her gaze, surprised by the protective look in his eyes. 'It was so hot at the wedding too. Remind me never to get married on a yacht again.'

It was meant as a joke, but he didn't smile.

'I'm dying of thirst,' she finished plaintively.

'That, at least, is easily remedied. I asked Kyria Diakou

to leave a bottle of champagne on ice. I'll go down and pour us a glass each.'

He hesitated, studying her. Something in her core awoke at the look in his eyes. Awoke and began to thaw rapidly, leaving her body humming with need.

'You really do look stunning in that dress,' he said. 'Every man on that yacht was staring at you. No doubt wishing he was the one marrying you.'

'Thank you.'

Her heart stuttered at the deep note in his voice, but she kept smiling, holding herself still with an effort.

'Now that we're home, though,' she added, realising with a start how soon she had come to think of Villa Rosa as 'home', 'I'd better slip into something cooler.'

This was not merely her excuse for having run upstairs on arriving. The wedding dress was fitted, and sat snugly about her breasts and hips—too tight for these long, Calistan summer evenings.

'I came up here to change and then got sidetracked.'

'Of course. Excuse me.'

He turned as though to leave her alone to change, but some devil made her call him back.

'Actually, I… I could do with a hand,' she burst out, and felt a rush of heat to her cheeks as he glanced back at her, dark brows raised. 'There's a tricky zip…'

Half of her expected him to see the bait and walk away. They had both signed that no-sex contract, after all. But that didn't mean she wasn't interested in him physically. Much to her hot-cheeked embarrassment…

Only he didn't say no.

'In that case, you'd better allow me.'

He walked towards her as she stood frozen in place and turned her gently to face the full-length mirror. His hands were warm on her shoulders. Staring into the mirror, she tried but couldn't read the expression in his eyes, shielded by long thick lashes.

'Ah, I see there's a hook…'

She held her breath as his fingers moved over her back, gently unfastening the top of her dress.

'And there's the "tricky zip"…'

As the zip was released, the dress sagged in a rustle of white silk, and she grabbed at the bodice to keep it in place, her heart thumping. Her mouth was dry—and not simply through the thirst she'd claimed.

Their eyes met in the mirror.

'Sabrina…' he whispered.

Electricity leapt between them like wildfire, just as it had done when he'd kissed her after the wedding ceremony. She heard the fierce intake of his breath as his hands moved to the thin spaghetti straps of her dress, slipping them off her shoulders, his fingers caressing her delicately. She turned, gazing up into his lean, dark face, her whole body aching. Her palms were damp, her breathing ragged.

What were they doing?

There was silence between them as their gazes locked.

Heat rushed to her core and she could have moaned out loud. Her whole body was tingling with excitement as she waited for his kiss.

But Rafael surprised her by releasing her and stepping back carefully. 'Maybe that champagne would be a good idea.'

'Um…okay, yeah.' Embarrassed, she swallowed hard, fighting for self-control against an inner tide of longing, all her nerves prickling and vibrant. 'You go. I'll be down in a minute,' she added, and even managed a fleeting smile. 'Thanks for your help with the dress.'

To her relief he didn't comment, but merely gave a nod and left the room. Hearing him go downstairs, Sabrina kicked the bedroom door shut, stepped out of the sensuous pool of silk and tulle, and sank onto the bed in bra and panties, shaking with reaction. Blood was rushing in her veins, its turbulent beat almost deafening.

What was wrong with her?

Enticing an experienced playboy like Rafael to get so close was asking for the kind of trouble she was ill-equipped to handle. She had slept with him once, yes. But she was still little more than an innocent when it came to sex. All she knew was that her breasts felt heavy and full, and heat was throbbing between her legs as she imagined him removing the wedding dress fully and lying down with her on this bed, like any other couple on their wedding day...

Her wide-eyed gaze met her own flushed reflection in the mirror, then dropped to his unexpected wedding gift— the crystal dolphin. Its blue-white glassy body leapt perpetually, like her heart, taking joy in this tiny Greek island.

He might have spotted the dolphin on a market stall in passing, but there had been nothing random about his choice. It was a gift that spoke to her deeply—not merely a reminder of her childhood here on Calista, but of what they had been to each other back then.

She could still taste the magic of their time together on this bee-rich island, with its cliffs swathed in rosemary, sage and purple-coloured thyme, where they had once lain on rocks together to watch dolphins at play in the glittering aquamarine waters. Simpler times...when their friendship had meant everything to each other.

Had those days gone for ever, or was it possible to get them back?

CHAPTER SEVEN

RAFAEL STRETCHED AND rolled over in the morning light, nude in the tangled sheets, covering his eyes with his forearm.

He was a married man. His new bride had eaten her dinner last night in a meek silence, eyes downcast, before retiring to bed without him.

He could have gone after her. Instead, he had kept to the contract and sat on the veranda long into the early hours, drinking whisky and staring out at the violet mass of the Aegean, breathing in the hot, dusty night air of Calista, his birthplace and spiritual home. Because he had known he dared not touch her. The risk to his sanity would be too great.

A tiny sound had him scrambling up in bed, abruptly aware that he was not alone in the bedroom.

Sabrina was slumped in an easy chair near his bed, wearing a short, flimsy nightdress that left little to the imagination, bare legs curled beneath her, eyes closed. Her blonde head was resting on her shoulder while her chest rose and fell gently under a delicate white lace and satin bodice.

Baffled, he threw back the covers, and she stirred, opening her eyes to peer sleepily across at him. Then he saw her blue gaze widen and her body stiffen as she realised he was naked.

'Good morning,' he said with heavy irony, making a swift grab for his shorts. 'Forgive the floor show. But what the hell are you doing in my bedroom?'

Red-cheeked, Sabrina stumbled to her feet and fled back to her own room without a word.

'Sabrina?' he called after her, but she didn't come back.

Astonished, Rafael stood beside the bed for a moment, racking his brains for a reason why she should have chosen to sleep on a chair in his room on their wedding night. Then he shrugged it away. No doubt once she'd woken up fully she would feel able to tell him.

Since he was unlikely to get back to sleep, he showered briskly to shake off his hangover before selecting an outfit to wear. But when he went to knock at Sabrina's door later he found her suite empty.

Downstairs, Kyria Diakou appeared on the veranda with a shy smile and a tray of fresh fruit and yoghurt. 'Breakfast, sir?'

'Only coffee today, thank you.' Wincing, he drew on reflective sunglasses against the morning glare. 'Have you seen my wife?'

'Why, yes, sir.' His housekeeper put down the tray and pointed to the pool below. 'Kyria Romano said she wished to swim before breakfast.'

Glancing that way with feigned nonchalance, he saw a sleek blonde head bobbing in the water. Sabrina was swimming lengths of the pool in a breaststroke, her rhythm swift but steady, the slender line of her body graceful as ever.

The housekeeper excused herself, saying she was going to fetch fresh coffee for him.

Rafael got up and sauntered down the steps to the pool. There was a towel over one of the loungers, and a pot of coffee with a solitary cup set on a low table.

Walking to the poolside, he waited for Sabrina to return

to that end. She was doing a front crawl now, low in the water, her movements more aggressive than before, though the splash was minimal and her technique super-efficient. Even through the distorting ripple of water he could see the lush swell of her breasts captured in a white bikini top, and was glad of his sunglasses masking his stare.

Reaching the wall of the pool, Sabrina stopped dead, gasping as she stared up at him, blue eyes wide with surprise. Blonde tendrils of hair stuck to her forehead and cheeks and she had no make-up on, her face beautifully natural.

'Oh!'

'Hello, again.'

His gaze dipped to the deep shadow between her breasts in the clinging white bikini and his arousal grew, suddenly urgent and uncomfortable.

Acting purely on instinct, he smiled as her gaze tangled with his. 'The pool looks refreshing in this heat. I'll join you, if I may.'

Before she could protest, he stripped off his white T-shirt, discarding it on the nearest lounger. Without a word, she swam slowly backwards, watching with an almost shocked expression as he drew off loose-fitting trousers to reveal a pair of black swimming trunks underneath.

Rafael dived in past her, cutting through the cool water for several meters before surfacing almost at the other end of the infinity pool. Shaking back his wet hair, he swam towards her, his arousal undiminished. In fact, the glimpse he'd enjoyed of her bare legs and midriff under the water had inflamed his desire.

'I'm sorry about earlier,' she volunteered. 'I... I heard you having a nightmare just before dawn, so I woke you and stayed with you a while.' She trod water, breathing fast, her eyes locked on his face. 'I only meant to sit there a few minutes. I must have dropped off to sleep.'

'A nightmare?' He frowned, made uncomfortable by the thought. 'I don't remember you waking me up. Did I speak to you?'

'Not really… You went straight back to sleep.'

There were dark shadows under her eyes; he studied them, frowning. 'I'm sorry if I disturbed you.'

'No, it's fine,' she said quickly. 'I was awake anyway… reading a book.' She licked her lips. 'I couldn't sleep. Too much champagne yesterday.'

Years ago, he had once shared a hotel room with a colleague on a team-building exercise. He'd told him the next day that he'd shouted out during his sleep. It had thrown him off balance, being made aware that he suffered bad dreams, and he wondered what embarrassing words he might have uttered while unconscious.

'Did I make a noise? Say something?'

When Sabrina hesitated, he moved closer. He couldn't help himself. It was as though an invisible cord was tugging them together.

'Tell me what I said.'

He could smell her light perfume even in the water. Her sleek hair hung wet about her face, and her delicate eyelashes were beaded with tiny jewels of water that shone and sparkled in the sunlight. Erotic fantasies chased through his mind even while he struggled to keep his thoughts out of his face.

No, not fantasies.

Memories of their night together in Paris…

He had known in advance that she would be at the charity ball. He'd considered backing out of the event at first, but his curiosity, once piqued, had got the better of him.

That first glance of her in Paris had shocked him to the

core. He'd seen photographs, of course. Even a few short videos. Sabrina Templeton had been everywhere on social media that year, as one of the youngest winners ever of a prestigious award for women in business. Yet he'd somehow convinced himself that how Sabrina looked on screen was not how she looked in real life. That the photographs and videos must have been touched up.

Because the Sabrina he'd known as a kid had been a completely different girl. Blonde hair, yes. But the flawless skin, the perfect make-up, the elegance and poise... All those belonged to a stranger.

Having worked through his disbelief at her appearance, Rafael had set out to get close to her. He'd never intended to seduce her—only to see how much of the old Sabrina was left under the expensive packaging.

But the bittersweet nostalgia of dancing and drinking champagne with the girl he'd known when they were both barefoot urchins in the dusty backstreets of Calista had drugged his senses, and before the night was out he'd suggested a nightcap at her nearby hotel.

It was the first time they'd been alone for years. The first time as adults. When he'd kissed her, unable to resist, her response had electrified him. Sabrina had been so eager, so willing, her passion naked and spontaneous, and he had allowed himself to be swept away...

Waking in her bed the next morning, he'd experienced an emotion he had only felt once before—the day Andrew Templeton had come to collect her from the orphanage.

Fear.

As a boy, he had not known that emotion for what it was. But that morning in Paris, seeing Sabrina's head on the pillow next to him, Rafael had recognised the stomach-churning emotion and recoiled from it. He had felt much the same terror when trying to protect his mother from his father—and failing abysmally.

Fear had gripped him as he'd stared at Sabrina's sleeping face. The fear of loss and inadequacy for the second time in his life.

Silently, he'd pulled on his clothes and left her lying there, still blissfully asleep, unaware of the turmoil in his heart.

Sabrina had called him later, shy and confused, asking where he'd gone and why he'd left without a word. Caught off guard, Rafael had said a few things he hadn't meant, and had known from the silence on the other end of the phone line that he'd hurt her deeply.

Better that, though, than have to live with his failure again. Because he wasn't perfect. One day he would disappoint her, or not be there for her when she needed him. One day he would fail her as he had failed his mother. And that awareness of his own inadequacy was too much to bear.

After Paris, he had vowed never to see Sabrina again. But then he'd managed to acquire the orphanage on Calista. And, hunting through its records one day, looking for details on another friend who'd been adopted and whom he'd wished to trace, he had stumbled across a dusty old folder of documents relating to Sabrina's arrival at the orphanage and her later adoption—records which had never been computerised, perhaps deliberately.

At first he had not understood what he was looking at, it had seemed so fantastical. Then, slowly, the truth had dawned on him.

Fury and disbelief pouring through him like acid, he had paced the deserted orphanage, cursing and smashing his fist repeatedly into the walls. But the person he had really wanted to hurt—the villain of the piece—had not only been thousands of miles away in London, but was Sabrina's father. And in hurting Templeton, exposing his behaviour to the world, he would be hurting Sabrina too.

She had still not answered his question, her wide gaze searching his face.

'Well? What was I shouting?'

He reached out and stroked an errant strand of wet hair from her cheek behind her ear. His heart was thumping and he could not seem to take his eyes off her.

'Come on… You used to tell me your dreams back in the orphanage and I would try to interpret them. Do you remember?'

'I remember,' she whispered.

'You always trusted me then.'

'Yes…'

The dazzle of sunlight on the water reflected off her throat and face, as if her skin was rippling with light. He recalled her broken face, the scar tissue she'd tried so hard to hide as a child, and could almost see it again as the sun bounced off the water droplets running down her cheek.

'So tell me what I was shouting in this nightmare. Maybe I can work out what it means.'

'I… I don't remember,' Sabrina muttered.

But he dismissed that. Especially when she lowered her gaze, ostensibly simply not meeting his eyes, but in truth studying his semi-naked body.

He was gradually learning to recognise that new, hungry look in her face. He felt it too, that hunger and yearning to be closer to her, to join with her as one miraculous whole, as they had done once before. But he knew how dangerous that would be. And he wasn't quite crazy enough to go there. Not after last time.

His heart accelerated like soft, distant thunder. 'You don't remember?' he demanded. 'Somehow I don't believe you.'

His gaze focused on the quick, nervous lick of her lips,

then dipped to the rise and fall of her chest. He knew her too well not to read the signs. She was trying to conceal something from him. But what?

His eyes narrowed on her face. 'What's the matter, Sabrina?' A thought struck him. 'Did I call out your name? Is that it?'

'What? No!'

Sabrina trod water, frantically trying to steer clear of the dangerous temptation of his body, hard and achingly muscular, muscles bulging in his chest and his flat abdomen visible through the water...

Yet still she kept drifting closer and closer, constantly having to back-pedal with her feet and legs, thrusting cooler currents of water between their two bodies, both of them so scantily clothed they might as well have been naked.

If only she had packed a one-piece swimsuit for this trip. But no, she'd chosen to pack this skimpy white and gold bikini, with its deep-plunge cleavage and tiny string briefs, thinking she would probably never wear it. And now his gaze kept straying unashamedly to her breasts, bobbing on top of the water in an embarrassing way.

Flustered, she sucked in a shaky breath, meaning to explain that she hadn't been able to interpret his incoherent dream shouts, and then he surprised her by moving closer. Startled, she stared up at him, deeply aware of his proximity, heat burning along all the pathways in her body until her skin was alight with it.

Idly, his fingers brushed her cheek again, then stroked down her throat towards the deep V of her cleavage, those dark, intelligent eyes watching for a response.

She began to say something, but the sunlight dazzled her. That and his broad shoulders, and the naked chest mere inches away, gleaming with water...

Desire burned through her in a hot flush and her eyes narrowed on his strong, muscular body. Her hands curled into fists as she battled the need to touch him in return. The world spun, frustration was molten inside her, and she gasped, abruptly light-headed, flailing her hands in the water as her head sank and water lapped at her lips.

'Sabrina…? What the hell?'

His face, dark and sombre, loomed over her, then his arms clamped about her frame and a few seconds later Rafael had lifted her bodily out of the water.

Dripping and helpless, she clung to his wet body, her hands slipping on his strong shoulders, feeling the muscles bulge and contract under her fingers.

He waded through shallow water to set her down on the pool steps, still waist-deep in water. 'What happened? Are you okay?'

'Sorry,' she whispered weakly. 'I… I got dizzy.'

'That's what comes of skipping breakfast before exercising,' Rafael chided her. He stepped back in the water, examining her with searching eyes. 'Or was it the heat? You never used to mind it. But I suppose you've been living in England a long time now.' He smiled, showing white teeth. 'Grown soft.'

She muttered something unflattering under her breath, and his smile broadened.

'I see you're feeling better,' he drawled.

It hadn't been the heat, of course, or her lack of breakfast. It had been her hyper-awareness of his body that had precipitated that sudden bout of weakness.

And he was even closer now.

All she could focus on was the sculpted perfection of his chest and the washboard abs that spoke of long hours in the gym. Her attention zigzagged wildly between the velvety darkness of his gaze and the muscular expanse of his biceps and pectorals, all manner of wickedly delicious thoughts wrecking her peace of mind.

Her self-control was beginning to shear away, leaving her defenceless.

'Hey, are you okay? You look flushed.'

Rafael lifted a hand to her cheek, and his touch inflamed her.

She had gone into this marriage with her eyes wide open, aware of how badly he could hurt her, and determined not to make a fool of herself again. But she couldn't keep fighting this attraction between them. It was tearing her apart, pretending not to want him...

Growling like an animal, she abandoned control and leant forward, setting her mouth hungrily against his with an impact that rocked them both.

As he staggered and shifted, steadying himself in the water, her arms rose to encircle his strong neck, her fingers running through sleek dark hair, grasping the back of his head.

'Rafael...' she moaned against his mouth, all pretence swept away by the hot, turbulent waves of desire washing through her. 'Yes!' she gasped, not answering his question so much as urging him on. 'Yes!'

It might be crazy, and it was definitely not in their contract. But nobody would ever know her like he did, she thought feverishly, and the only thing that could make their oneness more absolute was for them to bring each other to completion.

His tongue thrust between her lips and she sucked on it fiercely. Rafael groaned and thrust deeper, plundering her mouth. His strong hands lifted her from the pool steps and rooted her body against him, so she was straddling his hips. Leaning back, she rubbed herself suggestively against his arousal and felt him stiffen further, his clinging swim-trunks doing little to disguise his excitement.

Their kiss deepened. He cupped her breast, his hand warm and possessive, then pulled down the wet fabric to expose bare flesh. One thumb strummed across her nipple, bringing it instantly erect. Her heartbeat accelerated as their damp, half-naked bodies whirled and strained together in the sunlit water.

'*Thee mou*, woman,' he muttered, turning his head to kiss an explosive path down her neck.

His words were incoherent, hard to make out.

'You're simply gorgeous, stunning… You have the face of a goddess.'

CHAPTER EIGHT

SABRINA FROZE BENEATH HIM. The soft, panting goddess of Greek myth was abruptly an icy-eyed viper, hissing defiance as she planted both hands on his chest and heaved him free of her body.

'Get off me,' she spat.

Rafael staggered, caught off-guard, splashing backwards into deeper water. He stared up at her in confusion as she left the pool.

'What the hell was that for?' He launched himself upright again, his adrenalin levels spiking at this unexpected attack. 'What's the matter? Did I hurt you?'

But she'd already grabbed her towel and was charging up the steps to the villa as though the devil were at her heels, not looking back.

'Sabrina, come back!'

Dripping wet, he was halfway up the steps in pursuit when he caught sight of Kyria Diakou, standing shocked on the veranda, staring down at him, a tray in her hands.

Embarrassed, his heart thumping, Rafael slicked back his wet hair and slowly retraced his steps to the poolside.

An edge of defiance laced his hot thoughts. He'd broken the no-touching terms of their contract. But he clearly recalled *her* fingers wrapped in his hair, both *her* hands tugging him close, the provocative thrust of *her* tongue against his, and the hoarse 'Yes!' she'd uttered. Not once but *twice*.

With a sharp intake of breath he dived back into the refreshing depths of the pool, letting the water cool his ardour.

What had he done wrong? One minute she'd been urging him on, the next she'd shoved him aside. But perhaps he should give her some space to calm down before asking for an explanation. He didn't want to risk a full-blown row.

After a quick swim, he towelled off, got dressed again, and ate a light breakfast before heading upstairs to his wife's suite.

'Sabrina?' He knocked at her door. 'May I come in?'

Receiving no answer, he tried the handle and went in to find the lounge and bedroom empty. He checked the en-suite bathroom too, but she wasn't there.

Downstairs, he found Kyria Diakou dusting a large Grecian statue in the entrance hall. She looked flustered when he asked if she had seen Sabrina.

'Your wife has gone out, sir,' she told him in a faltering voice. 'Kyria Romano asked Nikos to drive her into town half an hour ago. A shopping trip, she said. I assumed you knew...'

It took all his willpower to nod with feigned calm, even muster a smile for her. 'Of course. I remember now.' He paused, made his tone casual. 'I'll join her in town.' Unhooking a baseball cap from the rack near the door, he settled it low over his forehead against the sun's glare. 'Thank you, Thea.'

Rafael always had a sports car brought to Villa Rosa for his visits. The blood-red Ferrari roared around the sharp bends of the coastal road and along the dusty straights, growling in the low gears as he slowed reluctantly for quiet villages, their windows shuttered against the heat of the day.

She could have caught a ferry by now. Gone back to the Greek mainland.

Unconsciously, he tightened his hands on the wheel and kicked his foot down on the accelerator. The Ferrari leaped forward with its characteristic throaty roar, spitting out a cloud of dust and grit behind him, visible in the rear-view mirror.

He'd gone too far in the pool—he acknowledged that. But Sabrina had initiated it…practically throwing herself at him.

A burning sense of injustice gripped him and his body tensed. He narrowed his eyes on the road ahead. He needed to master his desire for her. Yet every time he made an attempt, things slipped further out of his control.

He hadn't felt like this in years. Not since when, as a young boy, having finally broken out of the tiny space his father had imprisoned him in, he had cradled his dead mother's head in his lap, filled with self-loathing because he'd been too late to save her.

His therapist had taught him how to avoid triggering that memory 'wound', and what signs of trauma response to look for in himself. The nightmares he couldn't remember—like the one that had apparently woken Sabrina in the night—was one of those signs. And his permanently raised heart rate was another…his inability to calm down.

The rejection in Sabrina's eyes today had come dangerously close to reawakening the broken boy inside him—the one he'd lulled to sleep through therapy. And he still had no idea what he'd done to upset her.

But he was determined to find out.

The Ferrari growled as he was forced to slow down once again. The busy port was packed with tourist traffic as the incoming ferry discharged a long line of vehicles from its car deck. Rafael slotted the car neatly into the first parking space he found, then set off at a run for the terminal building, ignoring the stares of passers-by.

After grabbing Rafael in the pool and kissing him breathless, Sabrina had dashed back to her room, furious and shaking. She had dragged on a dress and begun angrily flinging clothes into her suitcase. She'd taken one look at him in that skimpy black swimwear and good old-fashioned lust had fogged up her brain until…

'You have the face of a goddess.'

Was that all he would ever see when he looked at her? The perfect mask her wealthy father had paid for so she could forget the horrors of her past? Would no longer have to face its legacy in the mirror every day?

How *dared* he, damn him?

The terrible scars she'd borne as a girl were long gone. Andrew Templeton's money had paid for the best plastic surgeons in the world.

'We'll fix you,' he'd assured her on the flight to England, flicking her scarred cheek. 'My ugly duckling will soon be a swan.'

Sure enough, within a year of arriving in England the face in the mirror had changed. She had become perfect and symmetrical. Everything smoothed out and tightened, every scar lifted, every blemish removed. Only her eyes had remained the same. Troubled and blue.

She still struggled to recognise the woman in the mirror at times. The one without the facial scars she'd lived with for so long as a child.

But her father had been delighted with the result.

'Every man on this planet is going to want you,' he'd said with satisfaction, walking around her, studying her from every angle. 'That's a weapon we can use. Once you're done with your education you can take some companies for a spin…try out that devastating smile in the boardroom.' He'd winked. 'Told you I'd fix you, didn't I? You're perfect now.'

And now, whenever she failed to achieve her goals, her father would express his disappointment, urging her to live up to her expensive face.

Andrew Templeton's love had always been conditional on her being 'perfect' inside and out. She had accepted that stark truth early on, fearful of losing her adoptive father as well as her birth mother by not living up to the potential he had seen in her at the orphanage.

Now she knew he had lied to her—been her true father all along. He had not picked her out of the crowd. She had been collected like a mislaid parcel from Left Luggage.

And now her husband had indicated that he too saw her in the same terms.

The face of a goddess, indeed!

Her face had been designed by her father and superimposed over the 'old' Sabrina—the one Rafael had never looked at twice in the orphanage, except as a friend.

Eventually common sense had reasserted itself, and Sabrina had stopped packing, sinking down on the bed instead. Rafael could theoretically sue her for breach of contract if she left now, and a court case would risk bringing their arrangement—and possibly her own personal history—into the public domain. She cringed at the thought.

But she had been determined to get out of the villa at least.

That shameless kiss in the pool…

After demanding a no-sex marriage, she had thrown herself at him without a shred of dignity. Talk about embarrassment!

Groaning, she had grabbed her handbag and run downstairs to find Nikos in the hallway, settling a wide-brimmed hat on his head as he headed outside with a gardening trug on his arm.

'Oh!' she'd said, smiling brightly. 'I don't suppose you're free to run me into town?' Nikos had looked surprised, and she'd added hurriedly, 'My husband says he won't be free to take me out for several hours, and I'd like to do some shopping this morning—before it gets too hot.'

To her relief, Nikos had agreed to drive her to the port, accepting without question her guilty lie that Rafael would be joining her later, so he need not wait for her. He had seemed uncertain about leaving her alone without any security, but she had laughed, insisting she was perfectly safe here in her birthplace.

Now she was alone, she headed for a harbourside café with tables set outside in the shade, ordered a cooling drink and turned on her phone.

The chime of messages arriving seemed never-ending. Since news of their wedding had broken her phone had received dozens of calls and messages from friends, colleagues and associates.

But the bulk were from her father.

Rage churned inside her as she read his arrogant, abusive messages. This man, who had lied and manipulated her for years, thought he could snap his fingers and she would come to heel. Tempting though it was to continue ignoring him, Sabrina knew it would be wiser to respond and play for time. But she mustn't allow herself to be drawn into confronting him about her past. Not yet...not while she still felt so fragile.

Taking a deep breath, she called him back.

Andrew Templeton answered after only two rings. 'Sabrina, thank God. I was hoping you'd call again. Are you all right?' Without waiting for an answer, he demanded, 'Is it true? Have you really lost your mind and married that low-life playboy Romano?'

She closed her eyes, battling to stay calm. If she flipped, this call would end in disaster and her father would not rest until he had found her. And right now she needed to sort this mess out for herself—not fall back on 'Daddy's' help.

'It was the only way to save the orphanage,' she said.

'Nonsense. We could have found some other leverage… These people always have a price.'

'I know,' she ground out, struggling against bitterness. 'And Rafael's price was me. But only for a year. Then we can go our separate ways. We've signed a contract.'

Her father was silent for a moment, then he said heavily, 'Very well. Give me your location. I'll send someone to bring you back home. We can get the lawyers involved and sort all this out once you're safely back on English soil.'

'I'm a big girl, Dad. I don't need to be rescued. Not this time.'

In her mind's eye she saw again Andrew Templeton's smiling face as he led her out of the orphanage, promising she would never be alone again. Naively, she had thought him the best man in the world.

'I didn't ring you for help or advice,' she added, almost choking.

It was harder than she'd expected not to admit what she knew and demand an explanation for his horrific behaviour. But her self-control was in tatters as it was. If she started down that particular path she would probably explode.

'I rang because I… I didn't want you to worry.'

'Without any friends or family present—only the paparazzi—you marry a man with Romano's criminal background…a man who treated you abominably in Paris…and you say I mustn't worry?' His voice was shaking. 'Sabrina, tell me where you are. Are you really in the Caribbean, or was that just a ruse to throw me off the scent? Because I swear, I'll soon find you.'

'Can't you just give me some space?' she pleaded.

He ignored her. 'I need to speak to you in person, and without Romano in the room. Is that clear? If you won't fly home, I'll come to you.'

'No, Dad, you mustn't try to find me,' she told him more firmly, determined not to cave to his demands. 'You need to let this go. I'll speak to you again after the honeymoon. Okay?'

Ending the call on his noisy protests, Sabrina closed her eyes, trying to calm her frazzled nerves. Slowly, she finished her drink, and then walked along the sunlit harbourside to watch the ferry reversing into its berth, lost in her own scattered thoughts and fears.

When a shout rang out along the harbour she turned at her name and found herself face to face with Rafael, her father's scathing disapproval still echoing in her ears.

'Hello, Sabrina. Going somewhere?' her husband asked tightly, jerking his head towards the ferry.

Sabrina dug her fingernails into her palms, her cheeks flaring with heat. 'It's true, I did consider catching a ferry and disappearing,' she admitted. 'But I've never given up on a business deal in my life and I won't start now.'

'So why run out on me?' he growled.

'Because you hurt my feelings and—'

'Hurt your feelings?' he repeated, incredulous. 'How?'

'Will you let me finish? If you don't, I'm catching the next ferry out of here.' She thrust her chin in the air at his frustrated look. 'I've just been speaking to my father. I can do without another lecture from an overbearing male who thinks he owns me, thank you very much.'

He sank his hands in his trouser pockets and glared at her

from under long dark lashes. She thought at first he would refuse. But then his lips thinned.

'Very well.' His brows lifted when she still hesitated. 'Go on. Tell me about your...*feelings*, then.'

Seconds later he was following her along the quayside as she spun on her heel and marched away, too angry even to speak to him.

'*Thee mou*, would you stop a minute?' When she turned, her eyes spitting fury, he said with a sigh, 'All right. That was a patronising thing to say. I apologise.'

Sabrina was surprised, even shocked by this unexpected admission. But she still said nothing, folding her arms defensively.

'Maybe you don't see our marriage as anything but a sham,' Rafael continued, a muscle jerking in his jaw, 'but I know you haven't forgotten our past. We were good friends once, and that's not a bad foundation for a marriage. Even a one-year arrangement like ours.'

His dark gaze grew velvety dark, hypnotising her again.

'Look, I don't want to start playing the blame game here, but in the pool, you kissed *me*—not the other way around. You *wanted* me. I felt it. Then you pushed me away like I'd tried to assault you.'

His last words crackled on the air, like static in her soul.

'Care to explain?' he asked.

Their eyes clashed as guilt and confusion warred inside her. He wasn't wrong. She *had* been to blame for what had happened earlier. Yet how to explain without baring her soul and risking the kind of rejection that would probably finish her?

There were people all around them on the busy quayside, glancing curiously their way. Alone, she might not have attracted much attention. But the two of them together—Sabrina and Rafael Romano, newlyweds—would make quite a photographic coup. And then her father would know for sure where they were honeymooning...

'Let's walk, shall we?' she suggested.

He said nothing, but followed as she stalked away, head high. They crossed the road between slow-moving cars, soon heading deep into the honeycomb of narrow streets and alleyways beyond the tourist traps. The whitewashed walls of traditional Calistan homes rose on either side of the narrow lanes, their windows shuttered against the heat of the day, flat roofs bathed in sunlight and draped with washing.

He must have brought his mobile with him, because she heard it ring. He drew it out of his pocket, hesitating before glancing at her.

'Go ahead,' she said lightly, continuing to walk. 'You might as well take advantage of having a signal here.'

Rafael stopped to answer the call, catching up with her a few minutes later, an energetic look in his face. 'Looks like that big deal I've been hoping for may be going ahead. Still early days, but the mood music has definitely changed. Thanks to you,' he added softly, 'it seems I'm no longer such a bitter pill for their conservative stakeholders to swallow.'

'I'm glad to hear it.'

He studied her face, then dropped the subject. They walked on together through the quiet maze of streets.

'So, are you ready to talk yet?' He sounded brusque, almost impatient.

'Please...this is difficult for me.' Sabrina wrapped her arms about herself like a nervous teenager. 'It's true, I did kiss you first in the pool,' she admitted in a whisper. 'But that wasn't why I ran.' She fixed her gaze on the dusty stones at their feet. 'It's just...when we were kids, you didn't care about any of that.'

'Any of what?' He sounded baffled.

'My looks.'

He was silent for a moment. 'You're talking about your scars?' he said slowly. 'You think I'm only attracted to you because you've had plastic surgery?'

Tongue-tied, she made a rough noise of assent, gripping her sides tightly. Tears squeezed out from under her lids and she looked away through blurred vision, hating her own weakness.

'*Thee mou*, Sabbie… Are you serious?' He came to a halt, and she stopped too. 'You mean it, don't you?'

'You never kissed me when we were younger.'

'Yes, because we were *kids*,' he exploded, and then reined himself in, seeing her flinch. 'My lovely idiot… I am absolutely *not* attracted to you because you've had your face fixed. This thing between us is about chemistry, not beauty. Got it?'

'But you said…' she gulped '… I had *the face of a goddess*.'

'And so you do. But that's not why I find you attractive. I've dated one or two of the world's most beautiful women, remember? They had nothing on you for sheer sex appeal—trust me.'

Heartened by this flattery, she peeped up at him through wet lashes. 'Only one or two?'

'Claws in, pussycat,' he drawled.

Their eyes met and everything inside her was drawn inexorably towards him, as though he'd bound a cord about her heart and was tugging on it. She drew a long breath and felt the tension begin to drain from her body. It was difficult to ignore their long bond of friendship, and just now, when she was feeling particularly lost and lonely over her father's betrayal, perhaps it would be stupid to try.

'Very well,' she agreed reluctantly, reaching for a tissue

from her bag and drying her eyes. 'Maybe I overreacted. My head's just so messed up at the moment. My father—'

'He really did a number on you, didn't he?' he said huskily.

'You don't understand. I always thought he'd arranged for plastic surgery to help me fit in better at that posh school… But he did it because he couldn't b-bear looking at my scars.'

'Sabrina, no.'

'It's true!' she burst out. 'Andrew Templeton hates any kind of imperfection. The first time he saw me, when he turned up at the orphanage, he shuddered. He actually *shuddered*.'

She felt again the searing humiliation of that moment, made a thousand times worse now, because she knew that he'd come to meet his own daughter for the first time that day.

'What a piece of work,' Rafael muttered.

'He's never let me forget it either. Whenever I make a mistake, he somehow always finds a way to reference the surgery…as though to remind me how imperfect I am under—' She choked. 'Under the mask.'

Rafael made a rough noise, trying to take her in his arms for a hug, but she stepped back, shaking her head. The last thing she wanted was to complicate matters by letting him get close again.

'No, I'm fine…' She dried her cheeks. 'I need to deal with this in my own way. Now, I'll come back to the villa with you. But—'

'I know,' he interrupted. 'No more touching.'

'Exactly.'

And no more swimming together either, she thought grimly, recalling the temptation of his bronzed semi-naked body gleaming with water.

'Better avoid kissing me, then,' he tossed back, as though reading her mind, 'if you want me to keep my hands off you. Especially when we're both wearing next to nothing.'

'No problem.'

She had spoken lightly, flippantly, but her heart was already racing again as they walked back to the car.

The real question was, could *she* keep her hands off *him*?

On the drive back to Villa Rosa, along the winding, dusty roads as familiar to him as the landscape of his mind, Rafael found it hard to concentrate on the road ahead, constantly glancing at his wife and wishing he could read her thoughts.

Her face was averted, as if she was studying the dramatic scenery of Calista, its distant, hazy hills punctuated by stately spikes of cypress thrusting dark into an azure sky.

'Did you ring your father while you were in town?' he asked.

'Yes.' She bit her lip deeply. 'I wanted to confront him. But in the end I didn't even bring it up. I couldn't trust myself not to scream at him.'

'Do you hate him now you know the truth?'

'Yes!' she said with venom, and then groaned. 'No, how can I? He's my father. But...' Her voice tailed off.

He nodded. 'It's complicated.'

She turned towards him. 'It must have been complicated for you too, though,' she said.

His hands tightened on the steering wheel, his nerves prickling as he guessed what was coming next.

'I mean, your dad... The things he did to you, and then...' She left the rest unspoken.

'Murdering my mother?' He made an effort to slow his breathing and turn his thoughts away from that flashback in his head. His mother's body, his wailing childish grief, and his hatred for the man who had done it. '"Complicated" doesn't cover it.'

'I'm sorry.'

'No need to be.' He shrugged, trying to stay casual. 'It was before you came to the orphanage.'

'True.' She was watching him curiously. 'But you never really told me what happened.'

'Would you have done, in my position?' His hands clenched even harder on the wheel, and he set his jaw as he slowed to round the next bend. 'I wanted to forget. To put it behind me.'

'I remember the boys calling you names…but I never understood why.'

'Because they were cruel. That's all you need to know. There's no point discussing ancient history.'

To his amazement, there were tears in his eyes.

Angrily, he blinked them away. 'It hardly matters now, does it?'

'I think it still matters to you.' She touched his arm. 'Though you're right—it shouldn't do. Whatever those boys thought, you've proved yourself a thousand times over since then.'

Rafael struggled to maintain focus on his driving. The villa was within sight now, its white domed roof bathed in sunlight. His refuge from the outside world. And he had never needed it more.

'Not everyone would agree with that appraisal,' he growled.

'What do you mean?'

But he only shook his head. 'Forget it.'

'Rafael—'

'I've had a few unpleasant comments, that's all. Sideways looks in the boardroom.'

'About what?'

He bared his teeth. 'My background.'

Her eyes widened. 'Don't tell me people have judged you for being an orphan, for God's sake? For coming from an underprivileged family?' There was outrage in her voice now. 'That's appalling.'

He shrugged, not wanting to make a big thing of it. 'I don't think it's held me back. I lack a few advantages, that's all. No blue blood or old school tie network.' He frowned. 'There were a few difficult moments early on in my career. I soon learnt not to advertise my personal history—let's put it like that.'

'I see...' Sabrina was silent for a moment as they approached the high gates to the villa complex. 'I hope my father doesn't take advantage of that to make your life difficult.'

'If he does, that will be my concern, not yours.'

Rafael raised a hand to the guard in the turreted gatehouse, who nodded in recognition and opened the electric gates for him to drive through.

'I'm your wife. That makes it my concern too.' Sabrina hesitated. 'And I never said a proper thank-you.'

'Thank you?' He glanced at her, puzzled. 'What for?'

Already Kyria Diakou was at the door, waiting for them, her face wreathed in smiles. No doubt she and Nikos had been unsettled by Sabrina's trip to the port alone. The older couple had not said anything, but he had not missed the unusual warmth they had shown Sabrina, and guessed they approved of his marriage and were keen for it to work.

'For telling me about my father,' Sabrina said now. 'I still feel stupid for not having realised on my own that Andrew Templeton was my biological parent. I mean, the physical resemblance between us is obvious now. Bone structure, colouring... I just didn't see it.' She shook her head. 'I'm such an idiot.'

'Don't say that.' He had spoken harshly, and she glanced at him, surprised. 'You're not to blame. Nobody could have guessed such a thing. You're the victim here.'

'Absolutely. Though I expect my father will find a way to frame it so I'm the one to blame.' She gathered her things as he parked the car. 'We're both victims of our fathers, aren't we?'

He turned off the engine and sat unmoving. 'I'd never thought of it like that before,' he said grudgingly. 'But I suppose we are, yes.'

'Then let's agree never to be victims again,' Sabrina suggested softly. 'How's that?'

He met her eyes and saw the vulnerability there. He wished that he could make her smile again. Really smile, the way she had done when they were kids, with all her face, as if a beam of light was shining out of her soul. Somehow, Templeton had extinguished that light when he'd taken her away from Calista.

'It's a deal,' he agreed.

CHAPTER NINE

THEY ATE THAT night in near silence, neither particularly hungry, both picking at the excellent dinner served to them by Kyria Diakou. Afterwards, once the housekeeper had cleared the table and retreated, they lingered over coffee and liqueurs while the sun set over the dusky Aegean and night fell softly across Calista.

'We could take a walk in the gardens,' he suggested at last, 'if you need to stretch your legs. I don't think you've had a chance to explore the grounds yet.'

Sabrina's gaze met his over her glass of rich raspberry liqueur. Unsmiling, she tipped the glass to her lips, the ruby liquid glinting in the candlelight. When she lowered the glass and licked her lips his eyes seized on that seductive gesture, his body restless and on fire.

'Why not?' she said lightly.

He held out a hand and to his surprise she took it. He led her around the sleeping villa until they reached the formal gardens—a square courtyard open to the sky, surrounded on all four sides by a colonnade. Flowers bloomed in ornate terracotta urns and troughs, while a dolphin fountain of his own design played into a shallow pool at the centre.

Slowly, they walked around the colonnade, their path illuminated at intervals by soft solar-powered lamps. Cicadas sang in the warm darkness, and the scent of jasmine was thick on the night air. Breathing in the sweet fragrance, Rafael felt the tension of the past few days begin to drain out of him.

He had often come out here after the villa was first renovated, finding sanctuary from his high-stress lifestyle in this place of peace.

Now he was sharing it with Sabrina.

With his wife.

He came to a halt at an opening into a wider courtyard. She looked like a water nymph in the lamplit darkness, wild and seductive, her long blonde tresses haloed with light.

He brushed a long finger under her chin, tilting her face towards him, and she did not flinch away. 'Sabbie...' His nickname for her as a girl hung in the air between them, a whisper from the past. 'Sabbie,' he repeated softly, 'I'm truly sorry about your father...the lies he told you.'

'None of that was your fault.'

'No, but now you're away from him I want you to be happy again. Carefree. Like you used to be.' He examined her face. 'Tell me how I can help with that.'

'I don't think it's possible.'

'Anything's possible.'

'Is it?'

Her smile was teasing, her gentle fragrance filling his senses.

'Well, I suppose we could...change the narrative.' Slowly, suggestively, she held his gaze. 'Rewrite the past.'

His heart was thumping violently, his body tingling. 'Could you be more explicit?'

'Must I?' she whispered, but she put a hand to his face, cupping his rough cheek. 'I guess, with everything that's happened recently, I'm just so tired of feeling hurt. I want to be held. To be loved.'

When he held his breath, hardly daring to move, her voice broke.

'Forget the contract. Make love to me tonight. Please, Rafe...'

Desire flared in him, a guzzling torch fed by the husky need in her voice, the gasoline of her touch on his stubble.

'Sabbie, are you sure?'

He didn't know why the hell he was asking that. She sounded one hundred percent sure. It was he who was unsure about letting his guard down, risking his sanity and his soul. All the same, taking her by the shoulders, he brushed his lips across hers, but tentatively, still giving her time to change her mind.

'Yes!' she gasped, quickly drawing his hand up to cup her mounded flesh through the soft sea-blue fabric of her dress. She wasn't wearing a bra. 'I need you to touch me.'

His heart accelerated.

Sabrina moaned and her head fell back, exposing her throat. Palming her unrestrained breast, he bent to kiss her throat, every nerve in his body burning with excitement as his lips met fevered skin.

It was like diving into the Aegean and feeling its warm depths close about him. After the frustration of days not being able to kiss her, to make love to her as he wished, the freedom was exhilarating. His skin prickled with lightning wherever her fingers touched, moving blindly as they explored his face...

Hungrily, he parted his lips to draw those two questing fingers inside, sucking on them fiercely until Sabrina gave a muffled sob, her eyes flying open, her turbulent blue gaze like storm-tossed waves.

He scooped her up, carrying her to the large, cushioned divan beside the fountain. There, he lay her down among the red and orange cushions and knelt beside her. His need was urgent, but he must not rush her, he knew, and forced himself to slow down, to make love…

'*Agape mou,*' he whispered in her ear.

Her jewelled sandals were quickly disposed of. Tantalised by the glittering silver anklet, he let his fingers play with it a moment, before sliding up her shapely calf to her knee, then slipping daringly beneath her shift dress, stroking the soft flesh of her thighs.

She moaned, the foaming blue fabric of her dress ebbing away as she drew up her knees, exposing what lay beneath. 'Rafe, I need you so badly.'

There was a flush in her cheeks, a glow that told him she was in the grip of the same fever that burnt him.

'Do…? Do you need *me*?' she added.

'Never doubt it,' he growled.

'Then show me.'

Impatiently, she sat up and dragged the flimsy dress over her head, tossing it to the ground. Beneath, she wore nothing but a pair of lacy blue panties, barely enough fabric to cover her sex. Staring at him hungrily, she knelt among the divan cushions, breasts jutting magnificently, her pale body gleaming near-nude in the darkness.

'Come here, Rafe,' she ordered him in Greek, her voice thickened by desire. She tugged at her panties. 'Don't make me wait any longer.'

Equally urgent, he helped her discard the panties, and then held her naked in his arms, stroking one breast while sucking firmly on the other, revelling in the sweet taste of her flesh. In Paris, she had been shy and inexperienced. This was a different Sabrina…a woman who knew what she wanted.

He felt a stab of jealousy, wondering who had been her lover since him, then the thought was lost in the swirl of heat between them.

His tongue worked on the aroused points of her nipples and Sabrina panted and cried out, writhing beneath him. His fingers explored the sweet flesh between her thighs, stroking softly and masterfully in the damp cleft while he continued to nuzzle her breasts.

'Rafe, please...'

Her knees parted for him, her hips arching high off the cushions as she pushed against him, each sinew of her lithe body urging him to go deeper, to bring her to completion.

Over and over he rubbed his thumb across the nub of flesh and heard her gasp. Then he bent his head there. Her hands gripped his hair, his neck, his shoulders, urging him closer, her nails digging into his back like claws. The sharp pain excited him. He hoped she had drawn blood...marked him as her lover.

Her cries rose to a throbbing crescendo and then she flung out her arms, gripping the cushions of the divan and fisting the soft material, her body jerking beneath him. He closed his eyes, driven by an urge so primitive he could no longer control it. At last Sabrina thrust up against his mouth, a reedy cry on her lips, and he felt a surge of triumph that he had brought her so much pleasure, and something else besides. A strange tenderness that shook him to the core.

He needed her too. But they had to be careful. This was not what they'd planned.

'Are you protected?' he asked, hesitating. 'Should I fetch—?'

'I'm on the pill,' she whispered.

He rose above her in relief, swiftly undressing now, kicking aside his trousers, his boxers. His desire was urgent, a hardness that was almost painful, that could only be assuaged in her softness.

'Sabrina...' he said huskily, bringing himself between her splayed thighs, finding again the wet heat that had welcomed his mouth and his fingers. 'You're mine,' he told her, thrilled by this simple truth. He stroked and caressed her slick core in readiness. 'My wife. My woman.' Perhaps she had taken other lovers since him. But he knew nobody else would ever know her as intimately. 'You will always be mine. My Sabrina.'

But Sabrina shook her head.

'No.' Gazing up at him through half-closed eyes, her skin still glowing with pleasure, she whispered, 'I don't belong to anyone, Rafe. I never will again. I'm done with belonging.'

'You're mine. My wife. My woman. You will always be mine. My Sabrina.'

Did he understand why she had to reject his words of possession? Not because she didn't want this consummation as desperately as he did, but because she was still smarting from the lies she'd been fed for years—the great deception that had stunted her childhood and her youth.

She needed to be free now, to be her own person, and Rafael would have to accept that if he wanted to be her lover.

She stilled for a beat, watching him anxiously, wondering if he would turn away. But he seemed to understand the fierceness of her response. His eyes glinted above her in the darkness, his mouth quirking, showing white teeth. Then he bent over her body like a worshipper, reverently kissing her throat and breasts as the hard ridge of his arousal pressed against her, demanding entry.

'No,' he agreed, and she caught an edge of regret in his voice. 'You're a free spirit, Sabbie. But tonight at least you're mine.'

And he slid home inside her wet flesh, with a demanding thrust that snatched her breath away and drove her body temperature several degrees hotter. She felt her cheeks flare and gasped as he began to make love to her, rising to meet his thrusts, knowing herself close to the tremulous edge.

She soared among the bright points of light above her, the stars of her childhood, of Calista, while he worked at her slick flesh, his maleness intoxicating her senses. Still deep inside her, he palmed a breast, bent his head to her taut nipple and sucked hard. The pain and pleasure were too exquisite…she could scarcely bear them. Her concentration frayed. She chewed her lip, thrashed her head from side to side, trying not to scream. And then she hissed and let go, her body shuddering into joy again.

'Yes…' His growl urged her on. His face was a mask of desire now, barely recognisable. His hands smoothed her hips down into the soft cushions as he rode her, a muscular god, driving into her again and again, his dark gaze hooked on her face. 'Sabbie,' he muttered, his pace increasing. 'My Sabbie.'

They were making love again at last. It was one of her recurring dreams and now it was true. She had imagined this reunion so many times…

Sabrina closed her eyes to his magnificent body, almost overwhelmed by his power and presence, his consummate skill as a lover. Rafael shifted with ease, a hand under each knee, raising her legs to cradle them about him.

His hips angled and he drove deeper still, working the soft hot metal at her core, remaking her. Sabrina gasped and let her head fall back, losing herself to a pleasure beyond anything she had ever known, gripping the sides of the divan, its hard edges the only thing anchoring her to reality.

Even that one glorious night with him in Paris had not been like this.

But they understood each other better now.

They connected.

They soared high and burnt together in the darkness. Her body was a river of fire.

She shivered with ecstasy, her eyes flying open at last. High above, the night sky dazzled her with its silent beauty. Black velvet studded with millions of tiny jewels, arcing over their heads.

His breathing became ragged, his thrusts erratic. 'Sabrina!' he cried out.

Beyond them, the fountain played endlessly, spilling liquid into the warm depths of the pool. They lay together on the divan for some time afterwards, bare limbs tangled, facing each other, while their hearts stopped thumping and their breathing returned to normal.

Sabrina's body ached and throbbed. Everything felt different, newly awoken, as though she had just learnt some fantastical truth about herself and the world.

She wanted to share her newfound joy with Rafael, with the rebellious boy she had once known as well as she knew herself. But what if he didn't understand? What if he was no longer the boy she remembered and he laughed at her moment of revelation? What if he turned away as he had done in Paris and left her wounded and dying inside?

So she lay there and said nothing, the joy slowly cooling in her heart, a tiny precious jewel she would need to hide from everyone—even from him.

'Did you have any special plans for today?'

At the sound of his wife's voice Rafael put down his coffee cup and glanced over his shoulder. He had left Sabrina sleeping when he'd come down for breakfast, her face flushed, blonde hair spread loosely on the pillow after another late night. Studying her, he had found his mind drifting ahead to the dim and distant future, when she would leave him and demand the divorce built into their marriage contract.

He had thrust the unsettling thought far away.

It shouldn't be as hard as he feared to let her go. This phase would pass and he would be free.

What was done was done.

They were now spending every night together.

Without a word, Sabrina had moved her clothes into his suite a few days ago, and after dinner and a moonlit walk each night they retired to bed and made love as passionately and intensely as though each time might be their last. They slept deeply between bouts of lovemaking, the bedsheets hot and crumpled, their naked limbs thrown over each other in exhausted abandon...

'Not particularly,' he said now. He watched as Kyria Diakou poured fresh coffee for them both before bustling away to fetch a jug of orange juice. 'Why?'

'I'd like to go and visit the orphanage.' Sabrina sipped her coffee, her thoughtful gaze on the cloudless blue skies above the Aegean.

He couldn't seem to take his eyes off her.

It was a hot summer's day, like all the days at Villa Rosa so far. A green lizard clung motionless, partway across the warm stone wall of the veranda, watching them. Sabrina sat back in a tight red dress with a plunge neckline, crossing smooth, honey-tanned legs, and Rafael's gaze was riveted to the sexy gesture, his shorts suddenly straining. The lizard must have caught the movement too, for the creature darted away and out of sight in a flash.

As what she'd said filtered through to his brain Rafael couldn't hide his surprise. 'Again? But—'

'The new orphanage. The one in town.' She put down her cup and selected a fresh-baked sweet roll from the wicker basket. 'I want to meet the children—if that's allowed?'

'Of course. The director said I could drop in any time.'

'Good. It's important to me to know how they feel about their new home.'

She smiled at him, biting into the roll with neat white teeth. As she ate, she played with the silver chain about her neck, its diamond pendant dangling between her breasts.

'How about this afternoon? We could have lunch in town first. At that discreet little restaurant in the square.'

'Whatever you like.'

His hand crumpled the napkin beside his plate as his gaze moved hotly over her cleavage and down to the sharp inward curve of her waist.

He was falling apart already. No need to wait until she'd left him.

His control blurred.

'Sabbie…'

He was on his feet, he realised, standing right in front of her. She looked up at him, startled, eyes wide.

'You have…crumbs.' He was still gripping the napkin in his fist. 'Allow me.'

Slowly, delicately, he dabbed at the cleavage of her red dress, where two or three crumbs dusted the scarlet fabric. Sabrina watched, perfectly still except for her tongue, which crept out to moisten her lips. He shifted his gaze to her mouth at once, dropping the napkin as he leant forward to claim her lips.

She gasped and her lips parted further, their kiss deepening. He was breathing heavily, his arousal urgent now.

A sound brought him around to find Kyria Diakou in the doorway, a jug of orange juice in her hands, looking embarrassed. 'Excuse me,' she murmured, and backed away. 'I'll come back later.'

Damn it.

'No, it's fine.' He pulled Sabrina to her feet, holding her

close when she would have wriggled free. 'I believe we've both finished breakfast.' He paused. 'There's no need to clear the table until later. In fact, why don't you and Nikos take the day off?'

'Sir...?' His housekeeper looked amazed.

'We'll fend for ourselves today.' When she began to stammer a protest, he shook his head. 'No, I insist.'

Once Kyria Diakou had gone, he turned to Sabrina, still clasped against him. 'How about a swim?'

'Okay, but I'll need to fetch my swimsuit.'

Rafael shook his head.

Her eyes grew large. 'Swim in the...the nude?'

'Why not?'

Her mouth opened, but then slowly closed again. A sultry look came into her face. 'You're incorrigible.'

'Maybe,' he agreed in a murmur. 'But you,' he continued, lifting her wrist to his mouth and kissing the delicate skin there, her feminine fragrance driving him wild, 'are my drug of choice. And I'm addicted.' He nuzzled her palm. 'I need to take you. And take you. And take you again.'

She swayed against him, a flush in her cheeks. 'Rafe...'

He scooped her up in his arms and carried her down the broad steps to the pool, setting her lightly on her feet by the shallow end. Holding her gaze, he drew her scarlet dress up over hips and breasts in one smooth movement, then past her head. Beneath, she was wearing matching bra and panties in flimsy red lace.

Hungrily, Rafael admired her stunning figure, then reached around to unsnap her bra, his gaze intent on the high bounce of her breasts as they were released. Then he hooked his thumbs in the waistband of her red panties and smiled as she helped him remove them too, lifting her ankles and kicking them impatiently aside.

Far from being shy in her nudity, Sabrina stood on tiptoe and set her mouth to his. He held her close, his hands sliding down to rest on her hips. Her tongue played against his, teasing and playful, and his groin throbbed with need.

'Now you,' she whispered against his mouth.

He grasped his T-shirt to drag it off, but she got there first, shaking her head.

'That's my job,' she told him, her eyes dancing.

Obediently, even though he was chafing to be free to do as he wished with her delectable body, he stood with his arms by his sides as she undressed him too, pulling off his T-shirt, then unzipping his shorts and drawing them off with painstaking care.

Rafael was breathing harshly by the time she bent with a smile to remove his distended trunks. He groaned at the maddening brush of her hands, arching his hips to meet her touch.

'Have pity, Sabrina,' he told her, his voice strangled.

She turned to descend into the shallows of the pool and his gaze followed her. There was a series of steps under the water, and she took these swiftly, sinking into the pool up to her waist before swimming away, her golden hair floating wide like a mermaid's.

He dived after her, pursuing her underwater for a few metres before surfacing close to the wall, his hands already on her waist, pulling her against his naked body. She turned to face him, her pale gleaming breasts pushing at his chest, their legs tangling…

'I need you,' he whispered against her damp throat. 'Now.'

'But what if the Diakous see us?'

'I told them to go home… If they're still here, too bad.'

Her wet lashes rose and fell and her gaze met his, those blue depths somehow strong and vulnerable at the same time.

Do it, she mouthed, almost daring him.

In one swift move he raised her effortlessly, shifting her full weight onto his hips, and draped her thighs around him. Their mouths met and his heart hammered, everything inside him straining towards her. His fingers found her core, the slippery flesh hot and yielding, more than ready for him. He worked at the delicate bud there, firm but gentle, sensing her climax as it built.

Once she'd moaned against his mouth he couldn't wait any longer. He speared inside her and felt Sabrina jerk at his entry, her cry one of satisfaction as she undulated against him.

At first he thought he had himself well under control. But then she leant back in the water, her firm thighs gripping him, and he drove deep, again and again, finally releasing himself into her with a hoarse shout. The pleasure that filled him at that moment was so intense, so overwhelming, he felt again the piercing sweetness he'd known in Paris…

Only he didn't weep this time. He closed his eyes against the water's dazzling brilliance and counted silently to ten as his heart rate returned to normal. This was a coping mechanism he used in other stressful situations, and Rafael wasn't sure why he'd chosen to do it now. Except that it allowed him to retain control.

He could barely stand afterwards, and yet somehow he managed to restore her to the shallow end, staggering towards the steps with her in his arms.

'I don't have a towel,' she protested as he set her on her feet beside the pool.

'So?' He flashed her an irreverent grin. 'Why not drip-dry?'

He waited, expecting some glib remark in response, but she stretched out on a lounger, saying nothing.

Rafael slicked back his wet hair, studying her averted

profile in surprise. They were still friends, but friends with benefits now. And the sex was incredible. Sabrina was fantastically responsive as a lover, and the way she had ridden him in the pool just now, with zero inhibitions, had blown his mind.

Yet there was a barrier between them that had not existed when they'd made love in Paris, and although there was no earthly reason why that should bother him, it did.

He turned away, saying lightly, 'I'm going for a shower,' and headed up the steps into the villa without waiting for a response.

This was only a temporary marriage of convenience, he reminded himself. They might be sleeping together now, but if Sabrina could play it casual, so could he.

Later that afternoon they traversed the dusty backstreets of the Calistan port together, coming out into a new-build area, pleasantly shaded, with a high-rise complex bordered by well-maintained gardens behind security fencing. She could smell cooking, and heard loud, cheerful music playing from inside.

Above the entrance doors was a sign in Greek that read, *Calista Children's Sunshine Centre*, with a smiley icon beside it in yellow and orange.

A dark-haired girl was peering out through one of the upper windows as they were buzzed through the security gate. Something about her wide-eyed stare reminded Sabrina of her own childhood in the old orphanage. She had thought herself all alone after her mother's death, adrift in a dark world. Yet her father had been aware of her existence the whole time and had left her to languish there for years.

She thrust the angry thought away, still smarting from her father's betrayal.

'This used to be the old market,' Rafael told her as she

stared about, taking in the bright, ultra-modern setting. 'When the orphanage came up for sale I had this site redeveloped and kitted out to accommodate the orphans.' He gestured up the steps to the entrance. 'Shall we?'

Sabrina smiled, but inwardly she was feeling shaky. The more they made love, the more distant Rafael was becoming. She didn't understand it, but wondered if it might be her fault. For she was aware of a growing coolness between them now that they were lovers. The marriage that had worked as a business arrangement seemed doomed to fall apart now that they were sharing a bed...

The new director, Anka, was a friendly Polish-born woman in her thirties, who seemed delighted to see Rafael and insisted on showing them around the whole orphanage herself. Her Greek was excellent. She told them several of the new children were from Poland and neighbouring Ukraine, which had inspired her to apply for the job.

Room after room was bright and sunny, with colourfully painted walls and soft matting underfoot. The kids had a large, well-equipped computer room, a television lounge with beanbags and huge sofas, a recreation area with a climbing wall and table tennis, and bedrooms with only one or two beds each, prettily decorated with ensuite bathroom facilities. Through the tinted windows, Sabrina looked down on shaded lawns and flowerbeds, and an enclosed playground for the younger children, plus a half-pipe and skater park for the older kids, all painted in bright graffiti style.

'This is marvellous,' Sabrina admitted. 'When I think of how you and I grew up... Not that the wardens didn't take care of us. But this is another world.'

Rafael nodded sombrely, his dark eyes intent on her face.

Anka gave them both a broad smile. 'And now, Kyria

Romano, perhaps you would like to meet some of the children?'

'Oh!' Sabrina put her hands to her cheeks. 'Could we?'

'Of course. I've asked my assistant to gather the older children together in here.'

The director led them into the lounge area.

Sabrina recalled herself as a teenager: wary, inquisitive, permanently poised to reject the world while simultaneously eager to engage with it. These youngsters were no different. Some scrambled to their feet, staring wide-eyed at the newcomers. Others turned their backs, arms folded, eyes downcast, determined not to show any interest. One boy—with spiky hair and a black T-shirt with a superhero on it—swore loudly, and the girl beside him, who had just dropped his hand, giggled nervously.

The director began to reprimand the boy for swearing but Rafael shook his head, saying it didn't matter. He strolled forward and held out a hand to the boy, who shook it after a moment's hesitation.

'I'm Rafael Romano. I don't believe we've met. I had a T-shirt like that when I was your age. Never too soon to be aspirational.' He grinned. 'What's your name?'

The boy introduced himself, adding, 'Romano? Are you the man who bought the orphanage?' When Rafael nodded, his eyes grew larger, his look more friendly. 'Thank you. This place is a…a miracle.'

'Especially the computer room,' one of the other kids burst out, coming closer.

'And the sports pitch.'

'Don't forget the skate park. That's awesome!'

A dark-haired girl who'd been reading in the corner put down her book, smiling up at him shyly. 'Thank you for the library too. So many stories… I'll never read them all.'

'This is Cora,' Anka said, beckoning the girl forward.

'She's a very clever girl, top of all her classes. Our resident bookworm too.'

She was the child at the window, who'd watched them come in through the gates, Sabrina realised, and she smiled at the girl warmly.

'I'm glad you approve, Cora,' her husband was saying. 'Though if you like books you really should speak to my wife, Kyria Romano. She loves reading too.'

Rafael turned to indicate Sabrina, who had not said much yet, almost as shy as the children.

'Back in the day, my wife was an orphan here on Calista, just like me. In fact, she's worried that some of you may miss the old orphanage.' He gave the children an encouraging smile. 'So, how about you tell Sabrina which one you prefer? This place or the old one?'

They spent some hours at the orphanage, chatting to the kids and later walking outside in the shade under fragrant pines. Sabrina got on well with young Cora, whose love of books and reading was expressed in short, ecstatic bursts followed by nervous laughter. It was obvious the young people loved their new location in the port and would rather not go back to the crumbling old orphanage.

After they'd finally said their goodbyes, Sabrina and Rafael wandered back to the car, smiling at each other shyly as they discussed what they'd seen. Meeting the children, so like themselves at the same age, seemed to have rekindled their friendship.

It was only when Rafael was driving them back to the villa that he broke the good mood.

'You're still coming to the charity ball in Paris, aren't you? You agreed to attend the event with me,' he reminded her, his eyes on the road ahead. 'To silence any remaining doubters and meet a few of my business associates.'

Her soul grew cold again at his words. For a short time

she'd forgotten this wasn't a real marriage, that she was only his wife for a year and had official duties to perform...like a hired escort.

'Of course,' she said without expression, and turned to study the rugged sunlit landscape flashing by. 'I'll be there.'

CHAPTER TEN

THE ELEGANT PARISIAN ballroom had been decorated for the charity ball with gigantic urns spilling over with flowers, each urn set at intervals in front of floor-to-ceiling mirrors, above which spanned a glorious ceiling mural depicting what looked like gods and goddesses. The space was packed with wealthy, young, designer-clad couples whirling gracefully, while big ticket donors chatted in groups, champagne glasses in hand. Musicians played on a central raised platform, and the music swelled to a crescendo as Rafael led Sabrina through the crowded space towards the dancers.

Her husband looked unspeakably edible in a sharp designer suit, his black jacket hanging open to reveal a white silk shirt left unbuttoned to partway down his chest.

As they stood on the edge of the dance floor, it became increasingly obvious they had become the centre of attention. Everywhere she looked eyes studied them covertly, curious and speculative. From the eyes of those gossiping behind their hands on the sidelines to the smiling, uniformed staff circulating discreetly with trays of champagne and dainty, exquisitely crafted canapés.

'Shall we?' Rafael asked.

The dark slash of his eyebrows arched in query at her hesitation.

'What? You don't want to dance?'

He placed their empty champagne flutes on a passing waiter's tray and reached for her hand, his touch electrifying. Sabrina caught her breath, her whole body tingling with sensation.

'We're supposed to be in love, remember?' His gaze clashed with hers when she stubbornly refused to move. 'How will it look if we come to a charity ball together, but don't dance?'

'It's not that,' she whispered, not wanting anyone else to hear. 'It's just…everyone's staring.'

'Of course they're staring.' His voice dipped. 'Isn't that why we're here? To be seen out in public as a couple?' His fingers curled about hers, strong and possessive. 'You're a blushing new bride, remember? Try to act the part.'

She gave an automatic smile, but behind it she felt slightly sick.

'Try to act the part.'

Had Rafael been acting a part since their wedding? Making love to her so passionately, sharing his days and nights with her, just to keep her from growing restless? The boy she had known had grown into a ruthless billionaire, after all, just like her father. She wouldn't put it past him to lull her into acquiescence with such tactics.

Her phone buzzed in her sparkly clutch bag, but she ignored it. It was probably another message from Andrew Templeton, in response to the text she'd sent him last night.

I know the truth about you, Dad. I never thought you could disappoint me. But I was wrong. Now I need time to think. Please leave me alone.

On Calista it had all felt too raw, too visceral for her to handle—remembering her childhood as an orphan, the appalling loneliness she'd experienced that first year after

losing her mother, the sense of having nobody to turn to…
Nobody except Rafael, that was.

But being in Paris again, where she had first escaped
Andrew Templeton's suffocating control, had switched on
a light inside her—a beam of courage to illuminate a new
path. It had taken her a long time to get the wording of her
message right. But the time had finally come to confront
her father, and she was determined to do it on her terms—
not his.

After hitting 'Send' and turning off her phone, she had
fallen into the soundest sleep she'd enjoyed in years, waking refreshed and with an odd feeling of liberation…like a
caged bird whose prison door had been left open.

They had taken an elite suite at the Paris Ritz, with two
opulent bedrooms and a huge gold and white sitting room
with a fabulous view of Place Vendôme and the city beyond.
It had not taken long for word to get around, and the paparazzi had come swarming into the hotel lobby in search
of a candid shot of the world's most famous new couple.

They had deliberately allowed themselves to be snapped,
even stopping sometimes to pose for the press, hand in hand
as they were now, smiling at each other. Keeping up the
appearance of happy newlyweds for the sake of his business contacts.

On Calista they had made love as though the world were
ending, and yet… She had never quite been sure what he
was thinking or feeling. Or indeed if he was feeling anything at all. Given the absence at the heart of both their
childhoods, she had often thought they should be more open
to the idea of love. Yet Rafael seemed to view emotion with
such disdain and suspicion, his difficult past no doubt colouring his responses.

Now they were in Paris, with its wide boulevards and elegant monuments...its intimate little restaurants and breath-taking views.

The city of love.

The irony was not lost on her.

Since their arrival in Paris, Rafael had spent every morning working, catching up with his PA in New York, while Sabrina had taken work-related calls from her own assistant, Shelley, in London. The afternoons had been spent together, exploring the famous European city and ignoring the curious looks of passers-by who recognised them.

They had taken a *bateau mouche* along the River Seine, toured the Louvre with guidebooks in hand, and strolled around the lively Rive Gauche area in the sunshine before heading to a lively club for dinner and dancing in Montmartre. Rafael was an interesting companion, keen on art, opinionated about politics without becoming dogmatic, and always able to make her laugh with a barbed remark or a clever play on words.

Paris was working its magic on them all over again. She had felt quite different in his company since arriving here, enjoying the two of them being out in the world together, openly a couple.

She was in danger of feeling something for this man that she couldn't risk admitting. Their lovemaking had lulled her into forgetting that this was a business partnership, nothing more. It would break her apart to trust him as she had trusted the younger Rafael...to open her heart only for him to walk away and abandon her exactly as he'd done before. As everyone else in her life had done, in fact.

Besides, she'd spent too many years in her father's shadow. She refused to escape from Andrew Templeton only to bind herself to yet another charismatic male—to become Rafael's lover and helpmate instead of an independent woman, walking her own path, making her own decisions.

The band had struck up a new tune with a sweeping rhythmic beat. A waltz.

They had danced a waltz last time, giggling as Rafael fumbled the steps, never having been taught ballroom dancing—unlike her.

Sabrina breathed hard through another cresting wave of anxiety, as traumatic memories jostled for space in her head. She had been so sure she could handle being in Paris with him again. Yet this was the same ballroom where they'd bumped into each other five years ago and ended up in bed...with such disastrous consequences for her heart.

Talk about *déjà-vu*.

Rafael tugged her hand, pulling her onto the dance floor. 'Come on, let's show them how to do it.'

Her eyes widened. 'But this is a waltz,' she reminded him in an urgent whisper. 'You know you can't waltz.'

He tucked his raised hand into hers, his gaze arrowing in on her face. 'After last time I made sure to take formal dance lessons. Like for horse-riding.' The dark gaze intensified, almost setting her alight, and his lip curled. 'Couldn't have the street urchin from Calista embarrassing himself in front of his betters again, could we?'

He swung her out among the other dancers, one arm anchored firmly about her waist, and suddenly they were waltzing. It felt more like flying...

'Oh!' She swallowed, looking him in the eye.

His hand clasped hers. Their bodies were intimately close. His muscular thighs brushed her body quite deliberately. The delicate silk of her blue evening gown was no barrier to the hard ridge of his arousal. Heat swamped her cheeks and her lips parted as she sought to control her breathing. His desire could not have been more prominent, though she took some comfort from the realisation that only the two of them knew about it.

His eyes glinted, his smile mocking her. 'Did I mention you look beautiful in that frock?'

'No,' she said faintly, 'but thank you.'

'You can thank me later,' he murmured, drawing her even closer as they swung around the edge of the dance floor, where a crowd of partygoers stood watching. His dark mocking gaze met hers. 'And stop looking so frightened.'

Her eyes flashed at him. 'I am *not* frightened. I told you. I don't like being stared at, that's all.'

'Yes, I remember that about you.' His voice dropped to a whisper that prickled her nerve-endings. 'But those days are over, Sabbie. You're not that lost little girl any more.'

'Aren't I?' Her hand trembled in his and she felt his grip tighten.

'Not even remotely,' he insisted.

She wished she could share his confidence. She had spent the morning trawling elite Parisian boutiques for tonight's ballgown, aware that this was a special performance—not merely for Rafael's more conservative business associates but for her father too. She knew he would scan any photos or footage of this evening like a detective looking for weaknesses in an alibi—it needed to be pitch-perfect.

Meanwhile, since that text she'd sent, her muted phone had become jammed with missed calls from Andrew Templeton, while the few messages he'd left had been brusque and uncompromising.

Call me. We need to talk. NOW.

So far she had ignored his demands, despite the nerves churning inside her at the thought of his growing anger, and had focused on herself instead.

Before the ball she'd been expertly made-up, her nails manicured and painted, her hair dressed to perfection, pampered and fussed over by the team of beauticians and an exclusive hairdresser who had come to their suite for added privacy. Then she had been helped into the snug-fitting blue silk gown, and added a few elegant diamonds to provide the finishing touches to her outfit.

Rafael, on the other hand, looked rough and on edge this evening, as though he'd barely slept in days. Still drop dead-gorgeous, though, and his designer stubble made her want to run her fingertips over his jutting chin.

'What are you thinking?'

His dark gaze scoured her face, a frown tugging his brows together.

When she didn't answer, he continued in a harsh voice, 'Forget the past. Forget your father. Think about the future, Sabrina.'

Her lips compressed as she took that in.

'Do you remember what you said when you left me in Paris last time?' she asked, daring to reopen that old wound. 'You said *I* was a part of your past, and all you wanted was to look ahead to the future.'

'Did I?' He glanced at her casually, and then looked away, though his arm tightened about her waist.

'If that was true,' she said, 'why come all the way from New York to see me on Calista? You could have explained about my father over the phone…or sent someone else to do it.'

He didn't answer for a moment, then growled, 'You know why.'

'No, I really don't.'

'Because I care for you,' he said, his voice dangerous. His stubborn chin jutted as he looked away, checking their path through the other dancers. 'We were always there for each other as children, Sabbie, and I knew I owed it to you to break the bad news in person.'

She swallowed, emotion churning inside her at his words. *'I care for you.'*

Was that as good as it was ever going to get between them?

But what did she feel for him? Did she even know?

Rafael glanced down at her, his dark gaze veiled by his lashes. 'Do you remember that summer festival on Calista, the year before Templeton took you away? You would have been fifteen… We slipped away from the orphanage that night and climbed onto the taverna roof to watch the procession go past.'

His hand gripped hers as she stared into his face, feeling the bittersweet memory burning her soul.

'Afterwards, there was dancing in the street until gone midnight.'

'I remember,' she said huskily.

'You said something to me that night,' he went on, his face stony, as unmoving as an ancient Greek statue. 'Something I've never forgotten.'

Heat bloomed in her cheeks as she realised what he meant. Lying on the taverna roof and watching the women in tight, colourful dresses below, gyrating with their partners in the street, she had whispered to him, 'The first time I dance like that, I want it to be with you, Rafe.'

Rafael had looked embarrassed at the time, and she'd regretted saying it. They had been friends, and that was all. Now, though, his eyes glowed as he met hers.

'When we met again here in Paris, what you'd said was in my head when I asked you to dance. Only I messed things up, didn't I?'

His hand tightened on hers and she knew he didn't mean the dance steps.

'For what it's worth,' he went on, his voice grating low in her ear, 'I'm sorry. I hurt you and that was unforgivable.'

He still hadn't explained why he'd left her so abruptly in Paris the morning after making love to her for the first time. But he had at least apologised for the hurt he'd caused her, and without being prompted to do so.

She hugged that sustaining thought to herself as they whirled about the floor for the last few sweeping beats of the dance, the two of them clamped together in a heated physical awareness of each other.

After the waltz came more champagne and canapés while they worked the room together, meeting other guests and celebrity ticket-holders. She struggled against the urge to drag him away to some private room where they could talk properly. This event was about him and his business. Not their marriage.

As the glittering evening wore on, Rafael introduced her to some high-profile business associates of his that he'd recognised across the ballroom, including one of the world's wealthiest men, and she smiled and chatted by his side about their wedding and their honeymoon, playing her part with ease.

He wanted a trophy wife? He could have a trophy wife.

But inside she longed for more—for this marriage to be real—all the while knowing it could never be. She didn't attract people; she repulsed them. Everyone she had ever loved had abandoned her. Why should this time be any different?

'Thank you,' Rafael murmured afterwards, steering her away from one of the conservative Americans he was eager to do business with. 'I appreciate you keeping your side of the bargain.'

She said nothing, but her heart plummeted. It was stupid to feel hurt by his reminder of their contract. This was why they had come to Paris, wasn't it? And yet she did feel hurt.

Towards midnight, the party began to break up, the

guests slowly drifting out of the grand Parisian ballroom towards the cloakrooms and the exit.

Sabrina, flagging with fatigue by then, was shocked to find herself face to face with an unexpected array of journalists and television cameras in the vast lobby. As she and Rafael descended the stairs together, arm in arm, the cameras began to flash wildly, dazzling and intimidating her. Suddenly traumatised afresh, still struggling to come to terms with her unfamiliar identity as Mrs Romano, she knew she couldn't stomach yet more questions from the paparazzi.

She trembled, looking around blindly. 'Quick, let's find another way out.'

But Rafael bent to her ear. 'No, this is why we came here. To be seen by the paparazzi.'

His intense gaze collided with hers—a jolt that ran through her like lightning.

'I never figured you for a coward, Sabrina.'

Dazed, and slightly the worse for champagne, she stumbled on the stairs in her high heels. Rafael caught her at once and pulled her close. Her hands pressed against his chest and their gazes meshed. Cameras flashed and a cry went up from the watching press. Wildly, she acknowledged bone, muscle, sinew...the heat of his body.

And the fact that he was right, of course.

This was why they had come to Paris, after all. To be publicly acknowledged as newlyweds. If she refused to speak to them now, the paps might run a story about how she was a reluctant bride, fuelling her father's paranoia about Rafael and casting doubt on their 'happiness'. Then their pretence tonight would have been for nothing.

'All right, I'll do it,' she whispered, and he led her forward to face the cameras and the shouting paparazzi, his arm about her waist.

'Miss Templeton!' came the shout. 'This way, Sabrina! Smile!'

More flash photography...and the overwhelming sense of being a creature under a microscope.

She drew herself up in front of the press, thankful at last for her training at the exclusive finishing school she'd hated. Her mouth even found a smile.

'I'm not Miss Templeton any more. Do I need to introduce my husband? Of course not—you all know him already. Rafael Romano...now a respectable married man.'

There was general laughter from the journalists.

'Is it true you've been forced into this marriage against your will, Sabrina?' one of the reporters shouted.

Rafael swore under his breath, then demanded in astonishment, 'Who the hell has been saying that?' as though he had no idea.

'Andrew Templeton,' the reporter replied. 'Your wife's father.'

They were all looking at her expectantly.

'I can't imagine why my father would say such a thing,' she told them, furious at Andrew Templeton's interference. 'I... I don't know what you've been told, but I certainly wasn't coerced into this marriage.'

It was tempting to expose her absent father for the liar and fraud that he was. But this was neither the time nor the place for such a revelation. Besides, that was not the kind of publicity they had sought in coming here.

'Rafael and I have known each other since we were children,' she continued, her voice wobbling a little. 'We grew up together on a beautiful Greek island called Calista. Both of us were orphans, with no one to turn to. My father clearly disapproves of our marriage, and that makes me sad. But I assure you that Rafael and I are very much in love.'

His fingers curled about hers, drawing her inexorably

closer to his side. Their hips bumped and her body flushed with heat. Her cheeks were on fire as she glanced up at his dark, forbidding face—a look that triggered another barrage of blinding camera flashes as the photographers scrabbled to capture the perfect shot of them together.

'I'm only sorry we couldn't invite more press to c-cover our wedding,' she stammered. 'But privacy is important to us. It's no fun getting married in a goldfish bowl.'

'What do you say to your father's accusation, then?' someone shouted from the back, and everyone looked at her expectantly. 'He claims Rafael's keeping you prisoner.'

Sabrina stared at the reporter, shocked. How much lower was her father prepared to go to keep control of the narrative?

'My…my father…' she began, sorely tempted to expose Andrew Templeton's true nature in front of the world's press.

And then she swallowed what felt like a throatful of broken glass, her vision blurred with tears. This was neither the time nor the place to accuse her father of wrongdoing. She had not even spoken to him in person yet. Yet these intrusive questions had her on the verge of weeping…unable to go on. A tearful, incoherent answer would make them think she really was a prisoner, when the only thing keeping her prisoner was her heart.

Rafael knew any rebuttal of that accusation must come from Sabrina or nobody would believe it. But he'd been gritting his teeth against the urge to protect her from these vultures, and when her voice had faltered one glance at her face had sent his blood pressure soaring.

Sabrina Templeton had matured into a confident businesswoman, sharp-witted and able to handle even the trickiest of negotiations. Yet he saw the vulnerability others missed, tucked away behind the smooth mask of perfection one of the world's finest plastic surgeons had created for her.

They had history together. To him, she would always be Sabbie, the scarred little girl who'd played with him in the dusty sunlit yard of the orphanage, and he missed the uncomplicated companionship of those days.

Her beauty was ethereal tonight. Her golden hair was worn up in a chignon, leaving her slender pale neck on display, adorned with a diamond necklace. She looked like a princess from a story book, he thought. A swan princess.

He recalled her sitting with young Cora in the library at the new orphanage, their heads bent together over a book, and an idea came to him.

Rafael smiled down at her encouragingly. 'I think we should tell them about our big plan, darling,' he said, raising his voice above the shouts of the paparazzi.

'Plan?' she repeated, blinking.

The reporters instantly forgot their previous question and went crazy, calling out, 'What's your big plan, Sabrina? Tell us!'

'Erm…' Sabrina drew a shaky breath, the fine silk sheen of her ballgown catching the light as her chest heaved. 'Why don't *you* tell them about it, Rafe?' she said. Her eyes sought his, their blue perfectly matched to her gown, a sea of churning intensity. 'Since it was your idea in the first place?'

Those eyes…

He had nearly drowned in them five years ago in this very building, reunited with her at the charity ball. He had felt the wildest leap of joy on seeing her across the ballroom, and then to his delight had seen an answering joy in her face as they'd rushed together and embraced. The years had fallen away, and with them the hurt of her long silence.

Seduced by her light, bubbling conversation, her infectious laughter and those shy, darting looks that had told him she wanted him as much as he wanted her, they had gone back to her hotel room and made love.

Their earlier friendship had been replaced by adult passion. Touching and kissing her that night had been as natural as breathing. And when she'd whispered in his ear, 'I'm on the pill,' he had wrongly assumed an experience she hadn't possessed.

Because she'd been a virgin. Her wide eyes and muffled cry as he'd entered her had told him as much, though he had said nothing, lost in the moment.

At first, Rafael had been thrilled by her innocence, imagining she must have been saving herself for him. He had lost control, felt tears in his eyes at the moment of climax, and had held her close for hours afterwards, all his hard certainties about life softened into an emotional blur. Then, after the most mind-blowing, exquisite night of lovemaking, he had woken in the sharp dawn light to realise he never wanted to let her go—that he was in love with her.

And he'd fled like a coward, barely able to look her in the face, after saying something unforgivable.

He had run out of fear. Fear of losing her as he'd lost his mother. Fear of not being strong enough to look after her. Fear that she must eventually realise his weakness and reject him...

He had behaved like an idiot by not admitting to his fears, allowing her to think he didn't care about her. And then he had compounded that error on Calista by convincing himself that she was merely a temporary solution to a business issue, afraid to look too deeply at his motives.

But he had not lost her yet. There was still time to make amends, wasn't there?

'As you wish, *agape mou*,' Rafael told her now. Smiling, he wove his fingers with hers, holding up their joined hands to the press pool. 'My wife and I plan to launch an international charity,' he announced, improvising swiftly. 'Our goal is to support and protect orphans all over the world.'

Shouts rang out from the assembled paparazzi, but he shook his head.

'I don't have all the details for you yet. But we'll be putting together a proposal soon. Orphans are very special and vulnerable members of any community, and not enough is being done on a global scale to help them—not only when they are children, and deserving of both loving care and secure, comfortable housing, but as young people in need of training and opportunities that might have been out of reach to them in the past.'

He saw surprise in Sabrina's eyes, and softening delight too, and raised her hand to his lips.

'Now, if you'll excuse us, my wife and I are still on our honeymoon—and, as the lady said, we'd appreciate some privacy.'

The paparazzi laughed and shouted more questions as the cameras flashed around them. But Rafael was already guiding Sabrina out to the limousine waiting for them by the kerb. They slid inside and the door closed, shutting out the chaos and the jagged, pulsing lights of the city.

'A charity for orphans... That's such a lovely idea,' she said huskily as the long, sleek car pulled away into the Parisian traffic, engine purring. 'Were you serious about it?'

He nodded. 'It's something I've been toying with for years.'

'Me too.'

'Then we'll do it,' he said firmly. 'Whatever else happens, at least we'll have built this charity together.'

CHAPTER ELEVEN

BACK IN HER bedroom at Villa Rosa, Sabrina woke with a start, sitting bolt-upright in bed. The sheet had fallen away, and her bare skin was icy-cold from the air conditioning.

She blinked at the darkness, confused.

Something had woken her.

According to the luminous digital clock beside her bed it was gone three o'clock in the morning. Roughly four hours since she and Rafael had returned to the villa. They had said a muted goodnight to each other before heading wearily for their own bedrooms, tired after their flight from Paris to Athens, followed by a turbulent helicopter ride back to Calista.

'Whatever else happens, at least we'll have built this charity together.'

His words echoed through her, slicing into her heart.

'Whatever else happens...'

Rafael was already bored and looking ahead to the end of their year together...to the no-contest divorce built into their contract. What else could he have meant?

She stumbled out of bed, dragging on a silk robe, and slid open the balcony window, listening to the lap of the Aegean against the rocks below in the warm, velvety darkness.

A hoarse cry split the silence, jolting her heart with fright, and she realised that was what had woken her earlier. Rafael was having another nightmare.

Sabrina hurried onto the landing, flicking on the light. 'Rafael?'

She caught a shout from inside his suite, and then a series of sobs, torn with anguish as if from a tortured soul, followed by the sound of gasping.

Tiptoeing along the landing, she tried the door to Rafael's suite. It opened onto darkness. She crept tentatively inside, groping her way along the wall and into the master bedroom. The light that trickled through the open door showed her the bronze of a hunched shoulder in his vast bed, a dark head lost amid a jumble of white pillows.

As usual, he was sleeping in the nude, only a sheet covering his lower half. The crumpled silk left little to the imagination, contouring his maleness and outlining strong, muscular thighs.

As she began to back away Rafael shuddered and gave another low cry, muttering in Greek, and she realised that he was still in the grip of the nightmare. He rolled over in a fast, convulsive movement, the sheet falling away to expose taut buttocks.

Clapping a hand to her mouth, Sabrina gasped. Her blood ran hot as she struggled to control her hunger for him.

Then Rafael cried out an obscenity. She was ripped from her dizzying need by that howl of pain, felt her face suffuse with guilt as she recalled why she had crept in here in the first place.

'Rafael, wake up...' she whispered, and hurried over to touch his shoulder. His skin was damp and hot, as though he were running a fever. Was he sick?

As she watched, he tipped onto his back again, his spine arching off the bed, feet pedalling as though running from some pursuer in his dream.

'No,' he muttered to himself. His body thrashed about, shaking the bed, and his feet tangled in the silk sheet. 'No...'

'You're having another nightmare,' she said, more loudly. 'Wake up!' When this didn't work, Sabrina reluctantly shook his shoulder. 'Rafael, you're dreaming. Can you hear me?'

To her alarm, his hand shot out, and with one smooth movement he dragged her onto the bed beside him. Before she could escape he rolled towards her, holding her close. His eyes were closed, his face flushed with sleep, and he was showing no awareness of his surroundings.

Gingerly, she attempted to slip out of his embrace and return to her room. But he seemed to sense this, his arms tightening around her in response.

He shuddered again and buried his face in her neck. 'No, please don't go... I'm sorry. I'll never do it again.'

He began to tremble violently again, abruptly releasing her.

'Wait, you can't leave me.'

Rolling over again, his back to her now, he began to claw at the sheet like a trapped animal.

'It's so hot and dark. I can't breathe. Please don't go, Papa!' His voice sounded like a frightened child's. 'Let me out of here!'

Papa.

She lay motionless beside him on the bed, listening to Rafael dreaming about his father—the man who had murdered his mother before killing himself. Only it sounded more like a memory than a dream...

Horror crept through her, turning her insides to ice.

'Rafael,' she whispered, and raised a hand to stroke his hair. 'It's Sabrina. I'm here. It's okay, you're not alone.'

He thrashed his legs again briefly, and then his breathing, which had become laboured, slowly began to return to normal.

She stayed where she was, nestled close at his back, until

the heat pumping from him forced her to sit up and peel the silk robe off her body, needing to cool down. At that instant he stirred and rolled towards her. She saw the glitter of his eyes through the darkness.

'Sabrina? What are you doing here?' His voice was hoarse with surprise. He sat up, noticing the open door to his suite, the light from the landing. 'What...? What is it? Is something wrong?'

'You had another bad dream,' she admitted, but didn't embarrass him with any details. 'I heard you cry out, so I came in to see if you were okay.' Acutely aware of her own nudity, she fumbled for the silk robe to cover herself, saying, 'You're awake now, so I'll go back to bed.'

'No,' he said thickly, catching at her hand as she tried to pull on the robe. His gaze crashed against hers, hotly demanding. 'Please don't go.'

'Please don't go.'

The refrain from his nightmare.

Her pity turned to desire at the look in his eyes. She held her breath, fearing to move. Something leapt between them in the darkness—a spark that raced greedily into flame and threatened to engulf her. Then he jerked her forward into his arms, and their naked bodies collided.

'Sabbie...'

He began kissing her mouth, her throat and her breasts, his hands gliding over her flesh, bringing her alive.

Sabrina gulped at the air. She knew she ought to go back to her room. Knew they should have kept this marriage platonic. Because this could only end in disaster.

But she couldn't help herself.

Gently, she pushed him onto his back, kneeling beside him and kissing down his flat abdomen to linger between his thighs. He was hard now, fully aroused, and she bent to take him into her mouth.

'Yes,' he groaned, his head thrown back in ecstasy, eyes closed. '*Thee mou*...you enchantress.'

Being in charge for once was a revelation. The power and the lust, and yet the sweetness too...the sudden understanding of his need and vulnerability.

'Enough...' he groaned after a while.

Looking up through a curtain of hair, she caught the hot glint of his eyes as he gazed upon her nudity. He shifted beneath her, slowly positioning her so her thighs straddled his strong body, her wet core flush with his hips.

'Put me inside you,' he instructed, his face a taut mask of need, and he groaned again as she complied, easing her core slowly down onto his broad crown. 'Yes, like that. Ah, that's good, *agape mou*.'

Cupping both breasts, he strummed his thumbs over her sensitive nipples until she whimpered, still straddling him. Then he thrust upwards, rocking her back and forth. She shook at his depth, her tenderness splayed wide, biting into her lower lip as her head tipped back, control fraying at the edges.

'Now, ride me.'

It was a command.

His hands gripped her hips, moving her in an age-old rhythm, teaching her how to ride his hard, muscular body until she shuddered and cried out. His breathing changed then, quickening. He rolled over, taking her with him, and thrust deep with a cry of triumph, on top of her now.

It felt so good. Sabrina lost all sense of time, gasping and kissing, raising her hips to meet his. Heat was pouring off them both in waves. He was hard as stone, his body like iron, and she was fluid, soft and flowing about him, wet and receptive.

She found herself mouthing the words *I love you*... over and over, but soft and soundless, under her breath so he couldn't hear. It was her secret, and she hugged it to herself even as mindless pleasure took her again…

In the depths of his nightmare Rafael had been a boy again, at home with his mother, holding her hand and soothing her tears with the comfort of his presence, which was all he'd had to give.

Then the door had crashed open and there was his father. *Papa.*

Next thing, pleading and crying, he was being pushed into the tiny space under the floor where Papa hid his contraband whenever the police came calling. Terrified, bent double, Rafael had slammed his fists against the dusty wooden boards that held him captive, while above his head his father had removed his belt and beat his mother.

'No!' he kept shouting. 'Please stop it! Leave her alone.'

Then his eyes had opened to find Sabrina there, and the nightmare was over. Her passionate kisses had melted the dream into nothing, her sweet sex burning his fears away.

Now he heard her cry out, and his soul recognised the emotion in her voice, felt his skin catching fire along with hers.

Gasping to completion, he jerked and groaned, filling her with his seed, and found himself wishing she was not on the contraceptive pill. He had always sworn he would never have a child himself, fearing his own fitness to be a good parent, coming from a man like his father. But now he knew what he wanted. To conceive a child with this woman…to become a father and watch their baby grow… safe, nurtured and loved as he had never been…

Waking late the next morning, Rafael found himself alone in bed.

Feeling curiously hollow inside, he took a shower,

dressed in blue jeans and a T-shirt, and went down to find Sabrina reading a novel by the pool.

'Good morning,' he said, feeling awkward, thrusting his hands in his jeans pockets.

He could still recall his nightmare, his desperate pleas to his father. She had admitted to hearing him cry out. How much had she heard last night before she'd come to his room?

She put down her book and looked up at him, sexy in skin-tight white shorts and a sky-blue midriff top that hugged her figure. Her gold-kissed skin glistened with sun oil. He couldn't decipher her expression, because large dark-framed sunglasses concealed her eyes. But her hands were clenched on the arms of the lounger, her body rigid.

'You had another nightmare,' she said, as though reading his mind.

'I remember.'

He drew up a lounger and sat beside her, watching the play of sunlight on the pool. His chest tightened as he moved his restless gaze over her gorgeous body, but he studiously avoided her face, afraid of what he might see there.

'I apologise. Did I frighten you?'

'No.' She put her novel aside. 'What was the dream about?'

'I don't want to discuss it.'

'You were shouting and moaning in your sleep,' she said softly, watching him. 'Something about your father? You sounded so desperate…so unhappy.'

He flushed, embarrassed by the thought of her witnessing his secret, long-buried pain. 'Flashback dream, my therapist calls them,' he admitted reluctantly.

'To the night your mother died?'

This was too close to the shame he kept hidden.

His jaw clenched hard. *'You were shouting and moaning in your sleep.'* She made him sound like a scared child...

'Yes,' he growled, and then, before she could mock him further, added in bitter self-loathing, 'And, yes, I *know* she died because I wasn't strong enough to protect her. You don't need to remind me.'

'What?' She stared at him, blinking.

'You always pretended you didn't know what had happened,' he ground out, unable to help himself. 'But everyone on Calista knew. It was all over the local paper.'

'Rafe, I genuinely have no idea what you're talking about. Your father murdered your mother and then shot himself. That's all I know. I certainly didn't read about it in the paper. I was barely ten at the time, remember?'

He gritted his teeth, struggling against the horrors of his past. But they refused to be suppressed any longer.

'My father often shoved me into a cubbyhole under the floor,' he burst out, 'the place where he hid stolen goods. It was his favourite punishment for me. But that night I had to listen as he beat my mother to death. I tried to get out of there, I swear. My hands were battered and bloody—' He broke off, and when he spoke again his voice was almost a howl. 'What kind of boy can't protect his own mother?'

There was horror in her face.

'You were only a child.' She shook her head, reaching out to him. 'There was nothing you could have done.'

'Mama trusted me. I let her down.'

'Hey, come here...'

Sabrina tried to hold him, but he jerked to his feet and turned away, his vision blurred with tears, unable to bear the thought of her pity.

'We've talked about this,' she continued gently. 'You can't blame yourself for what your father did. You were a victim too.'

'Is that the kind of man you want in your life, Sabbie? A victim?'

'You're not a victim any more—' she began, but he was no longer listening, struggling to hold onto his self-control.

'You went to bed in your own room last night.' His voice became clipped as he shifted topic to protect himself, busily tucking his painful past away, where it could no longer burst out and embarrass him. 'Is that how it's going to be from now on? Separate bedrooms?'

'You'd shut the door to your suite. I thought you didn't want me in there.'

'Not at all,' he said gruffly. 'I merely assumed you were tired after the Paris trip and needed time alone to sleep.' He thrust his hands into his pockets, glancing round at her. 'Talking of which…you left my bed in a hurry this morning. Couldn't wait to get away from me?'

He winced, falling silent. How needy that made him sound!

'Stop putting words in my mouth. Last night was…amazing.'

Amazing?

It had been incredible for him. But for her…?

She was being kind and comforting, of course. Because that was what friends did. Pain tore through him at the realisation that she saw him as vulnerable. Last night had revealed a terrible gaping hole at the centre of his being. He'd bared his past as he'd cried out like a frightened child in his sleep. He felt so ashamed, wishing she hadn't overheard his nightmare.

'But once you've left me,' he countered doggedly, trying to push his hurt and his fear deep down inside, where she couldn't see it, 'you won't waste any time thinking about me again. Just like when you left me behind at the orphanage. Out of sight, out of mind.'

'What the hell are you talking about, Rafe?'

She whipped off her sunglasses, glaring at him. Her eyes were red-rimmed, their lashes wet and stuck together. Had she been crying? The thought stunned him.

'I'm not planning on going anywhere. Besides, you're the one who forgot about *me*.'

'How do you work that out?'

'I wrote to you from London and never received a reply. In the end I just assumed you'd lost interest in me once I'd been adopted. And then in Paris—' Sabrina broke off and shook her head, her gaze dropping to the ground. 'Well, you certainly got your revenge that night. You must have laughed yourself sick when you realised it was my first time...'

Her voice was choked. He was astonished. He thought at first this must be another elaborate ruse to disarm him. Then he looked into her eyes and wanted to weep too, seeing the hurt she was no longer bothering to hide.

'Thee mou,' he groaned, at once snapping out of his self-pity. 'Laugh at you? For being a virgin? *Never.* Though it was a surprise,' he admitted guiltily, digging his hands into his pockets. 'You told me you were on the pill.'

'For medical reasons. Reasons that still exist, in fact.' She looked embarrassed. 'I take the pill to regulate my periods.'

'I see.' He grimaced, feeling like a fool. 'But how could you ever think I would make love to you out of revenge?' he threw back at her. 'Revenge for what?'

'For being adopted and leaving you behind.' Her whisper was agonised.

'No, I was overjoyed that someone had finally seen your true worth. And such a man. A billionaire. I knew you would live in the lap of luxury, that your days of suffering were at an end. I was delighted for you, *kardia mou.*'

'So why didn't you write to me?' she wailed, tears streaming down her face.

'What?' His lungs felt as if they were packed with broken glass, every breath a torment. 'I *did* write to you.' He raked a hand through his hair. 'I wrote to you every month for the first year and got no reply.' He swallowed hard, recalling the bitter unhappiness of those days. 'In the end I stopped writing. I assumed you didn't want to know me any more.'

She was shaking her head. 'No... No, you didn't write. I didn't get any letters from you. Not a single one.'

A bewildered silence stretched between them.

Then Rafael groaned, slapping himself in the forehead. 'Templeton. I should have known. He must have intercepted my letters. Probably read them, tore them up and threw them in the bin.' Fury gnawed at his insides. 'That *bastard.*'

Her damp blue eyes were stretched wide. She put her hand to her throat, gripping herself as though she was having difficulty breathing. 'My father...? Surely he couldn't have...?' She bared her teeth. 'But of course he did. He tried to stop me writing to you that first year in England too. So I sneaked my letters out of the house instead.'

'I never got them.'

She was breathing heavily. 'The wardens at the orphanage... They were in his pocket too. And it worked. When you never replied, I gave up.' She let out a cry of despair. '*I gave up.* I let you down.'

'No, Sabrina, never...'

But she didn't seem to be listening. 'I loved the orphanage. I thought of it as my real home, even years after I'd been adopted. Now I can't see it the same way any more. It's all tainted.' Her throat convulsed. 'I should have let you knock it down.'

Inwardly, he cursed all the men who had caused her so

much pain. Her father, the orphanage director, the wardens... But perhaps some good could come of that trauma.

'We could use the old orphanage as headquarters for our charity,' he suggested, following her as she walked away. 'Try to salvage something from this mess.'

There was a short silence. Slowly, she turned back to him. Her eyes were still swimming with tears. 'You still intend to go ahead with the charity?' Her voice was uncertain.

'Of course.' Rafael felt as if his heart was caught in a vice that was slowly tightening. 'Don't you want to work with me on that? To protect other orphans like ourselves?'

'Except I was never an orphan, was I? It was a lie. My father was still alive. I just didn't know it.'

Sabrina had stopped at the base of the steps up to the villa, her face half in sunlight, half in shadow. She looked so desolate it took his breath away.

'Marriage doesn't have to be a prison, Sabrina. It was for my mother, granted. But that's not what I want for us.'

Sabrina turned, came back to him. There was an odd look in her face. 'Then what *do* you want from our marriage, Rafe?' she asked softly.

He saw the trap too late.

Everything inside him was shaking. It was a seismic event in his soul. He could only control it by gritting his teeth and clenching his jaw. He wanted to reach for her, to kiss her fiercely and fold her in his arms for ever. To show her that they belonged to each other and always had.

But he knew she would push him away... Sooner or later she would see through his brash over-confidence to the weakness at his heart. Because he *must* be weak, mustn't he? Otherwise he would not have failed his own mother when she'd needed him most.

'For us to be friends,' he mumbled, not meeting her eyes. 'Soulmates.'

'And lovers?' she whispered, and she took his hand before he could snatch it away. 'For us to love each other, Rafe?'

The old familiar darkness gripped his heart and began to spread, tightening its stranglehold on his throat, his larynx.

'That's not possible,' he told her between numb lips. 'I'm not capable of love. It's not in my nature.'

'Everyone is capable of love.'

'Not me.' His smile was a grimace, showing his teeth. 'I don't deserve love. I've never done anything in my life to deserve a happy ending.'

'You've been my friend,' she pointed out unsteadily, her blue eyes glistening with tears he longed to kiss away. 'You've helped me escape my father...to see him for what he is.'

'That took no special skill. Only the truth.'

'And the orphans. You've helped them.'

'I only did what was necessary to hook you in,' he lied, hoping to make her hate him, because that would make everything easier. 'So I could get those US negotiations done. Make more money.'

'I don't believe you. And you *do* deserve love,' she insisted. 'We both do.'

But the tears were spilling down her cheeks now. She looked unhappier than ever, and Rafael knew with a plummeting heart that it was his fault. He had done this by marrying her. He had made Sabrina miserable, just as his father had made his mother miserable. And now they were locked in a spiralling fall from which only divorce could free them.

'No...' he croaked, as bitterness at his own failure flooded him. Everything inside him was hot and painful. 'Please don't cry,' he said hoarsely. 'I'm sorry if you misunderstood my motives. I didn't marry you in search of some fairy-tale ending, Sabbie. I married you because...'

He stopped, unable to say the words that would reveal his weakness. Because he knew how tender-hearted she could be, and he didn't want any decision she made about their marriage to be based on pity for an old friend. That would be unbearable.

'Well, none of that matters now. I guess we've both achieved our goals. So if you want that divorce straight away, I won't contest it.' His heart winced in agony, and it was all he could do not to cry out and beg her to stay. 'I can instruct my lawyers today. Just say the word.'

It wasn't what he wanted, but he couldn't bear the thought of her being locked into the misery and suffering of an unhappy marriage as his mother had been.

Clenching a fist against her mouth, Sabrina stared at him wide-eyed in silence—and then she stilled, looking up. A helicopter was approaching fast, a flash of silver in the azure sky. And multiple vehicles too. Rafael could hear the repeated bump of heavy tyres over the uneven track that led to the villa and he frowned.

More paparazzi?

Except he'd instructed the perimeter guards to keep all members of the press away from their home. So who the hell had let them through?

CHAPTER TWELVE

SABRINA STARED AT Rafael in consternation. Not because of the incoming helicopter—though she guessed from his frown that it meant trouble—but because it seemed their short marriage was over sooner than planned. Already he was talking of divorce.

In Paris, she had briefly dared to hope again, especially when he'd floated the idea of the charity for orphans... But she knew in her heart that even those few sweet hours together in the city of love had changed nothing. Sooner or later Rafael would walk away again, exactly as he'd done five years ago, proving her own worst fears correct.

The helicopter was landing. They heard feet on the steps down to the pool and then Kyria Diakou appeared on the veranda, looking embarrassed.

'Apologies, sir, madam!' the housekeeper called down to them breathlessly. 'But there are men at the door. One claims to be a lawyer and another is a police officer. They say you are keeping Kyria Romano here against her will and her father is coming to take her home.' She looked flustered. 'What should I do?'

Rafael said nothing but looked at Sabrina, his face a stony mask.

'I'll speak to them.' Sabrina swept up the steps to the

house without a backward look at her husband. 'It's time I put a stop to this nonsense.'

She was heartily sick of men treating her like a chattel, telling her what to think and how to live her life and always expecting her to obey.

When she threw open the front entrance door she found her father waiting impatiently on the other side of it. Behind him stood a small army of bodyguards, some men in suits, whom she presumed to be part of his vast legal team, and a police officer in Calistan uniform, looking uncomfortable.

'Dearest!' Andrew Templeton exclaimed, and embraced her before she could say a word. 'I'm relieved to see you looking so well. Now, listen…don't worry about this marriage to Romano. I can get you out of it in five minutes flat—just leave everything to me.'

She had too much pride to make a scene in front of an audience.

'You'd better come in, Dad,' was all she replied, speaking as calmly as she could manage while seething with emotion.

As soon as he'd stepped through the door, she closed it in the face of his entourage, ignoring their loud protests.

'But only you, and only for five minutes. Then you need to leave.'

'More games, Sabrina?'

Her father dominated the hallway, moving restlessly to examine the statues on display, his hat in his hand. Now she knew the truth about her parentage she could clearly see the features she'd inherited from him. The sculpted cheekbones, the wiry build, even the blond hair—though his was silvery now. At least she had her mother's blue eyes…

Her heart ached as she remembered the mother she'd lost, and she wished Cherie could have told her the truth.

'I'm not leaving Calista without you.' He turned to face her, hard authority in his voice. 'Pack your bags. My lawyers are here to serve annulment papers on Rafael Romano. Then I'm taking you home to London.'

Sabrina drew in a deep breath. 'No, you're not.'

'Why? Is there something else we need to clear up before you can leave?'

He looked impatiently about the villa, his polished shoes and severe dark suit and tie out of place in these relaxed surroundings.

'The clock is ticking, Sabrina. I need to get back in the air as soon as possible.' He grimaced. 'I've always hated this island.'

'Is that because you met my mother here?'

Her father turned to stare, arrested. 'Your *mother*? What on earth are you talking about?'

'You got my text, so don't pretend.'

'Your text?' He pulled out his mobile and nimbly flicked through the screens. 'You mean this nonsense about knowing who I am?'

'I know *everything*, Dad,' she told him, forestalling any attempt he might have made to keep lying. 'How you abandoned Cherie when she told you she was pregnant, and how you made the decision not to claim me after she died.'

She had thought she had herself under control, but her voice was shaking.

'How you left me to rot in that orphanage for years, and then swept in like a knight on a white charger to adopt me... All the while knowing you were my *actual* biological father.' She shook her head when he opened his mouth to deny it, adding sharply, 'No, don't waste your breath. I've got a dossier of evidence to prove it.'

Andrew Templeton blinked, taken aback by this direct attack. For once, he seemed lost for words.

'So you can forget about rescuing me from Rafael,' she went on raggedly, 'because you're the one who's leaving

Calista—not me.' She thrust her chin in the air to meet his stunned expression. 'And take your minions with you. They're not welcome here, and neither are you.'

'Sabrina...'

Her father took a step towards her but halted at her protest. A look of sly calculation came over his face.

'Okay, I can see how this might look bad,' he backtracked slowly. 'But I... I was in love with your mother. That's the honest truth.' He ran a hand through his thinning hair, his mouth compressed. 'It was just... I loved my wife more.'

There was a hint of despair in his voice—just enough to be believable.

'Cherie understood my dilemma. She never complained, so long as I took care of the two of you financially. I certainly didn't force that choice on her. You have to believe me.' He grimaced. 'She was born in England—I expect she told you that?'

When Sabrina nodded, he added, 'She left because of some trouble with the police. Some minor theft. She would have risked prison if she'd returned. That's why she was happy to stay on Calista with you...away from her past.' He shrugged. 'I helped that happen.'

That was news to her, and she wished her mother could have shared it with her. But it did make sense, at least.

'And after my mother died?' she asked.

He grimaced. 'I couldn't risk telling Barbara about the affair. Admit that I'd had a daughter by another woman. She would have left me.'

'So you threw me to the wolves instead.'

'Don't be so melodramatic.'

His brows tugged together in a look she knew well.

'I made sure you were well cared for. I paid the orphanage director a small fortune over the years to ensure it, and received regular updates on your health and progress. I did consider owning up... Only then Barbara got sick, and I couldn't hurt her like that when she was dying. After she passed away I flew straight out here to find you and take you back to England with me. Hardly *throwing you to the wolves*, is it?'

Andrew Templeton held out a hand, his look one of entreaty now. 'Come home and we can sort this mess out.'

She shook her head, hurt beyond measure to hear his candid confession. 'None of that explains why you "adopted" me...why you didn't admit who I was as soon as you'd taken me to England.'

'I couldn't have done that to your siblings. Tom and Pippa would have been devastated. They'd have hated me for betraying their mother, and would have found a way to blame you too.'

Sabrina could readily believe that, given how privileged her brother and sister were, and how they'd always looked down on her as an outsider to the family.

'But I've never begrudged you anything, have I?' her father went on. 'Since bringing you to live with me, I've given you the best education, clothes, jewellery, business opportunities... Because you're my daughter and I love you.'

'Is that why you refused treatment for my facial scars while I was in the orphanage? And told the director I wasn't to be adopted? Or why you hid Rafael's letters from me?' Pain wrenched at her. 'You let me think my closest friend had forgotten about me.'

'Barbara's cancer was terminal by the time the orphanage director approached me about facial surgery,' he told her, seeming unabashed by her accusations. 'I knew she didn't have long to live, and I wanted to wait until I could bring you home and get you the finest surgeons. As for that boy's letters... You were only a kid, for God's sake. I did it all for the best.'

'You did it for *yourself*,' she countered angrily. 'But you failed. Rafael and I still found each other again.'

'"*Found each other*"?' His lips twisted in a sneer. 'Do you know why Romano actually married you? For money. No other reason. He could have clicked his fingers and married any woman he likes. But he chose you.' He shook his head contemptuously. 'Romano found out I'm your real father and smelt a potential lawsuit. He knows you'll be a fabulously wealthy woman one day and he wants to jump on the gravy train.'

'He's already a billionaire, Dad.'

'You naïve little idiot.' He laughed harshly. 'A man can never have too much money. Have you learned nothing from living with me?' He cleared his throat, and that look of calculation was back in his face as he added, 'You can tell Romano I'm prepared to settle out of court if he agrees to keep this quiet.'

'I've heard enough.'

Sickened, Sabrina opened the front door. His men surged forward, trying to push past her. She held up a hand, announcing loudly in English, 'My father is leaving.' She turned to address the police officer in Greek. 'I'm sorry you've had a wasted trip. But my husband and I are on our honeymoon and would prefer not to be disturbed again.'

The police officer smiled politely. 'In that case, Kyria Romano, please accept my apologies and enjoy the rest of your honeymoon,' he said, and headed back to the gate.

The others fell back in his wake, confused, and her father had little choice but to leave the villa, gesturing for his men to return to their vehicles too.

'Goodbye, Dad,' she said coldly.

Andrew Templeton stepped into deep sunshine, a frown in his eyes. 'You're making a big mistake,' he warned her, resettling his hat on his silvery hair. 'I've had your husband investigated. I know all about his sordid affairs. He'll never stay faithful to you.'

Closing the door on her father, Sabrina stood with her head bowed, her whole body shaking. From beyond the villa walls she heard the sound of rotor blades whirring, louder and louder, and the steady retreat of vehicles along the dirt tracks of Calista.

She waited, expecting Rafael to appear, demanding to know what had been said.

But he didn't come.

Tears streamed down her face and she dashed them away. Of course he hadn't come to speak to her after her father left. He didn't care. He hadn't married her for some 'fairy-tale ending', as he'd said. It had all been strictly business.

'He'll never stay faithful to you.'

She bent over, sobbing silently, stifling the sound against her hand. Once again she was all alone in the world, with nobody to turn to for love and support.

Thea found her weeping and drew her gently into the lounge. 'Let me fetch you something cool to drink,' the housekeeper insisted, her eyes concerned, and bustled away to return with a glass of sharp-tasting home-made lemonade. 'This will help you feel better, *kyria*. It's the heat, that's all.'

But they both knew she was lying.

Feeling as if she'd been hit by a truck, Sabrina sipped the lemonade and then curled up on the couch, only meaning to close her eyes for a moment. But her body was exhausted…

She woke with a start some time later, catching the sound of someone saying her name. The Diakous were arguing softly in the hallway.

Groggily, she wandered out. 'What's the matter? I fell asleep.'

Thea turned to her, her kindly face creased in lines of anxiety. 'Oh, *kyria*, I apologise for disturbing you. We can't seem to find Kyrios Romano.'

'What do you mean?'

'I saw your husband leave the villa by the side door when your father arrived,' Nikos explained hesitantly. 'We don't know where he went. But he's taken the sports car.' His bushy brows tugged together in concern. 'I saw his face when he was leaving... He was so unhappy, *kyria*. I've never seen him look like that.'

Cold fear gripped Sabrina's heart. 'Like what?'

'Like he might do himself a mischief,' the man said bluntly, ignoring his wife's protest.

Sabrina felt a hollowness inside. Her skin cooled, her chest tight with dread. She ought to have gone to find Rafael as soon as her father had gone. Though perhaps he'd already left the villa by then. But she'd been in pieces...unable to breathe properly, let alone explain what had passed between her and her father.

Rafael had claimed he didn't deserve love. That he wasn't even capable of it himself. Her heart had broken to hear him say such things. But she didn't believe any of that. It was merely his past talking—his memory of a beloved mother lost to a violent bully he hadn't been able to defeat.

Guilt flooded her—and a hot tide of remorse. They'd always stood up for each other in the orphanage, pushing back against the bullies and the haters. In her scramble to escape what she'd seen as the trap of their marriage she'd forgotten the most essential thing that bound them together. They were soulmates.

'I think I know where he may have gone,' she said. 'But I'll need a lift.'

'At once, *kyria*,' Nikos agreed, beaming.

Eyes shut tight, Rafael drew his knees to his chin and hugged them. Dust settled about him in the silence of the old orphanage. As soon as he'd heard Sabrina invite Templeton inside he'd gone to listen, to be sure her father wasn't going to bully her, and prepared to leap to his wife's defence if necessary. But once she'd so bravely sent him packing Rafael had also left the villa, unseen via the side door.

He'd needed time alone to think.

He was proud of his wife. So fiercely proud he thought his heart would burst. The way she had handled her arrogant, overbearing father... Yet, despite her stubborn denials to her dad, he knew their marriage was still over. And deservedly so.

He couldn't give Sabrina love because he couldn't accept love in return.

'If you want that divorce straight away, I won't contest it. I can instruct my lawyers today. Just say the word.'

Their discussion had been interrupted by Templeton's arrival. But of *course* she would choose to divorce him. There was no doubt in his mind. Why would such a courageous, free-spirited woman, given the chance to escape, want to remain with a man as damaged as him?

This dark, cramped space was where Sabrina had hidden from the bullies as a child. Now he was hiding here too—but from himself. If he'd been a stronger person... if he'd spoken what was in his heart instead of fearing the darkness inside...perhaps he would have deserved her as a wife. Now he was going to lose her.

She had pointed out his appalling behaviour in Paris, how he'd so cruelly walked away after taking her virginity. An unforgivable act. Only he hadn't walked away. In truth, he'd run, and kept on running for years. Terrified by the sheer, fathomless depth of his love for her and his unfitness to share her life...

Rafael groaned, tugging violently on his hair. Sabrina didn't need him. She didn't need anyone and had just proved that. Besides, what did he know about love? He had made his fortune, become the infamous Rafael Romano, simply in order to impress her from afar. To prove he was more than the broken boy she'd known before—that he was somebody worth loving.

But the truth was, he was unlovable.

Looking to the future had always been one of his favourite ways to plan his next move. Yet all he could see ahead was loneliness. No woman except Sabrina had ever meant anything to him. Now she was going to leave him his life would be cold and barren. Barely worth living…

He heard a door thud and footsteps approaching his hiding place.

A memory rose up from the dark to scourge him, and he tensed, shaking his head. 'No!' he cried.

In his mind's eye Rafael saw his father tear open the cubbyhole under the floorboards, a long hairy arm reaching in to grab him and drag him out for another vicious beating.

He shrank back. 'I won't let you touch me!' He yelled into the void, down the turbulent spiral of years. 'Never again. You'll never touch me again, do you hear?'

Then the cupboard door was opening, dusty light pouring in, and he saw Sabrina crouched there, blue eyes wide with concern, golden hair spilling over her shoulders, exactly like the princess in a fairy story he had always known her to be.

'Okay,' she said huskily, and reached in to take his hand. 'Though for what it's worth, that would be a shame.'

Sabrina had guessed instinctively where he would be, knowing where *she* would have gone if it had felt like the end. Somewhere quiet and remote…somewhere she could retreat from the cruelties of the world.

On arrival at the old orphanage she'd spotted Rafael's sports car, drawn up outside, and told Nikos to go back to Villa Rosa without her.

'I'll come back later with my husband,' she'd assured him.

And sure enough she had found Rafael hiding there, and known it was fate. They were still soulmates, able to read each other's thoughts. All she needed now was to hear him say aloud what he was truly thinking and feeling, without trying to conceal it. Because without that it would all be pointless.

Together, they wandered out of the empty orphanage and stood in the fragrant silence, looking up at the crumbling, flower-bright façade.

'I'm sorry I walked out on you again,' he said gruffly.

'There's nothing to apologise for.'

'I listened to you and Templeton… I hope you don't mind. I heard you tell him to leave.' There was a grim smile on his face. 'I was so proud of you.'

'Thank you.' She expelled a long breath. 'Yes, that whole disgraceful charade is over. I made sure my father understood. Now I just have to decide what to do with that information.'

It was going to be a difficult few years, she thought. But she would get through it, with or without Rafael. She had found her strength now, and knew she didn't need anyone to hold her hand through this new phase of her life.

Though it would be nice not to do it alone…

She stared up into the blue Calistan sky, remembering their unconventional childhood here, the crazy dreams they had whispered to each other when no one else was listening.

'Are you going to ask me for a divorce?' Rafael's voice was bleak.

She took a deep breath and weighed up her options. 'Only if you don't tell me the truth, Rafe,' she said bluntly.

He flinched. 'The truth?'

'About why you left me in Paris after the first time we slept together.'

A muscle jerked in his cheek as he considered that. 'I

left because I was terrified,' he said at last, as if the words had been drawn from him grudgingly.

'Terrified?' She stared at him in disbelief.

He looked away, grimacing. 'I couldn't get out of your hotel room fast enough. I was utterly mesmerised by you, Sabbie. I'd never wanted a woman so much in my life. And suddenly we were in bed together. And it was perfect. Better than perfect...it was miraculous.' He sucked in an unsteady breath before adding, 'I know you didn't see, but I... I cried while we were making love.'

She felt her own eyes water at this startling admission, and a hollow ache in her chest. 'You *cried*?'

'I couldn't help it,' he grated, jaw clenched, looking for all the world like a man in front of a firing squad. 'Next morning, I looked at you and knew why.' There was a red tint along his cheekbones. 'Because I was head over heels in love with you.'

She gasped, hardly daring to believe it. 'In *love* with me? You?' Sweet joy flooded her as he nodded. 'This, from the man who claims he can't love anyone?'

'I had to say something,' he mumbled stiffly. 'To stop you suspecting.'

'Oh, Rafe...' She touched his stubbled cheek, wishing he wasn't such an idiot. 'But if that's how you felt, why hurt me by walking out? Why not just tell me?'

'I'm sorry. I didn't want to hurt you.' He was struggling, his eyes darkening. 'But I couldn't run the risk of losing you. Don't you see? I knew I wouldn't be able to keep you and it would all end in disaster. I didn't deserve you, and I had nothing to offer you. I mean, you already had everything you could possibly want.'

Except love, she thought, but said nothing, watching him in hope.

'The fear was intense... It was like watching a meteor

approaching. The end of everything.' He ran a hand across his eyes. 'So I got up and ran—like the coward I am.'

Her heart broke for him. 'You're no coward. The things you've done...the way you've risen above your past... All that took incredible courage and determination. And as for not deserving me—'

'Oh, I know all that. But deep inside,' he said hoarsely, jabbing at his chest, 'I still feel the guilt of my mother's death.' He looked at her, his expression poignant. 'I should be able to protect the woman I love.'

'I don't need protecting,' she assured him.

'But your father... I should have gone to meet him and knocked him down before he even reached the villa. Not let him anywhere near you.'

'It was my business and I sent him away on my own,' she reminded him. 'All I need from you is love, Rafe.' She swallowed at the magnitude of those words, her stomach full of butterflies. 'If you still have feelings for me, that is.'

'Are you kidding?'

He kissed her on the lips and the world spun.

When he spoke again his voice was gruff, uneven with emotion. 'I love you so much, Sabbie. More than words.'

'I love you too, Rafe.'

They clung together for a few miraculous minutes, just letting those words sink into the air between them.

'It's stupid, but for a long while after Paris I truly thought you'd only wanted me for this.' She touched her unscarred face. 'And that once you were bored, you'd leave me again. I always seem to lose what I love...'

'Your mother?' he asked, narrow-eyed.

She nodded, trembling as she remembered that first traumatic loss.

'I will never, ever get *bored*, as you put it, and I will never leave you. This is for ever. I know it the way I know my own name.' He laid his warm cheek against hers, whispering, 'That first time with you in Paris I lost control. I'd never cried in bed with a woman before and it blew my mind. That was when I realised you were the one, for sure. But I also knew that if I admitted how I felt and you *rejected* me I would be broken. I could never be whole again.'

'I'm not going to reject you, Rafael Romano,' she promised him, raising her head to look him in the eye. 'I'm going to love you until you can't stand.'

His mouth quirked. 'That sounds…acceptable.'

Sabrina glanced at the sun-drenched building behind them. At last its old walls seemed beloved to her again. The taint of her father's lies was gone for ever, and this new joy was blotting out the past.

'Is this what you intended when you bought the orphanage?' she asked him. 'To bring us back together?'

'Not consciously. But the heart wants what the heart wants…'

She gave a gasp of laughter, a lightness inside her that she hadn't known in years. Not since she'd been a little girl. 'This must be what happiness feels like,' she said wonderingly.

'Yes,' he agreed, his gaze arrowing down to her mouth. 'That,' he murmured, 'and this.'

And he kissed her.

EPILOGUE

Two years later

'THERE IT IS!' Rafael called above the noise of the rotor blades as Villa Rosa came into view of the helicopter.

It was mid-afternoon and the walls were bathed in golden light. The Aegean sparkled beyond them in a deep blue dream of summer.

'Are you glad to be back on the island at last?' Sabrina asked her daughter.

Now a shy thirteen-year-old, Cora had been their daughter for nearly a year, adopted from the Calistan orphanage to come and live with them in New York.

Now they were all coming home to Villa Rosa for a few weeks of relaxation.

'Of course,' Cora told them both eagerly, plaiting her shoulder-length dark hair. 'I can't wait to see all my old friends at the orphanage.'

She had kept in touch with the other orphans, and always gave little shrieks of joy whenever one of them found new parents.

'But I love New York too,' she added with an impish smile. 'All those bookshops… I could never have too many books.'

'Our little bookworm,' Rafael said, and there was warm pride in his voice.

Sabrina grinned approvingly.

As soon as the helicopter touched down they shepherded Cora towards Villa Rosa, where the Diakous stood waiting to welcome them, their faces wreathed in smiles.

'It's so hot… Can I jump in the pool straight away?' Cora pleaded.

'Give us ten minutes, then we'll all swim together,' Sabrina told her, watching happily as the girl dashed upstairs, her heavy rucksack bouncing on her back, full of paperbacks to be read over the holiday.

She and Rafael followed more slowly, heading for the master bedroom. It had been a long flight and she was jet lagged. But it was so lovely to be back on Calista.

Her heart swelled with joy as she took in the familiar views, and the sun glinting on water far below the cliffs. The bedroom had been redecorated in sea-blue, with fresh flowers arranged in every alcove and thick fleece rugs under their feet, and it welcomed them home. And the crystal dolphin Rafael had bought her as a wedding gift stood on display beside the vast bed, reminding them both of the origins of their love story.

Rafael put down the bag he'd been carrying and took her in his arms. 'It's good to be home.'

They kissed deeply, and Sabrina felt her bones turn to water. 'Not now,' she whispered, laughing. 'Cora is waiting to swim.'

'Of course.' His dark eyes glowed. 'But after she's gone to bed this evening, what do you say to a late candlelit dinner for two on the veranda? Just like our first night here.'

'I'd love that.' Sabrina sank her teeth deep into her lower lip and caught his arm as he turned away. 'Wait… There's something I need to tell you.'

Rafael readily came back into her arms, stroking his

hands down her spine, his intense gaze meeting hers. 'I'm all ears, my love.'

'And all hands too!' she exclaimed.

'I can't help it. Not with the way you're beginning to round out these days.' He caught her quick look and said hurriedly, 'Don't get me wrong. I love it. You look incredibly sexy.'

Sabrina blushed. It was time to tell him what she'd discovered only that morning. Especially since he was about to see her squeeze into a bikini for the first time in ages.

'Rafael, I know you said we'd wait until Cora was more settled, but it seems Nature had other ideas...' Seeing his stare, she added nervously, 'I'm pregnant.'

He stilled, his gaze dropping to the soft swell of her belly. 'We're having a baby?'

He gave a whoop of joy and spun her around, lifting her feet off the ground.

'Kardia mou,' he whispered against her cheek, his voice hoarse with emotion. 'You make me the happiest of men...' His gaze raked her face. 'You're happy too? This is what you want?'

'I've never been happier.' Tears of joy squeezed from under Sabrina's eyelids. 'I just hope Cora won't mind a little brother or sister. We'll love both our children equally.'

'Both equally,' Rafael agreed, and leant forward, breathing in her scent. 'Is it wrong that I have the craziest urge to make mad, passionate love to you?'

'Yes, very wrong.' She laughed at his frustrated expression. 'Later, darling, after that candlelit dinner. Then we can play at being newlyweds again.'

After changing for the pool, they went downstairs together to join Cora.

'Linda rang during the flight, by the way,' he told Sabrina softly. 'She says we're all set for the big launch next month.'

'That's wonderful.'

They'd set up their charity supporting orphans worldwide, and had been busy acquiring premises in major cities.

'We're still keeping Calista as our official headquarters, though?'

Rafael nodded. 'Tomorrow we'll take the helicopter to the old orphanage and see how the refurb is progressing.' He smiled at her excitement. 'Your vision is coming true, Sabrina.'

'I couldn't have done it without you,' she said, waving to Cora as they descended through the hot fragrant sunshine to the poolside. 'If you hadn't agreed not to demolish the orphanage, none of this would be happening.'

'And if you hadn't come to find me that day—'

'I will *always* find you,' she told him, stopping to kiss him on the lips. 'It's fate, Rafe. We were meant to be together.'

* * * * *

COMING SOON!

We really hope you enjoyed reading this book. If you're looking for more romance be sure to head to the shops when new books are available on

Thursday 28th September

To see which titles are coming soon, please visit
millsandboon.co.uk/nextmonth

MILLS & BOON

MILLS & BOON®

Coming next month

REDEEMED BY MY
FORBIDDEN HOUSEKEEPER
Heidi Rice

My taste buds were already dancing a jig as Jessie uncovered the feast she had prepared for me.

But as my gaze devoured her lean frame disguised in the baggy T-shirt and scuffed jeans she always wore, and I noticed the flushed dewy skin of her face devoid of makeup as she straightened and grinned at me, the swell of something hot and fluid blossomed in my groin. *Again.*

The irritation twisted into resentment in my gut.

Somehow, the housekeeper I didn't even like had begun to captivate me. I was actually beginning to look forward to seeing her each day, anticipating her arrival like a lovesick teenager.

"I'm sick of always eating vegetables," I added, knowing that my anger had nothing to do with her choice of menu and everything to do with the fact I could not act on my attraction to her, even if I had wanted to.

I did not sleep with my employees. Even ones that fascinated and—*damn it*—excited me.

Continue reading
REDEEMED BY MY
FORBIDDEN HOUSEKEEPER
Heidi Rice

Available next month
www.millsandboon.co.uk

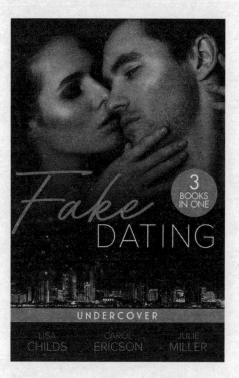

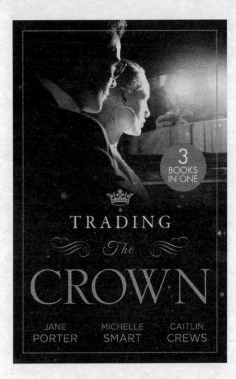

LET'S TALK
Romance

For exclusive extracts, competitions and special offers, find us online:

 MillsandBoon

 @MillsandBoon

 @MillsandBoonUK

 @MillsandBoonUK

Get in touch on 01413 063 232

For all the latest titles coming soon, visit
millsandboon.co.uk/nextmonth

MILLS & BOON

THE HEART OF ROMANCE

A ROMANCE FOR EVERY READER

MODERN

Prepare to be swept off your feet by sophisticated, sexy and seductive heroes, in some of the world's most glamourous and romantic locations, where power and passion collide.

HISTORICAL

Escape with historical heroes from time gone by. Whether your passion is for wicked Regency Rakes, muscled Vikings or rugged Highlanders, awaken the romance of the past.

MEDICAL

Set your pulse racing with dedicated, delectable doctors in the high-pressure world of medicine, where emotions run high and passion, comfort and love are the best medicine.

True Love

Celebrate true love with tender stories of heartfelt romance, from the rush of falling in love to the joy a new baby can bring, and a focus on the emotional heart of a relationship.

Desire

Indulge in secrets and scandal, intense drama and sizzling hot action with heroes who have it all: wealth, status, good looks…everything but the right woman.

HEROES

The excitement of a gripping thriller, with intense romance at its heart. Resourceful, true-to-life women and strong, fearless men face danger and desire - a killer combination!

To see which titles are coming soon, please visit

millsandboon.co.uk/nextmonth